House of Earth

The extraordinary *House of Earth* trilogy brings together three engrossing, best-selling novels—*The Good Earth, Sons,* and *A House Divided*—in the epic saga of the House of Wang that follows three generations of farmers, warlords, merchants, and students through the sweeping events of half a century.

"The mightiest monument of American letters"
—*Philadelphia Forum*

"An impressive achievement, revealing and rich in humanity"
—*The New York Times*

The Good Earth

"A comment upon the meaning and tragedy of life as it is lived in any age in any quarter of the globe"
—*The New York Times*

"One of the most important and revealing novels of our time"
—*Pittsburgh Post Gazette*

"One need never have lived in China or know anything about the Chinese to understand it or respond to its appeal."
—*Boston Transcript*

Books by Pearl S. Buck

The Angry Wife
A Bridge for Passing
Dragon Seed
The Exile
Fighting Angel
Fourteen Stories
The Goddess Abides
God's Men
The Good Earth
Hearts Come Home and Other Stories
The Hidden Flower
A House Divided
Kinfolk
Letter from Peking
The Living Reed
The Long Love
Mandala
The Mother
My Several Worlds
The New Year
Pavilion of Women
Peony
Portrait of a Marriage
The Rainbow
Sons
The Three Daughters of Madame Liang
The Time is Noon
The Townsman
Voices in the House

Published by POCKET BOOKS

PEARL S. BUCK

The Good Earth

PUBLISHED BY POCKET BOOKS NEW YORK

POCKET BOOKS, a Simon & Schuster division of
GULF & WESTERN CORPORATION
1230 Avenue of the Americas, New York, N.Y. 10020

ISBN: 0-671-43342-3

First Pocket Books printing January, 1939

95   94   93   92   91   90   89   88

POCKET and colophon are trademarks of Simon & Schuster.

Printed in the U.S.A.

I am always glad when any of my books can be put into an inexpensive edition, because I like to think that any people who might wish to read them can do so. Surely books ought to be within the reach of everybody.

". . . This was what Vinteuil had done for the little phrase. Swann felt that the composer had been content (with the instruments at his disposal) to draw aside its veil, to make it visible, following and respecting its outlines with a hand so loving, so prudent, so delicate and so sure, that the sound altered at every moment, blunting itself to indicate a shadow, springing back into life when it must follow the curve of some more bold projection. And one proof that Swann was not mistaken when he believed in the real existence of this phrase was that anyone with an ear at all delicate for music would have at once detected the imposture had Vinteuil, endowed with less power to see and to render its forms, sought to dissemble (by adding a line, here and there, of his own invention) the dimness of his vision or the feebleness of his hand."—*Swann's Way*, by MARCEL PROUST.

The
Good
Earth

1

IT WAS Wang Lung's marriage day. At first, opening his eyes in the blackness of the curtains about his bed, he could not think why the dawn seemed different from any other. The house was still except for the faint, gasping cough of his old father, whose room was opposite to his own across the middle room. Every morning the old man's cough was the first sound to be heard. Wang Lung usually lay listening to it and moved only when he heard it approaching nearer and when he heard the door of his father's room squeak upon its wooden hinges.

But this morning he did not wait. He sprang up and pushed aside the curtains of his bed. It was a dark, ruddy dawn, and through a small square hole of a window, where the tattered paper fluttered, a glimpse of bronze sky gleamed. He went to the hole and tore the paper away.

"It is spring and I do not need this," he muttered.

He was ashamed to say aloud that he wished the house to look neat on this day. The hole was barely large enough to admit his hand and he thrust it out to feel of the air. A small soft wind blew gently from the east, a wind mild and murmurous and full of rain. It was a good omen. The fields needed rain for fruition. There would be no rain this day, but within a few days, if this wind continued, there would be water. It was good. Yesterday he had said to his father that if this brazen, glittering sunshine continued, the wheat could not fill in the ear. Now it was as if Heaven had chosen this day to wish him well. Earth would bear fruit.

He hurried out into the middle room, drawing on his blue outer trousers as he went, and knotting about the fullness at his waist his girdle of blue cotton cloth. He left his upper body bare

1

until he had heated water to bathe himself. He went into the shed which was the kitchen, leaning against the house, and out of its dusk an ox twisted its head from behind the corner next the door and lowed at him deeply. The kitchen was made of earthen bricks as the house was, great squares of earth dug from their own fields, and thatched with straw from their own wheat. Out of their own earth had his grandfather in his youth fashioned also the oven, baked and black with many years of meal preparing. On top of this earthen structure stood a deep, round, iron cauldron.

This cauldron he filled partly full of water, dipping it with a half gourd from an earthen jar that stood near, but he dipped cautiously, for water was precious. Then, after a hesitation, he suddenly lifted the jar and emptied all the water into the cauldron. This day he would bathe his whole body. Not since he was a child upon his mother's knee had anyone looked upon his body. Today one would, and he would have it clean.

He went around the oven to the rear, and selecting a handful of the dry grass and stalks standing in the corner of the kitchen, he arranged it delicately in the mouth of the oven, making the most of every leaf. Then from an old flint and iron he caught a flame and thrust it into the straw and there was a blaze.

This was the last morning he would have to light the fire. He had lit it every morning since his mother died six years before. He had lit the fire, boiled water, and poured the water into a bowl and taken it into the room where his father sat upon his bed, coughing and fumbling for his shoes upon the floor. Every morning for these six years the old man had waited for his son to bring in hot water to ease him of his morning coughing. Now father and son could rest. There was a woman coming to the house. Never again would Wang Lung have to rise summer and winter at dawn to light the fire. He could lie in his bed and wait, and he also would have a bowl of water brought to him, and if the earth were fruitful there would be tea leaves in the water. Once in some years it was so.

And if the woman wearied, there would be her children to light the fire, the many children she would bear to Wang Lung. Wang Lung stopped, struck by the thought of children running in and out of their three rooms. Three rooms had always seemed much to them, a house half empty since his mother died. They were always having to resist relatives who were more crowded—his uncle, with his endless brood of children, coaxing,

"Now, how can two lone men need so much room? Cannot

2

father and son sleep together? The warmth of the young one's body will comfort the old one's cough."

But the father always replied, "I am saving my bed for my grandson. He will warm my bones in my age."

Now the grandsons were coming, grandsons upon grandsons! They would have to put beds along the walls and in the middle room. The house would be full of beds. The blaze in the oven died down while Wang Lung thought of all the beds there would be in the half empty house, and the water began to chill in the cauldron. The shadowy figure of the old man appeared in the doorway, holding his unbuttoned garments about him. He was coughing and spitting and he gasped,

"How is it that there is not water yet to heat my lungs?"

Wang Lung stared and recalled himself and was ashamed.

"This fuel is damp," he muttered from behind the stove. "The damp wind—"

The old man continued to cough perseveringly and would not cease until the water boiled. Wang Lung dipped some into a bowl, and then, after a moment, he opened a glazed jar that stood upon a ledge of the stove and took from it a dozen or so of the curled dried leaves and sprinkled them upon the surface of the water. The old man's eyes opened greedily and immediately he began to complain.

"Why are you wasteful? Tea is like eating silver."

"It is the day," replied Wang Lung with a short laugh. "Eat and be comforted."

The old man grasped the bowl in his shriveled, knotty fingers, muttering, uttering little grunts. He watched the leaves uncurl and spread upon the surface of the water, unable to bear drinking the precious stuff.

"It will be cold," said Wang Lung.

"True—true——" said the old man in alarm, and he began to take great gulps of the hot tea. He passed into an animal satisfaction, like a child fixed upon its feeding. But he was not too forgetful to see Wang Lung dipping the water recklessly from the cauldron into a deep wooden tub. He lifted his head and stared at his son.

"Now there is water enough to bring a crop to fruit," he said suddenly.

Wang Lung continued to dip the water to the last drop. He did not answer.

"Now then!" cried his father loudly.

"I have not washed my body all at once since the New Year," said Wang Lung in a low voice.

He was ashamed to say to his father that he wished his body to be clean for a woman to see. He hurried out, carrying the tub to his own room. The door was hung loosely upon a warped wooden frame and it did not shut closely, and the old man tottered into the middle room and put his mouth to the opening and bawled,

"It will be ill if we start the woman like this—tea in the morning water and all this washing!"

"It is only one day," shouted Wang Lung. And then he added, "I will throw the water on the earth when I am finished and it is not all waste."

The old man was silent at this, and Wang Lung unfastened his girdle and stepped out of his clothing. In the light that streamed in a square block from the hole he wrung a small towel from the steaming water and he scrubbed his dark slender body vigorously. Warm though he had thought the air, when his flesh was wet he was cold, and he moved quickly, passing the towel in and out of the water until from his whole body there went up a delicate cloud of steam. Then he went to a box that had been his mother's and drew from it a fresh suit of blue cotton cloth. He might be a little cold this day without the wadding of the winter garments, but he suddenly could not bear to put them on against his clean flesh. The covering of them was torn and filthy and the wadding stuck out of the holes, grey and sodden. He did not want this woman to see him for the first time with the wadding sticking out of his clothes. Later she would have to wash and mend, but not the first day. He drew over the blue cotton coat and trousers a long robe made of the same material—his one long robe, which he wore on feast days only, ten days or so in the year, all told. Then with swift fingers he unplaited the long braid of hair that hung down his back, and taking a wooden comb from the drawer of the small, unsteady table, he began to comb out his hair.

His father drew near again and put his mouth to the crack of the door.

"Am I to have nothing to eat this day?" he complained. "At my age the bones are water in the morning until food is given them."

"I am coming," said Wang Lung, braiding his hair quickly and smoothly and weaving into the strands a tasseled, black silk cord.

4

Then after a moment he removed his long gown and wound his braid about his head and went out, carrying the tub of water. He had quite forgotten the breakfast. He would stir a little water into corn meal and give it to his father. For himself he could not eat. He staggered with the tub to the threshold and poured the water upon the earth nearest the door, and as he did so he remembered he had used all the water in the cauldron for his bathing and he would have to start the fire again. A wave of anger passed over him at his father.

"That old head thinks of nothing except his eating and his drinking," he muttered into the mouth of the oven; but aloud he said nothing. It was the last morning he would have to prepare food for the old man. He put a very little water into the cauldron, drawing it in a bucket from the well near the door, and it boiled quickly and he stirred meal together and took it to the old man.

"We will have rice this night, my father," he said. "Meanwhile, here is corn."

"There is only a little rice left in the basket," said the old man, seating himself at the table in the middle room and stirring with his chopsticks the thick yellow gruel.

"We will eat a little less then at the spring festival," said Wang Lung. But the old man did not hear. He was supping loudly at his bowl.

Wang Lung went into his own room then, and drew about him again the long blue robe and let down the braid of his hair. He passed his hand over his shaven brow and over his cheeks. Perhaps he had better be newly shaven? It was scarcely sunrise yet. He could pass through the Street of the Barbers and be shaved before he went to the house where the woman waited for him. If he had the money he would do it.

He took from his girdle a small greasy pouch of grey cloth and counted the money in it. There were six silver dollars and a double handful of copper coins. He had not yet told his father he had asked friends to sup that night. He had asked his male cousin, the young son of his uncle, and his uncle for his father's sake, and three neighboring farmers who lived in the village with him. He had planned to bring back from the town that morning pork, a small pond fish, and a handful of chestnuts. He might even buy a few of the bamboo sprouts from the south and a little beef to stew with the cabbage he had raised in his own garden. But this only if there were any money left after the bean oil and the soybean sauce had been bought. If he shaved his head he could not, perhaps, buy the beef. Well, he would shave his head, he decided suddenly.

He left the old man without speech and went out into the early morning. In spite of the dark red dawn the sun was mounting the horizon clouds and sparkled upon the dew on the rising wheat and barley. The farmer in Wang Lung was diverted for an instant and he stooped to examine the budding heads. They were empty as yet and waiting for the rain. He smelled the air and looked anxiously at the sky. Rain was there, dark in the clouds, heavy upon the wind. He would buy a stick of incense and place it in the little temple to the Earth God. On a day like this he would do it.

He wound his way in among the fields upon the narrow path. In the near distance the grey city wall arose. Within that gate in the wall through which he would pass stood the great house where the woman had been a slave girl since her childhood, the House of Hwang. There were those who said, "It is better to live alone than to marry a woman who has been slave in a great house." But when he had said to his father, "Am I never to have a woman?" his father replied, "With weddings costing as they do in these evil days and every woman wanting gold rings and silk clothes before she will take a man, there remain only slaves to be had for the poor."

His father had stirred himself, then, and gone to the House of Hwang and asked if there were a slave to spare.

"Not a slave too young, and above all, not a pretty one," he had said.

Wang Lung had suffered that she must not be pretty. It would be something to have a pretty wife that other men would congratulate him upon having. His father, seeing his mutinous face, had cried out at him,

"And what will we do with a pretty woman? We must have a woman who will tend the house and bear children as she works in the fields, and will a pretty woman do these things? She will be forever thinking about clothes to go with her face! No, not a pretty woman in our house. We are farmers. Moreover, who has heard of a pretty slave who was virgin in a wealthy house? All the young lords have had their fill of her. It is better to be first with an ugly woman than the hundredth with a beauty. Do you imagine a pretty woman will think your farmer's hands as pleasing as the soft hands of a rich man's son, and your sun-black face as beautiful as the golden skin of the others who have had her for their pleasure?"

6

Wang Lung knew his father spoke well. Nevertheless, he had to struggle with his flesh before he could answer. And then he said violently,

"At least, I will not have a woman who is pock-marked, or who has a split upper lip."

"We will have to see what is to be had," his father replied.

Well, the woman was not pock-marked nor had she a split upper lip. This much he knew, but nothing more. He and his father had bought two silver rings, washed with gold, and silver earrings, and these his father had taken to the woman's owner in acknowledgment of betrothal. Beyond this, he knew nothing of the woman who was to be his, except that on this day he could go and get her.

He walked into the cool darkness of the city gate. Water carriers, just outside, their barrows laden with great tubs of water, passed to and fro all day, the water splashing out of the tubs upon the stones. It was always wet and cool in the tunnel of the gate under the thick wall of earth and brick; cool even upon a summer's day, so that the melon vendors spread their fruits upon the stones, melons split open to drink in the moist coolness. There were none yet, for the season was too early, but baskets of small hard green peaches stood along the walls, and the vendor cried out,

"The first peaches of spring—the first peaches! Buy, eat, purge your bowels of the poisons of winter!"

Wang Lung said to himself,

"If she likes them, I will buy her a handful when we return." He could not realize that when he walked back through the gate there would be a woman walking behind him.

He turned to the right within the gate and after a moment was in the Street of Barbers. There were few before him so early, only some farmers who had carried their produce into the town the night before in order that they might sell their vegetables at the dawn markets and return for the day's work in the fields. They had slept shivering and crouching over their baskets, the baskets now empty at their feet. Wang Lung avoided them lest some recognize him, for he wanted none of their joking on this day. All down the street in a long line the barbers stood behind their small stalls, and Wang Lung went to the furthest one and sat down upon the stool and motioned to the barber who stood chattering to his neighbor. The barber came at once and began quickly to pour hot water, from a kettle on his pot of charcoal, into his brass basin.

"Shave everything?" he said in a professional tone.

"My head and my face," replied Wang Lung.

"Ears and nostrils cleaned?" asked the barber.

"How much will that cost extra?" asked Wang Lung cautiously.

"Four pence," said the barber, beginning to pass a black cloth in and out of the hot water.

"I will give you two," said Wang Lung.

"Then I will clean one ear and one nostril," rejoined the barber promptly. "On which side of the face do you wish it done?" He grimaced at the next barber as he spoke and the other burst into a guffaw. Wang Lung perceived that he had fallen into the hands of a joker, and feeling inferior in some unaccountable way, as he always did, to these town dwellers, even though they were only barbers and the lowest of persons, he said quickly,

"As you will—as you will——"

Then he submitted himself to the barber's soaping and rubbing and shaving, and being after all a generous fellow enough, the barber gave him without extra charge a series of skilful poundings upon his shoulders and back to loosen his muscles. He commented upon Wang Lung as he shaved his upper forehead,

"This would not be a bad-looking farmer if he would cut off his hair. The new fashion is to take off the braid."

His razor hovered so near the circle of hair upon Wang Lung's crown that Wang Lung cried out,

"I cannot cut it off without asking my father!" And the barber laughed and skirted the round spot of hair.

When it was finished and the money counted into the barber's wrinkled, water-soaked hand, Wang Lung had a moment of horror. So much money! But walking down the street again with the wind fresh upon his shaven skin, he said to himself,

"It is only once."

He went to the market, then, and bought two pounds of pork and watched the butcher as he wrapped it in a dried lotus leaf, and then, hesitating, he bought also six ounces of beef. When all had been bought, even to fresh squares of beancurd, shivering in a jelly upon its leaf, he went to a candlemaker's shop and there he bought a pair of incense sticks. Then he turned his steps with great shyness toward the House of Hwang.

Once at the gate of the house he was seized with terror. How had he come alone? He should have asked his father—his uncle—even his nearest neighbor, Ching—anyone to come with him. He had never been in a great house before. How could he go in with his wedding feast on his arm, and say, "I have come for a woman?"

He stood at the gate for a long time, looking at it. It was closed fast, two great wooden gates, painted black and bound and studded with iron, closed upon each other. Two lions made of stone stood on guard, one at either side. There was no one else. He turned away. It was impossible.

He felt suddenly faint. He would go first and buy a little food. He had eaten nothing—had forgotten food. He went into a small street restaurant, and putting two pence upon the table, he sat down. A dirty waiting boy with a shiny black apron came near and he called out to him, "Two bowls of noodles!" And when they were come, he ate them down greedily, pushing them into his mouth with his bamboo chopsticks, while the boy stood and spun the coppers between his black thumb and forefinger.

"Will you have more?" asked the boy indifferently.

Wang Lung shook his head. He sat up and looked about. There was no one he knew in the small, dark, crowded room full of tables. Only a few men sat eating or drinking tea. It was a place for poor men, and among them he looked neat and clean and almost well-to-do, so that a beggar, passing, whined at him,

"Have a good heart, teacher, and give me a small cash—I starve!"

Wang Lung had never had a beggar ask of him before, nor had any ever called him teacher. He was pleased and he threw into the beggar's bowl two small cash, which are one fifth of a penny, and the beggar pulled back with swiftness his black claw of a hand, and grasping the cash, fumbled them within his rags.

Wang Lung sat and the sun climbed upwards. The waiting boy lounged about impatiently. "If you are buying nothing more," he said at last with much impudence, "you will have to pay rent for the stool."

Wang Lung was incensed at such impudence and he would have risen except that when he thought of going into the great House of Hwang and of asking there for a woman, sweat broke out over his whole body as though he were working in a field.

9

"Bring me tea," he said weakly to the boy. Before he could turn it was there and the small boy demanded sharply,

"Where is the penny?"

And Wang Lung, to his horror, found there was nothing to do but to produce from his girdle yet another penny.

"It is robbery," he muttered, unwilling. Then he saw entering the shop his neighbor whom he had invited to the feast, and he put the penny hastily upon the table and drank the tea at a gulp and went out quickly by the side door and was once more upon the street.

"It is to be done," he said to himself desperately, and slowly he turned his way to the great gates.

This time, since it was after high noon, the gates were ajar and the keeper of the gate idled upon the threshold, picking his teeth with a bamboo sliver after his meal. He was a tall fellow with a large mole upon his left cheek, and from the mole hung three long black hairs which had never been cut. When Wang Lung appeared he shouted roughly, thinking from the basket that he had come to sell something.

"Now then, what?"

With great difficulty Wang Lung replied,

"I am Wang Lung, the farmer."

"Well, and Wang Lung, the farmer, what?" retorted the gateman, who was polite to none except the rich friends of his master and mistress.

"I am come—I am come——" faltered Wang Lung.

"That I see," said the gateman with elaborate patience, twisting the long hairs of his mole.

"There is a woman," said Wang Lung, his voice sinking helplessly to a whisper. In the sunshine his face was wet.

The gateman gave a great laugh.

"So you are he!" he roared. "I was told to expect a bridegroom today. But I did not recognize you with a basket on your arm."

"It is only a few meats," said Wang Lung apologetically, waiting for the gateman to lead him within. But the gateman did not move. At last Wang Lung said with anxiety,

"Shall I go alone?"

The gateman affected a start of horror. "The Old Lord would kill you!"

Then seeing that Wang Lung was too innocent he said, "A little silver is a good key."

Wang Lung saw at last that the man wanted money of him.

10

"I am a poor man," he said pleadingly.

"Let me see what you have in your girdle," said the gateman.

And he grinned when Wang Lung in his simplicity actually put his basket upon the stones and lifting his robe took out the small bag from his girdle and shook into his left hand what money was left after his purchases. There was one silver piece and fourteen copper pence.

"I will take the silver," said the gateman coolly, and before Wang Lung could protest the man had the silver in his sleeve and was striding through the gate, bawling loudly,

"The bridegroom, the bridegroom!"

Wang Lung, in spite of anger at what had just happened and horror at this loud announcing of his coming, could do nothing but follow, and this he did, picking up his basket and looking neither to the right nor left.

Afterwards, although it was the first time he had ever been in a great family's house, he could remember nothing. With his face burning and his head bowed, he walked through court after court, hearing that voice roaring ahead of him, hearing tinkles of laughter on every side. Then suddenly when it seemed to him he had gone through a hundred courts, the gateman fell silent and pushed him into a small waiting room. There he stood alone while the gateman went into some inner place, returning in a moment to say,

"The Old Mistress says you are to appear before her."

Wang Lung started forward, but the gateman stopped him, crying in disgust,

"You cannot appear before a great lady with a basket on your arm—a basket of pork and beancurd! How will you bow?"

"True—true——" said Wang Lung in agitation. But he did not dare to put the basket down because he was afraid something might be stolen from it. It did not occur to him that all the world might not desire such delicacies as two pounds of pork and six ounces of beef and a small pond fish. The gateman saw his fear and cried out in great contempt,

"In a house like this we feed these meats to the dogs!" and seizing the basket he thrust it behind the door and pushed Wang Lung ahead of him.

Down a long narrow veranda they went, the roofs supported by delicate carven posts, and into a hall the like of which Wang Lung had never seen. A score of houses such as his whole house could have been put into it and have disappeared, so wide were the spaces, so high the roofs. Lifting his head in wonder to see

11

the great carven and painted beams above him he stumbled upon the high threshold of the door and would have fallen except that the gateman caught his arm and cried out,

"Now will you be so polite as to fall on your face like this before the Old Mistress?"

And collecting himself in great shame Wang Lung looked ahead of him, and upon a dais in the center of the room he saw a very old lady, her small fine body clothed in lustrous, pearly grey satin, and upon the low bench beside her a pipe of opium stood, burning over its little lamp. She looked at him out of small, sharp, black eyes, as sunken and sharp as a monkey's eyes in her thin and wrinkled face. The skin of her hand that held the pipe's end was stretched over her little bones as smooth and as yellow as the gilt upon an idol. Wang Lung fell to his knees and knocked his head on the tiled floor.

"Raise him," said the old lady gravely to the gateman, "these obeisances are not necessary. Has he come for the woman?"

"Yes, Ancient One," replied the gateman.

"Why does he not speak for himself?" asked the old lady.

"Because he is a fool, Ancient One," said the gateman, twirling the hairs of his mole.

This roused Wang Lung and he looked with indignation at the gateman.

"I am only a coarse person, Great and Ancient Lady," he said. "I do not know what words to use in such a presence."

The old lady looked at him carefully and with perfect gravity and made as though she would have spoken, except that her hand closed upon the pipe which a slave had been tending for her and at once she seemed to forget him. She bent and sucked greedily at the pipe for a moment and the sharpness passed from her eyes and a film of forgetfulness came over them. Wang Lung remained standing before her until in passing her eyes caught his figure.

"What is this man doing here?" she asked with sudden anger. It was as though she had forgotten everything. The gateman's face was immovable. He said nothing.

"I am waiting for the woman, Great Lady," said Wang Lung in much astonishment.

"The woman? What woman? . . ." the old lady began, but the slave girl at her side stooped and whispered and the lady recovered herself. "Ah, yes, I forgot for the moment—a small affair—you have come for the slave called O-lan. I remember we

12

promised her to some farmer in marriage. You are that farmer?"

"I am he," replied Wang Lung.

"Call O-lan quickly," said the old lady to her slave. It was as though she was suddenly impatient to be done with all this and to be left alone in the stillness of the great room with her opium pipe.

And in an instant the slave appeared leading by the hand a square, rather tall figure, clothed in clean blue cotton coat and trousers. Wang Lung glanced once and then away, his heart beating. This was his woman.

"Come here, slave," said the old lady carelessly. "This man has come for you."

The woman went before the lady and stood with bowed head and hands clasped.

"Are you ready?" asked the lady.

The woman answered slowly as an echo, "Ready."

Wang Lung, hearing her voice for the first time, looked at her back as she stood before him. It was a good enough voice, not loud, not soft, plain, and not ill-tempered. The woman's hair was neat and smooth and her coat clean. He saw with an instant's disappointment that her feet were not bound. But this he could not dwell upon, for the old lady was saying to the gateman,

"Carry her box out to the gate and let them begone." And then she called Wang Lung and said, "Stand beside her while I speak." And when Wang had come forward she said to him, "This woman came into our house when she was a child of ten and here she has lived until now, when she is twenty years old. I bought her in a year of famine when her parents came south because they had nothing to eat. They were from the north in Shantung and there they returned, and I know nothing further of them. You see she has the strong body and the square cheeks of her kind. She will work well for you in the field and drawing water and all else that you wish. She is not beautiful but that you do not need. Only men of leisure have the need for beautiful women to divert them. Neither is she clever. But she does well what she is told to do and she has a good temper. So far as I know she is virgin. She has not beauty enough to tempt my sons and grandsons even if she had not been in the kitchen. If there has been anything it has been only a serving man. But with the innumerable and pretty slaves running freely about the courts, I doubt if there has been anyone. Take her and use her well. She is a good slave, although somewhat slow and stupid, and had I not wished to acquire merit at the temple for my future existence by bringing more life into the world I should have kept her, for she is good enough for the kitchen. But I marry my slaves off if any will have them and the lords do not want them."

And to the woman she said,

"Obey him and bear him sons and yet more sons. Bring the first child to me to see."

"Yes, Ancient Mistress," said the woman submissively.

They stood hesitating, and Wang Lung was greatly embarrassed, not knowing whether he should speak or what.

"Well, go, will you!" said the old lady in irritation, and Wang Lung, bowing hastily, turned and went out, the woman after him, and after her the gateman, carrying on his shoulder the box. This box he dropped down in the room where Wang Lung returned to find his basket and would carry it no further, and indeed he disappeared without another word.

Then Wang Lung turned to the woman and looked at her for the first time. She had a square, honest face, a short, broad nose with large black nostrils, and her mouth was wide as a gash in her face. Her eyes were small and of a dull black in color, and were filled with some sadness that was not clearly expressed. It was a face that seemed habitually silent and unspeaking, as though it could not speak if it would. She bore patiently Wang Lung's look, without embarrassment or response, simply waiting until he had seen her. He saw that it was true there was not beauty of any kind in her face—a brown, common, patient face. But there were no pock-marks on her dark skin, nor was her lip split. In her ears he saw his rings hanging, the gold-washed rings he had bought, and on her hands were the rings he had given her. He turned away with secret exultation. Well, he had his woman!

"Here is this box and this basket," he said gruffly.

Without a word she bent over and picking up one end of the box she placed it upon her shoulder and, staggering under its weight, tried to rise. He watched her at this and suddenly he said,

"I will take the box. Here is the basket."

And he shifted the box to his own back, regardless of the best robe he wore, and she, still speechless, took the handle of the basket. He thought of the hundred courts he had come through and of his figure, absurd under its burden.

"If there were a side gate——" he muttered, and she nodded

after a little thought, as though she did not understand too quickly what he said. Then she led the way through a small unused court that was grown up with weed, its pool choked, and there under a bent pine tree was an old round gate that she pulled loose from its bar, and they went through and into the street.

Once or twice he looked back at her. She plodded along steadily on her big feet as though she had walked there all her life, her wide face expressionless. In the gate of the wall he stopped uncertainly and fumbled in his girdle with one hand for the pennies he had left, holding the box steady on his shoulder with the other hand. He took out two pence and with these he bought six small green peaches.

"Take these and eat them for yourself," he said gruffly.

She clutched them greedily as a child might and held them in her hand without speech. When next he looked at her as they walked along the margin of the wheat fields she was nibbling one cautiously, but when she saw him looking at her she covered it again with her hand and kept her jaws motionless.

And thus they went until they reached the western field where stood the temple to the earth. This temple was a small structure, not higher in all than a man's shoulder and made of grey bricks and roofed with tile. Wang Lung's grandfather, who had farmed the very fields upon which Wang Lung now spent his life, had built it, hauling the bricks from the town upon his wheelbarrow. The walls were covered with plaster on the outside and a village artist had been hired in a good year once to paint upon the white plaster a scene of hills and bamboo. But the rain of generations had poured upon this painting until now there was only a faint feathery shadow of bamboos left, and the hills were almost wholly gone.

Within the temple snugly under the roof sat two small, solemn figures, earthen, for they were formed from the earth of the fields about the temple. These were the god himself and his lady. They wore robes of red and gilt paper, and the god had a scant, drooping moustache of real hair. Each year at the New Year Wang Lung's father bought sheets of red paper and carefully cut and pasted new robes for the pair. And each year rain and snow beat in and the sun of summer shone in and spoiled their robes.

At this moment, however, the robes were still new, since the year was but well begun, and Wang Lung was proud of their spruce appearance. He took the basket from the woman's arm

15

and carefully he looked about under the pork for the sticks of incense he had bought. He was anxious lest they were broken and thus make an evil omen, but they were whole, and when he had found them he stuck them side by side in the ashes of other sticks of incense that were heaped before the gods, for the whole neighborhood worshipped these two small figures. Then fumbling for his flint and iron he caught, with a dried leaf for tinder, a flame to light the incense.

Together this man and this woman stood before the gods of their fields. The woman watched the ends of the incense redden and turn grey. When the ash grew heavy she leaned over and with her forefinger she pushed the head of ash away. Then as though fearful for what she had done, she looked quickly at Wang Lung, her eyes dumb. But there was something he liked in her movement. It was as though she felt that the incense belonged to them both; it was a moment of marriage. They stood there in complete silence, side by side, while the incense smouldered into ashes; and then because the sun was sinking, Wang Lung shouldered the box and they went home.

At the door of the house the old man stood to catch the last rays of the sun upon him. He made no movement as Wang Lung approached with the woman. It would have been beneath him to notice her. Instead he feigned great interest in the clouds and he cried,

"That cloud which hangs upon the left horn of the new moon speaks of rain. It will come not later than tomorrow night." And then as he saw Wang Lung take the basket from the woman he cried again, "And have you spent money?"

Wang Lung set the basket on the table. "There will be guests tonight," he said briefly, and he carried the box into the room where he slept and set it down beside the box where his own clothes were. He looked at it strangely. But the old man came to the door and said volubly,

"There is no end to the money spent in this house!"

Secretly he was pleased that his son had invited guests, but he felt it would not do to give out anything but complaints before his new daughter-in-law lest she be set from the first in ways of extravagance. Wang Lung said nothing, but he went out and took the basket into the kitchen and the woman followed him there. He took the food piece by piece from the basket and laid it upon the ledge of the cold stove and he said to her,

"Here is pork and here beef and fish. There are seven to eat. Can you prepare food?"

He did not look at the woman as he spoke. It would not have been seemly. The woman answered in her plain voice,

"I have been kitchen slave since I went into the House of Hwang. There were meats at every meal."

Wang Lung nodded and left her and did not see her again until the guests came crowding in, his uncle jovial and sly and hungry, his uncle's son an impudent lad of fifteen, and the farmers clumsy and grinning with shyness. Two were men from the village with whom Wang Lung exchanged seed and labor at harvest time, and one was his next door neighbor, Ching, a small, quiet man, ever unwilling to speak unless he were compelled to it. After they had been seated about the middle room with demurring and unwillingness to take seats, for politeness, Wang Lung went into the kitchen to bid the woman serve. Then he was pleased when she said to him,

"I will hand you the bowls if you will place them upon the table. I do not like to come out before men."

Wang Lung felt in him a great pride that this woman was his and did not fear to appear before him, but would not before other men. He took the bowls from her hands at the kitchen door and he set them upon the table in the middle room and called loudly,

"Eat, my uncle and my brothers." And when the uncle, who was fond of jokes, said, "Are we not to see the moth-browed bride?" Wang Lung replied firmly, "We are not yet one. It is not meet that other men see her until the marriage is consummated."

And he urged them to eat and they ate heartily of the good fare, heartily and in silence, and this one praised the brown sauce on the fish and that one the well-done pork, and Wang Lung said over and over in reply,

"It is poor stuff—it is badly prepared."

But in his heart he was proud of the dishes, for with what meats she had the woman had combined sugar and vinegar and a little wine and soy sauce and she had skilfully brought forth all the force of the meat itself, so that Wang Lung himself had never tasted such dishes upon the tables of his friends.

That night after the guests had tarried long over their tea and had done with their jokes, the woman still lingered behind the stove, and when Wang Lung had seen the last guest away he went in and she cowered there in the straw piles asleep

17

beside the ox. There was straw in her hair when he roused her, and when he called her she put up her arm suddenly in her sleep as though to defend herself from a blow. When she opened her eyes at last, she looked at him with her strange speechless gaze, and he felt as though he faced a child. He took her by the hand and led her into the room where that morning he had bathed himself for her, and he lit a red candle upon the table. In this light he was suddenly shy when he found himself alone with the woman and he was compelled to remind himself,

"There is this woman of mine. The thing is to be done."

And he began to undress himself doggedly. As for the woman, she crept around the corner of the curtain and began without a sound to prepare for the bed. Wang Lung said gruffly,

"When you lie down, put the light out first."

Then he lay down and drew the thick quilt about his shoulders and pretended to sleep. But he was not sleeping. He lay quivering, every nerve of his flesh awake. And when, after a long time, the room went dark, and there was the slow, silent, creeping movement of the woman beside him, an exultation filled him fit to break his body. He gave a hoarse laugh into the darkness and seized her.

2

THERE WAS this luxury of living. The next morning he lay upon his bed and watched the woman who was now wholly his own. She rose and drew about her her loosened garments and fastened them closely about her throat and waist, fitting them to her body with a slow writhe and twist. Then she put her feet into her cloth shoes and drew them on by the straps hanging at the back. The light from the small hole shone on her in a bar and he saw her face dimly. It looked unchanged. This was an astonishment to Wang Lung. He felt as though the night must have changed him; yet here was this woman rising from his bed as though she had risen every day of her life. The old man's cough rose querulously out of the dusky dawn and he said to her,

"Take to my father first a bowl of hot water for his lungs."

She asked, her voice exactly as it had been yesterday when she spoke, "Are there to be tea leaves in it?"

This simple question troubled Wang Lung. He would have liked to say, "Certainly there must be tea leaves. Do you think we are beggars?" He would have liked the woman to think that they made nothing of tea leaves in this house. In the House of Hwang, of course, every bowl of water was green with leaves. Even a slave, there, perhaps, would not drink only water. But he knew his father would be angry if on the first day the woman served tea to him instead of water. Besides, they really were not rich. He replied negligently, therefore,

"Tea? No—no—it makes his cough worse."

And then he lay in his bed warm and satisfied while in the kitchen the woman fed the fire and boiled the water. He would like to have slept, now that he could, but his foolish body, which he had made to arise every morning so early for all these years, would not sleep although it could, and so he lay there, tasting and savoring in his mind and in his flesh his luxury of idleness.

He was still half ashamed to think of this woman of his. Part of the time he thought of his fields and of the grains of the wheat and of what his harvest would be if the rains came and of the white turnip seed he wished to buy from his neighbor Ching if they could agree upon a price. But between all these thoughts which were in his mind every day there ran weaving and interweaving the new thought of what his life now was, and it occurred to him, suddenly, thinking of the night, to wonder if she liked him. This was a new wonder. He had questioned only of whether he would like her and whether or not she would be satisfactory in his bed and in his house. Plain though her face was and rough the skin upon her hands the flesh of her big body was soft and untouched and he laughed when he thought of it—the short hard laugh he had thrown out into the darkness the night before. The young lords had not seen, then, beyond that plain face of the kitchen slave. Her body was beautiful, spare and big boned yet rounded and soft. He desired suddenly that she should like him as her husband and then he was ashamed.

The door opened and in her silent way she came in bearing in both hands a steaming bowl to him. He sat up in bed and took it. There were tea leaves floating upon the surface of the water.

He looked up at her quickly. She was at once afraid and she said,

"I took no tea to the Old One—I did as you said—but to you I . . ."

Wang Lung saw that she was afraid of him and he was pleased and he answered before she finished, "I like it—I like it," and he drew his tea into his mouth with loud sups of pleasure.

In himself there was this new exultation which he was ashamed to make articulate even to his own heart, "This woman of mine likes me well enough!"

It seemed to him that during these next months he did nothing except watch this woman of his. In reality he worked as he always had. He put his hoe upon his shoulder and he walked to his plots of land and he cultivated the rows of grain, and he yoked the ox to the plow and he ploughed the western field for garlic and onions. But the work was luxury, for when the sun struck the zenith he could go to his house and food would be there ready for him to eat, and the dust wiped from the table, and the bowls and the chopsticks placed neatly upon it. Hitherto he had had to prepare the meals when he came in, tired though he was, unless the old man grew hungry out of time and stirred up a little meal or baked a piece of flat, unleavened bread to roll about a stem of garlic.

Now whatever there was, was ready for him, and he could seat himself upon the bench by the table and eat at once. The earthen floor was swept and the fuel pile replenished. The woman, when he had gone in the morning, took the bamboo rake and a length of rope and with these she roamed the countryside, reaping here a bit of grass and there a twig or a handful of leaves, returning at noon with enough to cook the dinner. It pleased the man that they need buy no more fuel.

In the afternoon she took a hoe and a basket and with these upon her shoulder she went to the main road leading into the city where mules and donkeys and horses carried burdens to and fro, and there she picked the droppings from the animals and carried it home and piled the manure in the dooryard for fertilizer for the fields. These things she did without a word and without being commanded to do them. And when the end of the day came she did not rest herself until the ox had been fed in the kitchen and until she had dipped water to hold to its muzzle to let it drink what it would.

And she took their ragged clothes and with thread she herself spun on a bamboo spindle from a wad of cotton she mended and contrived to cover the rents in their winter clothes. Their bedding she took into the sun on the threshold and ripped the coverings from the quilts and washed them and hung them upon a bamboo to dry, and the cotton in the quilts that had grown hard and grey from years she picked over, killing the vermin that had flourished in the hidden folds, and sunning it all. Day after day she did one thing after another, until the three rooms seemed clean and almost prosperous. The old man's cough grew better and he sat in the sun by the southern wall of the house, always half-asleep and warm and content.

But she never talked, this woman, except for the brief necessities of life. Wang Lung, watching her move steadily and slowly about the rooms on her big feet, watching secretly the stolid, square face, the unexpressed, half-fearful look of her eyes, made nothing of her. At night he knew the soft firmness of her body. But in the day her clothes, her plain blue cotton coat and trousers, covered all that he knew, and she was like a faithful, speechless serving maid, who is only a serving maid and nothing more. And it was not meet that he should say to her, "Why do you not speak?" It should be enough that she fulfilled her duty.

Sometimes, working over the clods in the fields, he would fall to pondering about her. What had she seen in those hundred courts? What had been her life, that life she never shared with him? He could make nothing of it. And then he was ashamed of his own curiosity and of his interest in her. She was, after all, only a woman.

But there is not that about three rooms and two meals a day to keep busy a woman who has been a slave in a great house and who has worked from dawn until midnight. One day when Wang Lung was hard pressed with the swelling wheat and was cultivating it with his hoe, day after day, until his back throbbed with weariness, her shadow fell across the furrow over which he bent himself, and there she stood, with a hoe across her shoulder.

"There is nothing in the house until nightfall," she said briefly, and without speech she took the furrow to the left of him and fell into steady hoeing.

The sun beat down upon them, for it was early summer, and her face was soon dripping with her sweat. Wang Lung had his coat off and his back bare, but she worked with her thin garment covering her shoulders and it grew wet and clung to her like skin. Moving together in a perfect rhythm, without a word, hour after hour, he fell into a union with her which took the pain from his labor. He had no articulate thought of anything; there was only this perfect sympathy of movement, of turning this earth of theirs over and over to the sun, this earth which formed their home and fed their bodies and made their gods. The earth lay rich and dark, and fell apart lightly under the points of their hoes. Sometimes they turned up a bit of brick, a splinter of wood. It was nothing. Some time, in some age, bodies of men and women had been buried there, houses had stood there, had fallen, and gone back into the earth. So would also their house, some time, return into the earth, their bodies also. Each had his turn at this earth. They worked on, moving together—together—producing the fruit of this earth— speechless in their movement together.

When the sun had set he straightened his back slowly and looked at the woman. Her face was wet and streaked with the earth. She was as brown as the very soil itself. Her wet, dark garments clung to her square body. She smoothed a last furrow slowly. Then in her usual plain way she said, straight out, her voice flat and more than usually plain in the silent evening air,

"I am with child."

Wang Lung stood still. What was there to say to this thing, then! She stooped to pick up a bit of broken brick and threw it out of the furrow. It was as though she had said, "I have brought you tea," or as though she had said, "We can eat." It seemed as ordinary as that to her! But to him—he could not say what it was to him. His heart swelled and stopped as though it met sudden confines. Well, it was their turn at this earth!

He took the hoe suddenly from her hand and he said, his voice thick in his throat, "Let be for now. It is a day's end. We will tell the old man."

They walked home, then, she half a dozen paces behind him as befitted a woman. The old man stood at the door, hungry for his evening's food, which, now that the woman was in the house, he would never prepare for himself. He was impatient and he called out,

"I am too old to wait for my food like this!"

But Wang Lung, passing him into the room, said,

"She is with child already."

He tried to say it easily as one might say, "I have planted the seeds in the western field today," but he could not. Although he spoke in a low voice it was to him as though he had shouted the words out louder than he would.

The old man blinked for a moment and then comprehended, and cackled with laughter.

"Heh-heh-heh——" he called out to his daughter-in-law as she came, "so the harvest is in sight!"

Her face he could not see in the dusk, but she answered evenly,

"I shall prepare food now."

"Yes—yes—food——" said the old man eagerly, following her into the kitchen like a child. Just as the thought of a grandson had made him forget his meal, so now the thought of food freshly before him made him forget the child.

But Wang Lung sat upon a bench by the table in the darkness and put his head upon his folded arms. Out of this body of his, out of his own loins, life!

3

WHEN THE HOUR for birth drew near he said to the woman,

"We must have someone to help at the time—some woman."

But she shook her head. She was clearing away the bowls after the evening food. The old man had gone to his bed and the two of them were alone in the night, with only the light that fell upon them from the flickering flame of a small tin lamp filled with bean oil, in which a twist of cotton floated for a wick.

"No woman?" he asked in consternation. He was beginning now to be accustomed to these conversations with her in which her part was little more than a movement of head or hand, or at most an occasional word dropped unwillingly from her wide mouth. He had even come to feel no lack in such conversing. "But it will be odd with only two men in the house!" he continued. "My mother had a woman from the village. I know nothing of these affairs. Is there none in the great house, no old slave with whom you were friends, who could come?"

It was the first time he had mentioned the house from which she came. She turned on him as he had never seen her, her narrow eyes widened, her face stirred with dull anger.

"None in that house!" she cried out at him.

He dropped his pipe which he was filling and stared at her. But her face was suddenly as usual and she was collecting the chopsticks as though she had not spoken.

"Well, here is a thing!" he said in astonishment. But she said nothing. Then he continued in argument, "We two men, we have no ability in childbirth. For my father it is not fitting to enter your room—for myself, I have never even seen a cow give birth. My clumsy hands might mar the child. Someone from the great house, now, where the slaves are always giving birth . . ."

She had placed the chopsticks carefully down in an orderly heap upon the table and she looked at him, and after a moment's looking she said,

"When I return to that house it will be with my son in my arms. I shall have a red coat on him and red-flowered trousers and on his head a hat with a small gilded Buddha sewn on the front and on his feet tiger-faced shoes. And I will wear new shoes and a new coat of black sateen and I will go into the kitchen where I spent my days and I will go into the great hall where the Old One sits with her opium, and I will show myself and my son to all of them."

He had never heard so many words from her before. They came forth steadily and without break, albeit slowly, and he realized that she had planned this whole thing out for herself. When she had been working in the fields beside him she had been planning all this out! How astonishing she was! He would have said that she had scarcely thought of the child, so stilly had she gone about her work, day in and day out. And instead she saw this child, born and fully clothed, and herself as his mother, in a new coat! He was for once without words himself, and he pressed the tobacco diligently into a ball between his thumb and forefinger, and picking up his pipe he fitted the tobacco into the bowl.

"I suppose you will need some money," he said at last with apparent gruffness.

"If you will give me three silver pieces . . ." she said fearfully. "It is a great deal, but I have counted carefully and I will waste no penny of it. I shall make the cloth dealer give me the last inch to the foot."

Wang Lung fumbled in his girdle. The day before he had

sold a load and a half of reeds from the pond in the western field to the town market and he had in his girdle a little more than she wished. He put the three silver dollars upon the table. Then, after a little hesitation, he added a fourth piece which he had long kept by him on the chance of his wanting to gamble a little some morning at the tea house. But he never did more than linger about the tables and look at the dice as they clattered upon the table, fearful lest he lose if he played. He usually ended by spending his spare hours in the town at the story-teller's booth, where one may listen to an old tale and pay no more than a penny into his bowl when it was passed about.

"You had better take the other piece," he said, lighting his pipe between the words, blowing quickly at the paper spill to set it aflame. "You may as well make his coat of a small remnant of silk. After all, he is the first."

She did not at once take the money, but she stood looking at it, her face motionless. Then she said in a half-whisper,

"It is the first time I have had silver money in my hand."

Suddenly she took it and clenched it in her hand and hurried into the bedroom.

Wang Lung sat smoking, thinking of the silver as it had lain upon the table. It had come out of the earth, this silver, out of his earth that he ploughed and turned and spent himself upon. He took his life from this earth; drop by drop by his sweat he wrung food from it and from the food, silver. Each time before this that he had taken the silver out to give to anyone, it had been like taking a piece of his life and giving it to someone carelessly. But now for the first time such giving was not pain. He saw, not the silver in the alien hand of a merchant in the town; he saw the silver transmuted into something worth even more than itself—clothes upon the body of his son. And this strange woman of his, who worked about, saying nothing, seeming to see nothing, she had first seen the child thus clothed!

She would have no one with her when the hour came. It came one night, early, when the sun was scarcely set. She was working beside him in the harvest field. The wheat had borne and been cut and the field flooded and the young rice set, and now the rice bore harvest, and the ears were ripe and full after the summer rains and the warm ripening sun of early autumn. Together they cut the sheaves all day, bending and cutting with short-handled scythes. She had stooped stiffly, because of the burden she bore, and she moved more slowly than he, so that they cut unevenly, his row ahead, and hers behind. She began to cut more and more slowly as noon wore on to afternoon and evening, and he turned to look at her with impatience. She stopped and stood up then, her scythe dropped. On her face was a new sweat, the sweat of a new agony.

"It is come," she said. "I will go into the house. Do not come into the room until I call. Only bring me a newly peeled reed, and slit it, that I may cut the child's life from mine."

She went across the fields toward the house as though there were nothing to come, and after he had watched her he went to the edge of the pond in the outer field and chose a slim green reed and peeled it carefully and slit it on the edge of his scythe. The quick autumn darkness was falling then and he shouldered his scythe and went home.

When he reached the house he found his supper hot on the table and the old man eating. She had stopped in her labor to prepare them food! He said to himself that she was a woman such as is not commonly found. Then he went to the door of their room and he called out,

"Here is the reed!"

He waited, expecting that she would call out to him to bring it in to her. But she did not. She came to the door and through the crack her hand reached out and took the reed. She said no word, but he heard her panting as an animal pants which has run for a long way.

The old man looked up from his bowl to say,

"Eat, or all will be cold." And then he said, "Do not trouble yourself yet—it will be a long time. I remember well when the first was born to me it was dawn before it was over. Ah me, to think that out of all the children I begot and your mother bore, one after the other—a score or so—I forget—only you have lived! You see why a woman must bear and bear." And then he said again, as though he had just thought of it newly, "By this time tomorrow I may be grandfather to a man child!" He began to laugh suddenly and he stopped his eating and sat chuckling for a long time in the dusk of the room.

But Wang Lung stood listening at the door to those heavy animal pants. A smell of hot blood came through the crack, a sickening smell that frightened him. The panting of the woman within became quick and loud, like whispered screams, but she made no sound aloud. When he could bear no more and was about to break into the room, a thin, fierce cry came out and he forgot everything.

"Is it a man?" he cried importunately, forgetting the woman. The thin cry burst out again, wiry, insistent. "Is it a man?" he cried again, "tell me at least this—is it a man?"

And the voice of the woman answered as faintly as an echo, "A man!"

He went and sat down at the table then. How quick it had all been! The food was long cold and the old man was asleep on his bench, but how quick it had all been! He shook the old man's shoulder.

"It is a man child!" he called triumphantly. "You are grandfather and I am father!"

The old man woke suddenly and began to laugh as he had been laughing when he fell asleep.

"Yes—yes—of course," he cackled, "a grandfather—a grandfather—" and he rose and went to his bed, still laughing.

Wang Lung took up the bowl of cold rice and began to eat. He was very hungry all at once and he could not get the food into his mouth quickly enough. In the room he could hear the woman dragging herself about and the cry of the child was incessant and piercing.

"I suppose we shall have no more peace in this house now," he said to himself proudly.

When he had eaten all that he wished he went to the door again and she called to him to come in and he went in. The odor of spilt blood still hung hot upon the air, but there was no trace of it except in the wooden tub. But into this she had poured water and had pushed it under the bed so that he could hardly see it. The red candle was lit and she was lying neatly covered upon the bed. Beside her, wrapped in a pair of his old trousers, as the custom was in this part, lay his son.

He went up and for the moment there were no words in his mouth. His heart crowded up into his breast and he leaned over the child to look at it. It had a round wrinkled face that looked very dark and upon its head the hair was long and damp and black. It had ceased crying and lay with its eyes tightly shut.

He looked at his wife and she looked back at him. Her hair was still wet with her agony and her narrow eyes were sunken. Beyond this, she was as she always was. But to him she was touching, lying there. His heart rushed out to these two and he said, not knowing what else there was that could be said,

27

"Tomorrow I will go into the city and buy a pound of red sugar and stir it into boiling water for you to drink."

And then looking at the child again, this burst forth from him suddenly as though he had just thought of it, "We shall have to buy a good basketful of eggs and dye them all red for the village. Thus will everyone know I have a son!"

4

THE NEXT DAY after the child was born the woman rose as usual and prepared food for them but she did not go into the harvest fields with Wang Lung, and so he worked alone until after the noon hour. Then he dressed himself in his blue gown and went into the town. He went to the market and bought fifty eggs, not new laid, but still well enough and costing a penny for one, and he bought red paper to boil in the water with them to make them red. Then with the eggs in his basket he went to the sweet shop, and there he bought a pound and a little more of red sugar and saw it wrapped carefully into its brown paper, and under the straw string which held it the sugar dealer slipped a strip of red paper, smiling as he did so.

"It is for the mother of a new-born child, perhaps,"

"A first-born son," said Wang Lung proudly.

"Ah, good fortune," answered the man carelessly, his eye on a well-dressed customer who had just come in.

This he had said many times to others, even every day to someone, but to Wang Lung it seemed special and he was pleased with the man's courtesy and he bowed and bowed again as he went from the shop. It seemed to him as he walked into the sharp sunshine of the dusty street that there was never a man so filled with good fortune as he.

He thought of this at first with joy and then with a pang of fear. It did not do in this life to be too fortunate. The air and the earth were filled with malignant spirits who could not endure the happiness of mortals, especially of such as are poor. He turned abruptly into the candlemaker's shop, who sold incense also, and there he bought four sticks of incense, one for each person in his house, and with these four sticks he went into the small temple of the gods of the earth, and he thrust them into the cold ashes of the incense he had placed there before, he and his wife together. He watched the four sticks well lit and then went homeward, comforted. These two small, protective figures, sitting staidly under their small roof—what a power they had!

And then, almost before one could realize anything, the woman was back in the fields beside him. The harvests were past, and the grain they beat out upon the threshing floor which was also the dooryard to the house. They beat it out with flails, he and the woman together. And when the grain was flailed they winnowed it, casting it up from great flat bamboo baskets into the wind and catching the good grain as it fell, and the chaff blew away in a cloud with the wind. Then there were the fields to plant for winter wheat again, and when he had yoked the ox and ploughed the land the woman followed behind with her hoe and broke the clods in the furrows.

She worked all day now and the child lay on an old torn quilt on the ground, asleep. When it cried the woman stopped and uncovered her bosom to the child's mouth, sitting flat upon the ground, and the sun beat down upon them both, the reluctant sun of late autumn that will not let go the warmth of summer until the cold of the coming winter forces it. The woman and the child were as brown as the soil and they sat there like figures made of earth. There was the dust of the fields upon the woman's hair and upon the child's soft black head.

But out of the woman's great brown breast the milk gushed forth for the child, milk as white as snow, and when the child suckled at one breast it flowed like a fountain from the other, and she let it flow. There was more than enough for the child, greedy though he was, life enough for many children, and she let it flow out carelessly, conscious of her abundance. There was always more and more. Sometimes she lifted her breast and let it flow out upon the ground to save her clothing, and it sank into the earth and made a soft, dark, rich spot in the field. The child was fat and good-natured and ate of the inexhaustible life his mother gave him.

Winter came on and they were prepared against it. There had been such harvests as never were before, and the small, three-roomed house was bursting. From the rafters of the thatched roof hung strings and strings of dried onions and garlic, and about the middle room and in the old man's room and in their own room were mats made of reeds and twisted into the shapes of great jars and these were filled full of wheat and rice. Much of this would be sold, but Wang Lung was frugal and he did not, like many of the villagers, spend his money freely at gambling or on foods too delicate for them, and so, like them, have to sell the grain at harvest when the price was low. Instead he saved it and sold it when the snow came on the ground or at the New Year when people in the towns will pay well for food at any price.

His uncle was always having to sell his grain before it was even well ripened. Sometimes he even sold it standing in the field to save himself the trouble of harvesting and threshing to get a little ready cash. But then his uncle's wife was a foolish woman, fat and lazy, and forever clamoring for sweet food and for this sort of thing and that and for new shoes bought in the town. Wang Lung's woman made all the shoes for himself and for the old man and for her own feet and the child's. He would not know what to make of it if she wished to buy shoes!

There was never anything hanging from the rafters in his uncle's crumbling old house. But in his own there was even a leg of pork which he had bought from his neighbor Ching when he killed his pig that looked as though it were sickening for a disease. The pig had been caught early before it lost flesh and the leg was a large one and O-lan had salted it thoroughly and hung it to dry. There were as well two of their own chickens killed and drawn and dried with the feathers on and stuffed with salt inside.

In the midst of all this plenty they sat in the house, therefore, when the winds of winter came out of the desert to the northeast of them, winds bitter and biting. Soon the child could almost sit alone. They had had a feast of noodles, which mean long life, on his month birthday, when he was a full moon of age, and Wang Lung had invited those who came to his wedding feast and to each he had given a round ten of the red eggs he had boiled and dyed, and to all those who came from the village to congratulate him he gave two eggs. And every one envied him his son, a great, fat, moony-faced child with high cheekbones like his mother. Now as winter came on he sat on the quilt placed on the earthen floor of the house instead of upon the fields, and they opened the door to the south for light, and the sun came in, and the wind on the north beat in vain against the thick earthen wall of the house.

The leaves were soon torn from the date tree on the threshold and from the willow trees and the peach trees near the fields. Only the bamboo leaves clung to the bamboos in the sparse clump to the east of the house, and even though the wind wrenched the stems double, the leaves clung.

With this dry wind the wheat seed that lay in the ground could not sprout and Wang Lung waited anxiously for the rains. And then the rains came suddenly out of a still grey day when the wind fell and the air was quiet and warm, and they all sat in the house filled with well-being, watching the rain fall full and straight and sink into the fields about the dooryard and drip from the thatched ends of the roof above the door. The child was amazed and stretched out his hands to catch the silver lines of the rain as it fell, and he laughed and they laughed with him and the old man squatted on the floor beside the child and said,

"There is not another child like this in a dozen villages. Those brats of my brother notice nothing before they walk." And in the fields the wheat seed sprouted and pushed spears of delicate green above the wet brown earth.

At a time like this there was visiting, because each farmer felt that for once Heaven was doing the work in the fields and their crops were being watered without their backs being broken for it, carrying buckets to and fro, slung upon a pole across their shoulders; and in the morning they gathered at this house and that, drinking tea here and there, going from house to house barefoot across the narrow path between the fields under great oiled paper umbrellas. The women stayed at home and made shoes and mended clothes, if they were thrifty, and thought of preparations for the feast of the New Year.

But Wang Lung and his wife were not frequent at visiting. There was no house in the village of small scattered houses, of which theirs was one of a half dozen, which was so filled with warmth and plenty as their own, and Wang Lung felt that if he became too intimate with the others there would be borrowing. New Year was coming and who had all the money he wanted for the new clothes and the feasting? He stayed in his house and while the woman mended and sewed he took his rakes of split bamboo and examined them, and where the string was broken he wove in new string made of hemp he grew himself,

31

and where a prong was broken out he drove in cleverly a new bit of bamboo.

And what he did for the farm implements, his wife, O-lan, did for the house implements. If an earthen jar leaked she did not, as other women did, cast it aside and talk of a new one. Instead she mixed earth and clay and welded the crack and heated it slowly and it was as good as new.

They sat in their house, therefore, and they rejoiced in each other's approval, although their speech was never anything more than scattered words such as these:

"Did you save the seed from the large squash for the new planting?" Or, "We will sell the wheat straw and burn the bean stalks in the kitchen." Or perhaps rarely Wang Lung would say, "This is a good dish of noodles," and O-lan would answer in deprecation, "It is good flour we have this year from the fields."

From the produce, Wang Lung in this good year had a handful of silver dollars over and above what they needed and these he was fearful of keeping in his belt or of telling any except the woman what he had. They plotted where to keep the silver and at last the woman cleverly dug a small hole in the inner wall of their room behind the bed and into this Wang Lung thrust the silver and with a clod of earth she covered the hole, and it was as though there was nothing there. But to both Wang and O-lan it gave a sense of secret richness and reserve. Wang Lung was conscious that he had money more than he need spend, and when he walked among his fellows he walked at ease with himself and with all.

5

THE NEW YEAR approached and in every house in the village there were preparations. Wang Lung went into the town to the candlemaker's shop and he bought squares of red paper on which were brushed in gilt ink the letter for happiness and some with the letter for riches, and these squares he pasted upon his farm utensils to bring him luck in the New Year. Upon his plow and upon the ox's yoke and upon the two buckets in which he carried his fertilizer and his water, upon each of these he pasted a square. And then upon the doors of his house he pasted long strips of red paper brushed with mottoes of good luck, and over his doorway he pasted a fringe of red paper cunningly cut into a flower pattern and very finely cut. And he bought red paper to make new dresses for the gods, and this the old man did cleverly enough for his old shaking hands, and Wang Lung took them and put them upon the two small gods in the temple to the earth and he burned a little incense before them for the sake of the New Year. And for his house he bought also two red candles to burn on the eve of the year upon the table under the picture of a god, which was pasted on the wall of the middle room above where the table stood.

And Wang Lung went again into the town and he bought pork fat and white sugar and the woman rendered the fat smooth and white and she took rice flour, which they had ground from their own rice between their millstones to which they could yoke the ox when they needed to do so, and she took the fat and the sugar and she mixed and kneaded rich New Year's cakes, called moon cakes, such as were eaten in the House of Hwang.

When the cakes were laid out upon the table in strips, ready for heating, Wang Lung felt his heart fit to burst with pride. There was no other woman in the village able to do what his had done, to make cakes such as only the rich ate at the feast. In some of the cakes she had put strips of little red haws and spots of dried green plums, making flowers and patterns.

"It is a pity to eat these," said Wang Lung.

The old man was hovering about the table, pleased as a child might be pleased with the bright colors. He said,

"Call my brother, your uncle, and his children—let them see!"

But prosperity had made Wang Lung cautious. One could not ask hungry people only to see cakes.

"It is ill luck to look at cakes before the New Year," he replied hastily. And the woman, her hands all dusty with the fine rice flour and sticky with the fat, said,

"Those are not for us to eat, beyond one or two of the plain ones for guests to taste. We are not rich enough to eat white sugar and lard. I am preparing them for the Old Mistress at the great house. I shall take the child on the second day of the New Year and carry the cakes for a gift."

Then the cakes were more important than ever, and Wang Lung was pleased that to the great hall where he had stood with so much timidity and in such poverty his wife should now go as visitor, carrying his son, dressed in red, and cakes made as these were, with the best flour and sugar and lard.

All else at that New Year sank into insignificance beside this visit. His new coat of black cotton cloth which O-lan had made, when he had put it on, only made him say to himself,

"I shall wear it when I take them to the gate of the great house."

He even bore carelessly the first day of the New Year when his uncle and his neighbors came crowding into the house to wish his father and himself well, all boisterous with food and drink. He had himself seen to it that the colored cakes were put away into the basket lest he might have to offer them to common men, although he found it very hard when the plain white ones were praised for their flavor of fat and sugar not to cry out,

"You should see the colored ones!"

But he did not, for more than anything he wished to enter the great house with pride.

Then on the second day of the New Year, when it is the day for women to visit each other, the men having eaten and drunk well the day before, they rose at dawn and the woman dressed the child in his red coat and in the tiger-faced shoes she had made, and she put on his head, freshly shaven by Wang Lung himself on the last day of the old year, the crownless red hat with the small gilt Buddha sewed on front, and she set him upon the bed. Then Wang Lung dressed himself quickly while his wife combed out afresh her long black hair and knotted it with the brass pin washed with silver which he had bought for her, and she put on her new coat of black that was made from the same piece as his own new robe, twenty-four feet of good cloth for the two, and two feet of cloth thrown in for good measure, as the custom is at cloth shops. Then he carrying the child and she the cakes in the basket, they set out on the path across the fields, now barren with winter.

Then Wang Lung had his reward at the great gate of the House of Hwang, for when the gateman came to the woman's call he opened his eyes at all he saw and he twirled the three long hairs on his mole and cried out,

"Ah, Wang the farmer, three this time instead of one!" And then seeing the new clothes they all wore and the child who was a son, he said further, "One has no need to wish you more fortune this year than you have had in the last."

Wang Lung answered negligently as one speaks to a man who is scarcely an equal, "Good harvests—good harvests—" and he stepped with assurance inside the gate.

The gateman was impressed with all he saw and he said to Wang Lung,

"Do you sit within my wretched room while I announce your woman and son within."

And Wang Lung stood watching them go across the court, his wife and his son, bearing gifts to the head of a great house. It was all to his honor, and when he could no longer see them when they had dwindled down the long vista of the courts one inside the other, and had turned at last wholly out of sight, he went into the gateman's house and there he accepted as a matter of course from the gateman's pock-marked wife the honorable seat to the left of the table in the middle room, and he accepted with only a slight nod the bowl of tea which she presented to him and he set it before him and did not drink of it, as though it were not good enough in quality of tea leaves for him.

It seemed a long time before the gateman returned, bringing back again the woman and child. Wang Lung looked closely at the woman's face for an instant trying to see if all were well, for he had learned now from that impassive square countenance to detect small changes at first invisible to him. She wore a look of heavy content, however, and at once he became impatient to hear her tell of what had happened in those courts of the ladies into which he could not go, now that he had no business there.

With short bows, therefore, to the gateman and to his pock-marked wife he hurried O-lan away and he took into his own arms the child who was asleep and lying all crumpled in his new coat.

"Well?" he called back to her over his shoulder as she followed him. For once he was impatient with her slowness. She drew a little nearer to him and said in a whisper,

"I believe, if one should ask me, that they are feeling a pinch this year in that house."

She spoke in a shocked tone as one might speak of gods being hungry.

35

"What do you mean?" said Wang Lung, urging her.

But she would not be hastened. Words were to her things to be caught one by one and released with difficulty.

"The Ancient Mistress wore the same coat this year as last. I have never seen this happen before. And the slaves had no new coats." And then after a pause she said, "I saw not one slave with a new coat like mine." And then after a while she said again, "As for our son, there was not even a child among the concubines of the Old Master himself to compare to him in beauty and in dress."

A slow smile spread over her face and Wang Lung laughed aloud and he held the child tenderly against him. How well he had done—how well he had done! And then as he exulted he was smitten with fear. What foolish thing was he doing, walking like this under an open sky, with a beautiful man child for any evil spirit passing by chance through the air to see! He opened his coat hastily and thrust the child's head into his bosom and he said in a loud voice,

"What a pity our child is a female whom no one could want and covered with smallpox as well! Let us pray it may die."

"Yes—yes——" said his wife as quickly as she could, understanding dimly what a thing they had done.

And being comforted with these precautions they had now taken, Wang Lung once more urged his wife.

"Did you find out why they are poorer?"

"I had but a moment for private talk with the cook under whom I worked before," she replied, "but she said, 'This house cannot stand forever with all the young lords, five of them, spending money like waste water in foreign parts and sending home woman after woman as they weary of them, and the Old Lord living at home adding a concubine or two each year, and the Old Mistress eating enough opium every day to fill two shoes with gold.' "

"Do they indeed!" murmured Wang Lung, spellbound.

"Then the third daughter is to be married in the spring," continued O-lan, "and her dowry is a prince's ransom and enough to buy an official seat in a big city. Her clothes she will have of nothing but the finest satins with special patterns woven in Soochow and Hangchow and she will have a tailor sent from Shanghai with his retinue of under tailors lest she find her clothes less fashionable than those of the women in foreign parts."

36

"Whom will she marry, then, with all this expense?" said Wang Lung, struck with admiration and horror at such pouring out of wealth.

"She is to marry the second son of a Shanghai magistrate," said the woman, and then after a long pause she added, "They must be getting poorer for the Old Mistress herself told me they wished to sell land—some of the land to the south of the house, just outside the city wall, where they have always planted rice each year because it is good land and easily flooded from the moat around the wall."

"Sell their land!" repeated Wang Lung, convinced. "Then indeed are they growing poor. Land is one's flesh and blood."

He pondered for a while and suddenly a thought came to him and he smote the side of his head with his palm.

"What have I not thought of!" he cried, turning to the woman. "We will buy the land!"

They stared at each other, he in delight, she in stupefaction.

"But the land—the land——" she stammered.

"I will buy it!" he cried in a lordly voice. "I will buy it from the great House of Hwang!"

"It is too far away," she said in consternation. "We would have to walk half the morning to reach it."

"I will buy it," he repeated peevishly as he might repeat a demand to his mother who crossed him.

"It is a good thing to buy land," she said pacifically. "It is better certainly than putting money into a mud wall. But why not a piece of your uncle's land? He is clamoring to sell that strip near to the western field we now have."

"That land of my uncle's," said Wang Lung loudly, "I would not have it. He has been dragging a crop out of it in this way and that for twenty years and not a bit has he put back of manure or bean cake. The soil is like lime. No, I will buy Hwang's land."

He said "Hwang's land" as casually as he might have said "Ching's land,"—Ching, who was his farmer neighbor. He would be more than equal to these people in the foolish, great, wasteful house. He would go with the silver in his hand and he would say plainly,

"I have money. What is the price of the earth you wish to sell?" Before the Old Lord he heard himself saying and to the Old Lord's agent, "Count me as anyone else. What is the fair price? I have it in my hand."

And his wife, who had been a slave in the kitchens of that

37

proud family, she would be wife to a man who owned a piece of the land that for generations had made the House of Hwang great. It was as though she felt his thought for she suddenly ceased her resistance and she said,

"Let it be bought. After all, rice land is good, and it is near the moat and we can get water every year. It is sure."

And again the slow smile spread over her face, the smile that never lightened the dullness of her narrow black eyes, and after a long time she said,

"Last year this time I was slave in that house."

And they walked on, silent with the fullness of this thought.

6

THIS PIECE of land which Wang Lung now owned was a thing which greatly changed his life. At first, after he had dug the silver from the wall and taken it to the great house, after the honor of speaking as an equal to the Old Lord's equal was past, he was visited with a depression of spirit which was almost regret. When he thought of the hole in the wall now empty that had been filled with silver he need not use, he wished that he had his silver back. After all, this land, it would take hours of labor again, and as O-lan said, it was far away, more than a *li* which is a third of a mile. And again, the buying of it had not been quite so filled with glory as he had anticipated. He had gone too early to the great house and the Old Lord was still sleeping. True, it was noon, but when he said in a loud voice,

"Tell his Old Honor I have important business—tell him money is concerned!" the gateman had answered positively,

"All the money in the world would not tempt me to wake the old tiger. He sleeps with his new concubine, Peach Blossom, whom he has had but three days. It is not worth my life to waken him." And then he added somewhat maliciously, pulling at the hairs on his mole, "And do not think that silver will waken him—he has had silver under his hand since he was born."

In the end, then, it had had to be managed with the Old Lord's agent, an oily scoundrel whose hands were heavy with the money that stuck to them in passing. So it seemed sometimes to Wang Lung that after all the silver was more valuable than the land. One could see silver shining.

Well, but the land was his! He set out one grey day in the second month of the new year to look at it. None knew yet that it belonged to him and he walked out to see it alone, a long square of heavy black clay that lay stretched beside the moat encircling the wall of the town. He paced the land off carefully, three hundred paces lengthwise and a hundred and twenty across. Four stones still marked the corners of the boundaries, stones set with the great seal character of the House of Hwang. Well, he would have that changed. He would pull up the stones later and he would put his own name there—not yet, for he was not ready for people to know that he was rich enough to buy land from the great house, but later, when he was more rich, so that it did not matter what he did. And looking at that long square of land he thought to himself,

"To those at the great house it means nothing, this handful of earth, but to me it means how much!"

Then he had a turn of his mind and he was filled with a contempt for himself that a small piece of land should seem so important. Why, when he had poured out his silver proudly before the agent the man had scraped it up carelessly in his hands and said,

"Here is enough for a few days of opium for the old lady, at any rate."

And the wide difference that still lay between him and the great house seemed suddenly impassable as the moat full of water in front of him, and as high as the wall beyond, stretching up straight and hoary before him. He was filled with an angry determination, then, and he said to his heart that he would fill that hole with silver again and again until he had bought from the House of Hwang enough land so that this land would be less than an inch in his sight.

And so this parcel of land became to Wang Lung a sign and a symbol.

Spring came with blustering winds and torn clouds of rain and for Wang Lung the half-idle days of winter were plunged into long days of desperate labor over his land. The old man looked after the child now and the woman worked with the man from dawn until sunset flowed over the fields, and when Wang Lung perceived one day that again she was with child, his first thought was of irritation that during the harvest she would be unable to work. He shouted at her, irritable with fatigue,

"So you have chosen this time to breed again, have you!"

She answered stoutly.

"This time it is nothing. It is only the first that is hard."

Beyond this nothing was said of the second child from the time he noticed its growth swelling her body until the day came in autumn when she laid down her hoe one morning and crept into the house. He did not go back that day even for his noon meal, for the sky was heavy with thunder clouds and his rice lay dead ripe for gathering into sheaves. Later before the sun set she was back beside him, her body flattened, spent, but her face silent and undaunted. His impulse was to say,

"For this day you have had enough. Go and lie upon your bed." But the aching of his own exhausted body made him cruel, and he said to himself that he had suffered as much with his labor that day as she with her childbirth, and so he only asked between the strokes of his scythe,

"Is it male or female?"

She answered calmly,

"It is another male."

They said nothing more to each other, but he was pleased, and the incessant bending and stooping seemed less arduous, and working on until the moon rose above a bank of purple clouds, they finished the field and went home.

After his meal and after he had washed his sunburnt body in cool water and had rinsed his mouth with tea, Wang Lung went in to look at his second son. O-lan had lain herself upon the bed after the cooking of the meal and the child lay beside her—a fat, placid child, well enough, but not so large as the first one. Wang Lung looked at him and then went back to the middle room well content. Another son, and another and another each year—one could not trouble with red eggs every year; it was enough to do it for the first. Sons every year; the house was full of good fortune—this woman brought him nothing but good fortune. He shouted to his father,

"Now, Old One, with another grandson we shall have to put the big one in your bed!"

The old man was delighted. He had for a long time been desiring this child to sleep in his bed and warm his chilly old flesh with the renewal of young bones and blood, but the child would not leave his mother. Now, however, staggering in with feet still unsteady with babyhood, he stared at this new child beside his mother, and seeming to comprehend with his grave eyes that another had his place, he allowed himself without protest to be placed in his grandfather's bed.

And again the harvests were good and Wang Lung gathered silver from the selling of his produce and again he hid it in the wall. But the rice he reaped from the land of the Hwangs brought him twice as much as that from his own rice land. The earth of that piece was wet and rich and the rice grew on it as weeds grow where they are not wanted. And everyone knew now that Wang Lung owned this land and in his village there was talk of making him the head.

7

WANG LUNG's uncle began at this time to become the trouble which Wang Lung had surmised from the beginning that he might be. This uncle was the younger brother of Wang Lung's father, and by all the claims of relationship he might depend upon Wang Lung if he had not enough for himself and his family. So long as Wang Lung and his father were poor and scantily fed the uncle made muster to scratch about on his land and gather enough to feed his seven children and his wife and himself. But once fed none of them worked. The wife would not stir herself to sweep the floor of their hut, nor did the children trouble to wash the food from their faces. It was a disgrace that as the girls grew older and even to marriageable age they still ran about the village street and left uncombed their rough sun-browned hair, and sometimes even talked to men. Wang Lung,

41

meeting his oldest girl cousin thus one day, was so angered for the disgrace done to his family that he dared to go to his uncle's wife and say,

"Now, who will marry a girl like my cousin, whom any man may look on? She has been marriageable these three years and she runs about and today I saw an idle lout on the village street lay his hand on her arm and she answered him only with brazen laughter!"

His uncle's wife had nothing active in her body except her tongue and this she now loosed upon Wang Lung.

"Well, and who will pay for the dowry and for the wedding and for the middleman's fees? It is all very well for those to talk who have more land than they know what to do with and who can yet go and buy more land from the great families with their spare silver, but your uncle is an unfortunate man and he has been so from the first. His destiny is evil and through no fault of his own. Heaven wills it. Where others can produce good grain, for him the seed dies in the ground and nothing but weeds spring up, and this though he break his back!"

She fell into loud, easy tears, and began to work herself up into a fury. She snatched at her knot of hair on the back of her head and tore down the loose hairs about her face and she began to scream freely,

"Ah, it is something you do not know—to have an evil destiny! Where the fields of others bear good rice and wheat, ours bear weeds; where the houses of others stand for a hundred years, the earth itself shakes under ours so that the walls crack; where others bear men, I, although I conceive a son, will yet give birth to a girl—ah, evil destiny!"

She shrieked aloud and the neighbor women rushed out of their houses to see and to hear. Wang Lung stood stoutly, however, and would finish what he came to say.

"Nevertheless," he said, "although it is not for me to presume to advise the brother of my father, I will say this: it is better that a girl be married away while she is yet virgin, and whoever heard of a bitch dog who was allowed on the streets who did not give birth to a litter?"

Having spoken thus plainly, he went away to his own house and left his uncle's wife screaming. He had it in his mind to buy more land this year from the House of Hwang and more land year after year as he was able, and he dreamed of adding a new room to his house and it angered him that as he saw himself and his sons rising into a landed family, this shiftless brood of his cousins should be running loose, bearing the same name as his own.

The next day his uncle came to the field where he was working. O-lan was not there, for ten moons had passed since the second child was born and a third birth was close upon her, and this time she was not so well and for a handful of days she had not come to the fields and so Wang Lung worked alone. His uncle came slouching along a furrow, his clothes never properly buttoned about him, but caught together and held insecurely with his girdle, so that it always seemed that if a gust of wind blew at him he might suddenly stand naked. He came to where Wang Lung was and he stood in silence while Wang Lung hoed a narrow line beside the broad beans he was cultivating. At last Wang Lung said maliciously and without looking up,

"I ask your pardon, my uncle, for not stopping in my work. These beans, must, if they are to bear, as you know, be cultivated twice and thrice. Yours, doubtless, are finished. I am very slow—a poor farmer—never finishing my work in time to rest."

His uncle understood perfectly Wang Lung's malice, but he answered smoothly,

"I am a man of evil destiny. This year out of twenty seed beans, one came up, and in such a poor growth as that there is no use in putting the hoe down. We shall have to buy beans this year if we eat them," and he sighed heavily.

Wang Lung hardened his heart. He knew that his uncle had come to ask something of him. He put his hoe down into the ground with a long even movement and with great care, breaking up the tiniest clod in the soft earth already well cultivated. The bean plants stood erect in thrifty order, casting as they stood little fringes of clear shadow in the sunshine. At last his uncle began to speak.

"The person in my house has told me," he said, "of your interest in my worthless oldest slave creature. It is wholly true what you say. You are wise for your years. She should be married. She is fifteen years old and for these three or four years could have given birth. I am terrified constantly lest she conceive by some wild dog and bring shame to me and to our name. Think of this happening in our respectable family, to me, the brother of your own father!"

Wang Lung put his hoe down hard into the soil. He would

43

have liked to have spoken plainly. He would have liked to have said,

"Why do you not control her, then? Why do you not keep her decently in the house and make her sweep and clean and cook and make clothes for the family?"

But one cannot say these things to an older generation. He remained silent, therefore, and hoed closely about a small plant and he waited.

"If it had been my good destiny," continued his uncle mournfully, "to have married a wife as your father did, one who could work and at the same time produce sons, as your own does also, instead of a woman like mine, who grows nothing but flesh and gives birth to nothing but females and that one idle son of mine who is less than a male for his idleness, I, too, might have been rich now as you are. Then might I have, willingly would I have, shared my riches with you. Your daughters I would have wed to good men, your son would I have placed in a merchant's shop as apprentice and willingly paid the fee of guaranty—your house would I have delighted to repair, and you I would have fed with the best I had, you and your father and your children, for we are of one blood."

Wang Lung answered shortly,

"You know I am not rich. I have the five mouths to feed now and my father is old and does not work and still he eats, and another mouth is being born in my house at this very moment, for aught I know."

His uncle replied shrilly,

"You are rich—you are rich! You have bought the land from the great house at the gods know what heavy price—is there another in the village who could do this thing?"

At this Wang Lung was goaded to anger. He flung down his hoe and he shouted suddenly, glaring at his uncle,

"If I have a handful of silver it is because I work and my wife works, and we do not, as some do, sit idling over a gambling table or gossiping on doorsteps never swept, letting the fields grow to weeds and our children go half-fed!"

The blood flew into his uncle's yellow face and he rushed at his nephew and slapped him vigorously on both cheeks.

"Now that," he cried, "for speaking so to your father's generation! Have you no religion, no morals, that you are so lacking in filial conduct? Have you not heard it said that in the Sacred Edicts it is commanded that a man is never to correct an elder?"

44

Wang Lung stood sullen and immoveable, conscious of his fault but angry to the bottom of his heart against this man who was his uncle.

"I will tell your words to the whole village!" screamed his uncle in a high cracked voice of fury. "Yesterday you attack my house and call aloud in the streets that my daughter is not a virgin; today you reproach me, who if your father passes on, must be as your own father to you! Now may my daughters all not be virgins, but not from one of them would I hear such talk!" And he repeated over and over, "I will tell it to the village—I will tell it to the village . . ." until at last Wang Lung said unwillingly, "What do you want me to do?"

It touched his pride that this matter might indeed be called out before the village. After all, it was his own flesh and blood.

His uncle changed immediately. Anger melted out of him. He smiled and he put his hand on Wang Lung's arm.

"Ah, I know you—good lad—good lad——" he said softly. "Your old uncle knows you—you are my son. Son, a little silver in this poor old palm—say, ten pieces, or even nine, and I could begin to have arrangements with a matchmaker for that slave of mine. Ah, you are right! It is time—it is time!" He sighed and shook his head and he looked piously to the sky.

Wang Lung picked up his hoe and threw it down again.

"Come to the house," he said shortly. "I do not carry silver on me like a prince," and he strode ahead, bitter beyond speech because some of the good silver with which he had planned to buy more land was to go into this palm of his uncle's, from whence it would slip on to the gambling table before night fell.

He strode into the house, brushing out of his way his two small sons who played, naked in the warm sunshine, about the threshold. His uncle, with easy good nature, called to the children and took from some recess in his crumpled clothing a copper coin for each child. He pressed the small fat shining bodies to him, and putting his nose into their soft necks he smelled of the sun-browned flesh with easy affection.

"Ah, you are two little men," he said, clasping one in either arm.

But Wang Lung did not pause. He went into the room where he slept with his wife and the last child. It was very dark, coming in as he did from the outer sunshine, and except for the bar of light from the hole, he could see nothing. But the smell of warm blood which he remembered so well filled his nostrils and he called out sharply,

45

"What now—has your time come?"

The voice of his wife answered from the bed more feebly than he had ever heard her speak,

"It is over once more. It is only a slave this time—not worth mentioning."

Wang Lung stood still. A sense of evil struck him. A girl! A girl was causing all this trouble in his uncle's house. Now a girl had been born into his house as well.

He went without reply then to the wall and felt for the roughness which was the mark of the hiding place and he removed the clod of earth. Behind it he fumbled among the little heap of silver and he counted out nine pieces.

"Why are you taking the silver out?" said his wife suddenly in the darkness.

"I am compelled to lend it to my uncle," he replied shortly.

His wife answered nothing at first and then she said in her plain, heavy way,

"It is better not to say lend. There is no lending in that house. There is only giving."

"Well I know that," replied Wang Lung with bitterness. "It is cutting my flesh out to give to him and for nothing except that we are of a blood."

Then going out into the threshold he thrust the money at his uncle and he walked quickly back to the field and there he fell to working as though he would tear the earth from its foundations. He thought for the time only of the silver; he saw it poured out carelessly upon a gambling table, saw it swept up by some idle hand—his silver, the silver he had so painfully collected from the fruits of his fields, to turn it back again for more earth for his own.

It was evening before his anger was spent and he straightened himself and remembered his home and his food. And then he thought of that new mouth come that day into his house and it struck him, with heaviness, that the birth of daughters had begun for him, daughters who do not belong to their parents, but are born and reared for other families. He had not even thought, in his anger at his uncle, to stop and see the face of this small, new creature.

He stood leaning upon his hoe and he was seized with sadness. It would be another harvest before he could buy that land now, a piece adjoining the one he had, and there was this new mouth in the house. Across the pale, oyster-colored sky of twilight a flock of crows flew, sharply black, and whirred over

46

him, cawing loudly. He watched them disappear like a cloud into the trees about his house, and he ran at them, shouting and shaking his hoe. They rose again slowly, circling and re-circling over his head, mocking him with their cries, and they flew at last into the darkening sky.

He groaned aloud. It was an evil omen.

8

IT SEEMED as though once the gods turn against a man they will not consider him again. The rains, which should have come in early summer, withheld themselves, and day after day the skies shone with fresh and careless brilliance. The parched and starving earth was nothing to them. From dawn to dawn there was not a cloud, and at night the stars hung out of the sky, golden and cruel in their beauty.

The fields, although Wang Lung cultivated them desperately, dried and cracked, and the young wheat stalks, which had sprung up courageously with the coming of spring and had prepared their heads for the grain, when they found nothing coming from the soil or the sky for them, ceased their growing and stood motionless at first under the sun and at last dwindled and yellowed into a barren harvest. The young rice beds which Wang Lung sowed at first were squares of jade upon the brown earth. He carried water to them day after day after he had given up the wheat, the heavy wooden buckets slung upon a bamboo pole across his shoulders. But though a furrow grew upon his flesh and a callus formed there as large as a bowl, no rain came.

At last the water in the pond dried into a cake of clay and the water even in the well sunk so low that O-lan said to him,

"If the children must drink and the old man have his hot water the plants must go dry."

Wang Lung answered with anger that broke into a sob,

47

"Well, and they must all starve if the plants starve." It was true that all their lives depended upon the earth.

Only the piece of land by the moat bore harvest, and this because at last when summer wore away without rain, Wang Lung abandoned all his other fields and stayed the day out at this one, dipping water from the moat to pour upon the greedy soil. This year for the first time he sold his grain as soon as it was harvested, and when he felt the silver upon his palm he gripped it hard in defiance. He would, he told himself, in spite of gods and drought, do that which he had determined. His body he had broken and his sweat he had spilled for this handful of silver and he would do what he would with it. And he hurried to the House of Hwang and he met the land agent there and he said without ceremony,

"I have that with which to buy the land adjoining mine by the moat."

Now Wang Lung had heard here and there that for the House of Hwang it had been a year verging upon poverty. The old lady had not had her dole of opium to the full for many days and she was like an old tigress in her hunger so that each day she sent for the agent and she cursed him and struck his face with her fan, screaming at him,

"And are there not acres of land left, yet?" until he was beside himself.

He had even given up the moneys which ordinarily he held back from the family transactions for his own use, so beside himself had he been. And as if this were not enough, the Old Lord took yet another concubine, a slave who was the child of a slave who had been his creature in her youth, but who was now wed to a man servant in the house, because the Old Lord's desire for her failed before he took her into his room as concubine. This child of the slave, who was not more than sixteen, he now saw with fresh lust, for as he grew old and infirm and heavy with flesh he seemed to desire more and more women who were slight and young, even to childhood, so that there was no slaking his lust. As the Old Mistress with her opium, so he with his lusts, and there was no making him understand there was not money for jade earrings for his favorites and not gold for their pretty hands. He could not comprehend the words "no money," who all his life had but to reach out his hand and fill it as often as he would.

And seeing their parents thus, the young lords shrugged their shoulders and said there must still be enough for their

48

lifetime. They united in only one thing and this was to berate the agent for his ill management of the estates, so that he who had once been oily and unctuous, a man of plenty and of ease, was now become anxious and harried and his flesh gone so that his skin hung upon him like an old garment.

Neither had Heaven sent rain upon the fields of the House of Hwang, and there, too, there were no harvests, and so when Wang Lung came to the agent crying, "I have silver," it was as though one came saying to the hungry, "I have food."

The agent grasped at it, and where before there had been dickering and tea-drinking, now the two men spoke in eager whispers, and more quickly than they could speak whole words, the money passed from one hand to the other and papers were signed and sealed and the land was Wang Lung's.

And once again Wang Lung did not count the passing of silver, which was his flesh and his blood, a hard thing. He bought with it the desire of his heart. He had now a vast field of good land, for the new field was twice as large as the first. But more to him than its dark fertility was the fact that it had belonged once to the family of a prince. And this time he told no one, not even O-lan, what he had done.

Month passed into month and still no rain fell. As autumn approached the clouds gathered unwillingly in the sky, small, light clouds, and in the village street one could see men standing about, idle and anxious, their faces upturned to the sky, judging closely of this cloud and that, discussing together as to whether any held rain in it. But before sufficient clouds could gather for promise, a bitter wind rose out of the northwest, the acrid wind of the distant desert, and blew the clouds from the sky as one gathers dust from a floor with a broom. And the sky was empty and barren, and the stately sun rose each morning and made its march and set solitary each night. And the moon in its time shone like a lesser sun for clearness.

From his fields Wang Lung reaped scanty harvest of hardy beans, and from his corn field, which he had planted in despair when the rice beds had yellowed and died before ever the plants had been set into the watered field, he plucked short stubby ears with the grains scattered here and there. There was not a bean lost in the threshing. He set the two little boys to sifting the dust of the threshing floor between their fingers after he and the woman had flailed the bean vines, and he shelled the

49

corn upon the floor in the middle room, watching sharply every grain that flew wide. When he would have put the cobs away for fuel, his wife spoke out,

"No—do not waste them in burning. I remember when I was a child in Shantung when years like this came, even the cobs we ground and ate. It is better than grass."

When she had spoken they all fell silent, even the children. There was foreboding in these strange brilliant days when the land was failing them. Only the girl child knew no fear. For her there were the mother's two great breasts as yet filled for her needs. But O-lan, giving her suck, muttered,

"Eat, poor fool—eat, while there is yet that which can be eaten."

And then, as though there were not enough evil, O-lan was again with child, and her milk dried up, and the frightened house was filled with the sound of a child continually crying for food.

If one had asked Wang Lung,

"And how are you fed through the autumn?" he would have answered, "I do not know—a little food here and there."

But there was none to ask him that. None asked of any other in the whole countryside, "How are you fed?" None asked anything except of himself, "How shall I be fed this day?" And parents said, "How shall we be fed, we and our children?"

Now Wang Lung's ox he had cared for as long as he could. He had given the beast a bit of straw and a handful of vines as long as these lasted and then he had gone out and torn leaves from the trees for it until winter came and these were gone. Then since there was no land to plough, since seed, if it were planted only dried in the earth, and since they had eaten all their seed, he turned the ox out to hunt for itself, sending the eldest boy to sit upon its back all day and hold the rope passed through its nostrils so that it would not be stolen. But latterly he had not dared even to do this, lest men from the village, even his neighbors, might overcome the lad and seize the ox for food, and kill it. So he kept the ox on the threshold until it grew lean as its skeleton.

But there came a day when there was no rice left and no wheat left and there were only a few beans and a meager store of corn, and the ox lowed with its hunger and the old man said,

"We will eat the ox, next."

Then Wang Lung cried out, for it was to him as though one

said, "We will eat a man next." The ox was his companion in the fields and he had walked behind and praised it and cursed it as his mood was, and from his youth he had known the beast, when they had bought it a small calf. And he said,

"How can we eat the ox? How shall we plough again?"

But the old man answered, tranquil enough,

"Well, and it is your life or the beast's, and your son's life or the beast's and a man can buy an ox again more easily than his own life."

But Wang Lung would not that day kill it. And the next day passed and the next and the children cried out for food and they would not be comforted and O-lan looked at Wang Lung, beseeching him for the children, and he saw at last that the thing was to be done. So he said roughly,

"Let it be killed then, but I cannot do it."

He went into the room where he slept and he laid himself upon the bed and he wrapped the quilt about his head that he might not hear the beast's bellowing when it died.

Then O-lan crept out and she took a great iron knife she had in the kitchen and she cut a great gash in the beast's neck, and thus she severed its life. And she took a bowl and caught its blood to cook for them to eat in a pudding, and she skinned and hacked to pieces the great carcass, and Wang Lung would not come out until the thing was wholly done and the flesh was cooked and upon the table. But when he tried to eat the flesh of his ox his gorge rose and he could not swallow it and he drank only a little of the soup. And O-lan said to him,

"An ox is but an ox and this one grew old. Eat, for there will be another one day and far better than this one."

Wang Lung was a little comforted then and he ate a morsel and then more, and they all ate. But the ox was eaten at last and the bones cracked for the marrow, and it was all too quickly gone, and there was nothing left of it except the skin, dried and hard and stretched upon the rack of bamboo O-lan had made to hold it spread.

At first there had been hostility in the village against Wang Lung because it was supposed that he had silver which he was hiding and food stored away. His uncle, who was among the first to be hungry, came importuning to his door, and indeed the man and his wife and his seven children had nothing to eat. Wang Lung measured unwillingly into the skin of his uncle's robe a small heap of beans and a precious handful of corn. Then he said with firmness,

"It is all I can spare and I have first my old father to consider, even if I had no children."

When his uncle came again Wang Lung cried out,

"Even filial piety will not feed my house!" and he sent his uncle empty away.

From that day his uncle turned against him like a dog that has been kicked, and he whispered about the village in this house and in that,

"My nephew there, he has silver and he has food, but he will give none of it to us, not even to me, and to my children, who are his own bones and flesh. We can do nothing but starve."

And as family after family finished its store in the small village and spent its last coin in the scanty markets of the town, and the winds of winter came down from the desert, cold as a knife of steel and dry and barren, the hearts of the villagers grew distraught with their own hunger and with the hunger of their pinched wives and crying children, and when Wang Lung's uncle shivered about the streets like a lean dog and whispered from his famished lips, "There is one who has food—there is one whose children are fat, still," the men took up poles and went one night to the house of Wang Lung and beat upon the door. And when he had opened to the voices of his neighbors, they fell upon him and pushed him out of the doorway and threw out of the house his frightened children, and they fell upon every corner, and they scrabbled every surface with their hands to find where he had hidden his food. Then when they found his wretched store of a few dried beans and a bowlful of dried corn they gave a great howl of disappointment and despair, and they seized his bits of furniture, the table and the benches and the bed where the old man lay, frightened and weeping.

Then O-lan came forward and spoke, and her plain, slow voice rose above the men,

"Not that—not that yet," she called out. "It is not yet time to take our table and the benches and the bed from our house. You have all our food. But out of your own houses you have not sold yet your table and your benches. Leave us ours. We are even. We have not a bean or a grain of corn more than you—no, you have more than we, now, for you have all of ours. Heaven will strike you if you take more. Now, we will go out together and hunt for grass to eat and bark from the trees, you for your children, and we for our three children, and for this fourth who is to be born in such times." She pressed her hand to her belly as she spoke, and the men were ashamed before her and went out

52

one by one, for they were not evil men except when they starved.

One lingered, that one called Ching, a small, silent yellow man with a face like an ape's in the best of times, and now hollowed and anxious. He would have spoken some good word of shame, for he was an honest man and only his crying child had forced him to evil. But in his bosom was a handful of beans he had snatched when the store was found and he was fearful lest he must return them if he spoke at all, and so he only looked at Wang Lung with haggard, speechless eyes and he went out.

Wang Lung stood there in his dooryard where year after year he had threshed his good harvests, and which had lain now for many months idle and useless. There was nothing left in the house to feed his father and his children—nothing to feed this woman of his who besides the nourishment of her own body had this other one to feed into growth, this other one who would, with the cruelty of new and ardent life, steal from the very flesh and blood of its mother. He had an instant of extreme fear. Then into his blood like soothing wine flowed this comfort. He said in his heart,

"They cannot take the land from me. The labor of my body and the fruit of the fields I have put into that which cannot be taken away. If I had the silver, they would have taken it. If I had bought with the silver to store it, they would have taken it all. I have the land still, and it is mine."

9

WANG LUNG, sitting at the threshold of his door, said to himself that now surely something must be done. They could not remain here in this empty house and die. In his lean body, about which he daily wrapped more tightly his loose girdle, there was a determination to live. He would not thus, just when he was coming into the fullness of a man's life, suddenly be robbed of it by a stupid fate. There was such anger in him now as he often could not express. At times it seized him like a frenzy so that he rushed out upon his barren threshing floor and shook his arms at the foolish sky that shone above him, eternally blue and clear and cold and cloudless.

"Oh, you are too wicked, you Old Man in Heaven!" he would cry recklessly. And if for an instant he were afraid, he would the next instant cry sullenly, "And what can happen to me worse than that which has happened!"

Once he walked, dragging one foot after another in his famished weakness, to the temple of the earth, and deliberately he spat upon the face of the small, imperturbable god who sat there with his goddess. There were no sticks of incense now before this pair, nor had there been for many moons, and their paper clothes were tattered and showed their clay bodies through the rents. But they sat there unmoved by anything and Wang Lung gnashed his teeth at them and walked back to his house groaning and fell upon his bed.

They scarcely rose at all now, any of them. There was no need, and fitful sleep took the place, for a while, at least, of the food they had not. The cobs of the corn they had dried and eaten and they stripped the bark from trees and all over the countryside people were eating what grass they could find upon the wintry hills. There was not an animal anywhere. A man might walk for a handful of days and see not an ox nor an ass nor any kind of beast or fowl.

The children's bellies were swollen out with empty wind, and one never saw in these days a child playing upon the village street. At most the two boys in Wang Lung's house crept to the door and sat in the sun, the cruel sun that never ceased its endless shining. Their once rounded bodies were angular and bony now, sharp small bones like the bones of birds, except for their ponderous bellies. The girl child never even sat alone, although the time was past for this, but lay uncomplaining hour after hour wrapped in an old quilt. At first the angry insistence of her crying had filled the house, but she had come to be quiet, sucking feebly at whatever was put into her mouth and never lifting up her voice. Her little hollowed face peered out at them all, little sunken blue lips like a toothless old woman's lips, and hollow black eyes peering.

This persistence of the small life in some way won her father's affection, although if she had been round and merry as the others had been at her age he would have been careless of her for a girl. Sometimes, looking at her he whispered softly,

"Poor fool—poor little fool——" And once when she essayed a weak smile with her toothless gums showing, he broke into tears and took into his lean hard hand her small claw and held the tiny grasp of her fingers over his forefinger. Thereafter he would sometimes lift her, all naked as she lay, and thrust her inside the scant warmth of his coat against his flesh and sit with her so by the threshold of the house, looking out over the dry, flat fields.

As for the old man, he fared better than any, for if there was anything to eat he was given it, even though the children were without. Wang Lung said to himself proudly that none should say in the hour of death he had forgotten his father. Even if his own flesh went to feed him the old man should eat. The old man slept day and night, and ate what was given him and there was still strength in him to creep about the dooryard at noon when the sun was warm. He was more cheerful than any of them and he quavered forth one day in his old voice that was like a little wind trembling among cracked bamboos,

"There have been worse days—there have been worse days. Once I saw men and women eating children."

"There will never be such a thing in my house," said Wang Lung, in extremest horror.

There was a day when his neighbor Ching, worn now to less than the shadow of a human creature, came to the door of Wang Lung's house and he whispered from his lips that were dried and black as earth,

"In the town the dogs are eaten and everywhere the horses and the fowls of every sort. Here we have eaten the beasts that ploughed our fields and the grass and the bark of trees. What now remains for food?"

Wang Lung shook his head hopelessly. In his bosom lay the slight, skeleton-like body of his girl child, and he looked down into the delicate bony face, and into the sharp, sad eyes that watched him unceasingly from his breast. When he caught those eyes in his glance, invariably there wavered upon the child's face a flickering smile that broke his heart.

Ching thrust his face nearer.

"In the village they are eating human flesh," he whispered. "It is said your uncle and his wife are eating. How else are they living and with strength enough to walk about—they, who, it is known, have never had anything?"

Wang Lung drew back from the death-like head which Ching

had thrust forward as he spoke. With the man's eyes close like this, he was horrible. Wang Lung was suddenly afraid with a fear he did not understand. He rose quickly as though to cast off some entangling danger.

"We will leave this place," he said loudly. "We will go south! There are everywhere in this great land people who starve. Heaven, however wicked, will not at once wipe out the sons of Han."

His neighbor looked at him patiently. "Ah, you are young," he said sadly. "I am older than you and my wife is old and we have nothing except one daughter. We can die well enough."

"You are more fortunate than I," said Wang Lung. "I have my old father and these three small mouths and another about to be born. We must go lest we forget our nature and eat each other as the wild dogs do."

And then it seemed to him suddenly that what he said was very right, and he called aloud to O-lan, who lay upon the bed day after day without speech, now that there was no food for the stove and no fuel for the oven.

"Come, woman, we will go south!"

There was cheer in his voice such as none had heard in many moons, and the children looked up and the old man hobbled out from his room and O-lan rose feebly from her bed and came to the door of their room and clinging to the door frame she said,

"It is a good thing to do. One can at least die walking."

The child in her body hung from her lean loins like a knotty fruit and from her face every particle of flesh was gone, so that the jagged bones stood forth rock-like under her skin. "Only wait until tomorrow," she said. "I shall have given birth by then. I can tell by this thing's movements in me."

"Tomorrow, then," answered Wang Lung, and then he saw his wife's face and he was moved with a pity greater than any he had had for himself. This poor creature was dragging forth yet another!

"How shall you walk, you poor creature!" he muttered, and he said unwillingly to his neighbor Ching, who still leaned against the house by the door, "If you have any food left, for a good heart's sake give me a handful to save the life of the mother of my sons, and I will forget that I saw you in my house as a robber."

Ching looked at him ashamed and he answered humbly,

"I have never thought of you with peace since that hour. It

was that dog, your uncle, who enticed me, saying that you had good harvests stored up. Before this cruel heaven I promise you that I have only a little handful of dried red beans buried beneath the stone of my doorway. This I and my wife placed there for our last hour, for our child and ourselves, that we might die with a little food in our stomachs. But some of it I will give to you, and tomorrow go south, if you can. I stay, I and my house. I am older than you and I have no son, and it does not matter whether I live or die."

And he went away and in a little while he came back, bringing tied in a cotton kerchief a double handful of small red beans, mouldy with the soil. The children clambered about at the sight of the food, and even the old man's eyes glistened, but Wang Lung pushed them away for once and he took the food in to his wife as she lay and she ate a little of it, bean by bean, unwilling except that her hour was upon her and she knew that if she had not any food she would die in the clutches of her pain.

Only a few of the beans did Wang Lung hide in his own hand and these he put into his own mouth and he chewed them into a soft pulp and then putting his lips to the lips of his daughter he pushed into her mouth the food, and watching her small lips move, he felt himself fed.

That night he stayed in the middle room. The two boys were in the old man's room and in the third room O-lan gave birth alone. He sat there as he had sat during the birth of his first-born son and listened. She would not even yet have him near her at her hour. She would give birth alone, squatting over the old tub she kept for the purpose, creeping about the room afterwards to remove the traces of what had been, hiding as an animal does the birth stains of its young.

He listened intently for the small sharp cry he knew so well, and he listened with despair. Male or female, it mattered nothing to him now—there was only another mouth coming which must be fed.

"It would be merciful if there were no breath," he muttered, and then he heard the feeble cry—how feeble a cry!—hang for an instant upon the stillness. "But there is no mercy of any kind in these days," he finished bitterly, and he sat listening.

There was no second cry, and over the house the stillness became impenetrable. But for many days there had been stillness everywhere, the stillness of inactivity and of people, each in his own house, waiting to die. This house was filled with such stillness. Suddenly Wang Lung could not bear it. He was afraid. He rose and went to the door of the room where O-lan was and he called into the crack and the sound of his own voice heartened him a little.

"You are safe?" he called to the woman. He listened. Suppose she had died as he sat there! But he could hear a slight rustling. She was moving about and at last she answered, her voice a sigh,

"Come!"

He went in, then, and she lay there upon the bed, her body scarcely raising the cover. She lay alone.

"Where is the child?" he asked.

She made a slight movement of her hand upon the bed and he saw upon the floor the child's body.

"Dead!" he exclaimed.

"Dead," she whispered.

He stooped and examined the handful of its body—a wisp of bone and skin—a girl. He was about to say, "But I heard it crying—alive——" and then he looked at the woman's face. Her eyes were closed and the color of her flesh was the color of ashes and her bones stuck up under the skin—a poor silent face that lay there, having endured to the utmost, and there was nothing he could say. After all, during these months he had had only his own body to drag about. What agony of starvation this woman had endured, with the starved creature gnawing at her from within, desperate for its own life!

He said nothing, but he took the dead child into the other room and laid it upon the earthen floor and searched until he found a bit of broken mat and this he wrapped about it. The round head dropped this way and that and upon the neck he saw two dark, bruised spots, but he finished what he had to do. Then he took the roll of matting, and going as far from the house as he had strength, he laid the burden against the hollowed side of an old grave. This grave stood among many others, worn down and no longer known or cared for, on a hillside just at the border of Wang Lung's western field. He had scarcely put the burden down before a famished, wolfish dog hovered almost at once behind him, so famished that although he took up a small stone and threw it and hit its lean flank with a thud, the animal would not stir away more than a few feet. At last Wang Lung felt his legs sinking beneath him and covering his face with his hands he went away.

58

"It is better as it is," he muttered to himself, and for the first time was wholly filled with despair.

The next morning when the sun rose unchanging in its sky of varnished blue it seemed to him a dream that he could ever have thought of leaving his house with these helpless children and this weakened woman and this old man. How could they drag their bodies over a hundred miles, even to plenty? And who knew whether or not even in the south there was food? One would say there was no end to this brazen sky. Perhaps they would wear out all their last strength only to find more starving people and these strangers to them as well. Far better to stay where they could die in their beds. He sat desponding on the threshold of the door and gazed bleakly over the dried and hardened fields from which every particle of anything which could be called food or fuel had been plucked.

He had no money. Long ago the last coin was gone. But even money would do little good now, for there was no food to buy. He had heard earlier that there were rich men in the town who were hoarding food for themselves and for sale to the very rich, but even this ceased to anger him. He did not feel this day that he could walk to the town, even to be fed without money. He was, indeed, not hungry.

The extreme gnawing in his stomach which he had had at first was now past and he could stir up a little of the earth from a certain spot in one of his fields and give it to the children without desiring any of it for himself. This earth they had been eating in water for some days—goddess of mercy earth, it was called, because it had some slight nutritious quality in it, although in the end it could not sustain life. But made into a gruel it allayed the children's craving for a time and put something into their distended, empty bellies. He steadfastly would not touch the few beans that O-lan still held in her hand, and it comforted him vaguely to hear her crunching them, one at a time, a long time apart.

And then, as he sat there in the doorway, giving up his hope and thinking with a dreamy pleasure of lying upon his bed and sleeping easily into death, someone came across the fields—men walking toward him. He continued to sit as they drew near and he saw that one was his uncle and with him were three men whom he did not know.

"I have not seen you these many days," called his uncle with loud and affected good humor. And as he drew nearer he said in the same loud voice, "And how well you have fared! And your father, my elder brother, he is well?"

Wang Lung looked at his uncle. The man was thin, it is true, but not starved, as he should be. Wang Lung felt in his own shriveled body the last remaining strength of life gathering into a devastating anger against this man, his uncle.

"How you have eaten—how you have eaten!" he muttered thickly. He thought nothing of these strangers or of any courtesy. He saw only his uncle with flesh on his bones, still. His uncle opened wide his eyes and threw up his hands to the sky.

"Eaten!" he cried. "If you could see my house! Not a sparrow even could pick up a crumb there. My wife—do you remember how fat she was? How fair and fat and oily her skin? And now she is like a garment hung on a pole—nothing but the poor bones rattling together in her skin. And of our children only four are left—the three little ones gone—gone—and as for me, you see me!" He took the edge of his sleeve and wiped the corner of each eye carefully.

"You have eaten," repeated Wang Lung dully.

"I have thought of nothing but of you and of your father, who is my brother," retorted his uncle briskly, "and now I prove it to you. As soon as I could, I borrowed from these good men in the town a little food on the promise that with the strength it gave me I would help them to buy some of the land about our village. And then I thought of your good land first of all, you, the son of my brother. They have come to buy your land and to give you money—food—life!" His uncle, having said these words, stepped back and folded his arms with a flourish of his dirty and ragged robes.

Wang Lung did not move. He did not rise nor in any way recognize the men who had come. But he lifted his head to look at them and he saw that they were indeed men from the town, dressed in long robes of soiled silk. Their hands were soft and their nails long. They looked as though they had eaten and blood still ran rapidly in their veins. He suddenly hated them with an immense hatred. Here were these men from the town, having eaten and drunk, standing beside him whose children were starving and eating the very earth of the fields; here they were, come to squeeze his land from him in his extremity. He looked up at them sullenly, his eyes deep and enormous in his bony, skull-like face.

"I will not sell my land," he said.

His uncle stepped forward. At this instant the younger of Wang Lung's two sons came creeping to the doorway upon his hands and knees. Since he had so little strength in these latter days the child at times had gone back to crawling as he used in his babyhood.

"Is that your lad?" cried the uncle, "the little fat lad I gave a copper to in the summer?"

And they all looked at the child and suddenly Wang Lung, who through all this time had not wept at all, began to weep silently, the tears gathering in great knots of pain in his throat and rolling down his cheeks.

"What is your price?" he whispered at last. Well, there were these three children to be fed—the children and the old man. He and his wife could dig themselves graves in the land and lie down in them and sleep. Well, but here were these.

And then one of the men from the city spoke, a man with one eye blind and sunken in his face, and unctuously he said,

"My poor man, we will give you a better price than could be got in these times anywhere for the sake of the boy who is starving. We will give you . . ." he paused and then he said harshly, "we will give you a string of a hundred pence for an acre!"

Wang Lung laughed bitterly. "Why, that," he cried, "that is taking my land for a gift. Why, I pay twenty times that when I buy land!"

"Ah, but not when you buy it from men who are starving," said the other man from the city. He was a small, slight fellow with a high thin nose, but his voice came out of him unexpectedly large and coarse and hard.

Wang Lung looked at the three of them. They were sure of him, these men! What will not a man give for his starving children and his old father! The weakness of surrender in him melted into an anger such as he had never known in his life before. He sprang up and at the men as a dog springs at an enemy.

"I shall never sell the land!" he shrieked at them. "Bit by bit I will dig up the fields and feed the earth itself to the children and when they die I will bury them in the land, and I and my wife and my old father, even he, we will die on the land that has given us birth!"

He was weeping violently and his anger went out of him as suddenly as a wind and he stood shaking and weeping. The men stood there smiling slightly, his uncle among them, unmoved.

61

This talk was madness and they waited until Wang's anger was spent.

And then suddenly O-lan came to the door and spoke to them, her voice flat and commonplace as though every day such things were.

"The land we will not sell, surely," she said, "else when we return from the south we shall have nothing to feed us. But we will sell the table and the two beds and the bedding and the four benches and even the cauldron from the stove. But the rakes and the hoe and the plow we will not sell, nor the land."

There was some calmness in her voice which carried more strength than all Wang Lung's anger, and Wang Lung's uncle said uncertainly,

"Will you really go south?"

At last the one-eyed man spoke to the others and they muttered among themselves and the one-eyed man turned and said,

"They are poor things and fit only for fuel. Two silver bits for the lot and take it or leave it."

He turned away with contempt as he spoke, but O-lan answered tranquilly,

"It is less than the cost of one bed, but if you have the silver give it to me quickly and take the things."

The one-eyed man fumbled in his girdle and dropped into her outstretched hand the silver and the three men came into the house and between them they took out the table and the benches and the bed in Wang Lung's room first with its bedding, and they wrenched the cauldron from the earthern oven in which it stood. But when they went into the old man's room Wang Lung's uncle stood outside. He did not wish his older brother to see him, nor did he wish to be there when the old man was laid on the floor and the bed taken from under him. When all was finished and the house was wholly empty except for the two rakes and the two hoes and the plow in one corner of the middle room, O-lan said to her husband,

"Let us go while we have the two bits of silver and before we must sell the rafters of the house and have no hole into which we can crawl when we return."

And Wang Lung answered heavily, "Let us go."

But he looked across the fields at the small figures of the men receding and he muttered over and over, "At least I have the land—I have the land."

THERE WAS nothing to do but to pull the door tight upon its wooden hinges and fasten the iron hasp. All their clothes they had upon them. Into each child's hands O-lan thrust a rice bowl and a pair of chopsticks and the two little boys grasped at them eagerly and held them tight as a promise of food to come. Thus they started across the fields, a dreary small procession moving so slowly that it seemed they would never be to the wall of the town.

The girl Wang Lung carried in his bosom until he saw that the old man would fall and then he gave the child to O-lan and stooping under his father he lifted him on his back and carried him, staggering under the old man's dry, wind-light frame. They went on in complete silence past the little temple with the two small stately gods within, who never noticed anything that passed. Wang Lung was sweating with his weakness in spite of the cold and bitter wind. This wind never ceased to blow on them and against them, so that the two boys cried of its cold. But Wang Lung coaxed them saying,

"You are two big men and you are travellers to the south. There is warmth there and food every day, white rice every day for all of us and you shall eat and you shall eat."

In time they reached the gate of the wall, resting continually every little way, and where Wang Lung had once delighted in its coolness now he clenched his teeth against the gust of wintry wind that swept furiously through its channel, as icy water will rush between cliffs. Beneath their feet the mud was thick and speared through with needles of ice and the little boys could make no headway and O-lan was laden with the girl and desperate under the weight of her own body. Wang Lung staggered through with the old man and set him down and then went back and lifted each child and carried him through, and then when it was over at last his sweat poured out of him like rain, spending all his strength with it, so that he had to lean for a long time against the damp wall, his eyes shut and his breath coming and going quickly, and his family stood shivering and waiting about him.

They were close to the gate of the great house now, but it was locked fast, the iron doors reared full to their height and the stone lions grey and windbitten on either side. Upon the doorsteps lay cowering a few dingy shapes of men and women who gazed, famished, upon the closed and barred gate, and when Wang Lung passed with his miserable little procession one cried out in a cracked voice,

"The hearts of these rich are hard like the hearts of the gods. They have still rice to eat and from the rice they do not eat they are still making wine, while we starve."

And another moaned forth,

"Oh, if I had an instant's strength in this hand of mine I would set fire to the gates and to those houses and courts within, even though I burned in the fire. A thousand curses to the parents that bore the children of Hwang!"

But Wang Lung answered nothing to all this and in silence they went on towards the south.

When they had passed through the town and had come out on the southern side, and this they did so slowly that it was evening and near to darkness, they found a multitude of people going toward the south. Wang Lung was beginning to think of what corner of the wall they had better choose for sleeping as well as they could huddled together, when he suddenly found himself and his family caught in a multitude, and he asked of one who pressed against him,

"Where is all this multitude going?"

And the man said,

"We are starving people and we are going to catch the firewagon and ride to the south. It leaves from yonder house and there are wagons for such as we for the price of less than a small silver piece."

Firewagons! One had heard of them. Wang Lung in days past in the tea shop had heard men tell of these wagons, chained one to the other and drawn neither by man nor beast, but by a machine breathing forth fire and water like a dragon.

He had said to himself many times then that on a holiday he would go and see it, but with one thing and another in the fields there was never time, he being well to the north of the city. Then there was always distrust of that which one did not know and understand. It is not well for a man to know more than is necessary for his daily living.

Now, however, he turned doubtfully to the woman and said, "Shall we also then go on this firewagon?"

They drew the old man and the children a little away from the passing crowd and looked at each other anxiously and afraid. At the instant's respite the old man sank upon the ground and the little boys lay down in the dust, heedless of the feet trampling everywhere about them. O-lan carried the girl child still, but the child's head hung over her arm with such a look of death on its closed eyes that Wang Lung, forgetting all else, cried out,

"Is the little slave already dead?"

O-lan shook her head.

"Not yet. The breath flutters back and forth in her. But she will die this night and all of us unless——"

And then as if she could say no other word she looked at him, her square face exhausted and gaunt. Wang Lung answered nothing but to himself he thought that another day of walking like this one and they would all be dead by night, and he said with what cheer there was to be found in his voice,

"Up, my sons, and help the grandfather up. We will go on the firewagon and sit while we walk south."

But whether or not they could have moved none knows, had there not come thundering out of the darkness a noise like a dragon's voice and two great eyes puffing fire out, so that everyone screamed and ran. And pressing forward in the confusion they were pushed hither and thither, but always clinging desperately together, until they were pushed somehow in the darkness and in the yelling and crying of many voices into a small open door and into a box-like room, and then with an incessant roaring the thing in which they rode tore forth into the darkness, bearing them in its vitals.

11

WITH HIS two pieces of silver Wang Lung paid for a hundred miles of road and the officer who took his silver from him gave him back a handful of copper pence, and with a few of these Wang Lung bought from a vendor, who thrust his tray of wares in at a hole in the wagon as soon as it stopped, four small loaves of bread and a bowl of soft rice for the girl. It was more than they had to eat at one time for many days, and although they were starved for food, when it was in their mouths desire left them and it was only by coaxing that the boys could be made to swallow. But the old man sucked perseveringly at the bread between his toothless gums.

"One must eat," he cackled forth, very friendly to all who pressed about him as the firewagon rolled and rocked on its way. "I do not care that my foolish belly is growing lazy after all these days of little to do. It must be fed. I will not die because it does not wish to work." And men laughed suddenly at the smiling, wizened little old man, whose sparse white beard was scattered all over his chin.

But not all the copper pence did Wang Lung spend on food. He kept back all he was able to buy mats to build a shed for them when they reached the south. There were men and women in the firewagon who had been south in other years; some who went each year to the rich cities of the south to work and to beg and thus save the price of food. And Wang Lung, when he had grown used to the wonder of where he was and to the astonishment of seeing the land whirl by the holes in the wagon, listened to what these men said. They spoke with the loudness of wisdom where others are ignorant.

"First you must buy six mats," said one, a man with coarse,

66

hanging lips like a camel's mouth. "These are two pence for one mat, if you are wise and do not act like a country bumpkin, in which case you will be charged three pence, which is more than is necessary, as I very well know. I cannot be fooled by the men in the southern cities, even if they are rich." He wagged his head and looked about for admiration. Wang Lung listened anxiously.

"And then?" he urged. He sat squatting upon his haunches on the bottom of the wagon, which was, after all, only an empty room made of wood and with nothing to sit upon, and the wind and the dust flying up through the cracks in the floor.

"Then," said the man more loudly still, raising his voice above the din of the iron wheels beneath them, "then you bind these together into a hut and then you go out to beg, first smearing yourself with mud and filth to make yourselves as piteous as you can."

Now Wang Lung had never in his life begged of any man and he disliked this notion of begging of strange people in the south.

"One must beg?" he repeated.

"Ah, indeed," said the coarse-mouthed man, "but not until you have eaten. These people in the south have so much rice that each morning you may go to a public kitchen and for a penny hold as much as you can in your belly of the white rice gruel. Then you can beg comfortably and buy beancurd and cabbage and garlic."

Wang Lung withdrew a little from the others and turned himself about to the wall and secretly with his hand in his girdle he counted out the pence he had left. There was enough for the six mats and enough each for a penny for rice and beyond that he had three pence left. It came over him with comfort that thus they could begin the new life. But the notion of holding up a bowl and begging of anyone who passed continued to distress him. It was very well for the old man and for the children and even for the women, but he had his two hands.

"Is there no work for a man's hands?" he asked of the man suddenly, turning about.

"Aye, work!" said the man with contempt, and he spat upon the floor. "You can pull a rich man in a yellow ricksha if you like, and sweat your blood out with heat as you run and have your sweat freeze into a coat of ice on you when you stand waiting to be called. Give me begging!" And he cursed a round curse, so that Wang Lung would not ask anything of him further.

But still it was a good thing that he had heard what the man said, for when the firewagon had carried them as far as it would and had turned them out upon the ground, Wang Lung had ready a plan and he set the old man and the children against a long grey wall of a house, which stood there, and he told the woman to watch them, and he went off to buy the mats, asking of this one and that where the market streets lay. At first he could scarcely understand what was said to him, so brittle and sharp was the sound which these southerners made when they spoke, and several times when he asked and they did not understand, they were impatient, and he learned to observe what sort of man he asked of and to choose one with a kindlier face, for these southerners had tempers which were quick and easily ruffled.

But he found the mat shop at last on the edge of the city and he put his pennies down upon the counter as one who knew the price of the goods and he carried away his roll of mats. When he returned to the spot where he had left the others, they stood there waiting, although when he came the boys cried out at him in relief, and he saw that they had been filled with terror in this strange place. Only the old man watched everything with pleasure and astonishment and he murmured at Wang Lung,

"You see how fat they all are, these southerners, and how pale and oily are their skins. They eat pork every day, doubtless."

But none who passed looked at Wang Lung and his family. Men came and went along the cobbled highway to the city, busy and intent and never glancing aside at beggars, and every little while a caravan of donkeys came pattering by, their small feet fitting neatly to the stones, and they were laden with baskets of brick for the building of houses and with great bags of grain crossed upon their swaying backs. At the end of each caravan the driver rode on the hindermost beast, and he carried a great whip, and this whip he cracked with a terrific noise over the backs of the beasts, shouting as he did so. And as he passed Wang Lung each driver gave him a scornful and haughty look, and no prince could have looked more haughty than these drivers in their rough work coats as they passed by the small group of persons, standing wondering at the edge of the roadway. It was the especial pleasure of each driver, seeing how strange Wang Lung and his family were, to crack his whip just as he passed them, and the sharp explosive cut of the air made them leap up, and seeing them leap the drivers guffawed, and Wang Lung was angry when this happened two and three times and he turned away to see where he could put his hut.

There were already other huts clinging to the wall behind them, but what was inside the wall none knew and there was no way of knowing. It stretched out long and grey and very high, and against the base the small mat sheds clung like fleas to a dog's back. Wang Lung observed the huts and he began to shape his own mats this way and that, but they were stiff and clumsy things at best, being made of split reeds, and he despaired, when suddenly O-lan said,

"That I can do. I remember it in my childhood."

And she placed the girl upon the ground and pulled the mats thus and thus, and shaped a rounded roof reaching to the ground and high enough for a man to sit under and not strike the top, and upon the edges of the mats that were upon the ground she placed bricks that were lying about and she sent the boys to picking up more bricks. When it was finished they went within and with one mat she had contrived not to use they made a floor and sat down and were sheltered.

Sitting thus and looking at each other, it seemed less than possible that the day before they had left their own house and their land and that these were now a hundred miles away. It was a distance vast enough to have taken them weeks of walking and at which they must have died, some of them, before it was done.

Then the general feeling of plenty in this rich land, where no one seemed even hungered, filled them and when Wang Lung said, "Let us go and seek the public kitchens," they rose up almost cheerfully and went out once more, and this time the small boys clattered their chopsticks against their bowls as they walked, for there would soon be something to put into them. And they found soon why the huts were built to that long wall, for a short distance beyond the northern end of it was a street and along the street many people walked carrying bowls and buckets and vessels of tin, all empty, and these persons were going to the kitchens for the poor, which were at the end of the street and not far away. And so Wang Lung and his family mingled with these others and with them they came at last to two great buildings made of mats, and everyone crowded into the open end of these buildings.

Now in the rear of each building were earthen stoves, but

larger than Wang Lung had ever seen, and on them iron cauldrons as big as small ponds; and when the great wooden lids were pried up, there was the good white rice bubbling and boiling, and clouds of fragrant steam rose up. Now when the people smelled this fragrance of rice it was the sweetest in the world to their nostrils, and they all pressed forward in a great mass and people called out and mothers shouted in anger and fear lest their children be trodden upon and little babies cried, and the men who opened the cauldrons roared forth,

"Now there is enough for every man and each in his turn!"

But nothing could stop the mass of hungry men and women and they fought like beasts until all were fed. Wang Lung caught in their midst could do nothing but cling to his father and his two sons and when he was swept to the great cauldron he held out his bowl and when it was filled threw down his pence, and it was all he could do to stand sturdily and not be swept on before the thing was done.

Then when they had come to the street again and stood eating their rice, he ate and was filled and there was a little left in his bowl and he said,

"I will take this home to eat in the evening."

But a man stood near who was some sort of a guard of the place for he wore a special garment of blue and red, and he said sharply,

"No, and you can take nothing away except what is in your belly." And Wang Lung marvelled at this and said,

"Well, if I have paid my penny what business is it of yours if I carry it within or without me?"

The man said then,

"We must have this rule, for there are those whose hearts are so hard that they will come and buy this rice that is given for the poor—for a penny will not feed any man like this—and they will carry the rice home to feed to their pigs for slop. And the rice is for men and not for pigs."

Wang Lung listened to this in astonishment and he cried,

"Are there men as hard as this!" And then he said, "But why should any give like this to the poor and who is it that gives?"

The man answered then,

"It is the rich and the gentry of the town who do it, and some do it for a good deed for the future, that by saving lives they may get merit in heaven, and some do it for righteousness that men may speak well of them."

"Nevertheless it is a good deed for whatever reason," said

Wang Lung, "and some must do it out of a good heart." And then seeing that the man did not answer him, he added in his own defense, "At least there are a few of these?"

But the man was weary of speaking with him and he turned his back, and he hummed an idle tune. The children tugged at Wang Lung then, and Wang Lung led them all back to the hut they had made, and there they laid themselves down and they slept until the next morning, for it was the first time since summer they had been filled with food, and sleep overcame them with fullness.

The next morning it was necessary that there be more money for they spent the last copper coin upon the morning's rice. Wang Lung looked at O-lan, doubtful as to what should be done. But it was not with the despair with which he had looked at her over their blank and empty fields. Here with the coming and going of well-fed people upon the streets, with meat and vegetables in the markets, with fish swimming in the tubs in the fish market, surely it was not possible for a man and his children to starve. It was not as it was in their own land, where even silver could not buy food because there was none. And O-lan answered him steadily, as though this were the life she had known always,

"I and the children can beg and the old man also. His grey hairs will move some who will not give to me."

And she called the two boys to her, for, like children, they had forgotten everything except that they had food again and were in a strange place, and they ran to the street and stood staring at all that passed, and she said to them,

"Each of you take your bowls and hold them thus and cry out thus——"

And she took her empty bowl in her hand and held it out and called piteously,

"A heart, good sir—a heart, good lady! Have a kind heart—a good deed for your life in heaven! The small cash—the copper coin you throw away—feed a starving child!"

The little boys stared at her, and Wang Lung also. Where had she learned to cry thus? How much there was of this woman he did not know! She answered his look saying,

"So I called when I was a child and so I was fed. In such a year as this I was sold a slave."

Then the old man, who had been sleeping, awoke, and they gave him a bowl and the four of them went out on the road to beg. The woman began to call out and to shake her bowl at

71

every passerby. She had thrust the girl child into her naked bosom, and the child slept and its head bobbed this way and that as she moved, running hither and thither with her bowl outstretched before her. She pointed to the child as she begged and she cried loudly,

"Unless you give, good sir, good lady—this child dies—we starve—we starve——" And indeed the child looked dead, its head shaking this way and that, and there were some, a few, who tossed her unwillingly a small cash.

But the boys after a while began to take the begging as play and the elder one was ashamed and grinned sheepishly as he begged, and then their mother perceiving it dragged them into the hut and she slapped them soundly upon their jaws and she scolded them with anger.

"And do you talk of starving and then laugh at the same time! You fools, starve then!" And she slapped them again and again until her own hands were sore and until the tears were running freely down their faces and they were sobbing and she sent them out again saying,

"Now you are fit to beg! That and more if you laugh again!"

As for Wang Lung, he went into the streets and asked hither and thither until he found a place where jinrickshas were for hire and he went in and hired one for the day for the price of half a round of silver to be paid at night and then dragged the thing after him out to the street again.

Pulling this rickety, wooden wagon on its two wheels behind him, it seemed to him that everyone looked at him for a fool. He was as awkward between its shafts as an ox yoked for the first time to the plow, and he could scarcely walk; yet must he run if he were to earn his living, for here and there and everywhere through the streets of this city men ran as they pulled other men in these. He went into a narrow side street where there were no shops but only doors of homes closed and private, and he went up and down for a while pulling to accustom himself, and just as he said to himself in despair that he had better beg, a door opened, and an old man, spectacled and garbed as teacher, stepped forth and hailed him.

Wang Lung at first began to tell him that he was too new at it to run, but the old man was deaf, for he heard nothing of what Wang Lung said, only motioning to him tranquilly to lower the shafts and let him step in, and Wang Lung obeyed, not knowing what else to do, and feeling compelled to it by the deafness of the old man and by his well-dressed and learned looks. Then the old man, sitting erect, said,

"Take me to the Confucian temple," and there he sat, erect and calm, and there was that in his calmness which allowed no question, so that Wang started forward as he saw others do, although he had no faintest knowledge of where the Confucian temple stood.

But as he went he asked, and since the road lay along crowded streets, with the vendors passing back and forth with their baskets and women going out to market, and carriages drawn by horses, and many other vehicles like the one he pulled, and everything pressing against another so that there was no possibility of running, he walked as swiftly as he was able, conscious always of the awkward bumping of his load behind him. To loads upon his back he was used, but not to pulling, and before the walls of the temple were in sight his arms were aching and his hands blistered, for the shafts pressed spots where the hoe did not touch.

The old teacher stepped forth out of the riksha when Wang Lung lowered it as he reached the temple gates, and feeling in the depths of his bosom he drew out a small silver coin and gave it to Wang Lung saying,

"Now I never pay more than this, and there is no use in complaint." And with this he turned away and went into the temple.

Wang Lung had not thought to complain for he had not seen this coin before, and he did not know for how many pence it could be changed. He went to a rice shop near by where money is changed, and the changer gave him for the coin twenty-six pence, and Wang Lung marvelled at the ease with which money comes in the south. But another ricksha puller stood near and leaned over as he counted and he said to Wang Lung,

"Only twenty-six. How far did you pull that old head?" And when Wang told him, the man cried out, "Now there is a small-hearted old man! He gave you only half the proper fare. How much did you argue for before you started?"

"I did not argue," said Wang Lung. "He said 'Come' and I came."

The other man looked at Wang Lung pityingly.

"Now there is a country lout for you, pigtail and all!" he called out to the bystanders. "Someone says come and he comes, and he never asks, this idiot born of idiots, 'How much will you give me if I come!' Know this, idiot, only white

73

foreigners can be taken without argument! Their tempers are like quick lime, but when they say 'Come' you may come and trust them, for they are such fools they do not know the proper price of anything, but let the silver run out of their pockets like water." And everyone listening, laughed.

Wang Lung said nothing. It was true that he felt very humble and ignorant in all this crowd of city people, and he pulled his vehicle away without a word in answer.

"Nevertheless, this will feed my children tomorrow," he said to himself stubbornly, and then he remembered that he had the rent of the vehicle to pay at night and that indeed there was not yet half enough to do that.

He had one more passenger during the morning and with this one he argued and agreed upon a price and in the afternoon two more called to him. But at night, when he counted out all his money in his hand he had only a penny above the rent of the ricksha, and he went back to his hut in great bitterness, saying to himself that for labor greater than the labor of a day in a harvest field he had earned only one copper penny. Then there came flooding over him the memory of his land. He had not remembered it once during this strange day, but now the thought of it lying back there, far away, it is true, but waiting and his own, filled him with peace, and so he came to his hut.

When he entered there he found that O-lan had for her day's begging received forty small cash, which is less than five pence, and of the boys, the elder had eight cash and the younger thirteen, and with these put together there was enough to pay for the rice in the morning. Only when they put the younger boy's in with all, he howled for his own, and he loved the money he had begged, and slept with it that night in his hand and they could not take it from him until he gave it himself for his own rice.

But the old man had received nothing at all. All day long he had sat by the roadside obediently enough, but he did not beg. He slept and woke and stared at what passed him, and when he grew weary he slept again. And being of the older generation, he could not be reproved. When he saw that his hands were empty he said merely.

"I have plowed and I have sown seed and I have reaped harvest and thus have I filled my rice bowl. And I have beyond this begotten a son and son's sons."

And with this he trusted like a child that now he would be fed, seeing that he had a son and grandsons.

12

Now AFTER the first sharpness of Wang Lung's hunger was over and he saw that his children daily had something to eat, and he knew there was every morning rice to be had, and of his day's labor and of O-lan's begging there was enough to pay for it, the strangeness of his life passed, and he began to feel what this city was, to whose fringes he clung. Running about the streets every day and all day long he learned to know the city after a fashion, and he saw this and that of its secret parts. He learned that in the morning the people he drew in his vehicle, if they were women, went to the market, and if they were men, they went to the schools and to the houses of business. But what sort of schools these were he had no way of knowing, beyond the fact that they were called such names as "The Great School of Western Learning" or as "The Great School of China," for he never went beyond the gates, and if he had gone in well he knew someone would have come to ask him what he did out of his place. And what houses of business they were to which he drew men he did not know, since when he was paid it was all he knew.

And at night he knew that he drew men to big tea houses and to places of pleasure, the pleasure that is open and streams out upon the streets in the sound of music and of gaming with pieces of ivory and bamboo upon a wooden table, and the pleasure that is secret and silent and hidden behind walls. But none of these pleasures did Wang Lung know for himself, since his feet crossed no threshold except that of his own hut, and his road was always ended at a gate. He lived in the rich city as alien as a rat in a rich man's house that is fed on scraps thrown away, and hides here and there and is never a part of the real life of the house.

So it was that, although a hundred miles are not so far as a thousand, and land road never so far as water road, yet Wang Lung and his wife and children were like foreigners in this southern city. It is true that the people who went about the streets had black hair and eyes as Wang Lung and all his family had, and as all did in the country where Wang Lung was born, and it is true that if one listened to the language of these southerners it could be understood, if with difficulty.

But Anhwei is not Kiangsu. In Anhwei, where Wang Lung was born, the language is slow and deep and it wells from the throat. But in the Kiangsu city where they now lived the people spoke in syllables which splintered from their lips and from the ends of their tongues. And where Wang Lung's fields spread out in slow and leisurely harvest twice a year of wheat and rice and a bit of corn and beans and garlic, here in the farms about the city men urged their land with perpetual stinking fertilizing of human wastes to force the land to a hurried bearing of this vegetable and that besides their rice.

In Wang Lung's country a man, if he had a roll of good wheat bread and a sprig of garlic in it, had a good meal and needed no more. But here the people dabbled with pork balls and bamboo sprouts and chestnuts stewed with chicken and goose giblets and this and that of vegetables, and when an honest man came by smelling of yesterday's garlic, they lifted their noses and cried out, "Now here is a reeking, pig-tailed northerner!" The smell of the garlic would make the very shopkeepers in the cloth shops raise the price of blue cotton cloth as they might raise the price for a foreigner.

But then the little village of sheds clinging to the wall never became a part of the city or of the countryside which stretched beyond, and once when Wang Lung heard a young man haranguing a crowd at the corner of the Confucian temple, where any man may stand, if he has the courage to speak out, and the young man said that China must have a revolution and must rise against the hated foreigners, Wang Lung was alarmed and slunk away, feeling that he was the foreigner against whom the young man spoke with such passion. And when on another day he heard another young man speaking—for this city was full of young men speaking—and he said at his street corner that the people of China must unite and must educate themselves in these times, it did not occur to Wang Lung that anyone was speaking to him.

It was only one day when he was on the street of the silk

76

markets looking for a passenger that he learned better than he had known, and that there were those who were more foriegn than he in this city. He happened on this day to pass by the door of a shop from whence ladies sometimes came after purchasing silks within, and sometimes thus he secured one who paid him better than most. And on this day someone did come out on him suddenly, a creature the like of whom he had never seen before. He had no idea of whether it was male or female, but it was tall and dressed in a straight black robe of some rough harsh material and there was the skin of a dead animal wrapped about its neck As he passed, the person, whether male or female, motioned to him sharply to lower the shafts and he did so, and when he stood erect again, dazed at what had befallen him, the person in broken accents directed that he was to go to the Street of Bridges. He began to run hurriedly, scarcely knowing what he did, and once he called to another puller whom he knew casually in the day's work,

"Look at this—what is this I pull?"

And the man shouted back at him,

"A forcigner—a female from America—you are rich——"

But Wang Lung ran as fast as he could for fear of the strange creature behind him, and when he reached the Street of Bridges he was exhausted and dripping with his sweat.

This female stepped out then and said in the same broken accents, "You need not have run yourself to death," and left him with two silver pieces in his palm, which was double the usual fare.

Then Wang Lung knew that this was indeed a foreigner and more foreign yet than he in this city, and that after all people of black hair and black eyes are one sort and people of light hair and light eyes of another sort, and he was no longer after that wholly foreign in the city.

When he went back to the hut that night with the silver he had received still untouched, he told O-lan and she said,

"I have seen them. I always beg of them, for they alone will drop silver rather than copper into my bowl."

But neither Wang Lung nor his wife felt that the foreigner dropped silver because of any goodness of heart but rather because of ignorance and not knowing that copper is more correct to give to beggars than silver.

Nevertheless, through this experience Wang Lung learned what the young men had not taught him, that he belonged to his own kind, who have black hair and black eyes.

Clinging thus to the outskirts of the great, sprawling, opulent city it seemed that at least there could not be any lack of food. Wang Lung and his family had come from a country where if men starve it is because there is no food, since the land cannot bear under a relentless heaven. Silver in the hand was worth little because it could buy nothing where nothing was.

Here in the city there was food everywhere. The cobbled streets of the fish market were lined with great baskets of big silver fish, caught in the night out of the teeming river; with tubs of small shining fish, dipped out of a net cast over a pool; with heaps of yellow crabs, squirming and nipping in peevish astonishment; with writhing eels for gourmands at the feasts. At the grain markets there were such baskets of grain that a man might step into them and sink and smother and none know it who did not see it; white rice and brown and dark yellow wheat and pale gold wheat, and yellow soybeans and red beans and green broad beans and canary-colored millet and grey sesame. And at the meat markets whole hogs hung by their necks, split open the length of their great bodies to show the red meat and the layers of goodly fat, the skin soft and thick and white. And duck shops hung row upon row, over their ceilings and in their doors, the brown baked ducks that had been turnd slowly on a spit before coals and the white salted ducks and the strings of duck giblets, and so with the shops that sold geese and pheasant and every kind of fowl.

As for the vegetables, there was everything which the hand of man could coax from the soil; glittering red radishes and white, hollow lotus root and taro, green cabbages and celery, curling bean sprouts and brown chestnuts and garnishes of fragrant cress. There was nothing which the appetite of man might desire that was not to be found upon the streets of the markets of that city. And going hither and thither were the vendors of sweets and fruits and nuts and of hot delicacies of sweet potatoes browned in sweet oils and little delicately spiced balls of pork wrapped in dough and steamed, and sugar cakes made from glutinous rice, and the children of the city ran out to the vendors of these things with their hands full of pennies and they bought and they ate until their skins glistened with sugar and oil.

Yes, one would say that in this city there could be none who starved.

Still, every morning a little after dawn Wang Lung and his family came out of their hut and with their bowls and chopsticks they made a small group in a long procession of people, each issuing from his hut, shivering in clothes too thin for the damp river fog, walking curved against the chill morning wind to the public kitchens, where for a penny a man may buy a bowl of thin rice gruel. And with all Wang Lung's pulling and running before his ricksha and with all O-lan's begging, they never could gain enough to cook rice daily in their own hut. If there was a penny over and above the price of the rice at the kitchens for the poor, they bought a bit of cabbage. But the cabbage was dear at any price, for the two boys must go to hunt for fuel to cook it between the two bricks O-lan had set up for a stove, and this fuel they had to snatch by handsful as they could from the farmers who carried the loads of reed and grass into the city fuel markets. Sometimes the children were caught and cuffed soundly and one night the elder lad, who was more timid than the younger and more ashamed of what he did, came back with an eye swollen shut from the blow of a farmer's hand. But the younger lad grew adept and indeed more adept at petty thieving than at begging.

To O-lan this was nothing. If the boy could not be without laughing and play, let them steal to fill their bellies. But Wang Lung, although he had no answer for her, felt his gorge rise at this thievery of his sons, and he did not blame the elder when he was slow at the business. This life in the shadow of the great wall was not the life Wang Lung loved. There was his land waiting for him.

One night he came late and there was in the stew of cabbage a good round piece of pork. It was the first time they had had flesh to eat since they killed their own ox, and Wang Lung's eyes widened.

"You must have begged of a foreigner this day," he said to O-lan. But she, according to her habit, said nothing. Then the younger boy, too young for wisdom and filled with his own pride of cleverness, said,

"I took it—it is mine, this meat. When the butcher looked the other way after he had sliced it from the big piece upon the counter, I ran under an old woman's arm who had come to buy it and seized it and ran into an alley and hid in a dry water jar at a back gate until Elder Brother came."

"Now will I not eat this meat!" cried Wang Lung angrily. "We will eat meat that we can buy or beg, but not that which we steal. Beggars we may be but thieves we are not." And he took the meat out of the pot with his two fingers and threw it upon the ground and was heedless of the younger lad's howling.

Then O-lan came forward in her stolid fashion and she picked up the meat and washed it off with a little water and thrust it back into the boiling pot.

"Meat is meat," she said quietly.

Wang Lung said nothing then, but he was angry and afraid in his heart because his sons were growing into thieves here in this city. And although he said nothing when O-lan pulled the tender cooked flesh apart with her chopsticks, and although he said nothing when she gave great pieces of it to the old man and to the boys and even filled the mouth of the girl with it and ate of it herself, he himself would have none of it, contenting himself with the cabbage he had bought. But after the meal was over he took his younger son into the street out of hearing of the woman and there behind a house he took the boy's head under his arm and cuffed it soundly on this side and that, and would not stop for the lad's bellowing.

"There and there and there!" he shouted. "That for a thief!"

But to himself he said when he had let the lad go snivelling home,

"We must get back to the land."

13

DAY BY DAY beneath the opulence of this city Wang Lung lived in the foundations of poverty upon which it was laid. With the food spilling out of the markets, with the streets of the silk shops flying brilliant banners of black and red and orange silk to announce their wares, with rich men clothed in satin and in velvet, soft-fleshed rich men with their skin covered with garments of silk and their hands like flowers for softness and perfume and the beauty of idleness, with all of these for the regal beauty of the city, in that part where Wang Lung lived there was not food enough to feed savage hunger and not clothes enough to cover bones.

Men labored all day at the baking of breads and cakes for feasts for the rich and children labored from dawn to midnight and slept all greasy and grimed as they were upon rough pallets on the floor and staggered to the ovens next day, and there was not money enough given them to buy a piece of the rich breads they made for others. And men and women labored at the cutting and contriving of heavy furs for the winter and of soft light furs for the spring and at the thick brocaded silks, to cut and shape them into sumptuous robes for the ones who ate of the profusion at the markets, and they themselves snatched a bit of coarse blue cotton cloth and sewed it hastily together to cover their bareness.

Wang Lung living among these who labored at feasting others, heard strange things of which he took little heed. The older men and women, it is true, said nothing to anyone. Greybeards pulled rickshas, pushed wheelbarrows of coal and wood to bakeries and palaces, strained their backs until the muscles stood forth like ropes and they pushed and pulled the heavy carts of merchandise over the cobbled roads, ate frugally of their scanty food, slept their brief nights out, and were silent. Their faces were like the face of O-lan, inarticulate, dumb. None knew what was in their minds. If they spoke at all it was of food or of pence. Rarely was the word silver upon their lips because rarely was silver in their hands.

Their faces in repose were twisted as though in anger, only it was not anger. It was the years of straining at loads too heavy for them which had lifted their upper lips to bare their teeth in a seeming snarl, and this labor had set deep wrinkles in the flesh about their eyes and their mouths. They themselves had no idea of what manner of men they were. One of them once, seeing himself in a mirror that passed on a van of household goods, had cried out, "There is an ugly fellow!" And when others laughed at him loudly he smiled painfully, never knowing at what they laughed, and looking about hastily to see if he had offended someone.

At home in the small hovels where they lived, around Wang Lung's hovel, heaped one upon another, the women sewed rags together to make a covering for the children they were forever

81

breeding, and they snatched at bits of cabbage from farmers' fields and stole handfuls of rice from the grain markets, and gleaned the year round the grass on the hillsides; and at harvest they followed the reapers like fowls, their eyes piercing and sharp for every dropped grain or stalk. And through these huts passed children; they were born and dead and born again until neither mother or father knew how many had been born or had died, and scarcely knew even how many were living, thinking of them only as mouths to be fed.

These men and these women and these children passed in and out of the markets and the cloth shops and wandered about the countryside that bordered on the city, the men working at this and that for a few pence and the women and children stealing and begging and snatching, and Wang Lung and his woman and his children were among them.

The old men and the old women accepted the life they had. But there came a time when the male children grew to a certain age, before they were old and when they ceased to be children, and then they were filled with discontent. There was talk among the young men, angry, growling talk. And later when they were fully men and married and the dismay of increasing numbers filled their hearts, the scattered anger of their youth became settled into a fierce despair and into a revolt too deep for mere words because all their lives they labored more severely than beasts, and for nothing except a handful of refuse to fill their bellies. Listening to such talk one evening Wang Lung heard for the first time what was on the other side of the great wall to which their rows of huts clung.

It was at the end of one of those days in late winter when for the first time it seems possible that spring may come again. The ground about the huts was still muddy with the melting snow and the water ran into the huts so that each family had hunted here and there for a few bricks upon which to sleep. But with the discomfort of the damp earth there was this night a soft mildness in the air and this mildness made Wang Lung exceedingly restless so that he could not sleep at once as was his wont after he had eaten, so that he went out to the street's edge and stood there idle.

Here his old father habitually sat squatting on his thighs and leaning against the wall and here he sat now, having taken his bowl of food there to sup it, now that the children filled the hut to bursting when they were clamoring. The old man held in one hand the end of a loop of cloth which O-lan had torn from her girdle, and within this loop the girl child staggered to and fro without falling. Thus he spent his days looking after this child who had now grown rebellious at having to be in her mother's bosom as she begged. Besides this, O-lan was again with child and the pressure of the larger child upon her from without was too painful to bear.

Wang Lung watched the child falling and scrambling and falling again and the old man pulling at the loop ends, and standing thus he felt upon his face the mildness of the evening wind and there arose within him a mighty longing for his fields.

"On such a day as this," he said aloud to his father, "the fields should be turned and the wheat cultivated."

"Ah," said the old man tranquilly, "I know what is in your thought. Twice and twice again in my years I have had to do as we did this year and leave the fields and know that there was no seed in them for fresh harvests."

"But you always went back, my father."

"There was the land, my son," said the old man simply.

Well, they also would go back, if not this year, then next, said Wang to his own heart. As long as there was the land! And the thought of it lying there waiting for him, rich with the spring rains, filled him with desire. He went back to the hut and he said roughly to his wife.

"If I had anything to sell I would sell it and go back to the land. Or if it were not for the old head, we would walk though we starved. But how can he and the small child walk a hundred miles? And you, with your burden!"

O-lan had been rinsing the rice bowls with a little water and now she piled them in a corner of the hut and looked up at him from the spot where she squatted.

"There is nothing to sell except the girl," she answered slowly.

Wang Lung's breath caught.

"Now, I would not sell a child!" he said loudly.

"I was sold," she answered very slowly. "I was sold to a great house so that my parents could return to their home."

"And would you sell the child, therefore?"

"If it were only I, she would be killed before she was sold . . . the slave of slaves was I! But a dead girl brings nothing. I would sell this girl for you—to take you back to the land."

"Never would I," said Wang Lung stoutly, "not though I spent my life in this wilderness."

But when he had gone out again the thought, which never

alone would have come to him, tempted him against his will. He looked at the small girl, staggering persistently at the end of the loop her grandfather held. She had grown greatly on the food given her each day, and although she had as yet said no word at all, still she was plump as a child will be on slight care enough. Her lips that had been like an old woman's were smiling and red, and as of old she grew merry when he looked at her and she smiled.

"I might have done it," he mused, "if she had not lain in my bosom and smiled like that."

And then he thought again of his land and he cried out passionately.

"Shall I never see it again! With all this labor and begging there is never enough to do more than feed us today."

Then out of the dusk there answered him a voice, a deep burly voice,

"You are not the only one. There are a hundred hundred like you in this city."

The man came up, smoking a short bamboo pipe, and it was the father of the family in the hut next but two to Wang Lung's hut. He was a man seldom seen in the daylight, for he slept all day and worked at night pulling heavy wagons of merchandise which were too large for the streets by day when other vehicles must continually pass each other. But sometimes Wang Lung saw him come creeping home at dawn, panting and spent, and his great knotty shoulders drooping. Wang Lung passed him thus at dawn as he went out to his own ricksha pulling, and sometimes at dusk before the night's work the man came out and stood with the other men who were about to go into their hovels to sleep.

"Well, and is it forever?" asked Wang Lung bitterly.

The man puffed at his pipe thrice and then spat upon the ground. Then he said,

"No, and not forever. When the rich are too rich there are ways, and when the poor are too poor there are ways. Last winter we sold two girls and endured, and this winter, if this one my woman bears is a girl, we will sell again. One slave I have kept—the first. The others it is better to sell than to kill, although there are those who prefer to kill them before they draw breath. This is one of the ways when the poor are too poor. When the rich are too rich there is a way, and if I am not mistaken, that way will come soon." He nodded and pointed

84

with the stem of his pipe to the wall behind them. "Have you seen inside that wall?"

Wang Lung shook his head, staring. The man continued,

"I took one of my slaves in there to sell and I saw it. You would not believe it if I told you how money comes and goes in that house. I will tell you this—even the servants eat with chopsticks of ivory bound with silver, and even the slave women hang jade and pearls in their ears and sew pearls upon their shoes, and when the shoes have a bit of mud upon them or a small rent comes such as you and I would not call a rent, they throw them away, pearls and all!"

The man drew hard on his pipe and Wang Lung listened, his mouth ajar. Over this wall, then, there were indeed such things!

"There is a way when men are too rich," said the man, and he was silent for a time and then as though he had said nothing he added indifferently,

"Well, work again," and was gone into the night.

But Wang Lung that night could not sleep for thinking of silver and gold and pearls on the other side of this wall against which his body rested, his body clad in what he wore day after day, because there was no quilt to cover him and only a mat upon bricks beneath him. And temptation fell on him again to sell the child, so that he said to himself,

"It would be better perhaps that she be sold into a rich house so that she can eat daintily and wear jewels, if it be that she grow up pretty and please a lord." But against his own wish he answered himself and he thought again, "Well, and if I did, she is not worth her weight in gold and rubies. If she bring enough to take us back to the land, where will come enough to buy an ox and a table and a bed and the benches once more? Shall I sell a child that we may starve there instead of here? We have not even seed to put into the land."

And he saw nothing of the way of which the man spoke when he said, "There is a way, when the rich are too rich."

14

Spring seethed in the village of huts. Out to the hills and the grave lands those who had begged now could go to dig the small green weeds, dandelions and shepherd's purse that thrust up feeble new leaves, and it was not necessary as it had been to snatch at vegetables here and there. A swarm of ragged women and children issued forth each day from the huts, and with bits of tin and sharp stones or worn knives, and with baskets made of twisted bamboo twigs or split reeds they searched the countrysides and the roadways for the food they could get without begging and without money. And every day O-lan went out with this swarm, O-Lan and the two boys.

But men must work on, and Wang Lung worked as he had before, although the lengthening warm days and the sunshine and sudden rains filled everyone with longings and discontents. In the winter they had worked and been silent, enduring stolidly the snow and ice under their bare, straw-sandalled feet, going back at dark to their huts and eating without words such food as the day's labor and begging had brought, falling heavily to sleep, men, women and children, together, to gain that for their bodies which the food was too poor and too scanty to give. Thus it was in Wang Lung's hut and well he knew it must be so in every other.

But with the coming of spring talk began to surge up out of their hearts and to make itself heard on their lips. In the evening when the twilight lingered they gathered out of their huts and talked together, and Wang Lung saw this one and that of the men who had lived near him and whom through the winter he had not known. Had O-lan been one to tell him things he might have heard, for instance, of this one who beat his wife, of that one who had a leprous disease that ate his cheeks out, of that one who was king of a gang of thieves. But she was silent beyond the spare questions and answers she asked and gave, and so Wang Lung stood diffidently on the edge of the circle and listened to the talk.

Most of these ragged men had nothing beyond what they took in the day's labor and begging, and he was always conscious that he was not truly one of them. He owned land and his land was waiting for him. These others thought of how they might tomorrow eat a bit of fish, or of how they might idle a bit, and even how they might gamble a little, a penny or two, since their days were alike all evil and filled with want and a man must play sometimes, though desperate.

But Wang Lung thought of his land and pondered this way and that, with the sickened heart of deferred hope, how he could get back to it. He belonged, not to this scum which clung to the walls of a rich man's house; nor did he belong to the rich man's house. He belonged to the land and he could not live with any fullness until he felt the land under his feet and followed a plow in the springtime and bore a scythe in his hand at harvest. He listened, therefore, apart from the others, because hidden in his heart was the knowledge of the possession of his land, the good wheat land of his fathers, and the strip of rich rice land which he had bought from the great house.

They talked, these men, always and forever of money; of what pence they had paid for a foot of cloth, and of what they had paid for a small fish as long as a man's finger, or of what they could earn in a day, and always at last of what they would do if they had the money which the man over the wall had in his coffers. Every day the talk ended with this:

"And if I had the gold that he has and the silver in my hand that he wears every day in his girdle and if I had the pearls his concubines wear and the rubies his wife wears . . ."

And listening to all the things they would do if they had these things, Wang Lung heard only of how much they would eat and sleep, and of what dainties they would eat that they had never yet tasted, and of how they would gamble in this great tea shop and in that, and of what pretty women they would buy for their lust, and above all, how none would ever work again, even as the rich man behind the wall never worked.

Then Wang Lung cried out suddenly,

"If I had the gold and the silver and the jewels, I would buy land with it, good land, and I would bring forth harvests from the land!"

At this they united in turning on him and in rebuking him,

"Now here is a pig-tailed country bumpkin who understands nothing of city life and of what may be done with money. He would go on working like a slave behind an ox or an ass!" And each one of them felt he was more worthy to have the riches than was Wang Lung, because they knew better how to spend it.

But this scorn did not change the mind of Wang Lung. It only made him say to himself instead of aloud for others to hear,

"Nevertheless, I would put the gold and the silver and the jewels into good rich lands."

And thinking this, he grew more impatient every day for the land that was already his.

Being possessed continually by this thought of his land, Wang Lung saw as in a dream the things that happened about him in the city every day. He accepted this strangeness and that without questioning why anything was, except that in this day this thing came. There was, for an example, the paper that men gave out here and there, and sometimes even to him.

Now Wang Lung had never in his youth or at any time learned the meaning of letters upon paper, and he could not, therefore, make anything out of such paper covered with black marks and pasted upon city gates or upon walls or sold by the handful or even given away. Twice had he had such paper given him.

The first time it was given by a foreigner such as the one he had pulled unwittingly in his ricksha one day, only this one who gave him the paper was a man, very tall, and lean as a tree that has been blown by bitter winds. This man had eyes as blue as ice and a hairy face, and when he gave the paper to Wang Lung it was seen that his hands were also hairy and red-skinned. He had, moreover, a great nose projecting beyond his cheeks like a prow beyond the sides of a ship and Wang Lung although frightened to take anything from his hand, was more frightened to refuse, seeing the man's strange eyes and fearful nose. He took what was thrust at him, then, and when he had courage to look at it after the foreigner had passed on, he saw on the paper a picture of a man, white-skinned, who hung upon a crosspiece of wood. The man was without clothes except for a bit about his loins, and to all appearances he was dead, since his head drooped upon his shoulder and his eyes were closed above his bearded lips. Wang Lung looked at the pictured man in horror and with increasing interest. There were characters beneath, but of these he could make nothing.

He carried the picture home at night and showed it to the old man. But he also could not read and they discussed its possible meaning, Wang Lung and the old man and the two boys. The two boys cried out in delight and horror,

"And see the blood streaming out of his side!"

And the old man said,

"Surely this was a very evil man to be thus hung."

But Wang Lung was fearful of the picture and pondered as to why a foreigner had given it to him, whether or not some brother of this foreigner's had not been so treated and the other brethren seeking revenge. He avoided, therefore, the street on which he had met the man and after a few days, when the paper was forgotten, O-lan took it and sewed it into a shoe sole together with other bits of paper she picked up here and there to make the soles firm.

But the next time one handed a paper freely to Wang Lung it was a man of the city, a young man well clothed, who talked loudly as he distributed sheets hither and thither among the crowds who swarm about anything new and strange in a street. This paper bore also a picture of blood and death, but the man who died this time was not white-skinned and hairy but a man like Wang Lung himself, a common fellow, yellow and slight and black of hair and eye and clothed in ragged blue garments. Upon the dead figure a great fat one stood and stabbed the dead figure again and again with a long knife he held. It was a piteous sight and Wang Lung stared at it and longed to make something of the letters underneath. He turned to the man beside him and he said,

"Do you know a character or two so that you may tell me the meaning of this dreadful thing?"

And the man said,

"Be still and listen to the young teacher; he tells us all."

And so Wang Lung listened, and what he heard was what he had never heard before.

"The dead man is yourselves," proclaimed the young teacher, "and the murderous one who stabs you when you are dead and do not know it are the rich and the capitalists, who would stab you even after you are dead. You are poor and downtrodden and it is because the rich seize everything."

Now that he was poor Wang Lung knew full well but he had

89

heretofore blamed it on a heaven that would not rain in its season, or having rained, would continue to rain as though rain were an evil habit. When there was rain and sun in proportion so that the seed would sprout in the land and the stalk bear grain, he did not consider himself poor. Therefore he listened in interest to hear further what the rich men had to do with this thing, that heaven would not rain in its season. And at last when the young man had talked on and on but had said nothing of this matter where Wang Lung's interest lay, Wang Lung grew bold and asked,

"Sir, is there any way whereby the rich who oppress us can make it rain so that I can work on the land?"

At this the young man turned on him with scorn and replied,

"Now how ignorant you are, you who still wear your hair in a long tail! No one can make it rain when it will not, but what has this to do with us? If the rich would share with us what they have, rain or not would matter none, because we would all have money and food."

A great shout went up from those who listened, but Wang Lung turned away unsatisfied. Yes, but there was the land. Money and food are eaten and gone, and if there is not sun and rain in proportion, there is again hunger. Nevertheless, he took willingly the papers the young man gave him, because he remembered that O-lan had never enough paper for the shoe soles, and so he gave them to her when he went home, saying,

"Now there is some stuff for the shoe soles," and he worked as before.

But of the men in the huts with whom he talked at evening there were many who heard eagerly what the young man said, the more eagerly because they knew that over the wall there dwelt a rich man and it seemed a small thing that between them and his riches there was only this layer of bricks, which might be torn down with a few knocks of a stout pole, such as they had, to carry their heavy burdens every day upon their shoulders.

And to the discontent of the spring there was now added the new discontent which the young man and others like him spread abroad in the spirits of the dwellers in the huts, the sense of unjust possession by others of those things which they had not. And as they thought day after day on all these matters and talked of them in the twilight, and above all as day after day their labor brought in no added wage, there arose in the hearts of the young and the strong a tide as irresistible as the tide of the river, swollen with winter snows—the tide of the fullness of savage desire.

But Wang Lung, although he saw this and he heard the talk and felt their anger with a strange unease, desired nothing but his land under his feet again.

Then in this city out of which something new was always springing at him, Wang Lung saw another new thing he did not understand. He saw one day, when he pulled his ricksha empty down a street looking for a customer, a man, seized as he stood by a small band of armed soldiers, and when the man protested, the soldiers brandished knives in his face, and while Wang Lung watched in amazement, another was seized and another, and it came to Wang Lung that those who were seized were all common fellows who worked with their hands, and while he stared, yet another man was seized, and this one a man who lived in the hut nearest his own against the wall.

Then Wang Lung perceived suddenly out of his astonishment that all these men seized were as ignorant as he as to why they were thus being taken, willy nilly, whether they would or not. And Wang Lung thrust his ricksha into a side alley and he dropped it and darted into the door of a hot water shop lest he be next and there he hid, crouched low behind the great cauldrons, until the soldiers passed. And then he asked the keeper of the hot water shop the meaning of the thing he had seen, and the man, who was old and shriveled with the steam rising continually about him out of the copper cauldrons of his trade, answered with indifference.

"It is but another war somewhere. Who knows what all this fighting to and fro is about? But so it has been since I was a lad and so will it be after I am dead and well I know it."

"Well, and but why do they seize my neighbor, who is as innocent as I who have never heard of this new war?" asked Wang Lung in great consternation. And the old man clattered the lids of his cauldrons and answered,

"These soldiers are going to battle somewhere and they need carriers for their bedding and their guns and their ammunition and so they force laborers like you to do it. But what part are you from? It is no new sight in this city."

"But what then?" urged Wang Lung breathless. "What wage—what return——"

Now the old man was very old and he had no great hope in

anything and no interest in anything beyond his cauldrons and he answered carelessly,

"Wage there is none and but two bits of dry bread a day and a sup from a pond, and you may go home when the destination is reached if your two legs can carry you."

"Well, but a man's family——" said Wang Lung, aghast.

"Well, and what do they know or care of that?" said the old man scornfully, peering under the wooden lid of the nearest cauldron to see if the water bubbled yet. A cloud of steam enveloped him and his wrinkled face could scarcely be seen peering into the cauldron. Nevertheless he was kindly, for when he came forth again out of the steam he saw what Wang Lung could not see from where he crouched, that once more the soldiers approached, searching the streets from which now every able-bodied working man had fled.

"Stoop yet more," he said to Wang Lung. "They are come again."

And Wang Lung crouched low behind the cauldrons and the soldiers clattered down the cobbles to the west, and when the sound of their leathern boots was gone Wang Lung darted out and seizing his ricksha he ran with it empty to the hut.

Then to O-lan, who had but just returned from the roadside to cook a little of the green stuff she had gathered, he told in broken, panting words what was happening and how nearly he had not escaped, and as he spoke this new horror sprang up in him, the horror that he be dragged to battlefields and not only his old father and his family left alone to starve, but he dying upon a battlefield and his blood spilled out, and nevermore able to see his own land. He looked at O-lan haggardly and he said,

"Now am I truly tempted to sell the little slave and go north to the land."

But she, after listening, mused and said in her plain and unmoved way,

"Wait a few days. There is strange talk about."

Nevertheless, he went out no more in the daylight but he sent the eldest lad to return the ricksha to the place from where he hired it and he waited until the night came and he went to the houses of merchandise and for half what he had earned before he pulled all night the great wagonloads of boxes, to each wagon a dozen men pulling and straining and groaning. And the boxes were filled with silks and with cottons and with fragrant tobacco, so fragrant that the smell of it leaked through the wood. And there were great jars of oils and of wines.

92

All night through the dark streets he strained against the ropes, his body naked and streaming with sweating, and his bare feet slipping on the cobbles, slimy and wet as they were with the dampness of the night. Before them to show the way ran a little lad carrying a flaming torch and in the light of this torch the faces and the bodies of the men and the wet stones glistened alike. And Wang Lung came home before dawn, gasping and too broken for food until he had slept. But during the bright day when the soldiers searched the street he slept safely in the furthermost corner of the hut behind a pile of straw O-lan gathered to make a shield for him.

What battles there were or who fought which other one Wang Lung did not know. But with the further coming of spring the city became filled with the unrest of fear. All during the days carriages drawn by horses pulled rich men and their possessions of clothing and satin-covered bedding and their beautiful women and their jewels to the river's edge where ships carried them away to other places, and some went to that other house where firewagons came and went. Wang Lung never went upon the streets in the day, but his sons came back with their eyes wide and bright, crying,

"We saw such an one and such an one, a man as fat and monstrous as a god in a temple, and his body covered with many feet of yellow silk and on his thumb a great gold ring set with green stone like a piece of glass, and his flesh was all bright with oil and eating!"

Or the elder cried,

"And we have seen such boxes and boxes and when I asked what was in them one said, 'There is gold and silver in them, but the rich cannot take all they have away, and some day it will all be ours.' Now, what did he mean by this, my father?" And the lad opened his eyes inquisitively to his father.

But when Wang Lung answered shortly, "How should I know what an idle city fellow means?" the lad cried wistfully,

"Oh, I wish we might go even now and get it if it is ours. I should like to taste a cake. I have never tasted a sweet cake with sesame seed sprinkled on the top."

The old man looked up from his dreaming at this and he said as one croons to himself,

"When we had a good harvest we had such cakes at the autumn feast, when the sesame had been threshed and before it was sold we kept a little back to make such cakes."

And Wang Lung remembered the cakes that O-lan had once

93

made at the New Year's feast, cakes of rice flour and lard and sugar, and his mouth watered and his heart pained him with longing for that which was passed.

"If we were only back on our land," he muttered.

Then suddenly it seemed to him that not one more day could he lie in this wretched hut, which was not wide enough for him even to stretch his length in behind the pile of straw, nor could he another night strain the hours through, his body bent against a rope cutting into his flesh, and dragging the load over the cobble stones. Each stone he had come to know now as a separate enemy, and he knew each rut by which he might evade a stone and so use an ounce less of his life. There were times in the black nights, especially when it rained and the streets were wet and more wet than usual, that the whole hatred of his heart went out against these stones under his feet, these stones that seemed to cling and to hang to the wheels of his inhuman load.

"Ah, the fair land!" he cried out suddenly and fell to weeping so that the children were frightened and the old man, looking at his son in consternation, twisted his face this way and that under his sparse beard, as a child's face twists when he sees his mother weep.

And again it was O-lan who said in her flat plain voice,

"Yet a little while and we shall see a thing. There is talk everywhere now."

From his hut where Wang Lung lay hid he heard hour after hour the passing of feet, the feet of soldiers marching to battle. Lifting sometimes a very little the mat which stood between them and him, he put one eye to the crack and he saw these feet passing, passing, leather shoes and cloth-covered legs, marching one after the other, pair by pair, score upon score, thousands upon thousands. In the night when he was at his load he saw their faces flickering past him, caught for an instant out of the darkness by the flaming torch ahead. He dared ask nothing concerning them, but he dragged his load doggedly, and he ate hastily his bowl of rice, and slept the day fitfully through in the hut behind the straw. None spoke in those days to any other. The city was shaken with fear and each man did quickly what he had to do and went into his house and shut the door.

There was no more idle talk at twilight about the huts. In the market places the stalls where food had been were now empty. The silk shops drew in their bright banners and closed the

fronts of their great shops with thick boards fitting one i
other solidly, so that passing through the city at noon it v
though the people slept.

It was whispered everywhere that the enemy approached
and all those who owned anything were afraid. But Wang
Lung was not afraid, nor the dwellers in the huts, neither were
they afraid. They did not know for one thing who this enemy
was, nor had they anything to lose since even their lives were no
great loss. If this enemy approached let him approach, seeing
that nothing could be worse than it now was with them. But
every man went on his own way and none spoke openly to any
other.

Then the managers of the houses of merchandise told the
laborers who pulled the boxes to and fro from the river's edge
that they need come no more, since there were none to buy and
sell in these days at the counters, and so Wang Lung stayed in
his hut day and night and was idle. At first he was glad, for it
seemed his body could never get enough rest and he slept as
heavily as a man dead. But if he did not work neither did he
earn, and in a few short days what they had of extra pence was
gone and again he cast about desperately as to what he could
do. And as if it were not enough of evil to befall them, the
public kitchens closed their doors also and those who had in
this way provided for the poor went into their own houses and
shut the doors and there was no food and no work, and no one
passing upon the streets of whom anyone could beg.

Then Wang Lung took his girl child into his arms and he sat
with her in the hut and he looked at her and said softly,

"Little fool, would you like to go to a great house where there
is food and drink and where you may have a whole coat to your
body?"

Then she smiled, not understanding anything of what he
said, and put up her small hand to touch with wonder his
staring eyes and he could not bear it and he cried out to the
woman,

"Tell me, and were you beaten in that great house?"

And she answered him flatly and somberly,

"Every day was I beaten."

And he cried again,

"But was it just with a girdle of cloth or was it with bamboo
or rope?"

And she answered in the same dead way,

95

"I was beaten with a leather thong which had been halter for one of the mules, and it hung upon the kitchen wall."

Well he knew that she understood what he was thinking, but he put forth his last hope and he said,

"This child of ours is a pretty little maid, even now. Tell me, were the pretty slaves beaten also?"

And she answered indifferently, as though it were nothing to her this way or that,

"Aye, beaten or carried to a man's bed, as the whim was, and not to one man's only but to any that might desire her that night, and the young lords bickered and bartered with each other for this slave or that and said, 'Then if you tonight, I tomorrow,' and when they were all alike wearied of a slave the men servants bickered and bartered for what the young lords left, and this before a slave was out of childhood—if she were pretty."

Then Wang Lung groaned and held the child to him and said over and over to her softly, "Oh, little fool—oh, poor little fool." But within himself he was crying as a man cries out when he is caught in a rushing flood and cannot stop to think, "There is no other way—there is no other way——"

Then suddenly as he sat there came a noise like the cracking of heaven and every one of them fell unthinking on the ground and hid their faces, for it seemed as though the hideous roar would catch them all up and crush them. And Wang Lung covered the girl child's face with his hand, not knowing what horror might appear to them out of this dreadful din, and the old man called out into Wang Lung's ear, "Now this I have never heard before in all my years," and the two boys yelled with fear.

But O-lan, when silence had fallen as suddenly as it had gone, lifted her head and said, "Now that which I have heard of has come to pass. The enemy has broken in the gates of the city." And before any could answer her there was a shout over the city, a rising shout of human voices, at first faint, as one may hear the wind of a storm approaching, and gathering in a deep howl, louder and more loud as it filled the streets.

Wang Lung sat erect then, on the floor of his hut, and a strange fear crept over his flesh, so that he felt it stirring among the roots of his hair, and everyone sat erect and they all stared at each other waiting for something they knew not. But there was only the noise of the gathering of human beings and each man howling.

Then over the wall and not far from them they heard the sound of a great door creaking upon its hinges and groaning as it opened unwillingly, and suddenly the man who had talked to Wang Lung once at dusk and smoked a short bamboo pipe, thrust his head in at the hut's opening and cried out,

"Now do you still sit here? The hour has come—the gates of the rich man are open to us!" And as if by magic of some kind O-lan was gone, creeping out under the man's arm as he spoke.

Then Wang Lung rose up, slowly and half dazed, and he set the girl child down and he went out and there before the great iron gates of the rich man's house a multitude of clamoring common people pressed forward, howling together the deep, tigerish howl that he had heard, rising and swelling out of the streets, and he knew that at the gates of all rich men there pressed this howling multitude of men and women who had been starved and imprisoned and now were for the moment free to do as they would. And the great gates were ajar and the people pressed forward so tightly packed together that foot was on foot and body wedged tightly against body so that the whole mass moved together as one. Others hurrying from the back caught Wang Lung and forced him into the crowd so that whether he would or not he was taken forward with them, although he did not himself know what his will was, because he was so amazed at what had come about.

Thus was he swept along over the threshold of the great gates, his feet scarcely touching the ground in the pressure of people, and like the continuous roar of angry beasts there went on all around the howling of the people.

Through court after court he was swept, into the very inner courts, and of those men and women who had lived in the house he saw not one. It was as though here were a palace long dead except that early lilies bloomed among the rocks of the gardens and the golden flowers of the early trees of spring blossomed upon bare branches. But in the rooms food stood upon a table and in the kitchens fire burned. Well this crowd knew the courts of the rich, for they swept past the front courts, where servants and slaves lived and where the kitchens are, into the inner courts, where the lords and ladies have their dainty beds and where stand their lacquered boxes of black and red and gold, their boxes of silken clothing, where carved tables and chairs are, and upon the walls painted scrolls. And upon these treasures the crowd fell, seizing at and tearing from each other what was revealed in every newly opened box or closet, so that clothing and bedding and curtains and dishes passed from hand to hand, each hand snatching that which another held, and none stopping to see what he had.

Only Wang Lung in the confusion took nothing. He had never in all his life taken what belonged to another, and not at once could he do it. So he stood in the middle of the crowd at first, dragged this way and that, and then coming somewhat to his senses, he pushed with perseverance toward the edge and found himself at last on the fringe of the multitude, and here he stood, swept along slightly as little whirlpools are at the edge of a pool of current; but still he was able to see where he was.

He was at the back of the innermost court where the ladies of the rich dwell, and the back gate was ajar, that gate which the rich have for centuries kept for their escape in such times, and therefore called the gate of peace. Through this gate doubtless they had all escaped this day and were hidden here and there through the streets, listening to the howling in their courts. But one man, whether because of his size or whether because of his drunken heaviness of sleep, had failed to escape, and this one Wang Lung came upon suddenly in an empty inner room from whence the mob had swept in and out again, so that the man, who had been hidden in a secret place and not been found, now crept out, thinking he was alone, to escape. And thus Wang Lung, always drifting away from the others until he too was alone, came upon him.

He was a great fat fellow, neither old nor young, and he had been lying naked in his bed, doubtless with a pretty woman, for his naked body gaped through a purple satin robe he held about him. The great yellow rolls of his flesh doubled over his breasts and over his belly and in the mountains of his cheeks his eyes were small and sunken as a pig's eyes. When he saw Wang Lung he shook all over and yelled out as though his flesh had been stuck with a knife, so that Wang Lung, weaponless as he was, wondered and could have laughed at the sight. But the fat fellow fell upon his knees and knocked his head on the tiles of the floor and he cried forth,

"Save a life—save a life—do not kill me. I have money for you—much money——"

It was this word "money" which suddenly brought to Wang Lung's mind a piercing clarity. Money! Aye, and he needed that! And again it came to him clearly, as a voice speaking, "Money—the child saved—*the land!*"

He cried out suddenly in a harsh voice such as he did not himself know was in his breast,

"Give me the money then!"

And the fat man rose to his knees, sobbing and gibbering, and feeling for the pocket of the robe, and he brought forth his yellow hands dripping with gold and Wang Lung held out the end of his coat and received it. And again he cried out in that strange voice that was like another man's,

"Give me more!"

And again the man's hands came forth dripping with gold and he whimpered,

"Now there is none left and I have nothing but my wretched life," and he fell to weeping, his tears running like oil down his hanging cheeks.

Wang Lung, looking at him as he shivered and wept, suddenly loathed him as he had loathed nothing in his life and he cried out with the loathing surging up in him,

"Out of my sight, lest I kill you for a fat worm!"

This Wang Lung cried, although he was a man so softhearted that he could not kill an ox. And the man ran past him like a cur and was gone.

Then Wang Lung was left alone with the gold. He did not stop to count it, but thrust it into his bosom and went out of the open gate of peace and across the small back streets to his hut. He hugged to his bosom the gold that was yet warm from the other man's body and to himself he said over and over,

"We go back to the land—tomorrow we go back to the land!"

15

BEFORE A HANDFUL of days had passed it seemed to Wang Lung that he had never been away from his land, as indeed, in his heart he never had. With three pieces of the gold he bought good seed from the south, full grains of wheat and of rice and of corn, and for very recklessness of riches he bought seeds the like of which he had never planted before, celery and lotus for his pond and great red radishes that are stewed with pork for a feast dish and small red fragrant beans.

With five gold pieces he bought an ox from a farmer ploughing in the field, and this before ever he reached his own land. He saw the man ploughing and he stopped and they all stopped, the old man and the children and the woman, eager as they were to reach the house and the land, and they looked at the ox. Wang Lung had been struck with its strong neck and noticed at once the sturdy pulling of its shoulder against the wooden yoke and he called out,

"That is a worthless ox! What will you sell it for in silver or gold, seeing that I have no animal and am hard put to it and willing to take anything?"

And the farmer called back,

"I would sooner sell my wife than this ox which is but three years old and in its prime," and he ploughed on and would not stop for Wang Lung.

Then it seemed to Wang Lung as if out of all the oxen the world held he must have this one, and he said to O-lan and to his father,

"How is it for an ox?"

And the old man peered and said, "It seems a beast well castrated."

And O-lan said, "It is a year older than he says."

But Wang Lung answered nothing because upon this ox he had set his heart because of its sturdy pulling of the soil and because of its smooth yellow coat and its full dark eye. With this ox he could plough his fields and cultivate them and with this ox tied to his mill he could grind the grain. And he went to the farmer and said,

"I will give you enough to buy another ox and more, but this ox I will have."

At last after bickering and quarrelling and false starts away the farmer yielded for half again the worth of an ox in those parts. But gold was suddenly nothing to Wang Lung when he looked at this ox, and he passed it over to the farmer's hand and he watched while the farmer unyoked the beast, and Wang Lung led it away with a rope through its nostrils, his heart burning with his possession.

When they reached the house they found the door torn away and the thatch from the roof gone and within their hoes and rakes that they had left were gone, so only the bare rafters and the earthen walls remained, and even the earthen walls were worn down with the belated snows and the rains of winter and early spring. But after the first astonishment all this was as nothing to Wang Lung. He went away to the town and he bought a good new plow of hard wood and two rakes and two hoes and mats to cover the roof until they could grow thatch again from the harvest.

Then in the evening he stood in the doorway of his house and looked across the land, his own land, lying loose and fresh from the winter's freezing, and ready for planting. It was full spring and in the shallow pool the frogs croaked drowsily. The bamboos at the corner of the house swayed slowly under a gentle night wind and through the twilight he could see dimly the fringe of trees at the border of the near field. They were peach trees, budded most delicately pink, and willow trees thrusting forth tender green leaves. And up from the quiescent, waiting land a faint mist rose, silver as moonlight, and clung about the tree trunks.

At first and for a long time it seemed to Wang Lung that he wished to see no human being but only to be alone on his land. He went to no houses of the village and when they came to him, those who were left of the winter's starving, he was surly with them.

"Which of you tore away my door and which of you have my rake and my hoe and which of you burned my roof in his oven?" Thus he bawled at them.

And they shook their heads, full of virtue; and this one said, "It was your uncle," and that one said, "Nay, with bandits and robbers roving over the land in these evil times of famine and war, how can it be said that this one or that stole anything? Hunger makes thief of any man."

Then Ching, his neighbor, came creeping forth from his house to see Wang Lung and he said,

"Through the winter a band of robbers lived in your house and preyed upon the village and the town as they were able. Your uncle, it is said, knows more of them than an honest man should. But who knows what is true in these days? I would not dare to accuse any man."

This man was nothing but a shadow indeed, so close did his skin stick to his bones and so thin and grey had his hair grown, although he had not yet reached forty-five years of his age. Wang Lung stared at him awhile and then in compassion he said suddenly,

"Now you have fared worse than we and what have you eaten?"

And the man sighed forth in a whisper,

"What have I not eaten? Offal from the streets like dogs when we begged in the town and dead dogs we ate and once before she died my woman brewed some soup from flesh I dared not ask what it was, except that I knew she had not the courage to kill, and if we ate it was something she found. Then she died, having less strength than I to endure, and after she died I gave the girl to a soldier because I could not see her starve and die also." He paused and fell silent and after a time he said, "If I had a little seed I would plant once more, but no seed have I."

"Come here!" cried Wang Lung roughly and dragged him into the house by the hand and he bade the man hold up the ragged tail of his coat and into it Wang Lung poured from the store of seed he had brought from the south. Wheat he gave him and rice and cabbage seed and he said,

"Tomorrow I will come and plough your land with my good ox."

Then Ching began to weep suddenly and Wang Lung rubbed his own eyes and cried out as if he were angry, "Do you think I have forgotten that you gave me that handful of beans?" But Ching could answer nothing, only he walked away weeping and weeping without stop.

It was joy to Wang Lung to find that his uncle was no longer in the village and where he was none knew certainly. Some said he had gone to a city and some said he was in far distant parts with his wife and his son. But there was not one left in his house in the village. The girls, and this Wang Lung heard with stout anger, were sold, the prettiest first, for the price they could bring, but even the last one, who was pock-marked, was sold for a handful of pence to a soldier who was passing through to battle.

Then Wang Lung set himself robustly to the soil and he begrudged even the hours he must spend in the house for food and sleep. He loved rather to take his roll of bread and garlic to the field and stand there eating, planning and thinking, "Here shall I put the black-eyed peas and here the young rice beds." And if he grew too weary in the day he laid himself into a furrow and there with the good warmth of his own land against his flesh, he slept.

And O-lan in the house was not idle. With her own hands she lashed the mats firmly to the rafters and took earth from the fields and mixed it with water and mended the walls of the house, and she built again the oven and filled the holes in the floor that the rain had washed.

Then she went into the town one day with Wang Lung and together they bought beds and a table and six benches and a great iron cauldron and then they bought for pleasure a red clay teapot with a black flower marked on it in ink and six bowls to match. Last of all they went into an incense shop and bought a paper god of wealth to hang on the wall over the table in the middle room, and they bought two pewter candlesticks and a pewter incense urn and two red candles to burn before the god, thick red candles of cow's fat and having a slender reed through the middle for wick.

And with this, Wang Lung thought of the two small gods in the temple to the earth and on his way home he went and peered in at them, and they were piteous to behold, their features washed from their faces with rain and the clay of their bodies naked and sticking through the tatters of their paper clothes. None had paid any heed to them in this dreadful year and Wang Lung looked at them grimly and with content and he said aloud, as one might speak to a punished child,

"Thus it is with gods who do evil to men!"

Nevertheless, when the house was itself again, and the pewter candlesticks gleaming and the candles burning in them shining red, and the teapot and the bowls upon the table and the beds in their places with a little bedding once more, and fresh paper pasted over the hole in the room where he slept and a new door hung upon its wooden hinges, Wang Lung was afraid of his happiness. O-lan grew great with the next child; his children tumbled like brown puppies about his threshold and against the southern wall his old father sat and dozed and smiled as he slept; in his fields the young rice sprouted as green as jade and more beautiful, and the young beans lifted their hooded heads from the soil. And out of the gold there was still enough left to feed them until the harvest, if they ate sparingly. Looking at the blue heaven above him and the white clouds driving across it, feeling upon his ploughed fields as upon his own flesh the sun and rain in proportion, Wang Lung muttered unwillingly,

"I must stick a little incense before those two in the small temple. After all, they have power over earth."

16

ONE NIGHT as Wang lay with his wife he felt a hard lump the size of a man's closed hand between her breasts and he said to her,

"Now what is this thing you have on your body?"

He put his hand to it and he found a cloth-wrapped bundle that was hard yet moved to his touch. She drew back violently at first and then when he laid hold of it to pluck it away from her she yielded and said,

"Well, look at it then, if you must," and she took the string which held it to her neck and broke it and gave him the thing.

It was wrapped in a bit of rag and he tore this away. Then suddenly into his hand fell a mass of jewels and Wang Lung gazed at them stupefied. There were such a mass of jewels as one had never dreamed could be together, jewels red as the inner flesh of watermelons, golden as wheat, green as young leaves in spring, clear as water trickling out of the earth. What the names of them were Wang did not know, having never heard names and seen jewels together in his life. But holding them there in his hand, in the hollow of his brown hard hand, he knew from the gleaming and the glittering in the half-dark room that he held wealth. He held it motionless, drunk with color and shape, speechless, and together he and the woman stared at what he held. At last he whispered to her, breathless,

"Where—where—"

And she whispered back as softly,

"In the rich man's house. It must have been a favorite's treasure. I saw a brick loosened in the wall and I slipped there carelessly so no other soul could see and demand a share. I pulled the brick away, caught the shining, and put them into my sleeve."

"Now how did you know?" he whispered again, filled with admiration, and she answered with the smile on her lips that was never in her eyes,

"Do you think I have not lived in a rich man's house? The rich are always afraid. I saw robbers in a bad year once rush into the gate of the great house and the slaves and the concubines and even the Old Mistress herself ran hither and thither and each had a treasure that she thrust into some secret place already planned. Therefore I knew the meaning of a loosened brick."

And again they fell silent, staring at the wonder of the stones. Then after a long time Wang Lung drew in his breath and said resolutely,

"Now treasure like this one cannot keep. It must be sold and put into safety—into land, for nothing else is safe. If any knew of this we should be dead by the next day and a robber would carry the jewels. They must be put into land this very day or I shall not sleep tonight."

He wrapped the stones in the rag again as he spoke and tied them hard together with the string, and opening his coat to thrust them into his bosom, by chance he saw the woman's face. She was sitting cross-legged upon the bed at its foot and her heavy face that never spoke of anything was moved with a dim yearning of open lips and face thrust forward.

"Well, and now what?" he asked, wondering at her.

"Will you sell them all?" she asked in a hoarse whisper.

"And why not then?" he answered, astonished. "Why should we have jewels like this in an earthen house?"

"I wish I could keep two for myself," she said with such helpless wistfulness, as of one expecting nothing, that he was moved as he might be by one of his children longing for a toy or for a sweet.

"Well, now!" he cried in amazement.

"If I could have two," she went on humbly, "only two small ones—two small white pearls even . . ."

"Pearls!" he repeated, agape.

"I would keep them —I would not wear them," she said, "only keep them." And she dropped her eyes and fell to twisting a bit of the bedding where a thread was loosened, and she waited patiently as one who scarcely expects an answer.

Then Wang Lung, without comprehending it, looked for an instant into the heart of this dull and faithful creature, who had labored all her life at some task at which she won no reward and who in the great house had seen others wearing jewels which she never even felt in her hand once.

"I could hold them in my hand sometimes," she added, as if she thought to herself.

And he was moved by something he did not understand and he pulled the jewels from his bosom and unwrapped them and handed them to her in silence, and she searched among the glittering colors, her hard brown hand turning over the stones delicately and lingeringly until she found the two smooth white pearls, and these she took, and tying up the others again, she gave them back to him. Then she took the pearls and she tore a bit of the corner of her coat away and wrapped them and hid them between her breasts and was comforted.

But Wang Lung watched her astonished and only half understanding, so that afterwards during the day and on other days he would stop and stare at her and say to himself,

"Well now, that woman of mine, she has those two pearls between her breasts still, I suppose." But he never saw her take them out or look at them and they never spoke of them at all.

As for the other jewels, he pondered this way and that, and at last he decided he would go to the great house and see if there were more land to buy.

To the great house he now went and there was in these days no gateman standing at the gate, twisting the long hairs of his mole, scornful of those who could not enter past him into the House of Hwang. Instead the great gates were locked and Wang Lung pounded against them with both fists and no one came. Men who passed in the streets looked up and cried out at him,

"Aye, you may pound now and pound again. If the Old Lord is awake he may come and if there is a stray dog of a slave about she may open, if she is inclined to it."

But at last he heard slow footsteps coming across the threshold, slow wandering footsteps that halted and came on by fits, and then he heard the slow drawing of the iron bar that held the gate and the gate creaked and a cracked voice whispered,

"Who is it?"

Then Wang Lung answered, loudly, although he was amazed,

"It is I, Wang Lung!"

Then the voice said peevishly,

"Now who is an accursed Wang Lung?"

And Wang Lung perceived by the quality of the curse u.
was the Old Lord himself, because he cursed as one ac
customed to servants and slaves. Wang Lung answered,
therefore, more humbly than before.

"Sir and lord, I am come on a little business, not to disturb
your lordship, but to talk a little business with the agent who
serves your honor."

Then the Old Lord answered without opening any wider the
crack through which he pursed his lips,

"Now curse him, that dog left me many months ago and he is
not here."

Wang Lung did not know what to do after this reply. It was
impossible to talk of buying land directly to the Old Lord,
without a middleman, and yet the jewels hung in his bosom
hot as fire, and he wanted to be rid of them and more than that
he wanted the land. With the seed he had he could plant as
much land again as he had, and he wanted the good land of the
House of Hwang.

"I came about a little money," he said hesitatingly.

At once the Old Lord pushed the gates together.

"There is no money in this house," he said more loudly than
he had yet spoken. "The thief and robber of an agent—and may
his mother and his mother's mother be cursed for him—took all
that I had. No debts can be paid."

"No—no——" called Wang Lung hastily, "I came to pay out,
not to collect debt."

At this there was a shrill scream from a voice Wang Lung
had not yet heard and a woman thrust her face suddenly out of
the gates.

"Now that is a thing I have not heard for a long time," she
said sharply, and Wang Lung saw a handsome, shrewish, high-
colored face looking out at him. "Come in," she said briskly and
she opened the gates wide enough to admit him and then behind
his back, while he stood astonished in the court, she barred
them securely again.

The Old Lord stood there coughing and staring, a dirty grey
satin robe wrapped about him, from which hung an edge of
bedraggled fur. Once it had been a fine garment, as anyone
could see, for the satin was still heavy and smooth, although
stains and spots covered it, and it was wrinkled as though it had
been used as a bedgown. Wang Lung stared back at the Old
Lord, curious, yet half-afraid, for all his life he half-feared the
people in the great house, and it seemed impossible that the

, of whom he had heard so much, was this old figure, dreadful than his old father, and indeed less so for his was a cleanly and smiling old man, and the Old Lord, who had been fat, was now lean, and his skin hung in folds about him and he was unwashed and unshaven and his hand was yellow and trembled as he passed it over his chin and pulled at his loose old lips.

The woman was clean enough. She had a hard, sharp face, handsome with a sort of hawk's beauty of high bridged nose and keen bright black eyes and pale skin stretched too tightly over her bones, and her cheeks and lips were red and hard. Her black hair was like a mirror for smooth shining blackness, but from her speech one could perceive she was not of the lord's family, but a slave, sharp voiced and bitter tongued. And besides these two, the woman and the Old Lord, there was not another person in the court where before men and women and children had run to and fro on their business of caring for the great house.

"Now about money," said the woman sharply. But Wang Lung hesitated. He could not well speak before the Old Lord and this the woman instantly perceived as she perceived everything more quickly than speech could be made about it, and she said to the old man shrilly, "Now off with you!"

And the aged lord, without a word, shambled silently away, his old velvet shoes flapping and off at his heels, coughing as he went. As for Wang Lung, left alone with this woman, he did not know what to say or do. He was stupefied with the silence everywhere. He glanced into the next court and still there was no other person, and about the court he saw heaps of refuse and filth and scattered straw and branches of bamboo trees and dried pine needles and the dead stalks of flowers, as though not for a long time had anyone taken a broom to sweep it.

"Now then, wooden head!" said the woman with exceeding sharpness, and Wang Lung jumped at the sound of her voice, so unexpected was its shrillness. "What is your business? If you have money, let me see it."

"No," said Wang Lung with caution, "I did not say that I had money. I have business."

"Business means money," returned the woman, "either money coming in or money going out, and there is no money to go out of his house."

"Well, but I cannot speak with a woman," objected Wang

Lung mildly. He could make nothing of the situation in which he found himself, and he was still staring about him.

"Well, and why not?" retorted the woman with anger. Then she shouted at him suddenly, "Have you not heard, fool, that there is no one here?"

Wang Lung stared at her feebly, unbelieving, and the woman shouted at him again, "I and the Old Lord—there is no one else!"

"Where then?" asked Wang Lung, too much aghast to make sense in his words.

"Well, and the Old Mistress is dead," retorted the woman. "Have you not heard in the town how bandits swept into the house and how they carried away what they would of the slaves and of the goods? And they hung the Old Lord up by his thumbs and beat him and the Old Mistress they tied in a chair and gagged her and everyone ran. But I stayed. I hid in a gong half full of water under a wooden lid. And when I came out they were gone and the Old Mistress sat dead in her chair, not from any touch they had given her but from fright. Her body was a rotten reed with the opium she smoked and she could not endure the fright."

"And the servants and the slaves?" gasped Wang Lung. "And the gateman?"

"Oh, those," she answered carelessly, "they were gone long ago—all those who had feet to carry them away, for there was no food and no money by the middle of the winter. Indeed," her voice fell to a whisper, "there are many of the men servants among the bandits. I saw that dog of a gateman myself—he was leading the way, although he turned his face aside in the Old Lord's presence, still I knew those three long hairs of his mole. And there were others, for how could any but those familiar with the great house know where jewels were hid and the secret treasure stores of things not to be sold? I would not put it beneath the old agent himself, although he would consider it beneath his dignity to appear publicly in the affair, since he is a sort of distant relative of the family."

The woman fell silent and the silence of the courts was heavy as silence can be after life has gone. Then she said,

"But all this was not a sudden thing. All during the lifetime of the Old Lord and of his father the fall of this house has been coming. In the last generation the lords ceased to see the land and took the moneys the agents gave them and spent it carelessly as water. And in these generations the strength of the land has gone from them and bit by bit the land has begun to go also."

"Where are the young lords?" asked Wang Lung, still staring about him, so impossible was it for him to believe these things.

"Hither and thither," said the woman indifferently. "It is good fortune that the two girls were married away before the thing happened. The elder young lord when he heard what had befallen his father and his mother sent a messenger to take the Old Lord, his father, but I persuaded the old head not to go. I said, 'Who will be in the courts, and it is not seemly for me, who am only a woman.'"

She pursed her narrow red lips virtuously as she spoke these words, and cast down her bold eyes, and again she said, when she had paused a little, "Besides, I have been my lord's faithful slave for these several years and I have no other house."

Wang Lung looked at her closely then and turned quickly away. He began to perceive what this was, a woman who clung to an old and dying man because of what last thing she might get from him. He said with contempt,

"Seeing that you are only a slave, how can I do business with you?"

At that she cried out at him, "He will do anything I tell him."

Wang Lung pondered over this reply. Well, and there was the land. Others would buy it through this woman if he did not.

"How much land is there left?" he asked her unwillingly, and she saw instantly what his purpose was.

"If you have come to buy land," she said quickly, "there is land to buy. He has a hundred acres to the west and to the south two hundred that he will sell. It is not all in one piece but the plots are large. It can be sold to the last acre."

This she said so readily that Wang Lung perceived she knew everything the old man had left, even to the last foot of land. But still he was unbelieving and not willing to do business with her.

"It is not likely the Old Lord can sell all the land of his family without the agreement of his sons," he demurred.

But the woman met his words eagerly.

"As for that, the sons have told him to sell when he can. The land is where no one of the sons wishes to live and the country is run over with bandits in these days of famine, and they have all said, 'We cannot live in such a place. Let us sell and divide the money.'"

"But into whose hand would I put the money?" asked Wang Lung, still unbelieving.

"Into the Old Lord's hand, and whose else?" replied the woman smoothly. But Wang Lung knew that the Old Lord's hand opened into hers.

He would not, therefore, talk further with her, but turned away saying, "Another day—another day—" and he went to the gate and she followed him, shrieking after him into the street,

"This time tomorrow—this time or this afternoon—all times are alike!"

He went down the street without answer, greatly puzzled and needing to think over what he had heard. He went into the small tea shop and ordered tea of the slavey and when the boy had put it smartly before him and with an impudent gesture had caught and tossed the penny he paid for it, Wang Lung fell to musing. And the more he mused the more monstrous it seemed that the great and rich family, who all his own life and all his father's and grandfather's lives long had been a power and a glory in the town, were now fallen and scattered.

"It comes of their leaving the land," he thought regretfully, and he thought of his own two sons, who were growing like young bamboo shoots in the spring, and he resolved that on this very day he would make them cease playing in the sunshine and he would set them to tasks in the field, where they would early take into their bones and their blood the feel of the soil under their feet, and the feel of the hoe hard in their hands.

Well, but all this time here were these jewels hot and heavy against his body and he was continually afraid. It seemed as though their brilliance must shine through his rags and someone cry out,

"Now here is a poor man carrying an emperor's treasure!"

And he could not rest until they were changed into land. He watched, therefore, until the shopkeeper had a moment of idleness and he called to the man and said,

"Come and drink a bowl at my cost, and tell me the news of the town, since I have been a winter away."

The shopkeeper was always ready for such talk, especially if he drank his own tea at another's cost, and he sat down readily at Wang Lung's table, a small weasel-faced man with a twisted and crossed left eye. His clothes were solid and black with grease down the front of his coat and trousers, for besides tea he sold food also, which he cooked himself, and he was fond of saying, "There is a proverb, 'A good cook has never a clean coat,' " and so he considered himself justly and necessarily filthy. He sat down and began at once,

"Well, and beyond the starving of people, which is no news, the greatest news was the robbery at the House of Hwang."

It was just what Wang Lung hoped to hear and the man went on to tell him of it with relish, describing how the few slaves left had screamed and how they had been carried off and how the concubines that remained had been raped and driven out and some even taken away, so that now none cared to live in that house at all. "None," the man finished, "except the Old Lord, who is now wholly the creature of a slave called Cuckoo, who has for many years been in the Old Lord's chamber, while others came and went, because of her cleverness."

"And has this woman command, then?" asked Wang Lung, listening closely.

"For the time she can do anything," replied the man. "And so for the time she closes her hand on everything that can be held and swallows all that can be swallowed. Some day, of course, when the young lords have their affairs settled in other parts they will come back and then she cannot fool them with her talk of a faithful servant to be rewarded, and out she will go. But she has her living made now, although she live to a hundred years."

"And the land?" asked Wang Lung at last, quivering with his eagerness.

"The land?" said the man blankly. To this shopkeeper land meant nothing at all.

"Is it for sale?" said Wang Lung impatiently.

"Oh, the land!" answered the man with indifference, and then as a customer came in he rose and called as he went, "I have heard it is for sale, except the piece where the family are buried for these six generations," and he went his way.

Then Wang Lung rose also, having heard what he came to hear, and he went out and approached again the great gates and the woman came to open to him and he stood without entering and he said to her,

"Tell me first this, will the Old Lord set his own seal to the deeds of sale?"

And the woman answered eagerly, and her eyes were fastened on his,

"He will—he will—on my life!"

Then Wang Lung said to her plainly,

"Will you sell the land for gold or for silver or for jewels?"

112

And her eyes glittered as she spoke and she said,
"I will sell it for jewels!"

Now Wang Lung had more land than a man with an ox
can plough and harvest, and more harvest than one man can
garner and so he built another small room to his house and he
bought an ass and he said to his neighbor Ching,

"Sell me the little parcel of land that you have and leave your
lonely house and come into my house and help me with my
land." And Ching did this and was glad to do it.

The heavens rained in season then; and the young rice grew
and when the wheat was cut and harvested in heavy sheaves,
the two men planted the young rice in the flooded fields, more
rice than Wang Lung had ever planted he planted this year, for
the rains came in abundance of water, so that lands that were
before dry were this year fit for rice. Then when this harvest
came he and Ching alone could not harvest it, so great it was,
and Wang Lung hired two other men as laborers who lived in
the village and they harvested it.

He remembered also the idle young lords of the fallen great
house as he worked on the land he had bought from the House
of Hwang, and he bade his two sons sharply each morning to
come into the fields with him and he set them at what labor
their small hands could do, guiding the ox and the ass, and
making them, if they could accomplish no great labor, at least to
know the heat of the sun on their bodies and the weariness of
walking back and forth along the furrows.

But O-lan he would not allow to work in the fields for he was
no longer a poor man, but a man who could hire his labor done
if he would, seeing that never had the land given forth such
harvests as it had this year. He was compelled to build yet
another room to the house to store his harvests in, or they would

not have had space to walk in the house. And he bought three pigs and a flock of fowls to feed on the grains spilled from the harvests.

Then O-lan worked in the house and made new clothes for each one and new shoes, and she made coverings of flowered cloth stuffed with warm new cotton for every bed, and when all was finished they were rich in clothing and in bedding as they had never been. Then she laid herself down upon her bed and gave birth again, although still she would have no one with her; even though she could hire whom she chose, she chose to be alone.

This time she was long at labor and when Wang Lung came home at evening he found his father standing at the door and laughing and saying,

"An egg with a double yolk this time!"

And when Wang Lung went into the inner room there was O-lan upon the bed with two new-born children, a boy and a girl as alike as two grains of rice. He laughed boisterously at what she had done and then he thought of a merry thing to say,

"So this is why you bore two jewels in your bosom!"

And he laughed again at what he had thought of to say, and O-lan, seeing how merry he was, smiled her slow, painful smile.

Wang Lung had, therefore, at this time no sorrow of any kind, unless it was this sorrow, that his eldest girl child neither spoke nor did those things which were right for her age, but only smiled her baby smile still when she caught her father's glance. Whether it was the desperate first year of her life or the starving or what it was, month after month went past and Wang Lung waited for the first words to come from her lips, even for his name which the children called him, "da-da." But no sound came, only the sweet, empty smile, and when he looked at her he groaned forth,

"Little fool—my poor little fool—"

And in his heart he cried to himself,

"If I had sold this poor mouse and they found her thus they would have killed her!"

And as if to make amends to the child he made much of her and took her into the field with him sometimes and she followed him silently about, smiling when he spoke and noticed her there.

In these parts, where Wang Lung had lived all his life and his father and his father's father had lived upon the land, there were famines once in five years or so, or if the gods were lenient, once in seven or eight or even ten years. This was because the heavens rained too much or not at all, or because the river to the north, because of rains and winter snows in distant mountains, came swelling into the fields over the dykes which had been built by men for centuries to confine it.

Time after time men fled from the land and came back to it, but Wang Lung set himself now to build his fortunes so securely that through the bad years to come he need never leave his land again but live on the fruits of the good years, and so subsist until another year came forth. He set himself and the gods helped him and for seven years there were harvests, and every year Wang Lung and his men threshed far more than could be eaten. He hired more laborers each year for his fields until he had six men and he built a new house behind his old one, a large room behind a court and two small rooms on each side of the court beside the large room. The house he covered with tiles, but the walls were still made of the hard tamped earth from the fields, only he had them brushed with lime and they were white and clean. Into these rooms he and his family moved, and the laborers, with Ching at their head, lived in the old house in front.

By this time Wang Lung had thoroughly tried Ching, and he found the man honest and faithful, and he set Ching to be his steward over the men and over the land and he paid him well, two silver pieces a month besides his food. But with all Wang Lung's urging Ching to eat and eat well, the man still put no flesh on his bones, remaining always a small, spare, lean man of great gravity. Nevertheless he labored gladly, pottering silently from dawn until dark, speaking in his feeble voice if there was anything to be said, but happiest and liking it best if there were nothing and he could be silent; and hour after hour he lifted his hoe and let it fall, and at dawn and sunset he would carry to the fields the buckets of water or of manure to put upon the vegetable rows.

But still Wang Lung knew that if any one of the laborers slept too long each day under the date trees or ate more than his share of the beancurd in the common dish or if any bade his wife or child come secretly at harvest time and snatch handfuls of the grain that was being beaten out under the flails, Ching would, at the end of the year when master and man feast together after the harvest, whisper to Wang Lung,

"Such an one and such an one do not ask back for the next year."

And it seemed that the handful of peas and of seed which had passed between these two men made them brothers, except that Wang Lung, who was the younger, took the place of the elder, and Ching never wholly forgot that he was hired and lived in a house which belonged to another.

By the end of the fifth year Wang Lung worked little in his fields himself, having indeed to spend his whole time, so increased were his lands, upon the business and the marketing of his produce, and in directing his workmen. He was greatly hampered by his lack of book knowledge and of the knowledge of the meaning of characters written upon a paper with a camel's hair brush and ink. Moreover, it was a shame to him when he was in a grain shop where grain was bought and sold again, that when a contract was written for so much and for so much of wheat or rice, he must say humbly to the haughty dealers in the town,

"Sir, and will you read it for me, for I am too stupid."

And it was a shame to him that when he must set his name to the contract another, even a paltry clerk, lifted his eyebrows in scorn and, with his brush pointed on the wet ink block, brushed hastily the characters of Wang Lung's name; and greatest shame that when the man called out for a joke,

"Is it the dragon character Lung or the deaf character Lung, or what?" Wang Lung must answer humbly,

"Let it be what you will, for I am too ignorant to know my own name."

It was on such a day one harvest time after he had heard the shout of laughter which went up from the clerks in the grain shop, idle at the noon hour and all listening to anything that went on, and all lads scarcely older than his sons, that he went home angrily over his own land saying to himself,

"Now, not one of those town fools has a foot of land and yet each feels he can laugh a goose cackle at me because I cannot tell the meanings of brush strokes over paper." And then as his indignation wore away, he said in his heart, "It is true that this is a shame to me that I cannot read and write. I will take my elder son from the fields and he shall go to a school in the town and he shall learn, and when I go into the grain markets he will read and write for me so that there may be an end of this hissing laughter against me, who am a landed man."

This seemed to him well and that very day he called to him his elder son, a straight tall lad of twelve years now, looking like his mother for his wide face bones and his big hands and feet but with his father's quickness of eye, and when the boy stood before him Wang Lung said,

"Come out of the fields from this day on, for I need a scholar in the family to read the contracts and to write my name so that I shall not be ashamed in the town."

The lad flushed a high dark red and his eyes shone.

"My father," he said, "so have I wished for these last two years that I might do, but I did not dare to ask it."

Then the younger boy when he heard of it came in crying and complaining, a thing he was wont to do, for he was a wordy, noisy lad from the moment he spoke at all, always ready to cry out that his share was less than that of others, and now he whined forth to his father,

"Well, and I shall not work in the fields, either, and it is not fair that my brother can sit at leisure in a seat and learn something and I must work like a hind, who am your son as well as he!"

Then Wang Lung could not bear his noise and he would give him anything if he cried loudly enough for it, and he said hastily,

"Well and well, go the both of you, and if Heaven in its evil take one of you, there will be the other one with knowledge to do the business for me."

Then he sent the mother of his sons into the town to buy cloth to make a long robe for each lad and he went himself to a paper and ink shop and he bought paper and brushes and two ink blocks, although he knew nothing of such things, and being ashamed to say he did not, was dubious at everything the man brought forward to show him. But at last all was prepared and arrangements made to send the boys to a small school near the city gate kept by an old man who had in past years gone up for government examinations and failed. In the central room of his house therefore he had set benches and tables and for a small sum at each feast day in the year he taught boys in the classics, beating them with his large fan, folded, if they were idle or if they could not repeat to him the pages over which they pored from dawn until sunset.

Only in the warm days of spring and summer did the pupils have a respite for then the old man nodded and slept after he had eaten at noon, and the dark small room was filled with the sound of his slumber. Then the lads whispered and played and drew pictures to show each other of this naughty thing and that, and snickered to see a fly buzzing about the old man's hanging, open jaw, and laid wagers with each other as to whether the fly would enter the cavern of his mouth or not. But when the old teacher opened his eyes suddenly—and there was no telling when he would open them as quickly and secretly as though he had not slept—he saw them before they were aware, and then laid about him with his fan, cracking this skull and that. And hearing the cracks of his stout fan and the cries of the pupils, the neighbors said,

"It is a worthy old teacher, after all." And this is why Wang Lung chose the school for the one where his sons should go to learn.

On the first day when he took them there he walked ahead of them, for it is not meet that father and son walk side by side, and he carried a blue kerchief filled with fresh eggs and these eggs he gave to the old teacher when he arrived. And Wang Lung was awed by the old teacher's great brass spectacles and by his long loose robe of black and by his immense fan, which he held even in winter, and Wang Lung bowed before him and said,

"Sir, here are my two worthless sons. If anything can be driven into their thick brass skulls it is only by beating them, and therefore if you wish to please me, beat them to make them learn." And the two boys stood and stared at the other boys on benches, and these others stared back at the two.

But going home again alone, having left the two lads, Wang Lung's heart was fit to burst with pride and it seemed to him that among all the lads in the room there were none equal to his two lads for tallness and robustness and bright brown faces. Meeting a neighbor coming from the village as he passed through the town gate, he answered the man's inquiry,

"This day I am back from my sons' school." And to the man's surprise he answered with seeming carelessness, "Now I do not need them in the fields and they may as well learn a stomachful of characters."

But to himself he said, passing by,

"It would not surprise me at all if the elder one should become a prefect with all this learning!"

And from that time on the boys were no longer called Elder and Younger, but they were given school names by the old teacher, and this old man, after inquiring into the occupation of their father, erected two names for the sons; for the elder, Nung En, and for the second Nung Wen, and the first word of each name signified one whose wealth is from the earth.

18

THUS WANG LUNG built the fortunes of his house and when the seventh year came and the great river to the north was too heavy with swollen waters, because of excessive rains and snows in the northwest where its source was, it burst it's bounds and came sweeping and flooding all over the lands of that region. But Wang Lung was not afraid. He was not afraid although two-fifths of his land was a lake as deep as a man's shoulders and more.

All through the late spring and early summer the water rose and at last it lay like a great sea, lovely and idle, mirroring cloud and moon and willows and bamboo whose trunks stood submerged. Here and there an earthen house, abandoned by the dwellers, stood up until after days of the water it fell slowly back into the water and the earth. And so it was with all houses that were not, like Wang Lung's built upon a hill, and these hills stood up like islands. And men went to and from town by boat and by raft, and there were those who starved as they ever had.

But Wang Lung was not afraid. The grain markets owed him money and his store-rooms were yet filled full with harvests of the last two years and his houses stood high so that the water was a long way off and he had nothing to fear.

But since much of the land could not be planted he was more idle than he had ever been in his life and being idle and full of good food he grew impatient when he had slept all he could sleep and done all there was to be done. There were, besides, the laborers, whom he hired for a year at a time, and it was foolish for him to work when there were those who ate his rice while they were half idle waiting day after day for the waters to recede. So after he had bade them mend the thatching of the old house and see to the setting of the tiles where the new roof leaked and had commanded them to mend the hoes and the rakes and the plows and to feed the cattle and to buy ducks to herd upon the water and to twist hemp into ropes—all those things which in the old days he did himself when he tilled his land alone—his own hands were empty and he did not know what to do with himself.

Now a man cannot sit all day and stare at a lake of water covering his fields, nor can he eat more than he is able to hold at one time, and when Wang Lung had slept, there was an end to sleeping. The house, as he wandered about it impatiently, was silent, too silent for his vigorous blood. The old man grew very feeble now, half blind and almost wholly deaf, and there was no need of speech with him except to ask if he were warm and fed or if he would drink tea. And it made Wang Lung impatient that the old man could not see how rich his son was and would always mutter if there were tea leaves in his bowl, "A little water is well enough and tea like silver." But there was no telling the old man anything for he forgot it at once and lived drawn into his own world and much of the time he dreamed he was a youth again and in his own fullness and he saw little of what passed him now.

The old man and the elder girl, who never spoke at all but sat beside her grandfather hour after hour, twisting a bit of cloth, folding and re-folding it and smiling at it, these two had nothing to say to a man prosperous and vigorous. When Wang Lung had poured the old man a bowl of tea and had passed his hand over the girl's cheek and received her sweet, empty smile, which passed with such sad swiftness from her face, leaving empty the dim and unshining eyes, there was nothing left. He always turned away from her with a moment's stillness, which was his daughter's mark of sadness on him, and he looked to his two younger children, the boy and the girl which O-lan had borne together, and who now ran about the threshold merrily.

But a man cannot be satisfied with the foolishness of little children and after a brief time of laughter and teasing they went off to their own games and Wang Lung was alone and filled with restlessness. Then it was that he looked at O-lan, his wife, as a man looks at the woman whose body he knows thoroughly and to satiation and who has lived beside him so closely that there is nothing he does not know of her and nothing new which he may expect or hope from her.

And it seemed to Wang Lung that he looked at O-lan for the first time in his life and he saw for the first time that she was a woman whom no man could call other than she was, a dull and common creature, who plodded in silence without thought of how she appeared to others. He saw for the first time that her hair was rough and brown and unoiled and that her face was large and flat and coarse-skinned, and her features too large altogether and without any sort of beauty or light. Her eyebrows were scattered and the hairs too few, and her lips were too wide, and her hands and feet were large and spreading. Looking at her thus with strange eyes, he cried out at her,

"Now anyone looking at you would say you were the wife of a common fellow and never of one who has land which he hires men to plow!"

It was the first time he had ever spoken of how she seemed to him and she answered with a slow painful gaze. She sat upon a bench threading a long needle in and out of a shoe sole and she stopped and held the needle poised and her mouth gaped open and showed her blackened teeth. Then as if she understood at last that he had looked at her as a man at a woman, a thick red flush crept up over her high cheek bones and she muttered,

"Since those two last ones were born together I have not been well. There is a fire in my vitals."

And he saw that in her simplicity she thought he accused her because for more than seven years she had not conceived. And he answered more roughly than he meant to do,

"I mean, cannot you buy a little oil for your hair as other women do and make yourself a new coat of black cloth? And those shoes you wear are not fit for a land proprietor's wife, such as you now are."

But she answered nothing, only looked at him humbly and without knowing what she did, and she hid her feet one over the other under the bench on which she sat. Then, although in his heart he was ashamed that he reproached this creature who through all these years had followed him faithfully as a dog, and although he remembered that when he was poor and labored in the fields himself she left her bed even after a child was born and came to help him in the harvest fields, yet he could not stem the irritation in his breast and he went on ruthlessly, although against his inner will,

"I have labored and have grown rich and I would have my wife look less like a hind. And those feet of yours——"

He stopped. It seemed to him that she was altogether hideous, but the most hideous of all were her big feet in their loose cotton cloth shoes, and he looked at them with anger so that she thrust them yet farther under the bench. And at last she said in a whisper,

"My mother did not bind them, since I was sold so young. But the girl's feet I will bind—the younger girl's feet I will bind."

But he flung himself off because he was ashamed that he was angry at her and angry because she would not be angry in return but only was frightened. And he drew his new black robe on him, saying fretfully,

"Well, and I will go to the tea shop and see if I can hear anything new. There is nothing in my house except fools and a dotard and two children."

His ill-temper grew as he walked to the town because he remembered suddenly that all these new lands of his he could not have bought in a lifetime if O-lan had not seized the handful of jewels from the rich man's house and if she had not given them to him when he commanded her. But when he remembered this he was the more angry and he said as if to answer his own heart rebelliously,

"Well, and but she did not know what she did. She seized them for pleasure as a child may seize a handful of red and green sweets, and she would have hidden them forever in her bosom if I had not found it out."

Then he wondered if she still hid the pearls between her breasts. But where before it had been strange and somehow a thing for him to think about sometimes and to picture in his mind, now he thought of it with contempt, for her breasts had grown flabby and pendulous with many children and had no beauty, and pearls between them were foolish and a waste.

But all this might have been nothing if Wang Lung were still a poor man or if the water was not spread over his fields. But he had money. There was silver hidden in the walls of his house and there was a sack of silver buried under a tile in the floor of his new house and there was silver wrapped in a cloth in the box in his room where he slept with his wife and silver sewed into the mat under their bed and his girdle was full of silver and he had no lack of it. So that now, instead of it passing from him like life blood draining from a wound, it lay in his girdle burning his fingers when he felt of it, and eager to be spent on this or that, and he began to be careless of it and to think what he could do to enjoy the days of his manhood.

Everything seemed not so good to him as it was before. The tea shop which he used to enter timidly, feeling himself but a common country fellow, now seemed dingy and mean to him. In the old days none knew him there and the tea boys were impudent to him, but now people nudged each other when he came in and he could hear a man whisper to another,

"There is that man Wang from the Wang village, he who bought the land from the House of Hwang that winter the Old Lord died when there was the great famine. He is rich, now."

And Wang Lung, hearing this sat down with seeming carelessness, but his heart swelled with pride at what he was. But on this day when he had reproached his wife even the deference he received did not please him and he sat gloomily drinking his tea and feeling that nothing was as good in his life as he had believed. And then he thought suddenly to himself,

"Now why should I drink my tea at this shop, whose owner is a cross-eyed weasel and whose earnings are less than the laborers upon my land, I who have land and whose sons are scholars?"

And he rose up quickly and threw his money on the table and went out before any could speak to him. He wandered forth upon the streets of the town without knowing what it was he wished. Once he passed by a story-teller's booth and for a little while he sat down upon the end of a crowded bench and listened to the man's tale of old days in the Three Kingdoms, when warriors were brave and cunning. But he was still restless and he could not come under the man's spell as the others did and the sound of the little brass gong the man beat wearied him and he stood up again and went on.

Now there was in the town a great tea shop but newly opened and by a man from the south, who understood such business, and Wang Lung had before this passed the place by, filled with horror at the thought of how money was spent there in gambling and in play and in evil women. But now, driven by his unrest from idleness and wishing to escape from the reproach of his own heart when he remembered that he had been unjust to his wife, he went toward this place. He was compelled by his restlessness to see or to hear something new. Thus he stepped across the threshold of the new tea shop into the great, glittering room, full of tables and open to the street as it was, and he went in, bold enough in his bearing and trying to be

123

the more bold because his heart was timid and he remembered that only in the last few years was he more than a poor man who had not at any time more than a silver piece or two, ahead, and a man who had even labored at pulling a ricksha on the streets of a southern city.

At first he did not speak at all in the great tea house but he bought his tea quietly and drank it and looked about him with wonder. This shop was a great hall and the ceiling was set about with gilt and upon the walls there were scrolls hung made of white silk and painted with the figures of women. Now these women Wang Lung looked at secretly and closely and it seemed to him they were women in dreams for none on earth had he seen like them. And the first day he looked at them and drank his tea quickly and went away.

But day after day while the waters held on his land he went to this tea shop and bought tea and sat alone and drank it and stared at the pictures of the beautiful women, and each day he sat longer, since there was nothing for him to do on his land or in his house. So he might have continued for many days on end, for in spite of his silver hidden in a score of places he was still a country-looking fellow and the only one in all that rich tea shop who wore cotton instead of silk and had a braid of hair down his back such as no man in a town will wear. But one evening when he sat drinking and staring from a table near the back of the hall, someone came down from a narrow stair which clung to the furthermost wall and led to the upper floor.

Now this tea shop was the only building in all that town which had an upper floor, except the Western Pagoda, which stood five stories high outside the West Gate. But the pagoda was narrow and more narrow toward the top, while the second floor of the tea shop was as square as that part of the building which stood upon the ground. At night the high singing of women's voices and light laughter floated out of the upper windows and the sweet strumming of lutes struck delicately by the hands of girls. One could hear the music streaming into the streets, especially after midnight, although where Wang Lung sat the clatter and noise of many men drinking tea and the sharp bony click of dice and sparrow dominoes muffled all else.

Thus it was that Wang Lung did not hear behind him on this night the footsteps of a woman creaking upon the narrow stair, and so he started violently when one touched him on the shoulder, not expecting that any would know him here. When he looked up it was into a narrow, handsome, woman's face, the face of Cuckoo, the woman into whose hands he had poured the jewels that day he bought land, and whose hand had held steady the Old Lord's shaking one and helped him to set aright his seal upon the deed of the sale. She laughed when she saw him, and her laughter was a sort of sharp whispering.

"Well, and Wang the farmer!" she said, lingering with malice on the word farmer, "and who would think to see you here!"

It seemed to Wang Lung then that he must prove at any cost to this woman that he was more than a mere country fellow, and he laughed and said too loudly,

"Is not my money as good to spend as another man's? And money I do not lack in these days. I have had good fortune."

Cuckoo stopped at this, her eyes narrow and bright as a snake's eyes, and her voice smooth as oil flowing from a vessel.

"And who has not heard it? And how shall a man better spend the money he has over and above his living than in a place like this, where rich men take their joy and elegant lords gather to take their joy in feasting and pleasure? There is no such wine as ours—have you tasted it, Wang Lung?"

"I have only drunk tea as yet," replied Wang Lung and he was half ashamed. "I have not touched wine or dice."

"Tea!" she exclaimed after him, laughing shrilly. "But we have tiger bone wine and dawn wine and wine of fragrant rice—why need you drink tea?" And as Wang Lung hung his head she said softly and insidiously,

"And I suppose you have not looked at anything else, have you, eh?—No pretty little hands, no sweet-smelling cheeks?"

Wang Lung hung his head yet lower and the red blood rushed into his face and he felt as though everyone near looked at him with mockery and listened to the voice of the woman. But when he took heart to glance about from under his lids, he saw no one paying any heed and the rattling of dice burst out anew and so he said in confusion,

"No—no—I have not—only tea—"

Then the woman laughed again and pointed to the painted silken scrolls and said,

"There they are, their pictures. Choose which one you wish to see and put the silver in my hand and I will place her before you."

"Those!" said Wang Lung, wondering. "I thought they were pictures of dream women, of goddesses in the mountain of Kwen Lwen, such as the story tellers speak of!"

"So they are dream women," rejoined Cuckoo, with mocking good humor, "but dreams such as a little silver will turn into flesh." And she went on her way, nodding and winking at the servants standing about and motioning to Wang Lung as at one of whom she said, "There is a country bumpkin!"

But Wang Lung sat staring at the pictures with a new interest. Up this narrow stairway then, in the rooms above him, there were these women in flesh and blood, and men went up to them—other men than he, of course, but men! Well, and if he were not the man he was, a good and working man, a man with a wife and sons, which picture would he, pretending as a child pretends that he might do a certain thing, pretending then, which would he pretend to take? And he looked at every painted face closely and with intensity as though each were real. Before this they had all seemed equally beautiful, before this when there had been no question of choosing. But now there were clearly some more beautiful than others, and out of the score and more he chose three most beautiful, and out of the three he chose again and he chose one most beautiful, a small, slender thing, a body light as a bamboo and a little face as pointed as a kitten's face, and one hand clasping the stem of a lotus flower in bud, and the hand as delicate as the tendril of a fern uncurled.

He stared at her and as he stared a heat like wine poured through his veins.

"She is like a flower on a quince tree," he said suddenly aloud, and hearing his own voice he was alarmed and ashamed and he rose hastily and put down his money and went out and into the darkness that had now fallen and so to his home.

But over the fields and the water the moonlight hung, a net of silver mist, and in his body his blood ran secret and hot and fast.

19

Now IF THE WATERS had at this time receded from Wang Lung's land, leaving it wet and smoking under the sun, so that in a few days of summer heat it would need to have been ploughed and harrowed and seed put in, Wang Lung might never have gone again to the great tea shop. Or if a child had fallen ill or the old man had reached suddenly to the end of his days, Wang Lung might have been caught up in the new thing and so forgotten the pointed face upon the scroll and the body of the woman slender as a bamboo.

But the waters lay placid and unmoved except for the slight summer wind that rose at sunset, and the old man dozed and the two boys trudged to school at dawn and were away until evening and in his house Wang Lung was restless and he avoided the eyes of O-lan who looked at him miserably as he went here and there and flung himself down in a chair and rose from it without drinking the tea she poured and without smoking the pipe he had lit. At the end of one long day, more long than any other, in the seventh month, when the twilight lingered murmurous and sweet with the breath of the lake, he stood at the door of his house, and suddenly without a word he turned abruptly and went into his room and put on his new coat, even the coat of black shining cloth, as shining almost as silk, that O-lan made for feast days, and with no word to anyone he went over the narrow paths along the water's edge and through the fields until he came to the darkness of the city gate and through this he went and through the streets until he came to the new tea shop.

There every light was lit, bright oil lamps which are to be bought in the foreign cities of the coast, and men sat under the lights drinking and talking, their robes open to the evening coolness, and everywhere fans moved to and fro and good laughter flowed out like music into the street. All the gayety which Wang Lung had never had from his labor on the land was held here in the walls of this house, where men met to play and never to work.

Wang Lung hesitated upon the threshold and he stood in the bright light which streamed from the open doors. And he might have stood there and gone away, for he was fearful and timid in his heart still, although his blood was rushing through his body fit to burst his veins, but there came out of the shadows on the edge of the light a woman who had been leaning idly against the doorway and it was Cuckoo. She came forward when she saw a man's figure, for it was her business to get customers for the women of the house, but when she saw who it was, she shrugged her shoulders and said,

"Ah, it is only the farmer!"

Wang was stung with the sharp carelessness in her voice, and his sudden anger gave him a courage he had not otherwise, so that he said,

"Well, and may I not come into the house and may I not do as other men?"

And she shrugged herself again and laughed and said,

"If you have the silver that other men have, you may do as they do."

And he wished to show her that he was lordly and rich enough to do as he liked, and he thrust his hand into his girdle and brought it out full of silver and he said to her,

"Is it enough and is it not enough?"

She stared at the handful of silver and said then without further delay,

"Come and say which one you wish."

And Wang Lung, without knowing what he said, muttered forth,

"Well, and I do not know that I want anything." And then his desire overcame him and he whispered, "That little one— that one with the pointed chin and the little small face, a face like a quince blossom for white and pink, and she holds a lotus bud in her hand."

The woman nodded easily and beckoning him she threaded her way between the crowded tables, and Wang Lung followed her at a distance. At first it seemed to him that every man looked up and watched him but when he took courage to see he

128

saw that none paid him any heed, except for one or two who called out, "Is it late enough, then, to go to the women?" and another called, "Here is a lusty fellow who needs must begin early!"

But by this time they were walking up the narrow straight stairway, and this Wang Lung did with difficulty, for it was the first time he had ever climbed steps in a house. Nevertheless, when they reached the top, it was the same as a house on the earth, except that is seemed a mighty way up when he passed a window and looked into the sky. The woman led the way down a close dark hall, then, and she cried as she went,

"Now here is the first man of the night!"

All along the hall doors opened suddenly and here and there girls' heads showed themselves in patches of light, as flowers burst out of their sheaths in the sun, but, Cuckoo called cruelly,

"No, not you—and not you—no one has asked for any of you! This one is for the little pink-faced dwarf from Soochow —for Lotus!"

A ripple of sound ran down the hall, indistinct, derisive, and one girl, ruddy as a pomegranate, called out in a big voice,

"And Lotus may have this fellow—he smells of the fields and of garlic!"

This Wang Lung heard, although he disdained to answer, although her words smote him like a dagger thrust because he feared that he looked indeed what he was, a farmer. But he went on stoutly when he remembered the good silver in his girdle, and at last the woman struck a closed door harshly with the flat palm of her hand and went in without waiting and there upon a bed covered with a flowered red quilt, sat a slender girl.

If one had told him there were small hands like these he would not have believed it, hands so small and bones so fine and fingers so pointed with long nails stained the color of lotus buds, deep and rosy. And if one had told him that there could be feet like these, little feet thrust into pink satin shoes no longer than a man's middle finger, and swinging childishly over the bed's edge—if anyone had told him he would not have believed it.

He sat stiffly on the bed beside her, staring at her, and he saw that she was like the picture and having seen the picture he would have known her if he had met her. But most of all her hand was like the painted hand, curling and fine and white as milk. Her two hands lay curling into each other upon the pink and silken lap of her robe, and he would not have dreamed that they were to be touched.

He looked at her as he had looked at the picture and he saw the figure slender as bamboo in its tight short upper coat; he saw the small pointed face set in its painted prettiness above the high collar lined with white fur; he saw the round eyes, the shape of apricots, so that now at last he understood what the story-tellers meant when they sang of the apricot eyes of the beauties of old. And for him she was not flesh and blood but the painted picture of a woman.

Then she lifted that small curling hand and put it upon his shoulder and she passed it slowly down the length of his arm, very slowly. And although he had never felt anything so light, so soft as that touch, although if he had not seen it, he would not have known that it passed, he looked and saw the small hand moving down his arm, and it was as though fire followed it and burned under through his sleeve and into the flesh of his arm, and he watched the hand until it reached the end of his sleeve and then it fell with an instant's practiced hesitation upon his bare wrist and then into the loose hollow of his hard dark hand. And he began to tremble, not knowing how to receive it.

Then he heard laughter, light, quick, tinkling as the silver bell upon a pagoda shaking in the wind, and a little voice like laughter said,

"Oh, and how ignorant you are, you great fellow? Shall we sit here the night through while you stare?"

And at that he seized her hand between both of his, but carefully, because it was like a fragile dry leaf, hot and dry, and he said to her imploringly and not knowing what he said,

"I do not know anything—teach me!"

And she taught him.

Now Wang Lung became sick with the sickness which is greater than any a man can have. He had suffered under labor in the sun and he had suffered under the dry icy winds of the bitter desert and he had suffered from starvation when the fields would not bear and he had suffered from the despair of laboring without hope upon the streets of a southern city. But under none of these did he suffer as he now did under this slight girl's hand.

Every day he went to the tea shop; every evening he waited until she would receive him, and every night he went in to her.

Each night he went in and each night again he was the country fellow who knew nothing, trembling at the door, sitting stiffly beside her, waiting for her signal of laughter, and then fevered, filled with a sickened hunger, he followed slavishly, bit by bit, her unfolding, until the moment of crisis, when, like a flower that is ripe for plucking, she was willing that he should grasp her wholly.

Yet never could he grasp her wholly, and this it was which kept him fevered and thirsty, even if she gave him his will of her. When O-lan had come to his house it was health to his flesh and he lusted for her robustly as a beast for its mate and he took her and was satisfied and he forgot her and did his work content. But there was no such content now in his love for this girl, and there was no health in her for him. At night when she would have no more of him, pushing him out of the door petulantly, with her small hands suddenly strong on his shoulders, his silver thrust into her bosom, he went away hungry as he came. It was as though a man, dying of thirst, drank the salt water of the sea which, though it is water, yet dries his blood into thirst and yet greater thirst so that in the end he dies, maddened by his very drinking. He went in to her and he had his will of her again and again and he came away unsatisfied.

All during that hot summer Wang Lung loved thus this girl. He knew nothing of her, whence she came or what she was; when they were together he said not a score of words and he scarcely listened to the constant running of her speech, light and interspersed with laughter like a child's. He only watched her face, her hands, the postures of her body, the meaning of her wide sweet eyes, waiting for her. He had never enough of her, and he went back to his house in the dawn, dazed and unsatisfied.

The days were endless. He would not sleep any more upon his bed, making a pretense of heat in the room, and he spread a mat under the bamboos and slept there fitfully, lying awake to stare into the pointed shadows of the bamboo leaves, his breast filled with a sweet sick pain he could not understand.

And if any spoke to him, his wife or his children, or if Ching came to him and said, "The waters will soon recede and what is there we should prepare of seed?" he shouted and said,

"Why do you trouble me?"

And all the time his heart was like to burst because he could not be satisfied of this girl.

Thus as the days went on and he lived only to pass the day until the evening came, he would not look at the grave faces of O-lan and of the children, suddenly sober in their play when he approached, nor even at his old father who peered at him and asked,

"What is this sickness that turns you full of evil temper and your skin as yellow as clay?"

And as these days went past to the night, the girl Lotus did what she would with him. When she laughed at the braid of his hair, although part of every day he spent in braiding and in brushing it, and said, "Now the men of the south do not have these monkey tails!" he went without a word and had it cut off, although neither by laughter or scorn had anyone been able to persuade him to it before.

When O-lan saw what he had done she burst out in terror, "You have cut off your life!"

But he shouted at her,

"And shall I look an old-fashioned fool forever? All the young men of the city have their hair cut short."

Yet he was afraid in his heart of what he had done, and yet so he would have cut off his life if the girl Lotus had commanded it or desired it, because she had every beauty which had ever come into his mind to desire in a woman.

His good brown body that he washed but rarely, deeming the clean sweat of his labor washing enough for ordinary times, his body he now began to examine as if it were another man's, and he washed himself every day so that his wife said, troubled,

"You will die with all this washing!"

He bought sweet-smelling soap in the shop, a piece of red scented stuff from foreign parts, and he rubbed it on his flesh, and not for any price would he have eaten a stalk of garlic, although it was a thing he had loved before, lest he stink before her.

And none in his house knew what to make of all these things.

He bought also new stuffs for clothes, and although O-lan had always cut his robes, making them wide and long for good measure and sewing them stoutly this way and that for strength, now he was scornful of her cutting and sewing and he took the stuffs to a tailor in the town and he had his clothes made as the men in the town had theirs, light grey silk for a robe, cut neatly to his body and with little to spare, and over this a black satin sleeveless coat. And he bought the first shoes he had

had in his life not made by a woman, and they were black velvet shoes such as the Old Lord had worn flapping at his heels.

But these fine clothes he was ashamed to wear suddenly before O-lan and his children. He kept them folded in sheets of brown oiled paper and he left them at the tea shop with a clerk he had come to know, and for a price the clerk let him go into an inner room secretly and put them on before he went up the stairs. And beyond this he bought a silver ring washed with gold for his finger, and as hair grew where it had been shaved above his forehead, he smoothed it with a fragrant foreign oil from a small bottle for which he had paid a whole piece of silver.

But O-lan looked at him in astonishment and did not know what to make from all this, except that one day after staring at him for a long time as they ate rice at noon, she said heavily,

"There is that about you which makes me think of one of the lords in the great house."

Wang Lung laughed loudly then and he said,

"And am I always to look like a hind when we have enough and to spare?"

But in his heart he was greatly pleased and for that day he was more kindly with her than he had been for many days.

Now the money, the good silver, went streaming out of his hands. There was not only the price he must pay for his hours with the girl, but there was the pretty demanding of her desires. She would sigh and murmur, as though her heart were half broken with her desire,

"Ah me—ah me!"

And when he whispered, having learned at last to speak in her presence, "What now, my little heart?" she answered, "I have no joy today in you because Black Jade, that one across the hall from me, has a lover who gave her a gold pin for her hair, and I have only this old silver thing, which I have had forever and a day."

And then for his life's sake he could not but whisper to her, pushing aside the smooth black curve of her hair that he might have the delight of seeing her small long-lobed ears,

"And so will I buy a gold pin for the hair of my jewel."

For all these names of love she had taught him, as one teaches new words to a child. She had taught him to say them to her and he could not say them enough for his own heart, even while he stammered them, he whose speech had all his life been only of planting and of harvests and of sun and rain.

Thus the silver came out of the wall and out of the sack, and O-lan, who in the old days might have said to him easily enough, "And why do you take the money from the wall," now said nothing, only watching him in great misery, knowing well that he was living some life apart from her and apart even from the land, but not knowing what life it was. But she had been afraid of him from that day on which he had seen clearly that she had no beauty of hair or of person, and when he had seen her feet were large, and she was afraid to ask him anything because of his anger that was always ready for her now.

There came a day when Wang Lung returned to his house over the fields and he drew near to her as she washed his clothes at the pool. He stood there silent for a while and then he said to her roughly, and he was rough because he was ashamed and would not acknowledge his shame in his heart,

"Where are those pearls you had?"

And she answered timidly, looking up from the edge of the pool and from the clothes she was beating upon a smooth flat stone,

"The pearls? I have them."

And he muttered, not looking at her but at her wrinkled, wet hands,

"There is no use in keeping pearls for nothing."

Then she said slowly,

"I thought one day I might have them set in earrings," and fearing his laughter she said again, "I could have them for the younger girl when she is wed."

And he answered her loudly, hardening his heart,

"Why should that one wear pearls with her skin as black as earth? Pearls are for fair women!" And then after an instant's silence he cried out suddenly, "Give them to me—I have need of them!"

Then slowly she thrust her wet wrinkled hand into her bosom and she drew forth the small package and she gave it to him and watched him as he unwrapped it; and the pearls lay in his hand and they caught softly and fully the light of the sun, and he laughed.

But O-lan returned to the beating of his clothes and when tears dropped slowly and heavily from her eyes she did not put up her hand to wipe them away; only she beat the more steadily with her wooden stick upon the clothes spread over the stone.

20

AND THUS it might have gone forever until all the silver was spent had not that one, Wang Lung's uncle, returned suddenly without explanation of where he had been or what he had done. He stood in the door as though he had dropped from a cloud, his ragged clothes unbuttoned and girdled loosely as ever about him, and his face as it always was but wrinkled and hardened with the sun and the wind. He grinned widely at them all as they sat about the table at their early morning meal, and Wang Lung sat agape, for he had forgotten that his uncle lived and it was like a dead man returning to see him. The old man his father blinked and stared and did not recognize the one who had come until he called out,

"Well, and Elder Brother and his son and his sons and my sister-in-law."

Then Wang Lung rose, dismayed in his heart but upon the surface of his face and voice courteous.

"Well, and my uncle and have you eaten?"

"No," replied his uncle easily, "but I will eat with you."

He sat himself down, then, and he drew a bowl and chopsticks to him and he helped himself freely to rice and dried salt fish and to salted carrots and to the dried beans that were upon the table. He ate as though he were very hungry and none spoke until he supped down loudly three bowls of the thin rice gruel, cracking quickly between his teeth the bones of the fish and the kernels of the beans. And when he had eaten he said simply and as though it was his right,

"Now I will sleep, for I am without sleep these three nights."

Then when Wang Lung, dazed and not knowing what else to do, led him to his father's bed, his uncle lifted the quilts and felt of the good cloth and of the clean new cotton and he looked at the wooden bedstead and at the good table and at the great wooden chair which Wang Lung had bought for his father's room, and he said,

"Well, and I heard you were rich but I did not know you were as rich as this," and he threw himself upon the bed and drew the quilt about his shoulders, all warm with summer though it was, and everything he used as though it was his own, and he was asleep without further speech.

Wang Lung went back to the middle room in great consternation for he knew very well that now his uncle would never be driven forth again, now that he knew Wang Lung had wherewith to feed him. And Wang Lung thought of this and thought of his uncle's wife with great fear because he saw that they would come to his house and none could stop them.

As he feared so it happened. His uncle stretched himself upon the bed at last after noon had passed and he yawned loudly three times and came out of the room, shrugging the clothes together upon his body and he said to Wang Lung,

"Now I will fetch my wife and my son. There are the three of us mouths, and in this great house of yours it will never be missed what we eat and the poor clothes we wear."

Wang Lung could do nothing but answer with sullen looks, for it is a shame to a man when he has enough and to spare to drive his own father's brother and son from the house. And Wang Lung knew that if he did this it would be a shame to him in the village where he was now respected because of his prosperity and so he did not dare to say anything. But he commanded the laborers to move altogether into the old house so that the rooms by the gate might be left empty and into these that very day in the evening his uncle came, bringing his wife and his son. And Wang Lung was exceedingly angry and the more angry because he must bury it all in his heart and answer with smiles and welcome his relatives. This, although when he saw the fat smooth face of his uncle's wife he felt fit to burst with his anger and when he saw the scampish, impudent face of his uncle's son, he could scarcely keep his hand down from slapping it. And for three days he did not go into the town because of his anger.

Then when they were all accustomed to what had taken place and when O-lan had said to him, "Cease to be angry. It is a thing to be borne," and Wang Lung saw that his uncle and his uncle's wife and son would be courteous enough for the sake of their food and their shelter, then his thoughts turned more violently than ever to the girl Lotus and he muttered to himself,

"When a man's house if full of wild dogs he must seek peace elsewhere."

And all the old fever and pain burned in him and he was still never satisfied of his love.

Now what O-lan had not seen in her simplicity nor the old man because of the dimness of his age nor Ching because of his friendship, the wife of Wang Lung's uncle saw at once and she cried out, the laughter slanting from her eyes,

"Now Wang Lung is seeking to pluck a flower somewhere." And when O-lan looked at her humbly, not understanding, she laughed and said again, "The melon must always be split wide open before you can see the seeds, eh? Well, then, plainly, your man is mad over another woman!"

This Wang Lung heard his uncle's wife say in the court outside his window as he lay dozing and weary in his room one early morning, exhausted with his love. He was quickly awake, and he listened further, aghast at the sharpness of this woman's eyes. The thick voice rumbled on, pouring like oil from her fat throat.

"Well, and I have seen many a man, and when one smooths his hair and buys new clothes and will have his shoes velvet all of a sudden, then there is a new woman and that is sure."

There came a broken sound from O-lan, what it was she said he could not hear, but his uncle's wife said again,

"And it is not to be thought, poor fool, that one woman is enough for any man, and if it is a weary hard-working woman who has worn away her flesh working for him, it is less than enough for him. His fancy runs elsewhere the more quickly, and you, poor fool, have never been fit for a man's fancy and little better than an ox for his labor. And it is not for you to repine when he has money and buys himself another to bring her to his house, for all men are so, and would my old do-nothing also, except the poor wretch has never had enough silver in his life to feed himself even."

This she said and more, but no more than this did Wang Lung hear upon his bed, for his thought stopped at what she had said. Now suddenly did he see how to satisfy his hunger and his thirst after this girl he loved. He would buy her and bring her to his house and make her his own so that no other man could come in to her and so could he eat and be fed and drink and be satisfied. And he rose up at once from his bed and he went out and motioned secretly to the wife of his uncle and he said, when she had followed him outside the gate and under the date tree where none could hear what he had to say,

"I listened and heard what you said in the courts and you are right. I have need of more than that one and why should I not, seeing that I have land to feed us all?"

She answered volubly and eagerly,

"And why not, indeed? So have all men who have prospered. It is only the poor man who must needs drink from one cup." Thus she spoke, knowing what he would say next, and he went on as she had planned,

"But who will negotiate for me and be the middleman? A man cannot go to a woman and say, 'Come to my house.'"

To this she answered instantly,

"Now do you leave this affair in my hands. Only tell me which woman it is and I will manage the affair."

Then Wang Lung answered unwillingly and timidly, for he had never spoken her name aloud before to anyone,

"It is the woman called Lotus."

It seemed to him that everyone must know and have heard of Lotus, forgetting how only a short two summers' moons before he had not known she lived. He was impatient, therefore, when his uncle's wife asked further,

"And where her home?"

"Now where," he answered with asperity, "where except in the great tea shop on the main street of the town?"

"The one called the House of Flowers?"

"And what other?" Wang Lung retorted.

She mused awhile, fingering her pursed lower lip, and she said at last,

"I do not know anyone there. I shall have to find a way. Who is the keeper of this woman?"

And when he told her it was Cuckoo, who had been slave in the great house, she laughed and said,

"Oh, that one? Is that what she did after the Old Lord died in her bed one night! Well, and it is what she would do." Then she laughed again, a cackling "Heh—heh—heh—" and she said easily,

"That one! But it is a simple matter, indeed. Everything is plain. That one! From the beginning that one would do anything, even to making a mountain, if she could feel silver enough in her palm for it."

And Wang Lung, hearing this, felt his mouth suddenly dry and parched and his voice came from him in a whisper,

"Silver, then! Silver and gold! Anything to the very price of my land!"

Then from a strange and contrary fever of love Wang Lung would not go again to the great tea house until the affair was arranged. To himself he said,

"And if she will not come to my house and be for me only, cut my throat and I will not go near her again."

But when he thought the words, "if she will not come," his heart stood still with fear, so that he continually ran to his uncle's wife saying,

"Now, lack of money shall not close the gate." And he said again, "Have you told Cuckoo that I have silver and gold for my will?" and he said, "Tell her she shall do no work of any kind in my house but she shall wear only silken garments and eat shark's fins if she will every day," until at last the fat woman grew impatient and cried out at him, rolling her eyes back and forth,

"Enough and enough! Am I a fool, or is this the first time I have managed a man and a maid? Leave me alone and I will do it. I have said everything many times."

Then there was nothing to do except to gnaw his fingers and to see the house suddenly as Lotus might see it and he hurried O-lan into this and that, sweeping and washing and moving tables and chairs, so that she, poor woman, grew more and more terror stricken for well she knew by now, although he said nothing, what was to come to her.

Now Wang Lung could not bear to sleep any more with O-lan and he said to himself that with two women in the house there must be more rooms and another court and there must be a place where he could go with his love and be separate. So while he waited for his uncle's wife to complete the matter, he called his laborers and commanded them to build another court to the house behind the middle room, and around the court three rooms, one large and two small on either side. And the laborers stared at him, but dared not reply and he would not tell them anything, but he superintended them himself, so that he need not talk with Ching even of what he did. And the men dug the earth from the fields and made the walls and beat them down, and Wang Lung sent to the town and bought tiles for the roof.

Then when the rooms were finished and the earth smoothed and beaten down for a floor, he had bricks bought and the men set them closely together and welded them with lime and there was a good brick floor to the three rooms for Lotus. And Wang Lung bought red cloth to hang at the doors for curtains and he bought a new table and two carved chairs to put on either side and two painted scrolls of pictured hills and water to hang upon the wall behind the table. And he bought a round red lacquered comfit dish with a cover, and in this he put sesame cakes and larded sweets and he put the box on the table. Then he bought a wide and deep carven bed, big enough for a small room in itself, and he bought flowered curtains to hang about it. But in all this he was ashamed to ask O-lan anything, and so in the evenings his uncle's wife came in and she hung the bed curtains and did the things a man is too clumsy for doing.

Then all was finished and there was nothing to do, and a moon of days had passed and the thing was not yet complete. So Wang Lung dallied alone in the little new court he had built for Lotus and he thought of a little pool to make in the center of the court, and he called a laborer and the man dug a pool three feet square and set it about with tiles, and Wang Lung went into the city and bought five goldfish for it. Then he could think of nothing more to be done, and again he waited impatient and fevered.

During all this time he said nothing to anyone except to scold the children if they were filthy at their noses or to roar out at O-lan that she had not brushed her hair for three days and more, so that at last one morning O-lan burst into tears and wept aloud, as he had never seen her weep before, even when they starved, or at any other time. He said harshly, therefore,

"Now what, woman? Cannot I say comb out your horse's tail of hair without this trouble over it?"

But she answered nothing except to say over and over, moaning,

"I have borne you sons—I have borne you sons—"

And he was silenced and uneasy and he muttered to himself for he was ashamed before her and so he let her alone. It was true that before the law he had no complaint against his wife, for she had borne him three good sons and they were alive, and there was no excuse for him except his desire.

Thus it went until one day his uncle's wife came and said,

"The thing is complete. The woman who is keeper for the

master of the tea house will do it for a hundred pieces of silver on her palm at one time, and the girl will come for jade earrings and a ring of jade and a ring of gold and two suits of satin clothes and two suits of silk clothes and a dozen pairs of shoes and two silken quilts for her bed."

Of all this Wang Lung heard only this part, "The thing is complete—" and he cried out,

"Let it be done—let it be done—" and he ran into the inner room and he got out silver and poured it into her hands, but secretly still, for he was unwilling that anyone should see the good harvests of so many years go thus, and to his uncle's wife he said, "And for yourself take a good ten pieces of silver."

Then she made a feint of refusal, drawing up her fat body and rolling her head this way and that and crying in a loud whisper,

"No, and I will not. We are one family and you are my son and I am your mother and this I do for you and not for silver." But Wang Lung saw her hand outstretched as she denied, and into it he poured the good silver and he counted it well spent.

Then he bought pork and beef and mandarin fish and bamboo sprouts and chestnuts, and he bought a snarl of dried birds' nests from the south to brew for soup, and he bought dried shark's fins and every delicacy he knew he bought and then he waited, if that burning, restless impatience within him could be called a waiting.

On a shining glittering fiery day in the eighth moon, which is the last end of summer, she came to his house. From afar Wang Lung saw her coming. She rode in a closed sedan chair of bamboo borne upon men's shoulders and he watched the sedan moving this way and that upon the narrow paths skirting the fields, and behind it followed the figure of Cuckoo. Then for an instant he knew fear and he said to himself,

"What am I taking into my house?"

And scarcely knowing what he did he went quickly into the room where he had slept for these many years with his wife and he shut the door and there in the darkness of the room he waited in confusion until he heard his uncle's wife calling loudly for him to come out, for one was at the gate.

Then abashed and as though he had never seen the girl before he went slowly out, hanging his head over his fine clothes, and his eyes looking here and there, but never ahead. But Cuckoo hailed him merrily,

"Well, and I did not know we would be doing business like this!"

Then she went to the chair which the men had set down and she lifted the curtain and clucked her tongue and she said,

"Come out, my Lotus Flower, here is your house and here your lord."

And Wang Lung was in an agony because he saw upon the faces of the chair men wide grins of laughter and he thought to himself,

"Now these are loafers from the town streets and they are worthless fellows," and he was angry that he felt his face hot and red and so he would not speak aloud at all.

Then the curtain was lifted and before he knew what he did he looked and he saw sitting in the shadowy recess of the chair, painted and cool as a lily, the girl Lotus. He forgot everything, even his anger against the grinning fellows from the town, everything but that he had bought this woman for his own and she had come to his house forever, and he stood stiff and trembling, watching as she rose, graceful as though a wind had passed over a flower. Then as he watched and could not take his eyes away, she took Cuckoo's hand and stepped out, keeping her head bowed and her eyelids drooped as she walked, tottering and swaying upon her little feet, and leaning upon Cuckoo. And as she passed him she did not speak to him, but she whispered only to Cuckoo, faintly,

"Where is my apartment?"

Then his uncle's wife came forward to her other side and between them they led the girl into the court and into the new rooms that Wang Lung had built for her. And of all Wang Lung's house there was none to see her pass, for he had sent the laborers and Ching away for the day to work on a distant field, and O-lan had gone somewhere he knew not and had taken the two little ones with her and the boys were in school and the old man slept against the wall and heard and saw nothing, and as for the poor fool, she saw no one who came and went and knew no face except her father's and her mother's. But when Lotus had gone in Cuckoo drew the curtains after her.

Then after a time Wang Lung's uncle's wife came out, laughing a little maliciously, and she dusted her hands together as though to free them of something that clung to them.

"She reeks of perfume and paint, that one," she said still laughing. "Like a regular bad one she smells." And then she said with a deeper malice, "She is not so young as she looks, my nephew! I will dare to say this, that if she had not been on the edge of an age when men will cease soon to look at her, it is doubtful whether jade in her ears and gold on her fingers and even silk and satin would have tempted her to the house of a farmer, and even a well-to-do farmer." And then seeing the anger on Wang Lung's face at this too plain speaking she added hastily, "But beautiful she is and I have never seen another more beautiful and it will be as sweet as the eight-jeweled rice at a feast after your years with the thick-boned slave from the House of Hwang."

But Wang Lung answered nothing, only he moved here and there through the house and he listened and he could not be still. At last he dared to lift the red curtain and to go into the court he had built for Lotus and then into the darkened room where she was and there he was beside her for the whole day until night.

All this time O-lan had not come near the house. At dawn she had taken a hoe from the wall and she called the children and she took a little cold food wrapped up in a cabbage leaf and she had not returned. But when night came on she entered, silent and earth-stained and dark with weariness, and the children silent behind her, and she said nothing to anyone, but she went into the kitchen and prepared food and set it upon the table as she always did, and she called the old man and put the chopsticks in his hand and she fed the poor fool and then she ate a little with the children. Then when they slept and Wang Lung still sat at the table dreaming she washed herself for sleeping and at last she went into her accustomed room and slept alone upon her bed.

Then did Wang Lung eat and drink of his love night and day. Day after day he went into the room where Lotus lay indolent upon her bed and he sat beside her and watched her at all she did. She never came forth in the heat of the early autumn days, but she lay while the woman Cuckoo bathed her slender body with lukewarm water and rubbed oil into her flesh and perfume and oil into her hair. For Lotus had said wilfully that Cuckoo must stay with her as her servant and she paid her prodigally so that the woman was willing enough to serve one instead of a score, and she and Lotus, her mistress, dwelt apart from the others in the new court that Wang Lung had made.

All day the girl lay in the cool darkness of her room, nibbling sweetmeats and fruits, and wearing nothing but single garments of green summer silk, a little tight coat cut to her waist and wide trousers beneath, and thus Wang Lung found her when he came to her and he ate and drank of his love.

Then at sunset she sent him away with her pretty petulance, and Cuckoo bathed and perfumed her again and put on her fresh clothes, soft white silk against her flesh and peach-colored silk outside, the silken garments that Wang Lung had given, and upon her feet Cuckoo put small embroidered shoes, and then the girl walked into the court and examined the little pool with its five gold fish, and Wang Lung stood and stared at the wonder of what he had. She swayed upon her little feet and to Wang Lung there was nothing so wonderful for beauty in the world as her pointed little feet and her curling helpless hands.

And he ate and drank of his love and he feasted alone and he was satisfied.

21

IT WAS not to be supposed that the coming of this one called Lotus and of her serving woman Cuckoo into Wang Lung's house could be accomplished altogether without stir and discord of some sort, since more than one woman under one roof is not for peace. But Wang Lung had not foreseen it. And even though he saw by O-lan's sullen looks and Cuckoo's sharpness that something was amiss, he would not pay heed to it and he was careless of anyone so long as he was still fierce with his desire.

Nevertheless, when day passed into night, and night changed into dawn, Wang Lung saw that it was true the sun rose in the morning, and this woman Lotus was there, and the moon rose in its season and she was there for his hand to grasp when it would, and his thirst of love was somewhat slaked and he saw things he had not seen before.

For one thing, he saw that there was trouble at once between O-lan and Cuckoo. This was an astonishment to him, for he was prepared for O-lan to hate Lotus, having heard many times of such things, and some women will even hang themselves upon a beam with a rope when a man takes a second woman into the house, and others will scold and contrive to make his life worthless for what he has done, and he was glad that O-lan was a silent woman for at least she could not think of words against him. But he had not foreseen that whereas she would be silent of Lotus, her anger would find its vent against Cuckoo.

Now Wang Lung had thought only of Lotus and when she begged him,

"Let me have this woman for my servant, seeing that I am altogether alone in the world, for my father and my mother died when I could not yet talk and my uncle sold me as soon as I was pretty to a life such as I have had, and I have no one."

This she said with her tears, always abundant and ready and glittering in the corners of her pretty eyes, and Wang Lung could have denied her nothing she asked when she looked up at him so. Besides, it was true enough that the girl had no one to serve her, and it was true she would be alone in his house, for it was plain enough and to be expected that O-lan would not serve the second one, and she would not speak to her or notice that she was in the house at all. There was only the uncle of Lotus then, and it was against Wang Lung's stomach to have that one peeping and prying and near to Lotus for her to talk to of him, and so Cuckoo was as good as any and he knew no other woman who would come.

But it seemed that O-lan, when she saw Cuckoo, grew angry with a deep and sullen anger that Wang Lung had never seen and did not know was in her. Cuckoo was willing enough to be friends, since she had her pay from Wang Lung, albeit she did not forget that in the great house she had been in the lord's chamber and O-lan a kitchen slave and one of many. Nevertheless, she called out to O-lan well enough when first she saw her,

"Well, and my old friend, here we are in a house together again, and you mistress and first wife—my mother—and how things are changed!"

But O-lan stared at her and when it came into her understanding who it was and what she was, she answered nothing but she put down the jar of water she carried and she went into the middle room where Wang Lung sat between his times of love, and she said to him plainly,

"What is this slave woman doing in our house?"

145

Wang Lung looked east and west. He would have liked to speak out to say in a surly voice of master, "Well, and it is my house and whoever I say may come in, she shall come in, and who are you to ask?" But he could not because of some shame in him when O-lan was there before him, and his shame made him angry, because when he reasoned it, there was no need for shame and he had done no more than any man may do who has silver to spare.

Still, he could not speak out, and he only looked east and west and feigned to have mislaid his pipe in his garments, and he fumbled in his girdle. But O-lan stood there solidly on her big feet and waited and when he said nothing she asked again plainly in the same words,

"What is this slave woman doing in our house?"

Then Wang Lung seeing she would have an answer, said feebly,

"And what is it to you?"

And O-lan said,

"I bore her haughty looks all during my youth in the great house and her running into the kitchen a score of times a day and crying out 'now tea for the lord'—'now food for the lord'—and it was always this is too hot and that is too cold, and that is badly cooked, and I was too ugly and too slow and too this and too that. . ."

But still Wang Lung did not answer, for he did not know what to say.

Then O-lan waited and when he did not speak, the hot, scanty tears welled slowly into her eyes, and she winked them to hold back the tears, and at last she took the corner of her blue apron and wiped her eyes and she said at last,

"It is a bitter thing in my house, and I have no mother's house to go back to anywhere."

And when Wang Lung was still silent and answered nothing at all, but he sat down to his pipe and lit it, and he said nothing still, she looked at him piteously and sadly out of her strange dumb eyes that were like a beast's eyes that cannot speak, and then she went away, creeping and feeling for the door because of her tears that blinded her.

Wang Lung watched her as she went and he was glad to be alone, but still he was ashamed and he was still angry that he was ashamed and he said to himself and he muttered the words aloud and restlessly, as though he quarreled with someone,

"Well, and other men are so and I have been good enough to

her, and there are men worse than I." And he said at last that O-lan must bear it.

But O-lan was not finished with it, and she went her way silently. In the morning she heated water and presented it to the old man, and to Wang Lung if he were not in the inner court she presented tea, but when Cuckoo went to find hot water for her mistress the cauldron was empty and not all her loud questionings would stir any response from O-lan. Then there was nothing but that Cuckoo must herself boil water for her mistress if she would have it. But then it was time to stir the morning gruel and there was not space in the cauldron for more water and O-lan would go steadily to her cooking, answering nothing to Cuckoo's loud crying,

"And is my delicate lady to lie thirsting and gasping in her bed for a swallow of water in the morning?"

But O-lan would not hear her; only she pushed more grass and straw into the bowels of the oven, spreading it as carefully and as thriftily as ever she had in the old days when one leaf was precious enough because of the fire it would make under food. Then Cuckoo went complaining loudly to Wang Lung and he was angry that his love must be marred by such things and he went to O-lan to reproach her and he shouted at her,

"And cannot you add a dipperful of water to the cauldron in the mornings?"

But she answered with a sullenness deeper than ever upon her face,

"I am not slave of slaves in this house at least."

Then he was angry beyond bearing and he seized O-lan's shoulder and he shook her soundly and he said,

"Do not be yet more of a fool. It is not for the servant but for the mistress."

And she bore his violence and she looked at him and she said simply,

"And to that one you gave my two pearls!"

Then his hand dropped and he was speechless and his anger was gone and he went away ashamed and he said to Cuckoo,

"We will build another stove and I will make another kitchen. The first wife knows nothing of the delicacies which the other one needs for her flower-like body and which you also enjoy. You shall cook what you please in it."

And so he bade the laborers build a little room and an earthen stove in it and he bought a good cauldron. And Cuckoo

147

was pleased because he said,"You shall cook what you please in it."

As for Wang Lung, he said to himself that at last his affairs were settled and his women at peace and he could enjoy his love. And it seemed to him freshly that he could never tire of Lotus and of the way she pouted at him with the lids drooped like lily petals over her great eyes, and at the way laughter gleamed out of her eyes when she glanced up at him.

But after all this matter of the new kitchen became a thorn in his body, for Cuckoo went to the town every day and she bought this and that of expensive foods that are imported from the southern cities. There were foods he had never even heard of: lichee nuts and dried honey dates and curious cakes of rice flour and nuts and red sugar, and horned fish from the sea and many other things. And these all cost money more than he liked to give out, but still not so much, he was sure, as Cuckoo told him, and yet he was afraid to say, "You are eating my flesh," for fear she would be offended and angry at him, and it would displease Lotus, and so there was nothing he could do except to put his hand unwillingly to his girdle. And this was a thorn to him day after day, and because there was none to whom he could complain of it, the thorn pierced more deeply continually, and it cooled a little of the fire of love in him for Lotus.

And there was yet another small thorn that sprang from the first, and it was that his uncle's wife, who loved good food, went often into the inner court at meal times, and she grew free there, and Wang Lung was not pleased that out of his house Lotus chose this woman for friend. The three women ate well in the inner courts, and they talked unceasingly, whispering and laughing, and there was something that Lotus liked in the wife of his uncle and the three were happy together, and this Wang Lung did not like.

But still there was nothing to be done, for when he said gently and to coax her,

"Now, Lotus, my flower, and do not waste your sweetness on an old fat hag like that one. I need it for my own heart, and she is a deceitful and untrustworthy creature, and I do not like it that she is near you from dawn to sunset."

Lotus was fretful and she answered peevishly, pouting her lips and hanging her head away from him,

"Now and I have no one except you and I have no friends and I am used to a merry house and in yours there is no one

148

except the first wife who hates me and these children of yours who are a plague to me, and I have no one."

Then she used her weapons against him and she would not let him into her room that night and she complained and said,

"You do not love me for if you did you would wish me to be happy."

Then Wang Lung was humbled and anxious and he was submissive and he was sorry and he said,

"Let it be only as you wish and forever."

Then she forgave him royally and he was afraid to rebuke her in any way for what she wished to do, and after that when he came to her Lotus, if she were talking or drinking tea or eating some sweetmeat with his uncle's wife, would bid him wait and was careless with him, and he strode away, angry that she was unwilling for him to come in when this other woman sat there, and his love cooled a little, although he did not know it himself.

He was angry, moreover, that his uncle's wife ate of the rich foods that he had to buy for Lotus and that she grew fat and more oily than she had been, but he could say nothing for his uncle's wife was clever and she was courteous to him and flattered him with good words, and rose when he came into the room.

And so his love for Lotus was not whole and perfect as it had been before, absorbing utterly his mind and his body. It was pierced through and through with small angers which were the more sharp because they must be endured and because he could no longer go even to O-lan freely for speech, seeing that now their life was sundered.

Then like a field of thorns springing up from one root and spreading here and there, there was yet more to trouble Wang Lung. One day his father, whom one would say saw nothing at any time so drowsy with age he was, woke suddenly out of his sleeping in the sun and he tottered, leaning on his dragon-headed staff which Wang Lung had bought for him on his seventieth birthday, to the doorway where a curtain hung between the main room and the court where Lotus walked. Now the old man had never noticed the door before nor when the court was built and seemingly he did not know whether anyone had been added to the house or not, and Wang Lung never told him, "I have another woman," for the old man was too deaf to make anything out of a voice if it told him something new and of which he had not thought.

But on this day he saw without reason this doorway and he

went to it and drew the curtain, and it happened that it was at an hour of evening when Wang Lung walked with Lotus in the court, and they stood beside the pool and looked at the fish, but Wang Lung looked at Lotus. Then when the old man saw his son standing beside a slender painted girl he cried out in his shrill cracked voice,

"There is a harlot in the house!" and he would not be silent although Wang Lung, fearing lest Lotus grow angry—for this small creature could shriek and scream and beat her hands together if she were angered at all—went forward and led the old man away into the outer court and soothed him, saying,

"Now calm your heart, my father. It is not a harlot but a second woman in the house."

But the old man would not be silent and whether he heard what was said or not no one knew only he shouted over and over, "There is a harlot here!" And he said suddenly, seeing Wang Lung near him, "And I had one woman and my father had one woman and we farmed the land." And again he cried out after a time, "I say it is a harlot!"

And so the old man woke from his aged and fitful sleeping with a sort of cunning hatred against Lotus. He would go to the doorway of her court and shout suddenly into the air,

"Harlot!"

Or he would draw aside the curtain into her court and then spit furiously upon the tiles. And he would hunt small stones and throw them with his feeble arm into the little pool to scare the fish, and in the mean ways of a mischievous child he expressed his anger.

And this too made a disturbance in Wang Lung's house, for he was ashamed to rebuke his father, and yet he feared the anger of Lotus, since he had found she had a pretty petulant temper that she loosed easily. And this anxiety to keep his father from angering her was wearisome to him and it was another thing to make of his love a burden to him.

One day he heard a shriek from the inner courts and he ran in for he heard it was the voice of Lotus, and there he found that the two younger children, the boy and the girl born alike, had between them led into the inner court his elder daughter, his poor fool. Now the four other children were constantly curious about this lady who lived in the inner court, but the two elder boys were conscious and shy and knew well enough why she was there and what their father had to do with her, although they never spoke of her unless to each other secretly. But the two younger ones could never be satisfied with their peepings and their exclamations, and sniffing of the perfume she wore and dipping their fingers in the bowls of food that Cuckoo carried away from her rooms after she had eaten.

Lotus complained many times to Wang Lung that his children were a plague to her and she wished there were a way to lock them out so that she need not be plagued with them. But this he was not willing to do, and he answered her in jest,

"Well, and they like to look at a lovely face as much as their father does."

And he did nothing except to forbid them to enter her courts and when he saw them they did not, but when he did not see them they ran in and out secretly. But the elder daughter knew nothing of anything, but only sat in the sun against the wall of the outer court, smiling and playing with her bit of twisted cloth.

On this day, however, the two elder sons being away at school, the two younger children had conceived the notion that the fool must also see the lady in the inner courts, and they had taken her hands and dragged her into the court and she stood before Lotus, who had never seen her and sat and stared at her. Now when the fool saw the bright silk of the coat Lotus wore and the shining jade in her ears, she was moved by some strange joy at the sight and she put out her hands to grasp the bright colors and she laughed aloud, a laugh that was only sound and meaningless. And Lotus was frightened and screamed out, so that Wang Lung came running in, and Lotus shook with her anger and leaped up and down on her little feet and shook her finger at the poor laughing girl and cried out,

"I will not stay in this house if that one comes near me, and I was not told that I should have accursed idiots to endure and if I had known it I would not have come—filthy children of yours!" and she pushed the little gaping boy who stood nearest her, clasping his twin sister's hand.

Then the good anger awoke in Wang Lung, for he loved his children, and he said roughly,

"Now I will not hear my children cursed, no and not by any one and not even my poor fool, and not by you who have no son in your womb for any man." And he gathered the children together and said to them, "Now go out, my son and my daughter, and come no more to this woman's court, for she does not love you and if she does not love you she does not love your father, either." And to the elder girl he said with great gentleness, "And you, my poor fool, come back to your place in

151

the sun." And she smiled and he took her by the hand and led her away.

For he was most angry of all that Lotus dared to curse this child of his and call her idiot, and a load of fresh pain for the girl fell upon his heart, so that for a day and two days he would not go near Lotus, but he played with the children and he went into the town and he bought a circle of barley candy for his poor fool and he comforted himself with her baby pleasure in the sweet sticky stuff.

And when he went in to Lotus again neither of them said anything that he had not come for two days, but she took special trouble to please him, for when he came his uncle's wife was there drinking tea, and Lotus excused herself and said,

"Now here is my lord come for me and I must be obedient to him for this is my pleasure," and she stood until the woman went away.

Then she went up to Wang Lung and took his hand and drew it to her face and she wooed him. But he, although he loved her again, loved her not so wholly as before, and never again so wholly as he had loved her.

There came a day when summer was ended and the sky in the early morning was clear and cold and blue as sea water and a clean autumn wind blew hard over the land, and Wang Lung woke as from a sleep. He went to the door of his house and he looked over his fields. And he saw that the waters had receded and the land lay shining under the dry cold wind and under the ardent sun.

Then a voice cried out in him, a voice deeper than love cried out in him for his land. And he heard it above every other voice in his life and he tore off the long robe he wore and he stripped off his velvet shoes and his white stockings and he rolled his trousers to his knees and he stood forth robust and eager and he shouted,

"Where is the hoe and where the plow? And where is the seed for the wheat planting? Come, Ching, my friend—come—call the men—I go out to the land!"

22

As HE had been healed of his sickness of heart when he came from the southern city and comforted by the bitterness he had endured there, so now again Wang Lung was healed of his sickness of love by the good dark earth of his fields and he felt the moist soil on his feet and he smelled the earthy fragrance rising up out of the furrows he turned for the wheat. He ordered his laborers hither and thither and they did a mighty day of labor, plowing here and plowing there, and Wang Lung stood first behind the oxen and cracked the whip over their backs and saw the deep curl of earth turning as the plow went into the soil, and then he called to Ching and gave him the ropes, and he himself took a hoe and broke up the soil into fine loamy stuff, soft as black sugar, and still dark with the wetness of the land upon it. This he did for the sheer joy he had in it and not for any necessity, and when he was weary he lay down upon his land and he slept and the health of the earth spread into his flesh and he was healed of his sickness.

When night came and the sun had gone blazing down without a cloud to dim it, he strode into his house, his body aching and weary and triumphant, and he tore aside the curtain that went into the inner court and there Lotus walked in her silken robes. When she saw him she cried out at the earth upon his clothes and shuddered when he came near her.

But he laughed and he seized her small, curling hands in his soiled ones and he laughed again and said,

"Now you see that your lord is but a farmer and you a farmer's wife!"

Then she cried out with spirit,

"A farmer's wife am I not, be you what you like!"

And he laughed again and went out from her easily.

He ate his evening rice all stained as he was with the earth and unwillingly he washed himself even before he slept. And washing his body he laughed again, for he washed it now for no woman, and he laughed because he was free.

Then it seemed to Wang Lung as though he had been for a long time away and there were suddenly a multitude of things he had to do. The land clamored for ploughing and planting and day after day he labored at it, and the paleness which the summer of his love had set on his flesh darkened to a deep brown under the sun and his hands, which had peeled off their calloused parts under the idleness of love, hardened again where the hoe pressed and where the plow handles set their mark.

When he came in at noon and at night he ate well of the food which O-lan prepared for him, good rice and cabbage and beancurd, and good garlic rolled into wheat bread. When Lotus held her small nose under her hand at his coming and cried out at his reek, he laughed and cared nothing and he breathed out his stout breath at her and she must bear it as she could for he would eat of what he liked. And now that he was full of health again and free of the sickness of his love he could go to her and be finished with her and turn himself to other things.

So these two women took their place in his house: Lotus for his toy and his pleasure and to satisfy his delight in beauty and in smallness and in the joy of her pure sex, and O-lan for his woman of work and the mother who had borne his sons and who kept his house and fed him and his father and his children. And it was a pride to Wang Lung in the village that men mentioned with envy the woman in his inner court; it was as though men spoke of a rare jewel or an expensive toy that was useless except that it was sign and symbol of a man who had passed beyond the necessity of caring only to be fed and clothed and could spend his money on joy if he wished.

And foremost among the men in the village who exclaimed over his prosperity was his uncle, for his uncle in these days was like a dog who fawns and desires to win favor. He said,

"There is my nephew, who keeps such an one for his pleasure as none of we common men have even seen." And again he said, "And he goes in to his woman, who wears robes of silk and satin like a lady in a great house. I have not seen it, but my woman tells me." And again he said, "My nephew, the son of my brother, is founding a great house and his sons will be the sons of a rich man and they need not work all their lives long."

Then men of the village, therefore, looked upon Wang Lung with increasing respect and they talked to him no more as to one of themselves but as to one who lived in a great house, and they came to borrow money of him at interest and to ask his advice concerning the marriage of their sons and daughters, and if any two had a dispute over the boundary of a field, Wang Lung was asked to settle the dispute and his decison was accepted, whatever it was.

Where Wang Lung had been busy with his love, then, he was now satisfied of it and was busied with many things. The rains came in season and the wheat sprouted and grew and the year turned to winter and Wang Lung took his harvests to the markets, for he saved his grain until prices were high, and this time he took with him his eldest son.

Now there is a pride a man has when he sees his eldest son reading aloud the letters upon a paper and putting the brush and ink to paper and writing that which may be read by others, and this pride Wang Lung now had. He stood proudly and saw this happen and he would not laugh when the clerks, who had scorned him before, now cried out,

"Pretty characters the lad makes and he is a clever one!"

No, Wang Lung would not pretend it was anything out of the common that he had a son like this, although when the lad said sharply as he read, "Here is a letter that has the wood radical when it should have the water radical," Wang Lung's heart was fit to burst with pride, so that he was compelled to turn aside and cough and spit upon the floor to save himself. And when a murmur of surprise ran among the clerks at his son's wisdom he called out merely,

"Change it, then! We will not put our name to anything wrongly written."

And he stood proudly and watched while his son took up the brush and changed the mistaken sign.

When it was finished and his son had written his father's name on the deed of sale of the grain and upon the receipt of the moneys, the two walked home together, father and son, and the father said within his heart that now his son was a man and his eldest son, and he must do what was right for his son, and he must see to it that there was a wife chosen and betrothed for his son so that the lad need not go begging into a great house as he had and pick up what was left there and what no one wanted, for his son was the son of a man who was rich and who owned land in his right.

Wang Lung set himself, therefore, to the seeking of a maid who might be his son's wife, and it was no slight task, for he would have no one who was a common and ordinary female. He talked of it one night to Ching, after the two of them had been alone in the middle room, taking account of what must be bought for spring planting and of what they had of their own seed. He talked not as one who expects great help, for he knew Ching was too simple, but still he knew the man was faithful as a good dog is faithful to its master, and it was relief to speak what he thought to such an one.

Ching stood humbly as Wang Lung sat at the table and spoke, for in spite of Wang Lung's urging, he would not, now that Wang Lung had become rich, sit in his presence as though they were equal, and he listened with fixed attention as Wang Lung spoke of his son and of the one he sought, and when Wang Lung was finished, Ching sighed and he said in his hesitant voice that was scarcely more than a whisper,

"And if my poor girl were here and sound you might have her for nothing at all and my gratitude, too, but where she is I do not know, and it may be she is dead and I do not know."

Then Wang Lung thanked him, but he forebore to say what was in his heart, that for his son there must be one far higher than the daughter of such an one as Ching, who although a good man was, besides that, only a common farmer on another's land.

Wang Lung kept his own counsel, therefore, only listening here and there in the tea shop when maids were spoken of, or men prosperous in the town who had daughters for marriage. But to his uncle's wife he said nothing, guarding his purpose from her. For she was well enough when he had need of a woman from a tea house for himself. She was such an one to arrange a matter like that. But for his son he would have no one like his uncle's wife, who could not know anyone he considered fit for his eldest son.

The year deepened into snow and the bitterness of winter and the New Year's festival came and they ate and drank, and men came to see Wang Lung, not only from the countryside but now from the town also, to wish him fortune, and they said,

"Well, and there is no fortune we can wish you greater than you have, sons in your house and women and money and land."

And Wang Lung, dressed in his silken robe with his sons in

156

good robes beside him on either hand, and sweet cakes and watermelon seeds and nuts upon the table, and red paper signs pasted upon his doors everywhere for the New Year and coming prosperity, knew that his fortune was good.

But the year turned to spring and the willows grew faintly green and the peach trees budded pink, and Wang Lung had not yet found the one he sought for his son.

Spring came in long, warm days scented with blossoming plum and cherry, and the willow trees sprouted their leaves fully and unfolded them, and the trees were green and the earth was moist and steaming and pregnant with harvest, and the eldest son of Wang Lung changed suddenly and ceased to be a child. He grew moody and petulant and would not eat this and that and he wearied of his books, and Wang Lung was frightened and did not know what to make of it and talked of a doctor.

There was no correction that could be made of the lad at all, for if his father said to him with anything beyond coaxing, "Now eat of the good meat and rice," the lad turned stubborn and melancholy, and if Wang Lung was angry at all, he burst into tears and fled from the room.

Wang Lung was overcome with surprise and he could make nothing of it, so that he went after the lad and he said gently as he was able,

"I am your father and now tell me what is in your heart." But the lad did nothing except sob and shake his head violently.

Moreover, he took a dislike to his old teacher and would not in the mornings rise out of his bed to go to school unless Wang Lung bawled at him or even beat him, and then he went sullenly and sometimes he spent whole days idling about the streets of the town, and Wang Lung only knew it at night, when the younger boy said spitefully,

"Elder Brother was not in school today."

Wang Lung was angry at his eldest son then and he shouted at him,

"And am I to spend good silver for nothing?"

And in his anger he fell upon the boy with a bamboo and beat him until O-lan, the boy's mother, heard it and rushed in from the kitchen and stood between her son and his father so that the blows rained upon her in spite of Wang Lung's turning this way and that to get at the boy. Now the strange thing was that whereas the boy might burst into weeping at a chance rebuke, he stood these beatings under the bamboo

157

without a sound, his face carven and pale as an image. And Wang Lung could make nothing of it, although he thought of it night and day.

He thought of it one evening thus after he had eaten his night's food, because on that day he had beaten his eldest son for not going to the school, and while he thought, O-lan came into the room. She came in silently and she stood before Wang Lung and he saw she had that which she wished to say. So he said,

"Say on. What is it, mother of my son?"

And she said, "It is useless for you to beat the lad as you do. I have seen this thing come upon the young lords in the courts of the great house, and it came on them melancholy, and when it came the Old Lord found slaves for them if they had not found any for themselves and the thing passed easily."

"Now and it need not be so," answered Wang Lung in argument. "When I was a lad I had no such melancholy and no such weepings and tempers, and no slaves, either."

O-lan waited and then she answered slowly, "I have not indeed seen it thus except with young lords. You worked on the land. But he is like a young lord and he is idle in the house."

Wang Lung was surprised, after he had pondered a while, for he saw truth in what she said. It was true that when he himself was a lad there was no time for melancholy, for he had to be up at dawn for the ox and out with the plow and the hoe and at harvest he must needs work until his back broke, and if he wept he could weep for no one heard him, and he could not run away as his son ran away from school, for if he did there was nothing for him to eat on return, and so he was compelled to labor. He remembered all this and he said to himself,

"But my son is not thus. He is more delicate than I was, and his father is rich and mine was poor, and there is no need for his labor, for I have labor in my fields, and besides, one cannot take a scholar such as my son is and set him to the plow."

And he was secretly proud that he had a son like this and so he said to O-lan,

"Well, and if he is like a young lord it is another matter. But I cannot buy a slave for him. I will betroth him and we will marry him early, and there is that to be done."

Then he rose and went in to the inner court.

23

Now Lotus, seeing Wang Lung distraught in her presence, and thinking of things other than her beauty, pouted and said,

"If I had known that in a short year you could look at me and not see me, I would have stayed in the tea house." And she turned her head away as she spoke and looked at him out of the corner of her eyes so that he laughed and seized her hand and he put it against his face and smelled of its fragrance and he answered,

"Well, and a man cannot always think of the jewel he has sewn on his coat, but if it were lost he could not bear it. These days I think of my eldest son and of how his blood is restless with desire and he must be wed and I do not know how to find the one he should wed. I am not willing that he marry any of the daughters of the village farmers, nor is it meet, seeing that we bear the common name of Wang. Yet I do not know one in the town well enough to say to him, 'Here is my son and there is your daughter,' and I am loath to go to a professional matchmaker, lest there be some bargain she has made with a man who has a daughter deformed or idiot."

Now Lotus, since the eldest son had grown tall and graceful with young manhood, looked on the lad with favor and she was diverted with what Wang Lung said to her and she replied, musing,

"There was a man who used to come in to me at the great tea house, and he often spoke of his daughter, because he said she was such an one as I, small and fine, but still only a child, and he said, 'And I love you with a strange unease as though you were my daughter; you are too like her, and it troubles me for it is not lawful,' and for this reason, although he loved me best, he went to a great red girl called Pomegranate Flower."

"What sort of man was this?" asked Wang Lung.

"He was a good man and his silver was ready and he did not promise without paying. We all wished him well, for he was not begrudging, and if a girl was weary sometimes he did not bawl out as some did that he had been cheated, but he always said courteously as a prince might, or some might from a learned and noble house, 'Well, and here is the silver, and rest, my child, until love blooms again.' He spoke very prettily to us." And Lotus mused until Wang Lung said hastily to waken her, for he did not like her to think on her old life,

"What was his business, then, with all this silver?"

And she answered,

"Now and I do not know but I think he was master of a grain market, but I will ask Cuckoo who knows everything about men and their money."

Then she clapped her hands and Cuckoo ran in from the kitchen, her high cheeks and nose flushed with the fire, and Lotus asked her,

"Who was that great, large, goodly man who came to me and then to Pomegranate Flower, because I was like his little daughter, so that it troubled him, although he ever loved me best?"

And Cuckoo answered at once, "Ah, and that was Liu, the grain dealer. Ah, he was a good man! He left silver in my palm whenever he saw me."

"Where is his market?" asked Wang Lung, although idly, because it was woman's talk and likely to come to nothing.

"In the street of the Stone Bridge," said Cuckoo.

Then before she finished the words Wang Lung struck his hands together in delight and he said,

"Now then, that is where I sell my grain, and it is a propitious thing and surely it can be done," and for the first time his interest was awake, because it seemed to him a lucky thing to wed his son to the daughter of the man who bought his grain.

When there was a thing to be done, Cuckoo smelled the money in it as a rat smells tallow, and she wiped her hands upon her apron and she said quickly,

"I am ready to serve the master."

Wang Lung was doubtful, and doubting, he looked at her crafty face, but Lotus said gaily,

"And that is true, and Cuckoo shall go and ask the man Liu, and he knows her well and the thing can be done, for Cuckoo is

160

clever enough, and she shall have the match-maker's fee, if it is well done."

"That will I do!" said Cuckoo heartily and she laughed as she thought of the fee of good silver on her palm, and she untied her apron from her waist and she said busily, "Now and at once will I go, for the meat is ready except for the moment of cooking and the vegetables are washed."

But Wang Lung had not pondered the matter sufficiently and it was not to be decided so quickly as this and he called out,

"No, and I have decided nothing. I must think of the matter for some days and I will tell you what I think."

The women were impatient, Cuckoo for the silver and Lotus because it was a new thing and she would hear something new to amuse her, but Wang Lung went out, saying,

"No, it is my son and I will wait."

And so he might have waited for many days, thinking of this and that, had not one early morning, the lad, his eldest son, come home in the dawn with his face hot and red with wine drinking, and his breath was fetid and his feet unsteady. Wang Lung heard him stumbling in the court and he ran out to see who it was, and the lad was sick and vomited before him, for he was unaccustomed to more than the pale mild wine they made from their own rice fermented, and he fell and lay on the ground in his vomit like a dog.

Wang Lung was frightened and he called for O-lan, and together they lifted the lad up and O-lan washed him and laid him upon the bed in her own room, and before she was finished with him the lad was asleep and heavy as one dead and could answer nothing to what his father asked.

Then Wang Lung went into the room where the two boys slept together, and the younger was yawning and stretching and tying his books into a square cloth to carry to school, and Wang Lung said to him,

"Was your elder brother not in the bed with you last night?"

And the boy answered unwillingly,

"No."

There was some fear in his look and Wang Lung, seeing it, cried out at him roughly,

"Where was he gone?" and when the boy would not answer, he took him by the neck and shook him and cried, "Now tell me all, you small dog!"

The boy was frightened at this, and he broke out sobbing and crying and said between his sobs,

"And Elder Brother said I was not to tell you and he said he would pinch me and burn me with a hot needle if I told and if I do not tell he gives me pence."

And Wang Lung, beside himself at this, shouted out,

"Tell what, you who ought to die?"

And the boy looked about him and said desperately, seeing that his father would choke him if he did not answer,

"He has been away three nights altogether, but what he does I do not know, except that he goes with the son of your uncle, our cousin."

Wang Lung loosed his hand then from the boy's neck and he flung him aside and he strode forth into his uncle's rooms, and there he found his uncle's son, hot and red of face with wine, even as his own son, but steadier of foot, for the young man was older and accustomed to the ways of men. Wang Lung shouted at him,

"Where have you led my son?"

And the young man sneered at Wang Lung and he said,

"Ah, that son of my cousin's needs no leading. He can go alone."

But Wang Lung repeated it and this time he thought to himself that he would kill this son of his uncle's now, this impudent scampish face, and he cried in a terrible voice,

"Where has my son been this night?"

Then the young man was frightened at the sound of his voice and he answered sullenly and unwillingly, dropping his impudent eyes,

"He was at the house of the whore who lives in the court that once belonged to the great house."

When Wang Lung heard this he gave a great groan, for the whore was one well known of many men and none went to her except poor and common men, for she was no longer young and she was willing to give much for little. Without stopping for food he went out of his gate and across his fields, and for once he saw nothing of what grew on his land, and noted nothing of how the crop promised, because of the trouble his son had brought to him. He went with his eyes fixed inward, and he went through the gate of the wall about the town, and he went to the house that had been great.

The heavy gates were swung back widely now, and none ever closed them upon their thick iron hinges, for any who would might come and go in these days, and he went in, and the courts and the rooms were filled with common people, who rented the rooms, a family of common people to a room. The place was filthy and the old pines hewed down and those left standing were dying, and the pools in the courts were choked with refuse.

But he saw none of this. He stood in the court of the first house and he called out,

"Where is the woman called Yang, who is a whore?"

There was a woman there who sat on a three-legged stool, sewing at a shoe sole, and she lifted her head and nodded toward a side door opening on the court and she took up her sewing again, as though many times she had been asked this question by men.

Wang Lung went to the door and he beat on it, and a fretful voice answered,

"Now go away, for I am done my business for this night and must sleep, since I work all night."

But he beat again, and the voice cried out, "Who is it?"

He would not answer, but he beat yet again, for he would go in whether or not, and at last he heard a shuffling and a woman opened the foor, a woman none too young and with a weary face and hanging, thick lips, and coarse white paint on her forehead and red paint she had not washed from her mouth and cheeks, and she looked at him and said sharply,

"Now I cannot before tonight and if you like you may come as early as you will then in the night, but now I must sleep."

But Wang Lung broke roughly into her talking, for the sight of her sickened him and the thought of his son here he could not bear, and he said,

"It is not for myself—I do not need such as you. It is for my son."

And he felt suddenly in his throat a thickening of weeping for his son. Then the woman asked,

"Well, and what of your son?"

And Wang Lung answered and his voice trembled,

"He was here last night."

"There were many sons of men here last night," replied the woman, "and I do not know which was yours."

Then Wang Lung said, beseeching her,

"Think and remember a little slight young lad, tall for his years, but not yet a man, and I did not dream he dared to try a woman."

163

And she, remembering, answered,

"Were there two, and was one a young fellow with his nose turned to the sky at the end and a look in his eye of knowing everything, and his hat over one ear? And the other, as you say, a tall big lad, but eager to be a man!"

And Wang Lung said, "Yes—yes—that is he—that is my son!"

"And what of your son?" said the woman.

Then Wang Lung said earnestly,

"This: if he ever comes again, put him off—say you desire men only—say what you will—but every time you put him off I will give you twice the fee of silver on your palm!"

The woman laughed then and carelessly and she said in sudden good humor,

"And who would not say aye to this, to be paid for not working? And so I say aye also. It is true enough that I desire men and little boys are small pleasure." And she nodded at Wang Lung as she spoke and leered at him and he was sickened at her coarse face and he said hastily,

"So be it, then."

He turned quickly and he walked home, and as he walked he spat and spat again to rid him of his sickness at the memory of the woman.

On this day, therefore, he said to Cuckoo,

"Let it be as you said. Go to the grain merchant and arrange the matter. Let the dowry be good but not too great if the girl is suitable and if it can be arranged."

When he had said this to Cuckoo he went back to the room and he sat beside his sleeping son and he brooded, for he saw how fair and young the boy lay there, and he saw the quiet face, asleep and smooth with its youth. Then when he thought of the weary painted woman and her thick lips, his heart swelled with sickness and anger and he sat there muttering to himself.

And as he sat O-lan came in and stood looking at the boy, and she saw the clear sweat standing on his skin and she brought vinegar in warm water and washed the sweat away gently, as they used to wash the young lords in the great house when they drank too heavily. Then seeing the delicate childish face and the drunken sleep that even the washing would not awaken, Wang Lung rose and went in his anger to his uncle's room, and he forgot the brother of his father and he remembered only that this man was father to the idle, impudent young man who had spoiled his own fair son, and he went in and he shouted,

"Now I have harbored an ungrateful nest of snakes and they have bitten me!"

His uncle was sitting leaning over a table eating his breakfast, for he never rose until midday, seeing there was no work he had to do, and he looked up at these words and he said lazily,

"How now?"

Then Wang Lung told him, half-choking, what had happened, but his uncle only laughed and he said,

"Well, and can you keep a boy from becoming a man? And can you keep a young dog from a stray bitch?"

When Wang Lung heard this laughter he remembered in one crowded space of time all that he had endured because of his uncle; how of old his uncle had tried to force him to the selling of his land, and how they lived here, these three, eating and drinking and idle, and how his uncle's wife ate of the expensive foods Cuckoo bought for Lotus, and now how his uncle's son had spoiled his own fair lad, and he bit his tongue between his teeth and he said,

"Now out of my house, you and yours, and no more rice will there be for any of you from this hour, and I will burn the house down rather than have it shelter you, who have no gratitude even in your idleness!"

But his uncle sat where he was and ate on, now from this bowl and now from that, and Wang Lung stood there bursting with his blood, and when he saw his uncle paid no heed to him, he stepped forward with his arm upraised. Then the uncle turned and said,

"Drive me out if you dare."

And when Wang Lung stammered and blustered, not understanding, "Well—and what —well and what—" his uncle opened his coat and showed him what was against its lining.

Then Wang Lung stood still and rigid, for he saw there a false beard of red hair and a length of red cloth, and Wang Lung stared at these things, and the anger went out of him like water and he shook because there was no strength left in him.

Now these things, the red beard and the red length of cloth were sign and symbol of a band of robbers who lived and marauded toward the northwest, and many houses had they burned and women they had carried away, and good farmers they had bound with ropes to the threshold of their own houses and men found them there next day, raving mad if they lived and burnt and crisp as roasted meat if they were dead. And Wang Lung stared and his eyes hung out of his head, and he turned and went away without a word. And as he went he heard his uncle's whispered laughter as he stooped again over his rice bowl.

Now Wang Lung found himself in such a coil as he had never dreamed of. His uncle came and went as before, grinning a little under the sparse and scattered hairs of his grey beard, his robes wrapped and girdled about his body as carelessly as ever, and Wang Lung sweated chilly when he saw him but he dared not speak anything except courteous words for fear of what his uncle might do to him. It was true that during all these years of his prosperity and especially during the years when there were no harvests or only very little and other men had starved with their children, never had bandits come to his house and his lands, although he had many times been afraid and had barred the doors stoutly at night. Until the summer of his love he had dressed himself coarsely and had avoided the appearance of wealth, and when among the villagers he heard stories of marauding he came home and slept fitfully and listened for sounds out of the night.

But the robbers never came to his house and he grew careless and bold and he believed he was protected by heaven and that he was a man of good fortune by destiny, and he grew heedless of everything, even of incense of the gods, since they were good enough to him without, and he thought of nothing except of his own affairs and of his land. And now suddenly he saw why he had been safe and why he would be safe so long as he fed the three of his uncle's house. When he thought of this he sweated heavy cold sweat, and he dared to tell no one what his uncle hid in his bosom.

But to his uncle he said no more of leaving the house, and to his uncle's wife he said with what urging he could muster,

"Eat what you like in the inner courts and here is a bit of silver to spend."

And to his uncle's son he said, although the gorge rose in his throat, yet he said,

"Here is a bit of silver, for young men will play."

But his own son Wang Lung watched and he would not allow him to leave the courts after sundown, although the lad grew angry and flung himself about and slapped the younger

166

children for nothing except his own ill-humor. So was Wang Lung encompassed about with his troubles.

At first Wang Lung could not work for thinking of all the trouble that had befallen him, and he thought of this trouble and that, and he thought, "I could turn my uncle out and I could move inside the city wall where they lock the great gates every night against robbers," but then he remembered that every day he must come to work on his fields, and who could tell what might happen to him as he worked defenseless, even on his own land? Moreover, how could a man live locked in a town and in a house in the town, and he would die if he were cut off from his land. There would surely come a bad year, moreover, and even the town could not withstand robbers, as it had not in the past when the great house fell.

And he could go into the town and go to the court where the magistrate lived and say to him,

"My uncle is one of the Redbeards."

But if he did this, who would believe him, who would believe a man when he told such a thing of his own father's brother? It was more likely that he would be beaten for his unfilial conduct rather than his uncle suffer, and in the end he would go in fear of his life, for if the robbers heard of it, they would kill him for revenge.

Then as if this were not enough Cuckoo came back from the grain merchant and although the affair of the betrothal had gone well, the merchant Liu was not willing that anything should take place now except the exchange of the betrothal papers, for the maid was too young for marriage, being but fourteen years old, and it must wait for another three years. Wang Lung was dismayed at three more years of this lad's anger and idleness and mooning eyes, for he would not go to school now two days out of ten, and Wang Lung shouted at O-lan that night when he ate,

"Well, and let us betroth these other children as soon as we are able, and the sooner the better, and let us marry them as soon as they begin to yearn, for I cannot have this over again three more times!"

And the next morning he had not slept but a little through the night, and he tore off his long robes and kicked off his shoes, and as was his wont when the affairs of his house became too deep for him, he took a hoe and he went to his fields, and he went through the outer court where the eldest girl sat smiling

167

and twisting her bit of cloth through her fingers and smoothing it, and he muttered,

"Well, and that poor fool of mine brings me more comfort than all the others put together."

And he went out to his land day after day for many days.

Then the good land did again its healing work and the sun shone on him and healed him and the warm winds of summer wrapped him about with peace. And as if to cure him of the root of his ceaseless thought of his own troubles, there came out of the south one day a small slight cloud. At first it hung on the horizon small and smooth as a mist, except it did not come hither and thither as clouds blown by the wind do, but it stood steady until it spread fanwise up into the air.

The men of the village watched it and talked of it and fear hung over them, for what they feared was this, that locusts had come out of the south to devour what was planted in the fields. Wang Lung stood there also, and he watched, and they gazed and at last a wind blew something to their feet, and one stooped hastily and picked it up and it was a dead locust, dead and lighter than the living hosts behind.

Then Wang Lung forgot everything that troubled him. Women and sons and uncle, he forgot them all, and he rushed among the frightened villagers, and he shouted at them,

"Now for our good land we will fight these enemies from the skies!"

But there were some who shook their heads, hopeless from the start, and these said,

"No, and there is no use in anything. Heaven has ordained that this year we shall starve, and why should we waste ourselves in struggle against it, seeing that in the end we must starve?"

And women went weeping to the town to buy incense to thrust before the earth gods in the little temple, and some went to the big temple in the town, where the gods of heaven were, and thus earth and heaven were worshipped.

But still the locusts spread up into the air and on over the land.

Then Wang Lung called his own laborers and Ching stood silent and ready beside him and there were others of the younger farmers, and with their own hands these set fire to certain fields and they burned the good wheat that stood almost ripe for cutting and they dug wide moats and ran water into them from the wells, and they worked without sleeping. O-lan

168

brought them food and the women brought their men food, and the men ate standing in the field, gulping it down as beasts do, as they worked night and day.

Then the sky grew black and the air was filled with the deep still roar of many wings beating against each other, and upon the land the locusts fell, flying over this field and leaving it whole, and falling upon that field, and eating it as bare as winter. And men sighed and said "So Heaven wills," but Wang Lung was furious and he beat the locusts and trampled on them and his men flailed them with flails and the locusts fell into the fires that were kindled and they floated dead upon the waters of the moats that were dug. And many millions of them died, but to those that were left it was nothing.

Nevertheless, for all his fighting Wang Lung had this as his reward: the best of his fields were spared and when the cloud moved on and they could rest themselves, there was still wheat that he could reap and his young rice beds were spared and he was content. Then many of the people ate the roasted bodies of the locusts, but Wang Lung himself would not eat them, for to him they were a filthy thing because of what they had done to his land. But he said nothing when O-lan fried them in oil and when the laborers crunched them between their teeth and the children pulled them apart delicately and tasted them, afraid of their great eyes. But as for himself he would not eat.

Nevertheless, the locusts did this for him. For seven days he thought of nothing but his land, and he was healed of his troubles and his fears, and he said to himself calmly,

"Well, and every man has his troubles and I must make shift to live with mine as I can, and my uncle is older than I and he will die, and three years must pass as they can with my son and I shall not kill myself."

And he reaped his wheat and the rains came and the young green rice was set into the flooded fields and again it was summer.

24

ONE DAY after Wang Lung had said to himself that peace was in his house, his eldest son came to him as he returned at noon from the land, and the lad said,

"Father, if I am to be a scholar, there is no more that this old head in the town can teach me."

Wang Lung had dipped from the cauldron in the kitchen a basin of boiling water and into this he dipped a towel and wrung it and holding it steaming against his face he said,

"Well, and how now?"

The lad hesitated and then he went on,

"Well, and if I am to be a scholar, I would like to go to the south to the city and enter a great school where I can learn what is to be learned."

Wang Lung rubbed the towel about his eyes and his ears and with his face all steaming he answered his son sharply, for his body ached with his labor in the fields,

"Well, and what nonsense is this? I say you cannot go and I will not be teased about it, for I say you cannot go. You have learning enough for these parts."

And he dipped the cloth in again and wrung it.

But the young man stood there and stared at his father with hatred and he muttered something and Wang Lung was angry for he could not hear what it was, and he bawled at his son,

"Speak out what you have to say!"

Then the young man flared at the noise of his father's voice and he said,

"Well, and I will, then, for go south I will, and I will not stay in this stupid house and be watched like a child, and in this little

170

town which is no better than a village! I will go out and learn something and see other parts."

Wang Lung looked at his son and he looked at himself, and his son stood there in a pale long robe of silver grey linen, thin and cool for the summer's heat, and on his lip were the first black hairs of his manhood, and his skin was smooth and golden and his hands under his long sleeves were soft and fine as a woman's. Then Wang Lung looked at himself and he was thick and stained with earth and he wore only trousers of blue cotton cloth girt about his knees and his waist and his upper body was naked, and one would have said he was his son's servant rather than his father. And this thought made him scornful of the young man's tall fine looks, and he was brutal and angry and he shouted out,

"Now then, get into the fields and rub a little good earth on yourself lest men take you for a woman, and work a little for the rice you eat!"

And Wang Lung forgot that he had ever had pride in his son's writing and in his cleverness at books, and he flung himself out, stamping his bare feet as he walked and spitting upon the floor coarsely, because the fineness of his son angered him for the moment. And the lad stood and looked at him with hatred, but Wang Lung would not turn back to see what the lad did.

Nevertheless, that night when Wang Lung went into the inner courts and sat beside Lotus as she lay upon the mat on her bed where Cuckoo fanned her as she lay, Lotus said to him idly as of a thing of no account, but only something to say,

"That big lad of yours is pining and desires to go away."

Then Wang Lung, remembering his anger against his son, said sharply,

"Well, and what is it to you? I will not have him in these rooms at his age."

But Lotus made haste to reply, "No—no—it is Cuckoo who says it." And Cuckoo made haste to say, "Anyone can see the thing and a lovely lad he is and too big for idleness and longing."

Wang Lung was led aside by this and he thought only of his anger against his son and he said,

"No, and he shall not go. I will not spend my money foolishly." And he would not speak of it any more and Lotus saw he was peevish from some anger, and she sent Cuckoo away and suffered him there alone.

Then for many days there was nothing said and the lad seemed suddenly content again, but he would not go to school any more and this Wang Lung allowed him, for the boy was nearly eighteen and large like his mother in frame of bones, and he read in his own room when his father came into the house and Wang Lung was content and he thought to himself,

"It was a whim of his youth and he does not know what he wants and there are only three years—it may be a little extra silver will make it two, or even one, if the silver is enough. One of these days when the harvests are well over and the winter wheat planted and beans hoed, I will see to it."

Then Wang Lung forgot his son, for the harvests, except what the locusts had consumed, were fair enough and by now he had gained once more what he had spent on the woman Lotus. His gold and his silver were precious to him once more, and at times he marvelled secretly at himself that he had ever spent so freely upon a woman.

Still, there were times when she stirred him sweetly, if not so strongly as at first, and he was proud to own her, although he saw well enough that what his uncle's wife had said was true, that she was none too young for all her smallness of stature, and she never conceived to bear a child for him. But for this he cared nothing, since he had sons and daughters, and he was willing enough to keep her for the pleasure she gave him.

As for Lotus, she grew lovelier as her fullness of years came on, for if before she had had a fault, it was her birdlike thinness that made too sharp the lines of her little pointed face and hollowed too much her temples. But now under the food which Cuckoo cooked for her, and under the idleness of her life with one man only, she became soft and rounded in body, and her face grew full and smooth at the temples, and with her wide eyes and small mouth she looked more than ever like a plump little cat. And she slept and ate and took on her body this soft smooth flesh. If she was no longer the lotus bud, neither was she more than the full-blown flower, and if she was not young, neither did she look old, and youth and age were equally far fom her.

With his life placid again and the lad content, Wang Lung might have been satisfied except that one night when he sat late and alone, reckoning on his fingers what he could sell of his corn and what he could sell of his rice, O-lan came softly into the room. This one, with the passing of the years had grown lean and gaunt and the rock-like bones of her face stood forth and her eyes were sunken. If one asked her how she did she said no more than this,

"There is a fire in my vitals."

Her belly was as great as though with child these three years, only there was no birth. But she rose at dawn and she did her work and Wang Lung saw her only as he saw the table or his chair or a tree in the court, never even so keenly as he might see one of the oxen drooping its head or a pig that would not eat. And she did her work alone and spoke no more than she could escape speaking with the wife of Wang Lung's uncle, and she never spoke at all to Cuckoo. Never once had O-lan gone into the inner courts, and rarely, if Lotus came out to walk a little in a place other than her own court, O-lan went into her room and sat until one said, "She is gone." And she said nothing but she worked at her cooking and at the washing at the pool even in the winter when the water was stiff with ice to be broken. But Wang Lung never thought to say,

"Well, and why do you not with the silver I have to spare, hire a servant or buy a slave?"

It did not occur to him that there was any need of this, although he hired laborers for his fields and to help with the oxen and asses and with the pigs he had, and in the summers when the river flooded, he hired men for the time to herd the ducks and geese he fed upon the waters.

On this evening, then, when he sat alone with only the red candles in the pewter stands alight, she stood before him and looked this way and that, and at last she said,

"I have something to say."

Then he stared at her in surprise and he answered,

"Well, and say on."

And he stared at her and at the shadowed hollows of her face and he thought again how there was no beauty in her and how for many years had he not desired her.

Then she said in a harsh whisper,

"The eldest son goes too often into the inner courts. When you are away he goes."

Now Wang Lung could not at first grasp what she said thus whispering and he leaned forward with his mouth agape and he said,

"What, woman?"

She pointed mutely to her son's room and pursed her thick dry lips at the door of the inner court. But Wang Lung stared at her, robust and unbelieving.

"You dream!" he said finally.

She shook her head at this, and, the difficult speech halting on her lips, she said further,

"Well, and my lord, come home unexpectedly." And again, after a silence, "It is better to send him away, even to the south." And then she went to the table and took his bowl of tea and felt of it and spilled the cool tea on the brick floor and filled the bowl again from the hot pot, and as she came she went, silent, and left him sitting there agape.

Well, and this woman, she was jealous he said to himself. Well, and he would not trouble about this, with his lad content and reading every day in his own room, and he rose and laughed and put it away from him, laughing at the small thoughts of women.

But when he went in that night to lie beside Lotus and when he turned upon the bed she complained and was petulant and she pushed him away saying,

"It is hot and you stink and I wish you would wash yourself before you come to lie beside me."

She sat up, then, and pushed her hair fretfully back from her face and she shrugged her shoulders when he would have drawn her to him, and she would not yield to his coaxing. Then he lay still and he remembered that she had yielded unwillingly these many nights, and he had thought it her whim and the heavy hot air of departing summer that depressed her, but now the words of O-lan stood out sharply and he rose up roughly and said,

"Well, and sleep alone then, and cut my throat if I care!"

He flung himself out of the room and strode into the middle room of his own house and he put two chairs together and stretched himself on them. But he could not sleep and he rose and went out of his gate and he walked among the bamboos beside the house wall, and there he felt the cool night wind upon his hot flesh, and there was the coolness of coming autumn in it.

Then he remembered this, that Lotus had known of his son's desire to go away, and how had she known? And he remembered that of late his son had said nothing of going away but had been content, and why was he content? And Wang Lung said to his heart, fiercely,

"I will see the thing for myself!"

And he watched the dawn come ruddy out of a mist over his land.

174

When the dawn was come and the sun showed a gold rim over the edge of the fields, he went in and he ate, and then he went out to oversee his men as his custom was in times of harvest and planting, and he went here and there over his land, and at last he shouted loudly, so that anyone in his house might hear,

"Now I am going to the piece by the moat of the town and I shall not be back early," and he set his face to the town.

But when he had gone half-way and reached as far as the small temple he sat down beside the road on a hillock of grass that was an old grave, now forgotten, and he plucked a grass and twisted it in his fingers and he meditated. Facing him were the small gods and on the surface of his mind he noted how they stared at him and how of old he had been afraid of them, but now he was careless, having become prosperous and in no need of gods, so that he scarcely saw them. Underneath he thought to himself, over and over,

"Shall I go back?"

Then suddenly he remembered the night before when Lotus had pushed him away, and he was angry because of all he had done for her and he said to himself,

"Well I know that she would not have lasted many years more at the tea house, and in my house she is fed and clothed richly."

And in the strength of his anger he rose and he strode back to his house by another way and he went secretly into his house and stood at the curtain that hung in the door to the inner court. And listening, he heard the murmuring of a man's voice, and it was the voice of his own son.

Now the anger that arose in Wang Lung's heart was an anger he had not known in all his life before, although as things had prospered with him and as men came to call him rich, he had lost his early timidity of a country fellow, and had grown full of small sudden angers, and he was proud even in the town. But this anger now was the anger of one man against another man who steals away the loved woman, and when Wang Lung remembered that the other man was his own son, he was filled with a vomiting sickness.

He set his teeth then, and he went out and chose a slim, supple bamboo from the grove and he stripped off the branches, except for a cluster of small branches at the top, thin and hard as cord, and he ripped off the leaves. Then he went in softly and suddenly he tore aside the curtain and there was his son, standing in the court, and looking down at Lotus, who sat on a small stool at the edge of the pool. And Lotus was dressed in her peach-colored silk coat, such as he had never seen her dressed in by the light of the morning.

These two talked together, and the woman laughed lightly and looked at the young man from the corner of her eyes, her head turned aside, and they did not hear Wang Lung. He stood and stared at them, his face whitening and his lips lifted back and snarling from his teeth, and his hands tightened about the bamboo. And still the two did not hear him and would not, except that the woman Cuckoo came out and saw him and shrieked and they saw.

Then Wang Lung leaped forward and he fell on his son, lashing him, and although the lad was taller than he, he was stronger from his labor in the fields and from the robustness of his mature body, and he beat the lad until the blood streamed down. When Lotus screamed and dragged at his arm he shook her off, and when she persisted, screaming, he beat her also and he beat her until she fled and he beat the young man until he stooped cowering to the ground, and covered his torn face in his hands.

Then Wang Lung paused and his breath whistled through his parted lips and the sweat poured down his body until he was drenched and he was weak as though with an illness. He threw down his bamboo and he whispered to the boy, panting,

"Now get you to your room and do not dare to come out of it until I am rid of you, lest I kill you!"

And the boy rose without a word and went out.

Wang Lung sat on the stool where Lotus had sat and he put his head in his hands and closed his eyes and his breath came and went in great gasps. No one drew near him and he sat thus alone until he was quieted and his anger gone.

Then he rose wearily and he went into the room and Lotus lay there on her bed, weeping aloud, and he went up to her and he turned her over, and she lay looking at him and weeping and there on her face lay the swollen purple mark of his whip.

And he said to her with great sadness,

"So must you ever be a whore and go a-whoring after my own sons!"

And she cried more loudly at this and protested,

"No, but I did not, and the lad was lonely and came in and you may ask Cuckoo if he ever came nearer to my bed than you saw him in the court!"

Then she looked at him frightened and piteous and she reached for his hand and drew it across the welt on her face and she whimpered.

"See what you have done to your Lotus—and there is no man in the world except you, and if it is your son, it is only your son, and what is he to me!"

She looked up at him, her pretty eyes swimming in her clear tears, and he groaned because this woman's beauty was more than he could wish and he loved her when he would not. And it seemed to him suddenly that he could not bear to know what had passed between these two and he wished never to know and it was better for him if he did not. So he groaned again and he went out. He passed his son's room and he called without entering.

"Well, and now put your things in the box and tomorrow go south to what you will and do not come home until I send for you."

Then he went on and there was O-lan sitting sewing on some garment of his, and when he passed she said nothing, and if she had heard the beating and the screaming, she made no sign of it. And he went on and out to his fields and into the high sun of noon, and he was spent as with the labor of a whole day.

25

WHEN THE eldest son was gone Wang Lung felt the house was purged of some surcharge of unrest and it was a relief to him. He said to himself that it was a good thing for the young man to be gone, and now he could look to his other children and see what they were, for what with his own troubles and the land which must be planted and harvested in season whatever might happen elsewhere, he hardly knew what he had for children after his eldest son. He decided, moreover, that he would early take the second lad out of school and he would apprentice him to a trade and not wait for the wildness of young manhood to catch him and make him a plague in the house as the older one had been.

Now the second son of Wang Lung was as unlike the elder as two sons in a house may be. Where the elder was tall and big-boned and ruddy faced as men of the north are and like his mother, this second one was short and slight and yellow-skinned, and there was that in him which reminded Wang Lung of his own father, a crafty, sharp, humorous eye, and a turn for malice if the moment came for it. And Wang Lung said,

"Well, and this boy will make a good merchant and I will take him out of school and see if he can be apprenticed in the grain market. It will be a convenient thing to have a son there where I sell my harvests and he can watch the scales and tip the weight a little in my favor."

Therefore he said to Cuckoo one day,

"Now go and tell the father of my eldest son's betrothed that I have something to say to him. And we should at any rate drink a cup of wine together, seeing that we are to be poured into one bowl, his blood and mine."

Cuckoo went, then, and came back saying,

"He will see you when you wish and if you can come to drink wine this noon it is well, and if you wish it he will come here instead."

But Wang Lung did not wish the town merchant to come to his house because he feared he would have to prepare this and that, and so he washed himself and put on his silk coat and he set out across the fields. He went first to the Street of Bridges, as Cuckoo had told him, and there before a gate which bore the name of Liu he stopped. Not that he knew the word himself, but he guessed the gate, two doors to the right of the bridge, and he asked one who passed and the letter was the letter of Liu. It was a respectable gate built plainly of wood, and Wang Lung struck it with the palm of his hand.

Immediately it opened and a woman servant stood there, wiping her wet hands on her apron as she spoke to ask who he was, and when he answered his name, she stared at him, and led him into the first court where the men lived and she took him into a room and bade him seat himself, and she stared at him again, knowing he was the father of the betrothed of the daughter of the house. Then she went out to call her master.

Wang Lung looked about him carefully, and he rose and felt of the stuffs of the curtains in the doorway, and examined the wood of the plain table, and he was pleased, for there was evidence of good living but not of extreme wealth. He did not want a rich daughter-in-law lest she be haughty and disobedient and cry for this and that of food and clothes and turn aside his son's heart from his parents. Then Wang sat down again and waited.

Suddenly there was a heavy step and a stout elderly man entered and Wang Lung rose and bowed and they both bowed, looking secretly at each other, and they liked each other, each respecting the other for what he was, a man of worth and prosperity. Then they seated themselves and they drank of the hot wine which the servant woman poured out for them, and they talked slowly of this and that, of crops and prices and what the price would be for rice this year if the harvest were good. And at last Wang Lung said,

"Well, and I have come for a thing and if it is not your wish, let us talk of other things. But if you have need for a servant in your great market, there is my second son, and a sharp one he is, but if you have no need of him, let us talk of other things."

Then the merchant said with great good humor,

"And so I have such need of a sharp young man, if he reads and writes."

And Wang Lung answered proudly,

"My sons are both good scholars and they can each tell when a letter is wrongly written, and whether the wood or the water radical is right."

"That is well," said Liu. "And let him come when he will and his wages at first are only his food until he learns the business, and then after a year if he do well, he may have a piece of silver at the end of every moon, and at the end of three years three pieces, and after that he is no longer apprentice, but he may rise as he is able in the business. And besides this wage, there is whatever fee he may extract from this buyer and that seller, and this I say nothing about if he is able to get it. And because our two families are united, there is no fee of guaranty I will ask of you for his coming."

Wang Lung rose then, well-pleased, and he laughed and said,

"Now we are friends, and have you no son for my second daughter?"

Then the merchant laughed richly, for he was fat and well-fed, and he said,

"I have a second son of ten whom I have not betrothed yet. How old is the girl?"

Wang Lung laughed again and answered,

"She is ten on her next birthday and she is a pretty flower."

Then the two men laughed together and the merchant said,

"Shall we tie ourselves together with a double rope?"

Then Wang Lung said no more, for it was not a thing that could be discussed face to face beyond this. But after he had bowed and gone away well-pleased, he said to himself, "The thing may be done," and he looked at his young daughter when he came home and she was a pretty child and her mother had bound her feet well, so that she moved about with small graceful steps.

But when Wang Lung looked at her thus closely he saw the marks of tears on her cheeks, and her face was a shade too pale and grave for her years, and he drew her to him by her little hand and he said,

"Now why have you wept?"

Then she hung her head and toyed with a button on her coat and said, shy and half-murmuring,

"Because my mother binds a cloth about my feet more tightly every day and I cannot sleep at night."

"Now I have not heard you weep," he said wondering.

"No," she said simply, "and my mother said I was not to weep aloud because you are too kind and weak for pain and you might say to leave me as I am, and then my husband would not love me even as you do not love her."

This she said as simply as a child recites a tale, and Wang Lung was stabbed at hearing this, that O-lan had told the child he did not love her who was the child's mother, and he said quickly,

"Well, and today I have heard of a pretty husband for you, and we will see if Cuckoo can arrange the matter."

Then the child smiled and dropped her head, suddenly a maid and no more a child. And Wang Lung said to Cuckoo on that same evening when he was in the inner court,

"Go and see if it can be done."

But he slept uneasily beside Lotus that night and he woke and fell to thinking of his life and of how O-lan had been the first woman he had known and how she had been a faithful servant beside him. And he thought of what the child said, and he was sad, because with all her dimness O-lan had seen the truth in him.

In the near days after this he sent his second son away into the town and he signed the papers for the second girl's betrothal and the dowry was decided upon and the gifts of clothing and jewelry for her marriage day were fixed. Then Wang Lung rested and he said to his heart,

"Well, and now all my children are provided for, and my poor fool can do nothing but sit in the sun with her bit of cloth and the youngest boy I will keep for the land and he shall not go to school, since two can read and it is enough."

He was proud because he had three sons and one was a scholar and one a merchant and one a farmer. He was content, then, and he gave over thinking any more about his children. But whether he would or not there came into his mind the thought of the woman who had borne them for him.

For the first time in his years with her Wang Lung began to think about O-lan. Even in the days of her new-coming he had not thought of her for herself and not further than because she was a woman and the first he had known. And it seemed to him that with this thing and that he had been busy and without time to spare, and only now, when his children were settled and his fields cared for and quiet under the coming of winter, and now, when his life with Lotus was regulated and she was submissive to him since he had beat her, now it seemed to him he had time to think of what he would and he thought of O-lan.

He looked at her, not because she was woman this time, and not that she was ugly and gaunt and yellow-skinned. But he looked at her with some strange remorse, and he saw that she had grown thin and her skin was sere and yellow. She had always been a dark woman, her skin ruddy and brown when she worked in the fields. Yet now for many years she had not gone into the fields except perhaps at harvest time, and not then for two years and more, for he disliked her to go, lest men say,

"And does your wife still work on the land and you rich?"

Nevertheless, he had not thought why she had been willing at last to stay in the house and why she moved slowly and more slowly about, and he remembered, now that he thought of it, that in the mornings sometimes he heard her groaning when she rose from her bed and when she stooped to feed the oven, and only when he asked, "Well, and what is it?" did she cease suddenly. Now, looking at her and at the strange swelling she had on her body, he was stricken with remorse, although he did not know why, and he argued with himself.

"Well, and it is not my fault if I have not loved her as one

181

loves a concubine, since men do not." And to himself he said for comfort, "I have not beat her and I have given her silver when she asked for it."

But still he could not forget what the child had said and it pricked him, although he did not know why, seeing that, when he came to argue the matter out, he had always been a good husband to her and better than most.

Because he could not be rid of this unease toward her, then, he kept looking at her as she brought in his food or as she moved about, and when she stooped to sweep the brick floor one day after they had eaten, he saw her face turn grey with some inner pain, and she opened her lips and panted softly, and she put her hand to her belly, although still stooping as though to sweep. He asked her sharply,

"What is it?"

But she averted her face and answered meekly,

"It is only the old pain in my vitals."

Then he stared at her and he said to the younger girl,

"Take the broom and sweep, for your mother is ill." And to O-lan he said more kindly than he had spoken to her in many years, "Go in and lie on your bed, and I will bid the girl bring you hot water. Do not get up."

She obeyed him slowly and without answer, and she went in to her room and he heard her dragging about it, and at last she lay down and moaned softly. Then he sat listening to this moaning until he could not bear it, and he rose and went in to the town to ask where a doctor's shop was.

He found a shop recommended to him by a clerk in the grain market where his second son now was, and he went to it. There the doctor sat idle over a pot of tea. He was an old man with a long grey beard and brass spectacles large as an owl's eyes over his nose, and he wore a dirty grey robe whose long sleeves covered his hands altogether. When Wang Lung told him what his wife's symptoms were, he pursed his lips and opened a drawer of the table at which he sat, and he took out a bundle wrapped in a black cloth and he said,

"I will come now."

When they came to O-lan's bed she had fallen into a light sleep and the sweat stood like dew on her upper lip and on her forehead, and the old doctor shook his head to see it. He put forth a hand as dried and yellowed as an ape's hand and he felt for her pulse, and then after he had held it for a long time, he shook his head again gravely, saying,

"The spleen is enlarged and the liver diseased. There is a rock as large as a man's head in the womb; the stomach is disintegrated. The heart barely moves and doubtless there are worms in it."

At these words Wang Lung's own heart stopped and he was afraid and he shouted out angrily,

"Well, and give her medicine, can you not?"

O-lan opened her eyes as he spoke and looked at them, not understanding and drowsy with pain. Then the old doctor spoke again,

"It is a difficult case. If you do not wish guarantee of recovery, I will ask for fee ten pieces of silver and I will give you a prescription of herbs and a tiger's heart dried in it and the tooth of a dog, and these boil together and let her drink the broth. But if you wish complete recovery guaranteed, then five hundred pieces of silver."

Now when O-lan heard the words, "five hundred pieces of silver" she came suddenly out of her languor and she said weakly,

"No, and my life is not worth so much. A good piece of land can be bought for so much."

Then when Wang Lung heard her say this all his old remorse smote him and he answered her fiercely,

"I will have no death in my house and I can pay the silver."

Now when the old doctor heard him say, "I can pay the silver," his eyes shone greedily enough, but he knew the penalty of the law if he did not keep his word and the woman died, and so he said, although with regret,

"Nay, and as I look at the color of the whites of her eyes, I see I was mistaken. Five thousand pieces of silver must I have if I guarantee full recovery."

Then Wang Lung looked at the doctor in silence and in sad understanding. He had not so many pieces of silver in the world unless he sold his land, but he knew that even though he sold his land it was no avail, for it was simply that the doctor said, "The woman will die."

He went out with the doctor, therefore, and he paid him the ten pieces of silver, and when he was gone Wang Lung went into the dark kitchen where O-lan had lived her life for the most part, and where, now that she was not there, none would see him, and he turned his face to the blackened wall, and he wept.

26

BUT THERE WAS no sudden dying of life in O-lan's body. She was scarcely past the middle of her span of years, and her life would not easily pass from her body, so that she lay dying on her bed for many months. All through the long months of winter she lay dying and upon her bed, and for the first time Wang Lung and his children knew what she had been in the house, and how she made comfort for them all and they had not known it.

It seemed now that none knew how to light the grass and keep it burning in the oven, and none knew how to turn a fish in the cauldron without breaking it or burning one side black before the other side was cooked, and none knew whether sesame oil or bean were right for frying this vegetable or that. The filth of the crumbs and dropped food lay under the table and none swept it unless Wang Lung grew impatient with the smell of it and called in a dog from the court to lick it up or shouted at the younger girl to scrape it up and throw it out.

And the youngest lad did this and that to fill his mother's place with the old man his grandfather, who was helpless as a little child now, and Wang Lung could not make the old man understand what had happened that O-lan no longer came to bring him tea and hot water and to help him lie down and stand up, and he was peevish because he called her and she did not come, and he threw his bowl of tea on the ground like a wilful child. At last Wang Lung led him in to O-lan's room and showed him the bed where she lay, and the old man stared out of his filmed and half blind eyes, and he mumbled and wept because he saw dimly that something was wrong.

Only the poor fool knew nothing, and only she smiled and twisted her bit of cloth as she smiled. Yet one had to think of her to bring her in to sleep at night and to feed her and to set her in the sun in the day and to lead her in if it rained. All this one of them had to remember. But even Wang Lung himself forgot, and once they left her outside through a whole night, and the next morning the poor wretch was shivering and crying in the early dawn, and Wang Lung was angry and cursed his son and daughter that they had forgotten the poor fool who was their sister. Then he saw that they were but children trying to take their mother's place and not able to do it, and he forebore and after that he saw to the poor fool himself night and morning. If it rained or snowed or a bitter wind blew he led her in and he let her sit among the warm ashes that dropped from the kitchen stove.

All during the dark winter months when O-lan lay dying Wang Lung paid no heed to the land. He turned over the winter's work and the men to the government of Ching, and Ching labored faithfully, and night and morning he came to the door of the room where O-lan lay and he asked twice each day thus in his piping whisper how she did. At last Wang Lung could not bear it because every day and every night he could only say,

"Today she drank a little soup from a fowl," or "today she ate a little thin gruel of rice."

So he commanded Ching to ask no more but to do the work well, and it would be enough.

All during the cold dark winter Wang Lung sat often beside O-lan's bed, and if she were cold he lit an earthen pot of charcoal and set it beside her bed for warmth, and she murmured each time faintly,

"Well, and it is too expensive."

At last one day when she said this he could not bear it and he burst forth,

"This I cannot bear! I would sell all my land if it could heal you."

She smiled at this and said in gasps, whispering,

"No, and I would not—let you. For I must die—sometime anyway. But the land is there after me."

But he would not talk of her death and he rose and went out when she spoke of it.

Nevertheless because he knew she must die and it was his duty, he went one day into the town to a coffin-maker's shop and he looked at every coffin that stood there ready to be bought, and he chose a good black one made from heavy and hard wood. Then the carpenter, who waited for him to choose, said cunningly,

"If you take two, the price is a third off for the two, and why do you not buy one for yourself and know you are provided?"

"No, and my sons can do it for me," answered Wang Lung, and then he thought of his own father and he had not yet a coffin for the old man and he was struck with the thought and he said again, "But there is my old father and he will die one day soon, weak as he is on his two legs and deaf and half blind, and so I will take the two."

And the man promised to paint the coffins again a good black and send them to Wang Lung's house. So Wang Lung told O-lan what he had done, and she was pleased that he had done it for her, and had provided well for her death.

Thus he sat by her many hours of the day, and they did not talk much for she was faint, and besides there had never been talk between them. Often she forgot where she was as he sat there in stillness and silence, and sometimes she murmured of her childhood, and for the first time Wang Lung saw into her heart, although even now only through such brief words as these,

"I will bring the meats to the door only—and well I know I am ugly and cannot appear before the great lord—" And again she said, panting, "Do not beat me—I will never eat of the dish again—" And she said over and over, "My father—my mother —my father—my mother——" and again and again, "Well I know I am ugly and cannot be loved—"

When she said this Wang Lung could not bear it and he took her hand and he soothed it, a big hard hand, stiff as though it were dead already. And he wondered and grieved at himself most of all because what she said was true, and even when he took her hand, desiring truly that she feel his tenderness towards her, he was ashamed because he could feel no tenderness, no melting of the heart such as Lotus could win from him with a pout of her lips. When he took this stiff dying hand he did not love it, and even his pity was spoiled with repulsion towards it.

And because of this, he was more kind to her and he bought her special food and delicate soups made of white fish and the hearts of young cabbages. Moreover, he could not take his pleasure of Lotus, for when he went in to her to distract his mind from its despair over this long agony of dying, he could not forget O-lan, and even as he held Lotus, he loosed her, because of O-lan.

There were times when O-lan woke to herself and to what was about her and once she called for Cuckoo, and when in great astonishment Wang Lung summoned the woman, O-lan raised herself trembling upon her arm, and she said plainly enough,

"Well, and you may have lived in the courts of the Old Lord, and you were accounted beautiful, but I have been a man's wife and I have borne him sons, and you are still a slave."

When Cuckoo would have answered angrily to this, Wang Lung besought her and led her out, saying,

"That one does not know what words mean, now."

When he went back into the room, O-lan still leaned her head upon her arms and she said to him,

"After I am dead that one nor her mistress neither is to come into my room or touch my things, and if they do, I will send my spirit back for a curse." Then she fell into her fitful sleep, and her head dropped upon the pillow.

But one day before the New Year broke, she was suddenly better, as a candle flickers brightly at its end, and she was herself as she had not been and she sat up in bed and twisted her hair for herself, and she asked for tea to drink, and when Wang Lung came she said,

"Now the New Year is coming and there are no cakes and no meats ready, and I have thought of a thing. I will not have that slave in my kitchen, but I would have you send for my daughter-in-law, who is betrothed to our eldest son. I have not seen her yet, but when she comes I will tell her what to do."

Wang Lung was pleased at her strength, although he cared nothing for festivities on this year, and he sent Cuckoo in to beseech Liu, the grain merchant, seeing how sad the case was. And after a while Liu was willing when he heard that O-lan would not live the winter out, perhaps, and after all the girl was sixteen and older than some who go to their husband's houses.

But because of O-lan there were no feasting. The maiden came quietly in a sedan chair, except that her mother and an old servant came with her, and her mother went back when she had delivered the maiden to O-lan, but the servant remained for the maiden's use.

Now the children were moved from the room where they had slept and the room was given to the new daughter-in-law, and all was arranged as it should be. Wang Lung did not speak with the maiden, since it was not fitting, but he inclined his head gravely when she bowed, and he was pleased with her, for she knew her duty and she moved about the house quietly with her eyes downcast. Moreover, she was a goodly maid, fair enough, but not too fair so as to be vain over it. She was careful and correct in all her behavior, and she went into O-lan's room and tended her, and this eased Wang Lung of his pain for his wife, because now there was a woman about her bed, and O-lan was very content.

O-lan was content for three days and more and then she thought of another thing and she said to Wang Lung when he came in the morning to see how she did through the night,

"There is another thing before I can die."

To this he replied angrily,

"You cannot speak of dying and please me!"

She smiled slowly then, the same slow smile that ended before it reached her eyes, and she answered,

"Die I must, for I feel it in my vitals waiting, but I will not die before my eldest son comes home and before he weds this good maid who is my daughter-in-law, and well she serves me, holding the hot water basin steadily and knowing when to bathe my face when I sweat in pain. Now I want my son to come home, because I must die, and I want him to wed this maid first, so that I may die easily, knowing your grandson is stirred into life and a great grandson for the old one."

Now these were many words for her at any time, even in health, and she said them more sturdily than she had said anything for many moons, and Wang Lung was cheered at the strength in her voice and with what vigor she desired this, and he would not cross her, although he would have liked more time for a great wedding for his eldest son. He only said heartily to her therefore,

"Well, and we will do this thing, and today I will send a man south and he shall search for my son and bring him home to be wed. And then you must promise me that you will gather your strength again and give over dying and grow well, for the house is like a cave for beasts without you."

This he said to please her and it pleased her, although she did not speak again, but lay back and closed her eyes, smiling a little.

Wang Lung despatched the man, therefore, and told him,

"Tell your young lord that his mother is dying and her spirit

188

cannot rest in ease until she sees him and sees him wed, and if he values me and his mother and his home, he must come back before he draws another breath, for on the third day from now I will have feasts prepared and guests invited and he will be wed."

And as Wang Lung said, so he did. He bade Cuckoo provide a feast as best she could, and she was to call in cooks from the shop in town to help her, and he poured silver into her hands and he said,

"Do as it would have been done in the great house at such an hour, and there is more silver than this."

Then he went into the village and invited guests, men and women, everyone whom he knew, and he went into the town and invited whom he knew at the tea shops and at the grain markets and everyone whom he knew. And he said to his uncle,

"Ask whom you will for my son's marriage, any of your friends or any of your son's friends."

This he said because he remembered always who his uncle was and Wang Lung was courteous to his uncle and treated him as an honored guest, and so he had done from the hour when he knew who his uncle was.

On the night of the day before his marriage, Wang Lung's eldest son came home, and he came striding into the room and Wang Lung forgot all that the young man had troubled him when he was at home. For two years and more had passed since he saw this son of his, and here he was and no longer a lad, but a tall man and a goodly one, with a great square body and high ruddy cheeks and short black hair, shining and oiled. And he wore a long dark red gown of satin such as one finds in the shops of the south, and a short black velvet jacket without sleeves, and Wang Lung's heart burst with pride to see his son, and he forgot everything except this, his goodly son, and he led him to his mother.

Then the young man sat beside his mother's bed and the tears stood in his eyes to see her thus, but he would not say anything except cheerful things such as these, "You look twice as well as they said and years away from death." But O-lan said simply,

"I will see you wed and then I must die."

Now the maid who was to be wed must not of course be seen by the young man and Lotus took her into the inner court to prepare her for marriage, and none could do this better than Lotus and Cuckoo and the wife of Wang Lung's uncle. These three took the maid and on the morning of her wedding day they washed her clean from head to foot, and bound her feet freshly with new white cloths under her new stockings, and Lotus rubbed into her flesh some fragrant almond oil of her own. Then they dressed her in garments she had brought from her home; white flowered silk next her sweet virgin flesh and then a light coat of sheep's wool of the finest and most curling kind, and then the red satin garments of marriage. And they rubbed lime upon her forehead and with a string tied skilfully they pulled out the hairs of her virginity, the fringe over her brow, and they made her forehead high and smooth and square for her new estate. Then they painted her with powder and with red paint, and with a brush they drew out in two long slender lines her eyebrows, and they set upon her head the bride's crown and the beaded veil, and upon her small feet they put shoes, embroidered, and they painted her fingertips and scented the palms of her hands, and thus they prepared her for marriage. To everything the maid was acquiescent, but reluctant and shy as was proper and correct for her.

Then Wang Lung and his uncle and his father and the guests waited in the middle room and the maid came in supported by her own slave and by the wife of Wang Lung's uncle, and she came in modestly and correctly with her head bowed, and she walked as though she were unwilling to wed a man and must be supported to it. This showed her great modesty and Wang Lung was pleased and said to himself that she was a proper maid.

After this Wang Lung's eldest son came in dressed as he had been in his red robe and his black jacket and his hair was smooth and his face fresh shaven. Behind him came his two brothers, and Wang Lung, seeing them, was fit to burst with pride at this procession of his goodly sons, who were to continue after him the life of his body. Now the old man, who had not understood what was happening at all and could hear only the fragments of what was shouted to him, now suddenly he understood, and he cackled out with cracked laughter and he said over and over in his piping old voice,

"There is a marriage and a marriage is children again and grandchildren!"

And he laughed so heartily that the guests all laughed to see his mirth and Wang Lung thought to himself that if only O-lan had been up from her bed it would have been a merry day.

All this time Wang Lung looked secretly and sharply at his

son to see if he glanced at the maid, and the young man did glance secretly and from the corner of his eyes, but it was enough, for he grew pleased and merry in his ways and Wang said proudly to himself,

"Well, and I have chosen one he likes for him."

Then the young man and the maid together bowed to the old man and to Wang Lung, and then they went into the room where O-lan lay, and she had caused herself to be dressed in her good black coat and she sat up when they came in and on her face there burned two fiery spots of red, which Wang Lung mistook for health, so that he said loudly, "Now she will be well, yet!"

And the two young persons went up and bowed to her and she patted the bed and said,

"Sit here and drink the wine and eat the rice of your marriage, for I would see it all and this will be your bed of marriage since I am soon to be finished with it and carried away."

Now none would answer her when she spoke thus but the two sat down side by side, shy and in silence of each other, and the wife of Wang Lung's uncle came in fat and important with the occasion, bearing two bowls of hot wine, and the two drank separately, and then mingled the wine of the two bowls and drank again, thus signifying that the two were now one, and they ate rice and mingled the rice and this signified that their life was now one, and thus they were wed. Then they bowed again to O-lan and to Wang Lung and then they went out and together they bowed to the assembled guests.

Then the feasting began and and the rooms and the courts were filled with tables and with the smell of cooking and with the sound of laughter, for the guests came from far and wide, those whom Wang Lung had invited and with them many whom Wang Lung had never seen, since it was known he was a rich man and food would never be missed or counted in his house at such a time. And Cuckoo had brought cooks from the town to prepare the feast, for there were to be many delicacies such as cannot be prepared in a farmer's kitchen and the town cooks came bearing great baskets of food ready cooked and only to be heated, and they made much of themselves and flourished their grimy aprons and bustled here and there in their zeal. And everyone ate more and yet more and drank all they were able to hold, and they were all very merry.

O-lan would have all the doors open and the curtains drawn so that she could hear the noise and the laughter and could smell the food, and she said again and again to Wang Lung, who came often to see how she did,

"And has everyone wine? And is the sweet rice dish in the middle of the feast very hot and have they put full measure of lard and sugar into it and the eight fruits?"

When he assured her that everything was as she wished it, she was content and lay listening.

Then it was over and the guests were gone and night came. And with the silence over the house and with the ebbing of merriment strength passed from O-lan and she grew weary and faint and she called to her the two who had been wed that day and she said,

"Now I am content and this thing in me may do as it will. My son, look to your father and your grandfather, and my daughter, look to your husband and your husband's father and his grandfather and the poor fool in the court, there is she. And you have no duty to any other."

This last she said, meaning Lotus, to whom she had never spoken. Then she seemed to fall into a fitful sleep, although they waited for her to speak further, and once more she roused herself to speak. Yet when she spoke it was as though she did not know they were there or indeed where she was, for she said, muttering and turning her head this way and that and her eyes closed,

"Well, and if I am ugly, still I have borne a son; although I am but a slave there is a son in my house." And again she said, suddenly, "How can that one feed him and care for him as I do? Beauty will not bear a man sons!"

And she forgot them all and lay muttering. Then Wang Lung motioned to them to go away, and he sat beside her while she slept and woke, and he looked at her. And he hated himself because even as she lay dying he saw how wide and ghastly her purpled lips drew back from her teeth. Then as he looked she opened her eyes wide and it seemed there was some strange mist over them, for she stared at him full and stared again, wondering and fixing her eyes on him, as though she wondered who he was. Suddenly her head dropped off the round pillow where it lay, and she shuddered and was dead.

Once she lay dead it seemed to Wang Lung that he could not bear to be near O-lan, and he called his uncle's wife to wash the body for burial, and when it was finished he would not go in again, but he allowed his uncle's wife and his eldest son and his daughter-in-law to lift the body from the bed and set it into the great coffin he had bought. But to comfort himself he busied himself in going to the town and calling men to seal the coffin according to custom and he went and found a geomancer and asked him for a lucky day for burials. He found a good day three months hence and it was the first good day the geomancer could find, so Wang Lung paid the man and went to the temple in the town and he bargained with the abbot there and rented a space for a coffin for three months, and there was O-lan's coffin brought to rest until the day of burial, for it seemed to Wang Lung he could not bear to have it under his eyes in the house.

Then Wang Lung was scrupulous to do all that should be done for the one dead, so he caused mourning to be made for himself and for his children, and their shoes were made of coarse white cloth, which is the color of mourning, and about their ankles they bound bands of white cloth, and the women in the house bound their hair with white cord.

After this Wang Lung could not bear to sleep in the room where O-lan had died and he took his possessions and moved altogether into the inner court where Lotus lived and he said to his eldest son,

"Go with your wife into that room where your mother lived and died, who conceived and bore you, and beget there your own sons."

So the two moved into it and were content.

Then as though death could not easily leave the house where it had come once, the old man, Wang Lung's father, who had been distraught ever since he saw them putting the stiff dead body of O-lan into the coffin, lay down on his bed one night for sleeping, and when the second daughter came in to him in the morning to bring him his tea, there he lay on his bed, his scattered old beard thrust up into the air, and his head thrown back in death.

She cried out at the sight and ran crying to her father and Wang Lung came in and found the old man so; his light, stiff old body was dry and cold and thin as a gnarled pine tree and he had died hours before, perhaps as soon as he had laid himself upon the bed. Then Wang Lung washed the old man himself and he laid him gently in the coffin he had bought for him and he had it sealed and he said,

"On the same day we will bury these two dead from our house and I will take a good piece of my hill land and we will bury them there together and when I die I will be laid there also."

So he did what he said he would do. When he had sealed the old man's coffin he set it upon two benches in the middle room and there it stood until the appointed day came. And it seemed to Wang Lung that it was a comfort to the old man to be there, even dead, and he felt near to his father in the coffin, for Wang Lung grieved for his father, but not unto death, because his father was very old and full of years, and for many years had been but half alive.

Then on the day appointed by the geomancer in the full of the spring of the year Wang Lung called priests from the Taoist temple and they came dressed in their yellow robes and their long hair knotted on their crowns, and he called priests from the Buddhist temples and they came in their long grey robes, their heads shaven and set with the nine sacred scars, and these priests beat drums and chanted the whole night through for the two who were dead. And whenever they stopped their chanting Wang Lung poured silver into their hands and they took breath again and chanted and did not cease until dawn rose.

Now Wang Lung had chosen a good place in his fields under a date tree upon a hill to set the graves, and Ching had the graves dug and ready and a wall of earth made about the graves, and there was space within the walls for the body of Wang Lung and for each of his sons and their wives, and there was space for sons' sons, also. This land Wang Lung did not begrudge, even though it was high land and good for wheat, because it was a sign of the establishment of his family upon their own land. Dead and alive they would rest upon their own land.

Then on the appointed day after the priests had finished the night of chanting, Wang Lung dressed himself in a robe of white sackcloth and he gave a robe like it to his uncle and his uncle's son, and to his own sons each a robe, and to his son's wife and to his own two daughters. He called chairs from the town to carry them, for it was not meet that they walk to the place of burial as though he were a poor man and a common fellow. So for the first time he rode on men's shoulders and behind the coffin where O-lan was. But behind his father's coffin his uncle rode first. Even Lotus, who in O-lan's lifetime could not appear before her, now that O-lan was dead, she came riding in a chair in order that before others she might appear dutiful to the first wife of her husband. So for his uncle's wife and for his uncle's son Wang Lung hired chairs also and for all of them he had robes of sackcloth, and even for the poor fool he made a robe and hired a chair and put her in it, although she was sorely bewildered and laughed shrilly when there should have been only weeping.

Then mourning and weeping loudly they went to the graves, the laborers and Ching following and walking and wearing white shoes. And Wang Lung stood beside the two graves. He had caused the coffin of O-lan to be brought from the temple and it was put on the ground to await the old man's burial first. And Wang Lung stood and watched and his grief was hard and dry, and he would not cry out loud as others did for there were no tears in his eyes, because it seemed to him that what had come about was come about, and there was nothing to be done more than he had done.

But when the earth was covered over and the graves smoothed, he turned away silently and he sent away the chair and he walked home alone with himself. And out of his heaviness there stood out strangely but one clear thought and it was a pain to him, and it was this, that he wished he had not taken the two pearls from O-lan that day when she was washing his clothes at the pool, and he would never bear to see Lotus put them in her ears again.

Thus thinking heavily, he went on alone and he said to himself,

"There in that land of mine is buried the first good half of my life and more. It is as though half of me were buried there, and now it is a different life in my house."

And suddenly he wept a little, and he dried his eyes with the back of his hand, as a child does.

27

During all this time Wang Lung had scarcely thought of what the harvests were, so busy had he been with the wedding feasts and funerals in his house, but one day Ching came to him and he said,

"Now that the joy and sorrow are over, I have that to tell you about the land."

"Say on, then," Wang Lung answered. "I have scarcely thought whether I had land or not these days except to bury my dead in."

Ching waited in silence for a few minutes in respect to Wang Lung when he spoke thus, and then he said softly,

"Now may Heaven avert it, but it looks as though there would be such a flood this year as never was, for the water is swelling up over the land, although it is not summer yet, and too early for it to come like this."

But Wang Lung said stoutly,

"I have never had any good from that old man in heaven, yet. Incense or no incense, he is the same in evil. Let us go and see the land." And as he spoke he rose.

Now Ching was a fearful and timid man and however bad the times were he did not dare as Wang Lung did to exclaim against Heaven. He only said "Heaven wills it," and he accepted flood and drought with meekness. Not so Wang Lung. He went out on his land, on this piece and that, and he saw it was as Ching said. All those pieces along the moat, along the waterways, which he had bought from the Old Lord of the House of Hwang, were wet and mucky from the full water oozing up from the bottom, so that the good wheat on this land had turned sickly and yellow.

The moat itself was like a lake and the canals were rivers, swift and curling in small eddies and whirlpools, and even a fool could see that with summer rains not yet come, there would be that year a mighty flood and men and women and children starving again. Then Wang Lung ran hastily here and there over his land and Ching came silently as a shadow behind him, and they estimated together which land could be planted to rice and which land before the young rice could be put on it would already be under water. And looking at the canals brimming already to the edge of their banks, Wang Lung cursed and said,

"Now that old man in heaven will enjoy himself, for he will look down and see people drowned and starving and that is what the accursed one likes."

This he said loudly and angrily so that Ching shivered and said,

"Even so, he is greater than anyone of us and do not talk so, my master."

But since he was rich Wang Lung was careless, and he was as angry as he liked and he muttered as he walked homeward to think of the water swelling up over his land and over his good crops.

Then it all came to pass as Wang Lung had foreseen. The river to the north burst its dykes, its furthermost dykes first, and when men saw what had happened, they hurried from this place to that to collect money to mend it, and every man gave as he was able, for it was to the interest of each to keep the river within its bounds. The money they entrusted, then, to the magistrate in the district, a man new and just come. Now this magistrate was a poor man and had not seen so much money in his lifetime before, being only newly risen to his position through the bounty of his father, who had put all the money he had and could borrow to buy this place for his son, so that from it the family might acquire some wealth. When the river burst again the people went howling and clamoring to this magistrate's house, because he had not done what he promised and mended the dykes, and he ran and hid himself because the money he had spent in his own house, even three thousand pieces of silver. And the common people burst into his house howling and demanding his life for what he had done, and when he saw he would be killed he ran and jumped into the water and drowned himself, and thus the people were appeased.

But still the money was gone, and the river burst yet another dyke and another before it was content with the space it had for itself, and then it wore away these walls of earth until none could tell where a dyke had been in that whole country and the river swelled and rolled like a sea over all the good farming land, and the wheat and the young rice were at the bottom of the sea.

One by one the villages were made into islands and men watched the water rising and when it came within two feet of their doorways they bound their tables and beds together and put the doors of their houses upon them for rafts, and they piled what they could of their bedding and their clothes and their women and children on these rafts. And the water rose into the earthern houses and softened the walls and burst them apart and they melted down into the water and were as if they had never been. And then as if water on earth drew water from heaven it rained as though the earth were in drought. Day after day it rained.

Wang Lung sat in his doorway and looked out over the waters that were yet far enough from his house that was built on a high wide hill. But he saw the waters covering his land and he watched lest it cover the new made graves, but it did not, although the waves of the yellow clay-laden water lapped about the dead hungrily.

There were no harvests of any kind that year and everywhere people starved and were hungry and were angry at what had befallen them yet again. Some went south, and some who were bold and angry and cared nothing for what they did joined the robber bands that flourished everywhere in the countryside. These even tried to beleaguer the town so that the townspeople locked the gates of the wall continually except for one small gate called the western water gate, and this was watched by soldiers and locked at night also. And besides those who robbed and those who went south to work and to beg, even as Wang Lung had once gone with his old father and his wife and children, there were others who were old and tired and timid, and who had no sons, like Ching, and these stayed and starved and ate grass and what leaves they could find on high places and many died upon the land and water.

Then Wang Lung saw that a famine such as he had never seen was upon the land, for the water did not recede in time to plant the wheat for winter and there could be no harvest then the next year. And he looked well to his own house and to the spending of money and food, and he quarreled heartily with Cuckoo because for a long time she would still buy meat every day in the town, and he was glad at last, since there must be flood, that the water crept between his house and the town so that she could no longer go to market when she would, for he would not allow the boats to be put forth except when he said, and Ching listened to him and not to Cuckoo, for all her sharpness of tongue.

Wang Lung allowed nothing to be bought and sold after the winter came except what he said, and he husbanded carefully all that they had. Every day he gave out to his daughter-in-law what food was needed in the house for that day, and to Ching he gave out what the laborers should have, although it hurt him to feed idle men, and it hurt him so greatly that at last when winter cold came and the water froze over, he bade the men begone to the south to beg and to labor until the spring came, when they might return to him. Only to Lotus he gave secretly sugar and oil, because she was not accustomed to hardship. Even on the New Year they did eat but a fish they caught themselves in the lake and a pig they killed from the farm.

Now Wang Lung was not so poor as he wished to seem, for he had good silver hidden away in the walls where his son slept with his wife, though his son and daughter-in-law did not know it, and he had good silver and even some gold hidden in a jar at the bottom of the lake under his nearest field, and he had some hidden among the roots of the bamboos, and he had grains from the year before which he had not sold at market, and there was no danger of starvation in his house.

But all around him there were people starving, and he remembered the cries of the starving at the gate of the great house once when he passed, and he knew that there were many who hated him well because he had still that which he could eat and feed to his children, and so he kept his gates barred and he let none in whom he did not know. But still he knew very well that even this could not have saved him in these times of robbers and lawlessness if it had not been for his uncle. Well did Wang Lung know that if it had not been for his uncle's power he would have been robbed and sacked for his food and for his money and for the women in his house. So he was courteous to his uncle and to his uncle's son and to his uncle's wife and the three were like guests in his house and they drank tea before others and dipped first with their chopsticks into the bowls at mealtime.

Now these three saw well enough that Wang Lung was afraid of them and they grew haughty and demanded this and that and complained of what they ate and drank. And especially did the woman complain, for she missed the delicacies she had eaten in the inner courts and she complained to her husband and the three of them complained to Wang Lung.

Now Wang Lung saw that although his uncle himself grew old and lazy and careless and would not have troubled to complain if he had been let alone, yet the young man, his son, and his wife goaded him, and one day when Wang Lung stood at the gate he heard these two urging the old man,

"Well, and he has money and food, and let us demand silver of him." And the woman said, "We will never have such a hold as this again, for well he knows that if you were not his uncle and the brother of his father he would be robbed and sacked and his house left empty and a ruin, since you stand next to the head of the Redbeards."

Wang Lung standing there secretly and hearing this grew so angry that his skin was like to burst on him, but he was silent with great effort and he tried to plan what he could do with these three, but he could think of nothing to do. When, therefore, his uncle came to him next day saying, "Well, and my good nephew, give me a handful of silver to buy me a pipe and a bit of smoke and my woman is ragged and needs a new coat," he could say nothing but he handed the old man the five pieces of silver from his girdle, although he gnashed his teeth secretly, and it seemed to him that never in the old days when silver was rare with him had it gone from him so unwillingly.

Then before two days were passed his uncle was at him again and again for silver and Wang Lung shouted at last,

"Well, and shall we all starve soon?"

And his uncle laughed and said carelessly,

"You are under a good heaven. There are men less rich than you who hang from the burnt rafters of their houses."

When Wang Lung heard this, cold sweat broke out on him and he gave the silver without a word. And so, although they went without meat in the house, these three must eat meat, and although Wang Lung himself scarcely tasted tobacco, his uncle puffed unceasingly at his pipe.

Now Wang Lung's eldest son had been engrossed in his marriage and he scarcely saw what happened except that he guarded his wife jealously from the gaze of his cousin so that now these two were no longer friends but enemies. Wang Lung's son scarcely let his wife stir from their room except in the evenings when the other man was gone with his father and during the day he made her stay shut in the room. But when he saw these three doing as they would with his father he grew angry, for he was of a quick temper, and he said,

"Well, and if you care more for these three tigers than you do for your son and his wife, the mother of your grandsons, it is a strange thing and we had better set up our house elsewhere."

Wang Lung told him plainly then what he had told no one,

"I hate these three worse than my life and if I could think of a way I would do it. But your uncle is lord of a horde of wild robbers, and if I feed him and coddle him we are safe, and no one can show anger toward them."

Now when the eldest son heard this he stared until his eyes hung out of his head, but when he had thought of it for a while he was more angry than ever and he said,

"How is this for a way? Let us push them all into the water one night. Ching can push the woman for she is fat and soft and helpless, and I will push the young one my cousin, whom I hate enough for he is always peeping at my wife, and you can push the man."

But Wang Lung could not kill; although he would rather have killed his uncle than his ox, he could not kill even when he hated and he said,

"No, and even if I could do this thing, to push my father's brother into the water I would not, for if the other robbers heard of it what should we do, and if he lives we are safe, and if he is gone we are become as other people who have a little and so are in danger in such times as these."

Then the two of them fell silent, each thinking heavily what to do, and the young man saw that his father was right and death was too easy for the trouble and that there must be another way. And Wang Lung spoke aloud at last, musing,

"If there were a way that we could keep them here but make them harmless and undesiring what a thing it would be, but there is no such magic as this!"

Then the young man smote his two hands together and cried out,

"Well, and you have told me what to do! Let us buy them opium to enjoy, and more opium, and let them have their will of it as rich people do. I will seem to be friends with my cousin again and I will entice him away to the tea house in the town where one can smoke and we can buy it for my uncle and his wife."

But Wang Lung, since he had not thought of the thing first himself, was doubtful.

"It will cost a great deal," he said slowly, "for opium is as dear as jade."

"Well, and it is dearer than jade to have them at us like this," the young man argued, "and to endure besides their haughtiness and the young man peeping at my wife."

But Wang Lung would not at once consent, for it was not so easy a thing to do, and it would cost a good bag of silver to do it.

It is doubtful whether the thing would ever have been done and they would have gone as they were until the waters chose to recede had not a thing happened.

This thing was that the son of Wang Lung's uncle cast his eyes upon the second daughter of Wang Lung, who was his cousin and by blood the same as his sister. Now the second daughter of Wang Lung was an exceedingly pretty girl, and she looked like the second son who was a merchant, but with her smallness and lightness, and she had not his yellow skin. Her skin was fair and pale as almond flowers and she had a little low nose and thin red lips and her feet were small.

Her cousin laid hold of her one night when she passed alone through the court from the kitchen. He laid hold of her roughly and he pressed his hand into her bosom and she screamed out, and Wang Lung ran out and beat the man about the head, but he was like a dog with a piece of stolen meat that he would not drop, so that Wang Lung had to tear his daughter away. Then the man laughed thickly and he said,

"It is only play and is she not my sister? Can a man do any evil with his sister?" But his eyes glittered with lust as he spoke and Wang Lung muttered and pulled the girl away and sent her into her own room.

And Wang Lung told his son that night what had come about, and the young man was grave and he said,

"We must send the maid into the town to the home of her betrothed; even if the merchant Liu says it is a year too evil for wedding we must send her, lest we cannot keep her virgin with this hot tiger in the house."

So Wang Lung did. He went the next day into the town and to the house of the merchant and he said,

"My daughter is thirteen years old and no longer a child and she is fit for marriage."

But Liu was hesitant and he said,

"I have not enough profit this year to begin a family in my house."

Now Wang Lung was ashamed to say, "There is the son of my uncle in the house and he is a tiger," so he said only,

"I would not have the care of this maid upon me, because her mother is dead and she is pretty and is of an age to conceive, and my house is large and full of this and that, and I cannot watch her every hour. Since she is to be your family, let her virginity be guarded here, and let her be wed soon or late as you like."

Then the merchant, being a lenient and kindly man, replied,

"Well, and if this is how it is, let the maid come and I will speak to my son's mother, and she can come and be safe here in the courts with her mother-in-law, and after the next harvest or so, she can be wed."

Thus the matter was settled and Wang Lung was well content, and he went away.

But on his way back to the gate in the wall, where Ching held a boat waiting for him, Wang Lung passed a shop where tobacco and opium are sold, and he went in to buy himself a little shredded tobacco to put in his water pipe in the evenings, and as the clerk had it on the scales, he said half unwillingly to the man,

"And how much is your opium if you have it?"

And the clerk said,

"It is not lawful in these days to sell it over the counter, and we do not sell it so, but if you wish to buy it and have the silver, it is weighed out in the room behind this, an ounce for a silver piece."

Then Wang Lung would not think further what he did, but he said quickly,

"I will take six ounces of it."

28

THEN AFTER the second daughter was sent away and Wang Lung was free of his anxiety about her, he said to his uncle one day,

"Since you are my father's brother, here is a little better tobacco for you."

And he opened the jar of opium and the stuff was sticky and sweet smelling and Wang Lung's uncle took it and smelled of it, and he laughed and was pleased and he said,

"Well now, I have smoked it a little but not often before this, for it is too dear, but I like it well enough."

And Wang Lung answered him, pretending to be careless,

"It is only a little I bought once for my father when he grew old and could not sleep at night and I found it today unused and I thought, 'There is my father's brother, and why should he not have it before me, who am younger and do not need it yet?' Take it then, and smoke it when you wish or when you have a little pain."

Then Wang Lung's uncle took it greedily, for it was sweet to smell and a thing that only rich men used, and he took it and bought a pipe and he smoked the opium, lying all day upon his bed to do it. Then Wang Lung saw to it that there were pipes bought and left here and there and he pretended to smoke himself, but he only took a pipe to his room and left it there cold. And his two sons in the house and Lotus he would not allow to touch the opium, saying as his excuse that it was too dear, but he urged it upon his uncle and upon his uncle's wife and son, and the courts were filled with the sweetish smell of the smoke, and the silver for this Wang Lung did not begrudge because it bought him peace.

Now as the winter wore away and the waters began to recede so that Wang Lung could walk abroad over his land it happened one day that his eldest son followed him and said to him proudly,

"Well, and there will soon be another mouth in the house and it will be the mouth of your grandson."

Then Wang Lung, when he heard this, turned himself about and he laughed and he rubbed his hands together and said,

"Here is a good day, indeed!"

And he laughed again, and went to find Ching and tell him to go to the town to buy fish and good food and he sent it in to his son's wife and said,

"Eat, make strong the body of my grandson."

Then all during the spring Wang Lung had the knowledge of this birth to come for his comfort. And when he was busy about

204

other things he thought of it, and when he was troubled he thought of it and it was a comfort to him.

And as the spring grew into summer, the people who had gone away from the floods came back again, one by one and group by group, spent and weary with the winter and glad to be back, although where their houses had been there was nothing now but the yellow mud of the water-soaked land. But out of this mud houses could be fashioned again, and mats bought to roof them, and many came to Wang Lung to borrow money, and he loaned it at high interest, seeing how greatly it was in demand, and the security he always said must be land. And with the money they borrowed they planted seed upon the earth that was fat with the richness of the dried water, and when they needed oxen and seed and plows and when they could borrow no more money, some sold land and part of their fields that they might plant what was left. And of these Wang Lung bought land and much land, and he bought it cheaply, since money men must have.

But there were some who would not sell their land, and when they had nothing wherewith to buy seed and plow and oxen, they sold their daughters, and there were those who came to Wang Lung to sell, because it was known he was rich and powerful and a man of good heart.

And he, thinking constantly of the child to come and of others to come from his sons when they were all wed, bought five slaves, two about twelve years of age with big feet and strong bodies, and two younger to wait upon them all and fetch and carry, and one to wait on the person of Lotus, for Cuckoo grew old and since the second girl was gone there had been none other to work in the house. And the five he bought in one day, for he was a man rich enough to do quickly what he decided upon.

Then one day many days later a man came bearing a small delicate maid of seven years or so, wanting to sell her, and Wang Lung said he would not have her at first, for she was so small and weak. But Lotus saw her and fancied her and she said pettishly,

"Now this one I will have because she is so pretty and the other one is coarse and smells like goat's meat and I do not like her."

And Wang Lung looked at the child and saw her pretty frightened eyes and her piteous thinness and he said partly to

humor Lotus and partly that he might see the child fed and fat-
tened,

"Well, and let it be so if you wish it."

So he bought the child for twenty pieces of silver and she
lived in the inner courts and slept on the foot of the bed where
Lotus slept.

Now it seened to Wang Lung that he could have peace in his
house. When the waters receded and summer came and the
land was to be planted to good seed, he walked hither and
thither and looked at every piece and he discussed with Ching
the quality of each piece of soil and what change there should
be of crops for the fertility of the land. And whenever he went
he took with him his youngest son, who was to be on the land
after him, that the lad might learn. And Wang Lung never
looked to see how the lad listened and whether he listened or
not, for the lad walked with his head downcast and he had a
sullen look on his face, and no one knew what he thought.

But Wang Lung did not see what the lad did, only that he
walked there in silence behind his father. And when everything
was planned Wang Lung went back to his house well content
and he said to his own heart,

"I am no longer young and it is not necessary for me to work
any more with my hands since I have men on my land and my
sons and peace in my house."

Yet when he went into his house there was no peace.
Although he had given his son a wife and although he had
bought slaves enough to serve them all, and although his uncle
and his uncle's wife were given enough of opium for their
pleasure all day, still there was no peace. And again it was
because of his uncle's son and his own eldest son.

It seemed as though Wang Lung's eldest son could never
give over his hatred of his cousin or his deep suspicion of his
cousin's evil. He had seen well enough with his own eyes in his
youth that the man, his cousin, was full of all sorts of evil, and
things had come to pass where Wang Lung's son would not
even leave the house to go to the tea shop unless the cousin
went also, and he watched the cousin and left only when he
left. And he suspected the man of evil with the slaves and even
of evil in the inner court with Lotus, although this was idle, for
Lotus grew fatter and older every day and had long since given
over caring for anything except her foods and her wines and
would not have troubled to look at the man had he come near,

and she was even glad when Wang Lung came to her less and less with his age.

Now when Wang Lung entered with his youngest son from the fields, his eldest son drew his father aside and he said,

"I will not endure that fellow my cousin in the house any more with his peepings and his lounging about with his robes unbuttoned and his eyes on the slaves." He did not dare to say further what he thought, "And even he dares to peep into the inner courts at your own woman," because he remembered with a sickness in his vitals that he himself had once hung about this woman of his father's, and now seeing her fat and older as she was, he could not dream that he had ever done this thing and he was bitterly ashamed of it and would not for anything have recalled it to his father's memory. So he was silent of that, and mentioned only the slaves.

Wang Lung had come in robustly from the fields and in high humor because the water was off the land and the air dry and warm and because he was pleased with his youngest son that he had gone with him, and he answered, angry at this fresh trouble in his house,

"Well, and you are a foolish child to be forever thinking of this. You have grown fond and too fond of your wife and it is not seemly, for a man ought not to care for his wife that his parents gave him above all else in the world. It is not meet for a man to love his wife with a foolish and overweening love, as though she were a harlot."

Then the young man was stung with this rebuke of his father against him, for more than anything he feared any who accused him of behavior that was not correct, as though he were common and ignorant, and he answered quickly,

"It is not for my wife. It is because it is unseemly in my father's house."

But Wang Lung did not hear him. He was musing in anger and he said again,

"And am I never to be done with all this trouble in my house between male and female? Here am I passing into my age and my blood cools and I am freed at last from lusts and I would have a little peace, and must I endure the lusts and jealousies of my sons?" And then after a little silence, he shouted again, "Well, and what would you have me do?"

Now the young man had waited patiently enough for his father's anger to pass, for he had something to say, and this

Wang Lung saw clearly when he shouted, "What would you have me do?" The young man then answered steadily,

"I wish we could leave this house and that we could go into the town and live. It is not meet that we go on living in the country like hinds and we could go and we could leave my uncle and his wife and my cousin here and we could live safely in the town behind the gates."

Wang Lung laughed bitterly and shortly when his son said this, and he threw the desire of the young man aside for something worthless and not to be considered.

"This is my house," he said stoutly, seating himself at the table and drawing his pipe toward him from where it stood, "and you may live in it or not. My house and my land it is, and if it were not for the land we should all starve as the others did, and you could not walk about in your dainty robes idle as a scholar. It is the good land that has made you something better than a farmer's lad."

And Wang Lung rose and tramped about loudly in the middle room and he behaved roughly and he spat upon the floor and acted as a farmer may, because although one side of his heart triumphed in his son's fineness, the other side was robust and scornful of him and this although he knew he was secretly proud of his son, and proud because none who looked at this son could dream that he was but one generation removed from the land itself.

But the eldest son was not ready to give over. He followed his father saying,

"Well, and there is the old great house of the Hwangs. The front part of it is filled with this and that of common people but the inner courts are locked and silent and we could rent them and live there peacefully and you and my youngest brother could come to and fro to the land and I would not be angered by this dog, my cousin." And then he persuaded his father and he allowed the tears to come into his eyes and he forced them upon his cheeks and did not wipe them away and he said again, "Well, and I try to be a good son and I do not gamble and smoke opium and I am content with the woman you have given me and I ask a little of you and it is all."

Now whether the tears would have alone moved Wang Lung he did not know, but he was moved by the words of his son when he said "the great house of the Hwangs."

Never had Wang Lung forgotten that once he had gone crawling into that great house and stood ashamed in the

208

presence of those who lived there so that he was frightened of even the gateman, and this had remained a memory of shame to him all his life and he hated it. Through all his life he had the sense that he was held in the eyes of men a little lower than those who lived in the town, and when he stood before the Old Mistress of the great house, this sense became crisis. So when his son said, "We could live in the great house," the thought leaped into his mind as though he saw it actually before his eyes, "I could sit on that seat where that old one sat and from whence she bade me stand like a serf, and now I could sit there and so call another into my presence." And he mused and he said to himself again, "This I could do if I wished."

And he toyed with the thought and he sat silent and he did not answer his son, but he put tobacco in his pipe and lit it with a spill that stood ready and he smoked and he dreamed of what he could do if he wished. So not because of his son and not because of his uncle's son he dreamed that he could live in the House of Hwang, which was to him forever the great house.

Therefore although he was not willing at first to say that he would go or that he would change anything, yet thereafter he was more than ever displeased with the idleness of his uncle's son, and he watched the man sharply and he saw that it was true he did cast eyes at the maids and Wang Lung muttered and said,

"Now I cannot live with this lustful dog in my house."

And he looked at his uncle and he saw that he grew thin as he smoked his opium and his skin was yellow with opium and he was bent and old and he spat blood when he coughed; and he looked at his uncle's wife and she was a cabbage of a woman who took eagerly to her opium pipe and was satisfied with it and drowsy; and these were little trouble enough now, and the opium had done what Wang Lung wished it would do.

But here was the uncle's son, this man, still unwed, and a wild beast for his desires, and he would not yield to opium easily as the two old ones had done and take out his lusts in dreams. And Wang Lung would not willingly let him wed in the house, because of the spawn he would breed and one like him was enough. Neither would the man work, since there was no need and none to drive him to it, unless the hours he spent away at night could be called work. But even these grew less frequent, for as men returned to the land order came back to the villages and to the town and the robbers withdrew to the hills in the northwest, and the man would not go with them, preferring to live on Wang Lung's bounty. Thus he was a thorn in the household and he hung about everywhere, talking and idling and yawning, and half dressed even at noon.

One day, therefore, when Wang Lung went into the town to see his second son at the grain market he asked him,

'Well, my second son, what say you of the thing your elder brother desires, that we move into the town to the great house if we can rent part of it?"

The second son was grown a young man by now and he had grown smooth and neat and like the other clerks in the shop, although still small of stature and yellow-skinned and with crafty eyes, and he answered smoothly,

"It is an excellent thing and it would suit me well, for then I could wed and have my wife there also and we would all be under one roof as a great family is."

Now Wang Lung had done nothing toward the wedding of this son, for he was a cool youth and cool-blooded and there had never been any sign of lust in him and Wang Lung had much else to trouble him. Now, however, he said in some shame, for he knew he had not done well by his second son, "Well, now I have said to myself this long time that you should be wed, but what with this thing and that I have not had time, and with this last famine and having to avoid all feasting—but now that men may eat again, the thing shall be done."

And he cast about secretly in his mind where he should find a maid. The second son said then,

"Well, and wed I will then, for it is a good thing and better than spending money on a jade when the need comes, and it is right for a man to have sons. But do not get me a wife from a house in town, such as my brother has, for she will talk forever of what was in her father's house and make me spend money and it will be an anger to me."

Wang Lung heard this with astonishment, for he had not known that his daughter-in-law was thus, seeing only that she was a woman careful to be correct in her behavior and fair enough in her looks. But it seemed to him wise talk and he was rejoiced that his son was sharp and clever for the saving of money. This lad he had, indeed, scarcely known at all, for he grew up weak beside the vigor of the elder brother, and except for his piping tales he was not a child or a youth to whom one would pay great heed, so that when he went into the shop, Wang Lung forgot him day after day, except to answer when anyone asked him how many children he had, "Well, and I have three sons."

Now he looked at the youth, his second son, and he saw his smooth-cut hair, oiled and flat, and his clean gown of small-patterned grey silk, and he saw the youth's neat movements and steady, secret eyes and he said to himself in his surprise,

"Well, and this also is my son!" And aloud he said, "What sort of a maid would you have, then?"

Then the young man answered as smoothly and steadily as if he had the thing planned before,

"I desire a maid from a village, of good landed family and without poor relatives, and one who will bring a good dowry with her, neither plain nor fair to look upon, and a good cook, so that even though there are servants in the kitchen she may watch them. And she must be such a one that if she buys rice it will be enough and not a handful over and if she buys cloth the garment will be well cut so that the scraps of cloth left over should lie in the palm of her hand. Such an one I want."

Now Wang Lung was the more astonished when he heard this talk, for here was a young man whose life he had not seen, even though it was his own son. It was not such blood as this that ran in his own lusty body when he was young, nor in the body of his eldest son; yet he admired the wisdom of the young man and he said laughing,

"Well, and I shall seek such a maid and Ching shall look for her among the villages."

Still laughing, he went away and he went down the street of the great house and he hesitated between the stone lions and then, since there was none to stop him, he went in and the front courts were as he remembered them when he came in to seek the whore whom he feared for his son. The trees were hung with drying clothes and women sat everywhere gossiping as they drove their long needles back and forth through shoe soles they made, and children rolled naked and dusty upon the tiles of the courts and the place reeked with the smell of common people who swarm into the courts of the great when the great are gone. And he looked towards the door where the whore had lived, but the door stood ajar and another lived there now, an old man, and for this Wang Lung was glad and he went on.

Now Wang Lung in the old days when the great family were there would have felt himself one of these common people and against the great and half hating, half fearful of them. But now that he had land and that he had silver and gold hidden safely away, he despised these people who swarmed everywhere, and he said to himself that they were filthy and he picked his way among them with his nose up and breathing lightly because of the stink they made. And he despised them and was against them as though he himself belonged to the great house.

He went back through the courts, although it was for idle curiosity and not because he had decided anything, but still he went on and at the back he found a gate locked into a court and beside it an old woman drowsing, and he looked and he saw that this was the pock-marked wife of the man who had been gateman. This astonished him, and he looked at her, whom he had remembered as buxom and middleaged, now haggard and wrinkled and white haired, and her teeth were yellow snags loose in her jaws, and looking at her thus he saw in a full moment how many and how swift were the years that had passed since he was a young man coming with his first-born son in his arms, and for the first time in his life Wang Lung felt his age creeping upon him.

Then he said somewhat sadly to the old woman,

"Wake and let me into the gate."

And the old woman started up blinking and licking her dry lips, and she said,

"I am not to open except to such as may rent the whole inner courts."

And Wang Lung said suddenly,

"Well, and so I may, if the place please me."

But he did not tell her who he was, only he went in after her and he remembered the way well and he followed her. There the courts stood in silence; there the little room where he had left his basket; here the long verandas supported by the delicate, red-varnished pillars. He followed her into the great hall itself, and his mind went back how quickly over the years past when he had stood there waiting to wed a slave of the house. There before him was the great carven dais where the old lady had sat, her fragile, tended body wrapped in silvery satin.

And moved by some strange impulse he went forward and he sat down where she had sat and he put his hand on the table and from the eminence it gave him he looked down on the bleary face of the old hag who blinked at him and waited in silence for what he would do. Then some satisfaction he had longed for all his days without knowing it swelled up in his heart and he smote the table with his hand and he said suddenly,

"This house I will have!"

29

In these days when Wang Lung had decided a thing he could not do it quickly enough. As he grew older he grew impatient to have done with things and to sit in the latter part of the day at peace and idle and to watch the late sun and sleep a little after he had strolled about his land. So he told his elder son what he had decided and he commanded the young man to arrange the matter, and he sent for his second son to come and help with the moving and on a day when they were ready they moved, first Lotus and Cuckoo and their slaves and goods, and then Wang Lung's eldest son and his wife and their servants and the slaves.

But Wang Lung himself would not go at once, and he kept with him his youngest son. When the moment came for leaving the land whereon he was born he could not do it easily nor so quickly as he had thought and he said to his sons when they urged him,

"Well then, prepare a court for me to use alone and on a day that I wish I will come, and it will be a day before my grandson is born, and when I wish I can come back to my land."

And when they urged him yet again, he said,

"Well, and there is my poor fool and whether to take her with me or not I do not know, but take her I must, for there is no one who will see if she is fed or not unless I do it."

This Wang Lung said in some reproach to the wife of his eldest son, for she would not suffer the poor fool near her, but was finicking and squeamish and she said, "Such an one should not be alive at all, and it is enough to mar the child in me to look at her." And Wang Lung's eldest son remembered the dislike of

213

his wife and so now he was silent and said no more. Then Wang Lung repented his reproach and he said mildly,

"I will come when the maid is found who is to wed the second son, for it is easier to stay here where Ching is until the matter is completed."

The second son, therefore, gave over his urging.

There was left in the house, then, none but the uncle and his wife and son and Ching and the laboring men, besides Wang Lung and his youngest son and the fool. And the uncle and his wife and son moved into the inner courts where Lotus had been and they took it for their own, but this did not grieve Wang Lung unduly, for he saw clearly there were not many days of life left for his uncle and when the idle old man was dead Wang Lung's duty to that generation was over and if the younger man did not do as he was told none would blame Wang Lung if he cast him out. Then Ching moved into the outer rooms and the laborers with him, and Wang Lung and his son and the fool lived in the middle rooms, and Wang Lung hired a stout woman to be servant to them.

And Wang Lung slept and rested himself and took no heed of anything, for he was suddenly very weary and the house was peaceful. There was none to trouble him, for his youngest son was a silent lad who kept out of his father's way and Wang Lung scarcely knew what he was, so silent a lad was he.

But at last Wang Lung stirred himself to bid Ching find a maid for his second son to wed.

Now Ching grew old and withered and lean as a reed, but there was the strength of an old and faithful dog in him yet, although Wang Lung would no longer let him lift a hoe in his hand or follow the oxen behind the plow. But still he was useful for he watched the labor of others and he stood by when the grain was weighed and measured. So when he heard what Wang Lung wished him to do he washed himself and put on his good blue cotton coat and he went hither and thither to this village and that and he looked at many maidens and at last he came back and he said,

"Now would I lief have to choose a wife for myself than for your son. But if it were I and I young, there is a maid three villages away, a good, buxom, careful maid with no fault except a ready laugh, and her father is willing and glad to be tied to your family by his daughter. And the dowry is good for these times, and he has land. But I said I could give no promise until you gave it."

214

It seemed to Wang Lung then that this was good enough and he was anxious to be done with it and so he gave his promise and when the papers were come he set his mark to them, and he was relieved and he said,

"Now there is but one more son and I am finished with all this wedding and marrying and I am glad I am so near my peace."

And when it was done and the wedding day set, he rested and sat in the sun and slept even as his father had done before him.

Then it seemed to Wang Lung that as Ching grew feeble with age and since he himself grew heavy and drowsy with his food and his age and his third son was yet too young for responsibility, that it would be well to rent some of his farthest fields to others in the village. This Wang Lung did, then, and many of the men in the villages near by came to Wang Lung to rent his land and to become his tenants, and the rent was decided upon, half of the harvest to go to Wang Lung because he owned the land, and half to the one who hired because of his labor, and there were other things which each must furnish besides: Wang Lung certain stores of manure and beancake and of sesame refuse from his oil mill after the sesame was ground, and the tenant to reserve certain crops for the use of Wang Lung's house.

And then, since there was not the need for his management that there had been, Wang Lung went sometimes into the town and slept in the court which he caused to be prepared for him, but when day came he was back upon his land, walking through the gate in the wall about the town as soon as it was open after dawn came. And he smelled the fresh smell of the fields and when he came to his own land he rejoiced in it.

Then as if the gods were kind for the once and had prepared peace for his old age his uncle's son, who grew restless in the house now quiet and without women save for the stout serving woman who was wife to one of the laborers, this uncle's son heard of a war to the north and he said to Wang Lung,

"It is said there is a war to the north of us and I will go and join it for something to do and to see. This I will if you will give me silver to buy more clothes and my bedding and a foreign firestick to put over my shoulder."

Then Wang Lung's heart leaped with pleasure but he hid his pleasure artfully and he demurred in pretense and he said,

"Now you are the only son of my uncle and after you there are none to carry on his body and if you go to war what will happen?"

But the man answered, laughing,

"Well, and I am no fool and I will not stand anywhere that my life is in danger. If there is to be a battle I will go away until it is over. I wish for a change and a little travel and to see foreign parts before I am too old to do it."

So Wang Lung gave him the silver readily and this time again the giving was not hard so that he poured the money out into the man's hand and he said to himself,

"Well, and if he likes it there is an end to this curse in my house, for there is always a war somewhere in the nation." And again he said to himself, "Well, and he may even be killed, if my good fortune holds, for sometimes in wars there are those who die."

He was in high good humor, then, although he concealed it, and he comforted his uncle's wife when she wept a little to hear of her son's going, and he gave her more opium and lit her pipe for her and he said,

"Doubtless he will rise to be a military official and honor will come to us all through him."

Then at last there was peace, for there were only the two old sleeping ones in the house in the country besides his own, and in the house in the town the hour grew near for the birth of Wang Lung's grandson.

Now Wang Lung, as this hour drew near, stayed more and more in the house in town and he walked about the courts and he could never have done with musing on what had happened, and he could never have his fill of wonder at this, that here in these courts where the great family of Hwang had once lived now he lived with his wife and his sons and their wives and now a child was to be born of a third generation.

And his heart swelled within him so that nothing was too good for his money to buy and he bought lengths of satin and of silk for them all for it looked ill to see common cotton robes upon the carved chairs and about the carved tables of southern blackwood, and he bought lengths of good blue and black cotton for the slaves so not one of them needed to wear a garment ragged. This he did, and he was pleased when the friends that his eldest son had found in the town came into the courts and proud that they should see all that was.

And Wang Lung took it into his heart to eat dainty foods, and he himself, who once had been well satisfied with good wheaten bread wrapped about a stick of garlic, now that he slept late in the day and did not work with his own hands on the land, now he was not easily pleased with this dish and that, and he tasted winter bamboo and shrimps' roe and southern fish and shellfish from the northern seas and pigeons' eggs and all those things which rich men use to force their lagging appetites. And his sons ate and Lotus also, and Cuckoo, seeing all that had come about, laughed and said,

"Well, and it is like the old days when I was in these courts, only this body of mine is withered and dried now and not fit even for an old lord."

Saying this, she glanced slyly at Wang Lung and laughed again, and he pretended not to hear her lewdness, but he was pleased, nevertheless, that she had compared him to the Old Lord.

So with this idle and luxurious living and rising when they would and sleeping when they would, he waited for his grandson. Then one morning he heard the groans of a woman and he went into the courts of his eldest son and his son met him and said,

"The hour is come, but Cuckoo says it will be long, for the woman is narrowly made and it is a hard birth."

So Wang Lung went back to his own court and he sat down and listened to the cries, and for the first time in many years he was frightened and felt the need of some spirit's aid. He rose and went to the incense shop and he bought incense and he went to the temple in the town where the goddess of mercy dwells in her gilded alcove and he summoned an idling priest and gave him money and bade him thrust the incense before the goddess saying,

"It is ill for me, a man, to do it, but my first grandson is about to be born and it is a heavy labor for the mother, who is a town woman and too narrowly made, and the mother of my son is dead, and there is no woman to thrust in the incense."

Then as he watched the priest thrust it in the ashes of the urn before the goddess he thought with sudden horror, "And what if it be not a grandson but a girl!" and he called out hastily,

"Well, and if it is a grandson I will pay for a new red robe for the goddess, but nothing will I do if it is a girl!"

He went out in agitation because he had not thought of this thing, that it might be not a grandson but a girl, and he went and bought more incense, although the day was hot and in the streets the dust was a span's depth, and he went out in spite of this to the small country temple where the two sat who watched over fields and land and he thrust the incense in and lit it and he muttered to the pair,

"Well now, and we have cared for you, my father and I and my son, and now here comes the fruit of my son's body, and if it is not a son there is nothing more for the two of you."

Then having done all he could, he went back to the courts, very spent, and he sat down at his table and he wished for a slave to bring him tea and for another to bring him a towel dipped and wrung from steaming water to wipe his face, but though he clapped his hands none came. No one heeded him, and there was running to and fro, but he dared to stop no one to ask what sort of a child had been born or even if any had been born. He sat there dusty and spent and no one spoke to him.

Then at last when it seemed to him it must soon be night, so long he had waited, Lotus came in waddling upon her small feet because of her great weight and leaning upon Cuckoo, and she laughed and said loudly

"Well, and there is a son in the house of your son, and both mother and son are alive. I have seen the child and it is fair and sound."

Then Wang Lung laughed also and he rose and he slapped his hands together and laughed again and he said,

"Well, and I have been sitting here like a man with his own first son coming and not knowing what to do of this and that and afraid of everything."

And then when Lotus had gone on to her room and he sat again he fell to musing and he thought to himself,

"Well, and I did not fear like this when that other one bore her first, my son." And he sat silent and musing and he remembered within himself that day and how she had gone alone into the small dark room and how alone she had borne him sons and again sons and daughters and she bore them silently, and how she had come to the fields and worked beside him again. And here was this one, now the wife of his son, who cried like a child with her pains, and who had all the slaves running in the house, and her husband there by her door.

And he remembered as one remembers a dream long past how O-lan rested from her work a little while and fed the child richly and the white rich milk ran out of her breast and spilled upon the ground. And this seemed too long past ever to have been.

Then his son came in smiling and important and he said loudly,

"The man child is born, my father, and now we must find a woman to nurse him with her breasts, for I will not have my wife's beauty spoiled with the nursing and her strength sapped with it. None of the women of position in the town do so."

And Wang Lung said sadly, although why he was sad he did not know,

"Well, and if it must be so, let it be so, if she cannot nurse her own child."

When the child was a month old Wang Lung's son, its father, gave the birth feasts, and to it he invited guests from the town and his wife's father and mother, and all the great of the town. And he had dyed scarlet many hundreds of hens' eggs, and these he gave to every guest and to any who sent guests, and there was feasting and joy through the house, for the child was a goodly fat boy and he had passed his tenth day and lived and this was a fear gone, and they all rejoiced.

And when the birth feast was over Wang Lung's son came to his father and he said,

"Now that there are the three generations in this house, we should have the tablets of ancestors that great families have, and we should set the tablets up to be worshipped at the feast days for we are an established family now."

This pleased Wang Lung greatly, and so he ordered it and so it was carried out, and there in the great hall the row of tablets was set up, his grandfather's name on one and then his father's, and the spaces left empty for Wang Lung's name and his son's when they should die. And Wang Lung's son bought an incense urn and set it before the tablets.

When this was finished Wang Lung remembered the red robe he had promised the goddess of mercy and so he went to the temple to give the money for it.

And then, on his way back, as if the gods cannot bear to give freely and not hide sting somewhere in the gift one came running from the harvest fields to tell him that Ching lay dying suddenly and had asked if Wang Lung would come to see him die. Wang Lung hearing the panting runner, cried angrily,

"Now I suppose that accursed pair in the temple are jealous

because I gave a red robe to a town goddess and I suppose they do not know they have no power over childbirth and only over land."

And although his noon meal stood ready for him to eat he would not take up his chopsticks, although Lotus called loudly to him to wait until after the evening sun came; he would not stay for her, and he went out. Then when Lotus saw he did not heed her she sent a slave after him with an umbrella of oiled paper, but so fast did Wang Lung run that the stout maid had difficulty in holding the umbrella over his head.

Wang Lung went at once to the room where Ching had been laid and he called out loudly to anyone,

"Now how did all this come about?"

The room was full of laborers crowding about and they answered in confusion and haste,

"He would work himself at the threshing . . ." "We told him not at his age . . ." "There was a laborer who is newly hired . . ." "He could not hold the flail rightly and Ching would show him . . ." "It is labor too hard for an old man . . ."

Then Wang Lung called out in a terrible voice,

"Bring me this laborer!"

And they pushed the man in front before Wang Lung, and he stood there trembling and his bare knees knocking together, a great, ruddy, coarse, country lad, with his teeth sticking out in a shelf over his lower lip and round dull eyes like an ox's eyes. But Wang Lung had no pity on him. He slapped the lad on both his cheeks and he took the umbrella from the slave's hand and he beat the lad about the head, and none dared stop him lest his anger go into his blood and at his age poison him. And the bumpkin stood it humbly, blubbering a little and sucking his teeth.

Then Ching moaned from the bed where he lay and Wang Lung threw down the umbrella and he cried out,

"Now this one will die while I am beating a fool!"

And he sat down beside Ching and took his hand and held it, and it was as light and dry and small as a withered oak leaf and it was not possible to believe that any blood ran through it, so dry and light and hot it was. But Ching's face, which was pale and yellow every day, was now dark and spotted with his scanty blood, and his half-opened eyes were filmed and blind and his breath came in gusts. Wang Lung leaned down to him and said loudly in his ear,

"Here am I and I will buy you a coffin second to my father's only!"

But Ching's ear were filled with his blood, and if he heard Wang Lung he made no sign, but he only lay there panting and dying and so he died.

When he was dead Wang Lung leaned over him and he wept as he had not wept when his own father died, and he ordered a coffin of the best kind, and he hired priests for the funeral and he walked behind wearing white mourning. He made his eldest son, even, wear white bands on his ankles as though a relative had died, although his son complained and said,

"He was only an upper servant, and it is not suitable so to mourn for a servant."

But Wang Lung compelled him for three days. And if Wang Lung had had his way wholly, he would have buried Ching inside the earthen wall where his father and O-lan were buried. But his sons would not have it and they complained and said,

"Shall our mother and grandfather lie with a servant? And must we also in our time?"

Then Wang Lung, because he could not contend with them and because at his age he would have peace in his house, buried Ching at the entrance to the wall and he was comforted with what he had done, and he said,

"Well, and it is meet, for he has ever stood guardian to me against evil." And he directed his sons that when he himself died he should lie nearest to Ching.

Then less than ever did Wang Lung go to see his lands, because now Ching was gone it stabbed him to go alone and he was weary of labor and his bones ached when he walked over the rough fields alone. So he rented out all his land that he could and men took it eagerly, for it was known to be good land. But Wang Lung would never talk of selling a foot of any piece, and he would only rent it for an agreed price for a year at a time. Thus he felt it all his own and still in his hand.

And he appointed one of the laborers and his wife and children to live in the country house and to care for the two old opium dreamers. Then seeing his youngest son's wistful eyes, he said,

"Well, and you may come with me into the town, and I will take my fool with me too, and she can live in my court where I am. It is too lonely for you now that Ching is gone, and with him gone, I am not sure that they will be kind to the poor fool seeing there will be none to tell if she is beaten or ill fed. And there is no one now to teach you concerning the land, now that Ching is gone."

So Wang Lung took his youngest son and his fool with him and thereafter he came scarcely at all for a long time to the house on his land.

30

NOW TO WANG LUNG it seemed there was nothing left to be desired in his condition, and now he could sit in his chair in the sun beside his fool and he could smoke his water pipe and be at peace since his land was tended and the money from it coming into his hand without care from him.

And so it might have been if it had not been for that eldest son of his who was never content with what was going on well enough but must be looking aside for more. So he came to his father saying,

"There is this and that which we need in this house and we must not think we can be a great family just because we live in these inner courts. Now there is my younger brother's wedding due in a bare six months and we have not chairs enough to seat the guests and we have not bowls enough nor tables enough nor anything enough in these rooms. It is a shame, moreover, to ask guests to come through the great gates and through all that common swarm with their stinks and their noise, and with my brother wed and his children and mine to come we need those courts also."

Then Wang Lung looked at his son standing there in his handsome raiment and he shut his eyes and drew hard on his pipe and he growled forth,

"Well, and what now and what again?"

The young man saw his father was weary of him but he said stubbornly, and he made his voice a little louder,

"I say we should have the outer courts also and we should

have what befits a family with so much money as we have and good land as we have."

Then Wang Lung muttered into his pipe,

"Well, and the land is mine and you have never put your hand to it."

"Well, and my father," the young man cried out at this, "it was you who would have me a scholar and when I try to be a fitting son to a man of land you scorn me and would make a hind of me and my wife." And the young man turned himself away stormily and made as though he would knock his brains out against a twisted pine tree that stood there in the court.

Wang Lung was frightened at this, lest the young man do himself an injury, since he had been fiery always, and so he called out,

"Do as you like—do as you like—only do not trouble me with it!"

Hearing this, the son went away quickly lest his father change and he went well pleased. As quickly as he was able, then, he bought tables and chairs from Soochow, carved and wrought, and he bought curtains of red silk to hang in the doorways and he bought vases large and small and he bought scrolls to hang on the wall and as many as he could of beautiful women, and he bought curious rocks to make rockeries in the courts such as he had seen in southern parts, and thus he busied himself for many days.

With all this coming and going he had to pass many times through the outer courts, even every day, and he could not pass among the common people without sticking his nose up and he could not bear them, so that the people who lived there laughed at him after he had passed and they said,

"He has forgotten the smell of the manure in the dooryard on his father's farm!"

But still none dared to speak thus as he passed, for he was a rich man's son. When the feast came when rents are decided upon these common people found that the rent for the rooms and the courts where they lived had been greatly raised, because another would pay that much for them, and they had to move away. Then they knew it was Wang Lung's eldest son who had done this, although he was clever and said nothing and did it all by letters to the son of the old Lord Hwang in foreign parts, and this son of the Old Lord cared for nothing except where and how he could get the most money for the old house.

The common people had to move, then, and they moved complaining and cursing because a rich man could do as he would and they packed their tattered possessions and went away swelling with anger and muttering that one day they would come back even as the poor do come back when the rich are too rich.

But all this Wang Lung did not hear, since he was in the inner courts and seldom came forth, since he slept and ate and took his ease as his age came on, and he left the thing in the hands of his eldest son. And his son called carpenters and clever masons and they repaired the rooms and the moon gates between the courts that the common people had ruined with their coarse ways of living, and he built again the pools and he bought flecked and golden fish to put in them. And after it was all finished and made beautiful as far as he knew beauty, he planted lotus and lilies in the pools, and the scarlet-berried bamboo of India and everything he could remember he had seen in southern parts. And his wife came out to see what he had done and the two of them walked about through every court and room and she saw this and that still lacking, and he listened with great heed to all she said that he might do it.

Then people on the streets of the town heard of all that Wang Lung's eldest son did, and they talked of what was being done in the great house, now that a rich man lived there again. And people who had said Wang The Farmer now said Wang The Big Man or Wang The Rich Man.

The money for all these doings had gone out of Wang Lung's hand bit by bit, so that he scarcely knew when it went, for the eldest son came and said,

"I need a hundred pieces of silver here"; or he said, "There is a good gate which needs only an odd bit of silver to mend it as good as new"; or he said, "There is a place where a long table should stand."

And Wang Lung gave him the silver bit by bit, as he sat smoking and resting in his court, for the silver came in easily from the land at every harvest and whenever he needed it, and so he gave it easily. He would not have known how much he gave had not his second son come into his court one morning when the sun was scarcely over the wall and he said,

"My father, is there to be no end to all this pouring out of money and need we live in a palace? So much money lent out at twenty per cent would have brought in many pounds of silver, and what is the use of all these pools and flowering trees that bear no fruit even, and all these idle, blooming lilies?"

Wang Lung saw that these two brothers would quarrel over this yet, and he said hastily, lest he never have any peace,

"Well, and it is all in honor of your wedding."

Then the young man answered, smiling crookedly and without any meaning of mirth,

"It is an odd thing for the wedding to cost ten times as much as the bride. Here is our inheritance, that should be divided between us when you are dead, being spent now for nothing but the pride of my elder brother."

And Wang Lung knew the determination of this second son of his and he knew he would never have done with him if talk began, so he said hastily,

"Well—well—I will have an end to it—I will speak to your brother and I will shut my hand. It is enough. You are right!"

The young man had brought out a paper on which was written a list of all the moneys his brother had spent, and Wang Lung saw the length of the list and he said quickly,

"I have not eaten yet and at my age I am faint in the morning until I eat. Another time for this." And he turned and went into his own room and so dismissed his second son.

But he spoke that same evening to his eldest son, saying,

"Have done with all this painting and polishing. It is enough. We are, after all, country folk."

But the young man answered proudly,

"That we are not. Men in the town are beginning to call us the great family Wang. It is fitting that we live somewhat suitably to that name, and if my brother cannot see beyond the meaning of silver for its own sake, I and my wife, we will uphold the honor of the name."

Now Wang Lung had not known that men so called his house, for as he grew older he went seldom even to the tea shops and no more to the grain markets since there was his second son to do his business there for him, but it pleased him secretly and so he said,

"Well, even great families are from the land and rooted in the land."

But the young man answered smartly,

"Yes, but they do not stay there. They branch forth and bear flowers and fruits."

Wang Lung would not have his son answering him too easily and quickly like this, so he said,

"I have said what I have said. Have done with pouring out silver. And roots, if they are to bear fruits, must be kept well in the soil of the land."

Then since evening came on, he wished his son would go away out of this court and into his own. He wished the young man to go away and leave him in peace in the twilight and alone. But there was no peace for him with this son of his. This son was willing to obey his father now for he was satisfied in the rooms and the courts, at least for the time, and he had done what he would do, but he began again,

"Well, let it be enough, but there is another thing."

Then Wang Lung flung his pipe down upon the ground and he shouted,

"Am I never to be in peace?"

And the young man went on stubbornly,

"It is not for myself or for my son. It is for my youngest brother who is your own son. It is not fit that he grow up so ignorant. He should be taught something."

Wang Lung stared at this for it was a new thing. He had long ago settled the life of his youngest son, what it was to be, and he said now,

"There is no need for any more stomachsful of characters in this house. Two is enough, and he is to be on the land when I am dead."

"Yes, and for this he weeps in the night, and this is why he is so pale and so reedy a lad," answered the eldest son.

Now Wang Lung had never thought to ask his youngest son what he wished to do with his life, since he had decided one son must be on the land, and this that his eldest son had said struck him between the brows and he was silent. He picked up his pipe from the ground slowly and pondered about his third son. He was a lad not like either of his brothers, a lad as silent as his mother, and because he was silent none paid any attention to him.

"Have you heard him say this?" asked Wang Lung of his eldest son, uncertainly.

"Ask him for yourself, my father," replied the young man.

"Well, but one lad must be on the land," said Wang Lung suddenly in argument and his voice was very loud.

"But why, my father?" urged the young man. "You are a man who need not have any sons like serfs. It is not fitting. People will say you have a mean heart. 'There is a man who makes his son into a hind while he lives like a prince.' So people will say."

Now the young man spoke cleverly for he knew that his father cared mightily what people said of him, and he went on,

"We could call a tutor and teach him and we could send him to a southern school and he could learn and since there is I in your house to help you and my second brother in his good trade, let the lad choose what he will."

Then Wang Lung said at last,

"Send him here to me."

After a while the third son came and stood before his father and Wang Lung looked at him to see what he was. And he saw a tall and slender lad, who was neither his father nor his mother, except that he had his mother's gravity and silence. But there was more beauty in him than there had been in his mother, and for beauty alone he had more of it than any of Wang Lung's children except the second girl who had gone to her husband's family and belonged no more to the house of Wang. But across the lad's forehead and almost a mar to his beauty were his two black brows, too heavy and black for his young, pale face, and when he frowned, and he frowned easily, these black brows met, heavy and straight, across his brow.

And Wang Lung stared at his son and after he had seen him well, he said,

"Your eldest brother says you wish to learn to read."

And the boy said, scarcely stirring his lips,

"Aye."

Wang Lung shook the ash from his pipe and pushed the fresh tobacco in slowly with his thumb.

"Well, and I suppose that means you do not want to work on the land and I shall not have a son on my own land, and I with sons and to spare."

This he said with bitterness, but the boy said nothing. He stood there straight and still in his long white robe of summer linen, and at last Wang Lung was angry at his silence and he shouted at him,

"Why do you not speak? Is it true you do not want to be on the land?"

And again the boy answered only the one word,

"Aye."

And Wang Lung looking at him said to himself at last that these sons of his were too much for him in his old age and they were a care and burden to him and he did not know what to

227

do with them, and he shouted again, feeling himself ill-used by these sons of his,

"What is it to me what you do? Get away from me!"

Then the boy went away swiftly and Wang Lung sat alone and he said to himself that his two girls were better after all than his sons, one, poor fool that she was, never wanted anything more than a bit of any food and her length of cloth to play with, and the other one married and away from his house. And the twilight came down over the court and shut him into it alone.

Nevertheless, as Wang Lung always did when his anger passed, he let his sons have their way, and he called his elder son and he said,

"Engage a tutor for the third one if he wills it, and let him do as he likes, only I am not to be troubled about it."

And he called his second son and said,

"Since I am not to have a son on the land it is your duty to see to the rents and to the silver that comes in from the land at each harvest. You can weigh and measure and you shall be my steward."

The second son was pleased enough for this meant the money would pass through his hands at least, and he would know what came in and he could complain to his father if more than enough was spent in the house.

Now this second son of his seemed more strange to Wang than any of his sons, for even at the wedding day, which came on, he was careful of the money spent on meats and on wines and he divided the tables carefully, keeping the best meats for his friends in the town who knew the cost of the dishes, and for the tenants and the country people who must be invited he spread tables in the courts, and to these he gave only the second best in meat and wine, since they daily ate coarse fare, and a little better was very good to them.

And the second son watched the money and the gifts that came in, and he gave to the slaves and servants the least that could be given them, so that Cuckoo sneered when into her hand he put a paltry two pieces of silver and she said in the hearing of many,

"Now a truly great family is not so careful of its silver and one can see that this family does not rightly belong in these courts."

The eldest son heard this, and he was ashamed and he was afraid of her tongue and he gave her more silver secretly and he was angry with his second brother. Thus there was trouble between them even on the very wedding day when the guests sat about the tables and when the bride's chair was entering the courts.

And of his own friends the eldest son asked but a few of the least considered to the feast, because he was ashamed of his brother's parsimony and because the bride was but a village maid. He stood aside scornfully, and he said,

"Well, and my brother has chosen an earthen pot when he might, from my father's position, have had a cup of jade."

And he was scornful and nodded stiffly when the pair came and bowed before him and his wife as their elder brother and sister. And the wife of the eldest son was correct and haughty and bowed only the least that could be considered proper for her position.

Now of all of them who lived in these courts it seemed there was none wholly at peace and comfortable there except the small grandson who had been born to Wang Lung. Even Wang Lung himself, waking within the shadows of the great carved bed where he slept in his own room that was next to the court where Lotus lived, even he woke to dream sometimes that he was back in the simple, dark, earth-walled house where a man could throw his cold tea down where he would not splatter a piece of carven wood, and where a step took him into his own fields.

As for Wang Lung's sons, there was continual unrest, the eldest son lest not enough be spent and they be belittled in the eyes of men and lest the villagers come walking through the great gate when a man from the town was there to call, and so make them ashamed before him; and the second son lest there was waste and money gone; and the youngest son striving to make repair the years he had lost as a farmer's son.

But there was one who ran staggering hither and yon and content with his life and it was the son of the eldest son. This small one never thought of any other place than this great house and to him it was neither great nor small but only his house, and here was his mother and here his father and grandfather and all those who lived but to serve him. And from this one did Wang Lung secure peace, and he could never have enough of watching him and laughing at him and picking him up when he fell. He remembered also what his own father had done, and he delighted to take a girdle and put it about the

229

child and walk, holding him thus from falling, and they went from court to court, and the child pointed at the darting fish in the pools and jabbered this and that and snatched the head of a flower and was at ease in the midst of everything, and only thus did Wang Lung find peace.

Nor was there only this one. The wife of the eldest son was faithful and she conceived and bore and conceived and bore regularly and faithfully, and each child as it was born had its slave. Thus Wang Lung each year saw more children in the courts and more slaves, so that when one said to him, "There is to be another mouth again in the eldest son's court," he only laughed and said,

"Eh—eh—well, there is rice and enough for all since we have the good land."

And he was pleased when his second son's wife bore also in her season, and she gave birth to a girl first as was fitting and it was seemly out of respect to her sister-in-law. Wang Lung, then, in the space of five years had four grandsons and three grand-daughters and the courts were filled with their laughter and their weeping.

Now five years is nothing in a man's life except when he is very young and very old, and if it gave to Wang Lung these others, it took away also that old dreamer, his uncle, whom he had almost forgotten except to see that he and his old wife were fed and clothed and had what they wished of opium.

On the winter of the fifth year it was very cold, more cold than any thirty years before, so that for the first time in Wang Lung's memory the moat froze about the wall of the town and men could walk back and forth on it. A continual icy wind blew also from the northeast and there was nothing, no garment of goatskin or fur, that could keep a man warm. In every room in the great house they burned braziers of charcoal and still it was cold enough to see a man's breath when he blew it out.

Now Wang Lung's uncle and his wife had long since smoked all the flesh off their bones and they lay day in and day out on their beds like two old dry sticks, and there was no warmth in them. And Wang Lung heard his uncle could not sit up even any more in his bed and he spat blood whenever he moved at all, and he went out to see and he saw there were not many hours left for the old man.

Then Wang Lung bought two coffins of wood good enough

but not too good, and he had the coffins taken into the room where his uncle lay that the old man might see them and die in comfort, knowing there was a place for his bones. And his uncle said, his voice a quavering whisper,

"Well, and you are a son to me and more than that wandering one of my own."

And the old woman said, but she was still stouter than the man,

"If I die before that son comes home, promise me you will find a good maid for him, so that he may have sons for us yet." And Wang Lung promised it.

What hour his uncle died Wang Lung did not know, except that he lay dead one evening when the serving woman went in to take a bowl of soup, and Wang Lung buried him on a bitter cold day when the wind blew the snow over the land in clouds, and he put the coffin in the family enclosure beside his father, only a little lower than his father's grave, but above the place where his own was to be.

Then Wang Lung caused mourning to be made for the whole family and they wore the sign of mourning for a year, not because any truly mourned the passing of this old man who had never been anything but a care to them, but because it is fitting so to do in a great family when a relative dies.

Then Wang Lung moved his uncle's wife into the town where she would not be alone, and he gave her a room at the end of a far court for her own, and he told Cuckoo to supervise a slave in the care of her, and the old woman sucked her opium pipe and lay on her bed in great content, sleeping day after day, and her coffin was beside her where she could see it for her comfort.

And Wang Lung marvelled to think that once he had feared her for a great fat blowsy country woman, idle and loud, she who lay there now shrivelled and yellow and silent, and as shrivelled and yellow as the Old Mistress had been in the fallen House of Hwang.

31

Now ALL HIS life long Wang Lung had heard of war here and there but he had never seen the thing come near except the once that he wintered in the southern city when he was young. It had never come nearer to him than that, although he had often heard men say from the time he was a child, "There is a war to the west this year," or they said, "War is to the east or the northeast."

And to him war was a thing like earth and sky and water and why it was no one knew but only that it was. Now and again he heard men say, "We will go to the wars." This they said when they were about to starve and would rather be soldiers than beggars; and sometimes men said it when they were restless at home as the son of his uncle had said it, but however this was, the war was always away and in a distant place. Then suddenly like a reasonless wind out of heaven the thing came near.

Wang Lung heard of it first from his second son who came home from the market one day for his noon rice and he said to his father,

"The price of grain has risen suddenly, for the war is to the south of us now and nearer every day, and we must hold our stores of grain until later for the price will go higher and higher as the armies come nearer to us and we can sell for a good price."

Wang Lung listened to this as he ate and he said,

"Well, and it is a curious thing and I shall be glad to see a war for what it is, for I have heard of it all my life and never seen it."

To himself then he remembered that once he had been afraid because he would have been seized against his will, but now he was too old for use and besides he was rich and the rich need not fear anything. So he paid no great heed to the matter beyond this and he was not moved by more than a little curiosity and he said to his second son,

"Do as you think well with the grain. It is in your hands."

And in the days to come he played with his grandchildren when he was in the mood, and he slept and ate and smoked and sometimes he went to see his poor fool who sat in a far corner of his court.

Then sweeping out of the northwest like a swarm of locusts there came one day in early summer a horde of men. Wang Lung's small grandson stood at the gate with a man servant to see what passed one fine sunny morning in early spring and when he saw the long ranks of grey-coated men, he ran back to his grandfather and he cried out,

"See what comes, Old One!"

Then Wang Lung went back to the gate with him to humor him, and there the men were filling the street, filling the town, and Wang Lung felt as though air and sunlight had been suddenly cut off because of the numbers of grey men tramping heavily and in unison through the town. Then Wang Lung looked at them closely and he saw that every man held an implement of some sort with a knife sticking out of the end, and the face of every man was wild and fierce and coarse; even though some were only lads, they were so. And Wang Lung drew the child to him hastily when he saw their faces and he murmured,

"Let us go and lock the gate. They are not good men to see, my little heart."

But suddenly, before he could turn, one saw him from among the men and shouted out at him,

"Ho there, my old father's nephew!"

Wang Lung looked up at this call, and he saw the son of his uncle, and he was clad like the others and dusty and grey, but his face was wilder and more fierce than any. And he laughed harshly and called out to his fellows,

"Here we may stop, my comrades, for this is a rich man and my relative!"

Before Wang Lung could move in his horror, the horde was pouring past him into his own gates and he was powerless in their midst. Into his courts they poured like evil filthy water, filling every corner and crack, and they laid themselves down on the floors and they dipped with their hands in the pools and drank, and they clattered their knives down upon carven tables and they spat where they would and shouted at each other.

Then Wang Lung, in despair over what had happened, ran back with the child to find his eldest son. He went into his son's courts and there his son sat reading a book and he rose when his father entered, and when he heard what Wang Lung gasped forth, he began to groan and he went out.

But when he saw his cousin he did not know whether to curse him or to be courteous to him. But he looked and he groaned forth to his father who was behind him,

"Every man with a knife!"

So he was courteous then and he said,

"Well, and my cousin, welcome to your home again."

And the cousin grinned widely and said,

"I have brought a few guests."

"They are welcome, being yours," said Wang Lung's eldest son, "and we will prepare a meal so that they may eat before they go on their way."

Then the cousin said, still grinning,

"Do, but make no haste afterwards, for we will rest a handful of days or a moon or a year or two, for we are to be quartered on the town until the war calls."

Now when Wang Lung and his son heard this they could scarcely conceal their dismay, but still it must be concealed because of the knives flashing everywhere through the courts, so they smiled what poor smiles they could muster and they said,

"We are fortunate—we are fortunate—"

And the eldest son pretended he must go to prepare and he took his father's hand and the two of them rushed into the inner court and the eldest son barred the door, and then the two, father and son, stared at each other in consternation, and neither knew what to do.

Then the second son came running and he beat upon the door and when they let him in he fell in and scarcely could save himself in his haste and he panted forth,

"There are soldiers everywhere in every house—even in the houses of the poor—and I came running to say you must not protest, for today a clerk in my shop, and I knew him well—he stood beside me every day at the counter—and he heard and went to his house and there were soldiers in the very room where his wife lay ill, and he protested and they ran a knife through him as though he were made of lard—as smoothly as that—and it came through him clean to the other side!

Whatever they wish we must give, but let us only pray that the war move on to other parts before long!"

Then the three of them looked at each other heavily, and thought of their women and of these lusty, hungry men. And the eldest son thought of his goodly, proper wife, and he said,

"We must put the women together in the innermost court and we must watch there day and night and keep the gates barred and the back gate of peace ready to be loosed and opened."

Thus they did. They took the women and the children and they put them all into the inner court where Lotus had lived alone with Cuckoo and her maids, and there in discomfort and crowding they lived. The eldest son and Wang Lung watched the gate day and night and the second son came when he could, and they watched as carefully by night as by day.

But there was that one, the cousin, and because he was a relative none could lawfully keep him out and he beat on the gate and he would come in and he walked about at will, carrying his knife shining and glittering and open in his hand. The eldest son followed him about, his face full of bitterness, but still not daring to say anything, for there was the knife open and glittering, and the cousin looked at this and that and appraised each woman.

He looked at the wife of the eldest son and he laughed his hoarse laugh and he said,

"Well, and it is a proper dainty bit you have, my cousin, a town lady and her feet as small as lotus buds!" And to the wife of the second son he said, "Well, here is a good stout red radish from the country—a piece of sturdy red meat!"

This he said because the woman was fat and ruddy and thick in the bone, but still not uncomely. And whereas the wife of the eldest son shrank away when he looked at her and hid her face behind her sleeve, this one laughed out, good humored and robust as she was, and she answered pertly,

"Well, and some men like a taste of hot radish, or a bite of red meat."

And the cousin answered back, promptly,

"That do I!" and he made as if to seize her hand.

All this time the eldest son was in agony of shame at this byplay between man and woman who ought not even to speak to each other, and he glanced at his wife because he was ashamed of his cousin and of his sister-in-law before her who had been more gently bred than he, and his cousin saw his timidity before his wife and said with malice,

"Well, and I had rather eat red meat any day than a slice of cold and tasteless fish like this other one!"

At this the wife of the eldest son rose in dignity and withdrew herself into an inner room. Then the cousin laughed coarsely and he said to Lotus, who sat there smoking her water pipe,

"These town women are too finicking, are they not, Old Mistress?" Then he looked at Lotus attentively and he said, "Well, and Old Mistress indeed, and if I did not know my cousin Wang Lung were rich I should know by looking at you, such a mountain of flesh you have become, and well you have eaten and how richly! It is only rich men's wives who can look like you!"

Now Lotus was mightily pleased that he called her Old Mistress, because it is a title that only the ladies of great families may have, and she laughed, deep and gurgling, out of her fat throat and she blew the ash out of her pipe and handed the pipe to a slave to fill again, and she said, turning to Cuckoo,

"Well, this coarse fellow has a turn for a joke!"

And as she said this she looked at the cousin out of her eyes coquettishly, although such glances, now that her eyes were no longer large and apricot-shaped in her great cheeks, were less coy than they once were, and seeing the look she gave him, the cousin laughed in uproar and cried out,

"Well, and it is an old bitch still!" and he laughed again loudly.

And all this time the eldest son stood there in anger and in silence.

Then when the cousin had seen everything he went to see his mother and Wang Lung went with him to show where she was. There she lay on her bed, asleep so her son could hardly wake her, but wake her he did, clapping the thick end of his gun upon the tiles of the floor at her bed's head. Then she woke and stared at him out of a dream, and he said impatiently,

"Well, and here is your son and yet you sleep on!"

She raised herself then in her bed and stared at him again and she said wondering,

"My son—it is my son——" and she looked at him for a long time and at last as though she did not know what else to do she proffered him her opium pipe, as if she could think of no greater good than this, and she said to the slave that tended her, "Prepare some for him."

And he stared back at her and he said,

236

"No, I will not have it."

Wang Lung stood there beside the bed and he was suddenly afraid lest this man should turn on him and say,

"What have you done to my mother that she is sere and yellow like this and all her good flesh gone?"

So Wang said hastily himself,

"I wish she were content with less, for it runs into a handful of silver a day for her opium, but at her age we do not dare to cross her and she wants it all." And he sighed as he spoke, and he glanced secretly at his uncle's son, but the man said nothing, only stared to see what his mother had become, and when she fell back and into her sleep again, he rose and clattered forth, using his gun as a stick in his hand.

None of the horde of idle men in the outer courts did Wang Lung and his family hate and fear as they did this cousin of theirs; this, although the men tore at the trees and the flowering shrubs of plum and almond and broke them as they would, and though they crushed the delicate carvings of chairs with their great leathern boots, and though they sullied with their private filth the pools where the flecked and golden fish swam, so that the fish died and floated on the water and rotted there, with their white bellies upturned.

For the cousin ran in and out as he would and he cast eyes at the slaves and Wang Lung and his sons looked at each other out of their eyes haggard and sunken because they dared not sleep. Then Cuckoo saw it and she said,

"Now there is only one thing to do, he must be given a slave for his pleasure while he is here, or else he will be taking where he should not."

And Wang Lung seized eagerly on what she said because it seemed to him he could not endure his life any more with all the trouble there was in his house, and so he said,

"It is a good thought."

And he bade Cuckoo go and ask the cousin what slave he would have since he had seen them all.

So Cuckoo did, then, and she came back and she said,

"He says he will have the little pale one who sleeps on the bed of the mistress."

Now this pale slave was called Pear Blossom and the one Wang Lung had bought in a famine year when she was small and piteous and half-starved, and because she was delicate always they had petted her and allowed her only to help Cuckoo and to do the lesser things about Lotus, filling her pipe and pouring her tea, and it was thus the cousin had seen her.

Now when Pear Blossom heard this she cried out as she poured the tea for Lotus, for Cuckoo said it all out before them in the inner court where they sat, and she dropped the pot and it broke into pieces on the tiles and the tea all streamed out, but the maid did not see what she had done. She only threw herself down before Lotus and she knocked her head on the tiles and she moaned forth,

"Oh, my mistress, not I—not I— I am afraid of him for my life——"

And Lotus was displeased with her and she answered pettishly,

"Now he is only a man and a man is no more than a man with a maid and they are all alike, and what is this ado?" And she turned to Cuckoo and said, "Take this slave and give her to him."

Then the young maid put her hands together piteously and cried as though she would die of weeping and fear and her little body was all trembling with her fear, and she looked from this face to that, beseeching with her weeping.

Now the sons of Wang Lung could not speak against their father's wife, nor could their wives speak if they did not, nor could the youngest son, but he stood there staring at her, his hands clenched on his bosom and his brows drawn down over his eyes, straight and black. But he did not speak. The children and the slaves looked and were silent, and there was only the sound of this dreadful, frightened weeping of the young girl.

But Wang Lung was made uncomfortable by it, and he looked at the young girl doubtfully, not caring to anger Lotus, but still moved, because he had always a soft heart. Then the maid saw his heart in his face and she ran and held his feet with her hands and she bent her head down to his feet and wept on in great sobs. And he looked down at her and saw how small her shoulders were and how they shook and he remembered the great, coarse, wild body of his cousin, now long past his youth, and a distaste for the thing seized him and he said to Cuckoo, his voice mild,

"Well now, it is ill to force the young maid like this."

These words he said mildly enough, but Lotus cried out sharply,

"She is to do as she is told, and I say it is foolish, all this weeping over a small thing that must happen soon or late with all women."

But Wang Lung was indulgent and he said to Lotus,

"Let us see first what else can be done, and let me buy for you another slave if you will, or what you will, but let me see what can be done."

Then Lotus, who had long been minded for a foreign clock and a new ruby ring, was suddenly silent and Wang Lung said to Cuckoo,

"Go and tell my cousin the girl has a vile and incurable disease, but if he will have her with that, then well enough and she shall come to him, but if he fears it as we all do, then tell him we have another and a sound one."

And he cast his eyes over the slaves who stood about and they turned away their faces and giggled and made as if they were ashamed, all except one stout wench, who was already twenty or so, and she said with her face red and laughing,

"Well, and I have heard enough of this thing and I have a mind to try it, if he will have me, and he is not so hideous a man as some."

Then Wang Lung answered in relief,

"Well, go then!"

And Cuckoo said,

"Follow close behind me, for it will happen, I know, that he will seize the fruit nearest to him." And they went out.

But the little maid still clung to Wang Lung's feet, only now she ceased her weeping and lay listening to what took place. And Lotus was still angry with her, and she rose and went into her room without a word. Then Wang Lung raised the maid gently and she stood before him, drooping and pale, and he saw that she had a little, soft, oval face, egg-shaped, exceedingly delicate and pale, and a little pale red mouth. And he said kindly,

"Now keep away from your mistress for a day or two, my child, until she is past her anger, and when that other one comes in, hide, lest he desire you again."

And she lifted her eyes and looked at him full and passionately, and she passed him, silent as a shadow, and was gone.

The cousin lived there for a moon and a half and he had the wench when he would and she conceived by him and boasted in the courts of it. Then suddenly the war called and the horde went away quickly as chaff caught and driven by the wind, and there was nothing left except the filth and destruction they had wrought. And Wang Lung's cousin girded his knife to his waist and he stood before them with his gun over his shoulder and he said mockingly,

"Well, and if I come not back to you I have left you my second self and a grandson for my mother, and it is not every man who can leave a son where he stops for a moon or two, and it is one of the benefits of the soldier's life—his seed springs up behind him and others must tend it!"

And laughing at them all, he went his way with the others.

32

WHEN THE SOLDIERS were gone Wang Lung and his two elder sons for once agreed and it was that all trace of what had just passed must be wiped away, and they called in carpenters and masons again, and the men servants cleaned the courts, and the carpenters mended cunningly the broken carvings and tables, and the pools were emptied of their filth and clean fresh water put in, and again the elder son bought flecked and golden fish and he planted once more the flowering trees and he trimmed the broken branches of the trees that were left. And within a year the place was fresh and flowering again and each son had moved again into his own court and there was order once more everywhere.

The slave who had conceived by the son of Wang Lung's uncle he commanded to wait upon his uncle's wife as long as she lived, which could not be long now, and to put her into the coffin when she died. And it was a matter for joy to Wang Lung that this slave gave birth only to a girl, for if it had been a boy she would have been proud and have claimed a place in the family, but being a girl it was only slave bearing slave, and she was no more than before.

Nevertheless, Wang Lung was just to her as to all, and he said to her that she might have the old woman's room for her own if she liked when the old one was dead, and she could have the bed also, and one room and one bed would not be missed from the sixty rooms in the house. And he gave the slave a little silver, and the woman was content enough except for one thing, and this she told to Wang Lung when he gave her the silver.

"Hold the silver as dowry for me, my master," she said, "and if it is not a trouble to you, wed me to a farmer or to a good poor man. It will be merit to you, and having lived with a man, it is hardship to me to go back to my bed alone."

Then Wang Lung promised easily, and when he promised he was struck with a thought and it was this. Here was he promising a woman to a poor man, and once he had been a poor man come into these very courts for his woman. And he had not for half a lifetime thought of O-lan, and now he thought of her with sadness that was not sorrow but only heaviness of memory and things long gone, so far distant was he from her now. And he said heavily,

"When the old opium dreamer dies, I will find a man for you, then, and it cannot be long."

And Wang Lung did as he said. The woman came to him one morning and said,

"Now redeem your promise, my master, for the old one died in the early morning without waking at all, and I have put her in her coffin."

And Wang Lung thought what man he knew now on his land and he remembered the blubbering lad who had caused Ching's death, and the one whose teeth were a shelf over his lower lip, and he said,

"Well, and he did not mean the thing he did, and he is as good as any and the only one I can think of now."

So he sent for the lad and he came, and he was a man grown now, but still he was rude and still his teeth were as they were. And it was Wang Lung's whim to sit on the raised dais in the great hall and to call the two before him and he said slowly, that he might taste the whole flavor of the strange moment,

"Here, fellow, is this woman, and she is yours if you will have her, and none has known her except the son of my own uncle."

And the man took her gratefully, for she was a stout wench and good-natured, and he was a man too poor to wed except to such an one.

And Wang Lung came down off the dais and it seemed to him that now his life was rounded off and he had done all that he said he would in his life and more than he could ever have dreamed he could, and he did not know himself how it had all come about. Only now it seemed to him that peace could truly come to him and he could sleep in the sun. It was time for it, also, for he was close to sixty-five years of his age and his grandsons were like young bamboos about him, three the sons of his eldest son, and the eldest of these nearly ten years old, and two the sons of his second son. Well, and there was the third son to wed one day soon, and with that over there was nothing left to trouble him in his life, and he could be at peace.

But there was no peace. It seemed as though the coming of the soldiers had been like the coming of a swarm of wild bees that leave behind them stings wherever they can. The wife of the eldest son and the wife of the second son who had been courteous enough to each other until they lived in one court together, now had learned to hate each other with a great hatred. It was born in a hundred small quarrels, the quarrels of women whose children must live and play together and fight each other like cats and dogs. Each mother flew to the defense of her child, and cuffed the other's children heartily but spared her own, and her own had always the right in any quarrel, and so the two women were hostile.

And then on that day when the cousin had commended the country wife and laughed at the city wife, that had passed which could not be forgiven. The wife of the elder son lifted her head haughtily when she passed her sister-in-law and she said aloud one day to her husband as she passed,

"It is a heavy thing to have a woman bold and ill-bred in the family, so that a man may call her red meat and she laughs in his face."

And the second son's wife did not wait but she answered back loudly,

"Now my sister-in-law is jealous because a man called her only a piece of cold fish!"

And so the two fell to angry looks and hatred, although the elder, being proud of her correctness, would deal only in silent scorn, careful to ignore the other's very presence. But when her children would go out of their own court she called out,

"I would have you stay away from ill-bred children!"

This she called out in the presence of her sister-in-law who stood within sight in the next court, and that one would call out to her own children,

"Do not play with snakes or you will be bitten!"

So the two women hated each other increasingly, and the

thing was the more bitter because the two brothers did not love each other well, the elder always being fearful lest his birth and his family seem lowly in the eyes of his wife who was town bred and better born than he, and the younger fearful lest his brother's desire for expenditure and place lead them into wasting their heritage before it was divided. Moreover, it was a shame to the elder brother that the second brother knew all the money their father had and what was spent and the money passed through his hands, so that although Wang Lung received and dispensed all the moneys from his lands, still the second brother knew what it was and the elder did not, but must go and ask his father for this and that like a child. So when the two wives hated each other, their hatred spread to the men also and the courts of the two were full of anger and Wang Lung groaned because there was no peace in his house.

Wang Lung had also his own secret trouble with Lotus since the day when he had protected her slave from the son of his uncle. Ever since that day the young maid had been in disfavor with Lotus, and although the girl waited on her silently and slavishly, and stood by her side all day filling her pipe and fetching this and that, and rising in the night at her complaint that she was sleepless and rubbing her legs and her body to soothe her, still Lotus was not satisfied.

And she was jealous of the maid and she sent her from the room when Wang Lung came in and she accused Wang Lung that he looked at the maid. Now Wang Lung had not thought of the girl except as a poor small child who was frightened and he cared as he might care for his poor fool and no more. But when Lotus accused him he took thought to look and he saw it was true that the girl was very pretty and pale as a pear blossom, and seeing this, something stirred in his old blood that had been quiet these ten years and more.

So while he laughed at Lotus saying, "What—are you thinking I am still a-lust, when I do not come into your room thrice a year?" yet he looked sidelong at the girl and he was stirred.

Now Lotus, for all she was ignorant in all ways except the one, in the way of men with women she was learned and she knew that men when they are old will wake once again to a brief youth, and so she was angry with the maid and she talked of selling her to the tea house. But still Lotus loved her comfort and Cuckoo grew old and lazy and the maid was quick and

243

used about the person of Lotus and saw what her mistress needed before she knew it herself, and so Lotus was loath to part with her and yet she would part with her, and in this unaccustomed conflict Lotus was the more angry because of her discomfort and she was more hard than usual to live with. Wang Lung stayed away from her court for many days at a time because her temper was too ill to enjoy. He said to himself that he would wait, thinking it would pass, but meanwhile he thought of the pretty pale young maid more than he himself would believe he did.

Then as though there was not enough trouble with the women of his house all awry, there was Wang Lung's youngest son. Now his youngest son had been so quiet a lad, so bent on his belated books, that none thought of him except as a reedy slender youth with books always under his arm and an old tutor following him about like a dog.

But the lad had lived among the soldiers when they were there and he had listened to their tales of war and plunder and battle, and he listened rapt to it all, saying nothing. Then he begged novels of his old tutor, stories of the wars of the three kingdoms and of the bandits who lived in ancient times about the Swei Lake, and his head was full of dreams.

So now he went to his father and he said,

"I know what I will do. I will be a soldier and I will go forth to wars."

When Wang Lung heard this, he thought in great dismay that it was the worst thing that could yet happen to him and he cried out with a great voice,

"Now what madness is this, and am I never to have any peace with my sons!" And he argued with the lad and he tried to be gentle and kindly when he saw the lad's black brows gather into a line and he said, "My son, it is said from ancient times that men do not take good iron to make a nail nor a good man to make a soldier, and you are my little son, my best little youngest son, and how shall I sleep at night and you wandering over the earth here and there in a war?"

But the boy was determined and he looked at his father and drew down his black brows and he said only,

"I will go."

Then Wang Lung coaxed him and said,

"Now you may go to any school you like and I will send you to the great schools of the south or even to a foreign school to learn curious things, and you shall go anywhere you like for

244

study if you will not be a soldier. It is a disgrace to a man like me, a man of silver and of land, to have a son who is a soldier." And when the lad was still silent, he coaxed again, and he said, "Tell your old father why you want to be a soldier?"

And the lad said suddenly, and his eyes were alight under his brows,

"There is to be a war such as we have not heard of—there is to be a revolution and fighting and war such as never was, and our land is to be free!"

Wang Lung listened to this in the greatest astonishment he had yet had from his three sons.

"Now what all this stuff is, I do not know," he said wondering. "Our land is free already—all our good land is free. I rent it to whom I will and it brings me silver and good grains and you eat and are clothed and are fed with it, and I do not know what freedom you desire more than you have."

But the boy only muttered bitterly,

"You do not understand—you are too old—you understand nothing."

And Wang Lung pondered and he looked at this son of his and he saw the suffering young face, and he thought to himself,

"Now I have given this son everything, even his life. He has everything from me. I have let him leave the land, even, so that I have not a son after me to see to the land, and I have let him read and write although there is no need for it in my family with two already." And he thought and he said to himself further, still staring at the lad. "Everything this son has from me."

Then he looked closely at his son and he saw that he was tall as a man already, though still reedy with youth, and he said, doubtfully, muttering and half-aloud, for he saw no sign of lust in the boy,

"Well, it may be he needs one thing more." And he said aloud then and slowly, "Well, and we will wed you soon, my son."

But the boy flashed a look of fire at his father from under his heavy gathered brows and he said scornfully,

"Then I will run away indeed, for to me a woman is not answer to everything as it is to my elder brother!"

Wang Lung saw at once that he was wrong and so he said hastily to excuse himself,

"No—no—we will not wed you—but I mean, if there is a slave you desire——"

And the boy answered with lofty looks and with dignity, folding his arms on his breast,

"I am not the ordinary young man. I have my dreams. I wish for glory. There are women everywhere." And then as though he remembered something he had forgotten, he suddenly broke from his dignity and his arms dropped and he said in his usual voice, "Besides, there never were an uglier set of slaves than we have. If I cared—but I do not—well, there is not a beauty in the courts except perhaps the little pale maid who waits on the one in the inner courts."

Then Wang knew he spoke of Pear Blossom and he was smitten with a strange jealousy. He suddenly felt himself older than he was—a man old and too thick of girth and with whitening hair, and he saw his son a man slim and young, and it was not for this moment father and son, but two men, one old and one young, and Wang Lung said angrily,

"Now keep off the slaves—I will not have the rotten ways of young lords in my house. We are good stout country folk and people with decent ways, and none of this in my house!"

Then the boy opened his eyes and lifted his black brows and shrugged his shoulders and he said to his father,

"You spoke of it first!" and then he turned away and went out.

Then Wang Lung sat there alone in his room by his table and he felt dreary and alone, and he muttered to himself,

"Well, and I have no peace anywhere in my house."

He was confused with many angers, but, although he could not understand why, this anger stood forth most clearly; his son had looked on a little pale young maid in the house and had found her fair.

33

WANG LUNG could not cease from his thought of what his youngest son had said of Pear Blossom and he watched the maid incessantly as she came and went and without his knowing it the thought of her filled his mind and he doted on her. But he said nothing to anyone.

One night in the early summer of that year, at the time when the night air is thick and soft with the mists of warmth and fragrance, he sat at rest in his own court alone under a flowering cassia tree and the sweet heavy scent of the cassia flowers filled his nostrils and he sat there and his blood ran full and hot like the blood of a young man. Through the day he had felt his blood so and he had been half of a mind to walk out on his land and feel the good earth under his feet and take off his shoes and his stockings and feel it on his skin.

This he would have done but he was ashamed lest men see him, who was no longer held a farmer within the gates of the town, but a landowner and a rich man. So he wandered restlessly about the courts and he stayed away altogether from the court where Lotus sat in the shade and smoked her water pipe, because well she knew when a man was restless and she had sharp eyes to see what was amiss. He went alone, then, and he had no mind to see either of his two quarreling daughters-in-law, nor even his grandchildren, in whom was his frequent delight.

So the day had passed very long and lonely and his blood was full and coursing under his skin. He could not forget his youngest son, how he had looked standing tall and straight and his black brows drawn together in the gravity of his youth, and he could not forget the maid. And to himself he said,

"I suppose they are of an age—the boy must be well on eighteen and she not over eighteen."

Then he remembered that he himself would before many years be seventy and he was ashamed of his coursing blood, and he thought,

"It would be a good thing to give the maid to the lad," and this he said to himself again and again, and everytime he said it the thing stabbed like a thrust on flesh already sore, and he could not but stab and yet he could not but feel the pain.

And so the day passed very long and lonely for him.

When night came he was still alone and he sat in his court alone and there was not one in all his house to whom he could go as friend. And the night air was thick and soft and hot with the smell of the flowers of the cassia tree.

And as he sat there in the darkness under the tree one passed

247

beside where he was sitting near the gate of his court where the tree stood, and he looked quickly and it was Pear Blossom.

"Pear Blossom!" he called, and his voice came in a whisper.

She stopped suddenly, her head bent in listening.

Then he called again and his voice would scarcely come from his throat,

"Come here to me!"

Then hearing him she crept fearfully through the gate and stood before him and he could scarcely see her standing there in the blackness, but he could feel her there and he put out his hand and laid hold of her little coat and he said, half choking,

"Child——!"

There he stopped with the word. He said to himself that he was an old man and it was a disgraceful thing for a man with grandsons and grand-daughters nearer to this child's age than he was, and he fingered her little coat.

Then she, waiting, caught from him the heat of his blood and she bent over and slipped, like a flower crumpling upon its stalk, to the ground, and she clasped his feet and lay there. And he said slowly,

"Child—I am an old man—a very old man——"

And she said, and her voice came out of the darkness like the very breath of the cassia tree,

"I like old men—I like old men—they are so kind—"

He said again, tenderly, stooping to her a little,

"A little maid like you should have a tall straight youth—a little maid like you!" And in his heart he added, "Like my son ——" but aloud he could not say it, because he might put the thought into her mind, and he could not bear it.

But she said,

"Young men are not kind—they are only fierce."

And hearing her small childish voice quavering up from about his feet his heart welled up in a great wave of love for this maid, and he took her and raised her gently, and then led her into his own courts.

When it was done, this love of his age astonished him more than any of his lusts before, for with all his love for Pear Blossom he did not seize upon her as he had seized upon the others whom he had known.

No, he held her gently and he was satisfied to feel her light youth against his heavy old flesh, and he was satisfied merely with the sight of her in the day and with the touch of her fluttering coat against his hand and with the quiet resting of her

248

body near him in the night. And he wondered at the love of old age, which is so fond and so easily satisfied.

As for her, she was a passionless maid and she clung to him as to a father, and to him she was indeed more than half child and scarcely woman.

Now the thing that Wang Lung had done did not quickly come out, for he said nothing at all, and why should he, being master in his own house?

But the eye of Cuckoo marked it first and she saw the maid slipping at dawn out of his court and she laid hold on the girl and laughed, and her old hawk's eyes glittered.

"Well!" she said. "And so it is the Old Lord over again!"

And Wang Lung in his room, hearing her, girded his robe about him quickly and he came out and smiled sheepishly and half proudly and he said muttering,

"Well, and I said she had better take a young lad and she would have the old one!"

"It will be a pretty thing to tell the mistress," Cuckoo said, then, and her eyes sparkled with malice.

"I do not know myself how the thing happened," answered Wang Lung slowly. "I had not meant to add another woman to my courts, and the thing came about of itself." Then when Cuckoo said, "Well, and the mistress must be told," Wang Lung, fearing the anger of Lotus more than anything begged Cuckoo and he said again, "Do you tell her, if you will, and if you can manage it without anger to my face I will give you a handful of money for it."

So Cuckoo, still laughing and shaking her head, promised, and Wang Lung went back to his court and he would not come forth for a while until Cuckoo came back and said,

"Well, and the thing is told, and she was angry enough until I reminded her she wanted and has wanted this long time the foreign clock you promised her, and she will have a ruby ring for her hand and a pair so that there will be one on each hand, and she will have other things as she thinks of them and a slave to take Pear Blossom's place, and Pear Blossom is not to come to her any more, and you are not to come soon either, because the sight of you sickens her."

And Wang Lung promised eagerly and he said,

"Get her what she wills and I do not begrudge anything."

And he was pleased that he need not see Lotus soon and until anger was cooled with the fulfillment of her wishes.

There were left yet his three sons, and he was strangely

ashamed before them of what he had done. And he said to himself again and again,

"Am I not master in my own house and may I not take my own slave I bought with my silver?"

But he was ashamed, and yet half proud too, as one feels himself who is still lusty and a man when others hold him to be only grandfather. And he waited for his sons to come into his court.

They came one by one, separately, and the second one came first. Now this one when he came talked of the land and of the harvest and of the summer drought which would this year divide the harvest by three. But Wang Lung considered nothing in these days of rain or drought, for if the harvest of the year brought him in little there was silver left from the year before and he kept his courts stuffed with silver and there was money owing to him at the grain markets and he had much money let out at high interest that his second son collected for him, and he looked no more to see how the skies were over his land.

But the second son talked on thus, and as he talked he looked here and there about the rooms with his eyes veiled and secret and Wang Lung knew that he looked for the maid to see if what he had heard was true, and so he called Pear Blossom from where she hid in the bed-room, and he called out,

"Bring me tea, my child, and tea for my son!"

And she came out, and her delicate pale face was rosy as a peach and she hung her head and crept about on her little silent feet, and the second son stared at her as if he had heard but could not believe until now.

But he said nothing at all except that the land was thus and so and this tenant and that must be changed at the end of the year, and the other one, because he smoked opium and would not gather from the land what it could bear. And Wang Lung asked his son how his children did, and he answered they had the hundred days' cough, but it was a slight thing now that the weather was warm.

This they talked back and forth drinking tea, and the second son took his fill of what he saw and he went away, and Wang Lung was eased of his second son.

Then the eldest son came in before the same day was half over and he came in tall and handsome and proud with the years of his maturity, and Wang Lung was afraid of his pride, and he did not call out Pear Blossom at first, but he waited and smoked his pipe. The eldest son sat there then stiff with his pride and his dignity and he asked after the proper manner for his father's health and for his welfare. Then Wang Lung answered quickly and quietly that he was well, and as he looked at his son his fear went out of him.

For he saw his eldest for what he was: a man big in body but afraid of his own town wife and more afraid of not appearing nobly born than of anything. And the robustness of the land that was strong in Wang Lung even when he did not know it swelled up in him, and he was careless again of this eldest son as he had been before, and careless of his proper looks, and he called easily of a sudden to Pear Blossom,

"Come, my child, and pour out tea again for another son of mine!"

This time she came out very cold and still and her small oval face was white as the flower of her name. Her eyes dropped as she came in and she moved stilly and did only what she was told to do and she went quickly out again.

Now the two men had sat silent while she poured the tea, but when she was gone and they lifted their bowls, Wang Lung looked fully into his son's eyes, and he caught there a naked look of admiration, and it was the look of one man who envies another man secretly. Then they drank their tea and the son said at last in a thick, uneven voice,

"I did not believe it was so."

"Why not?" replied Wang Lung tranquilly. "It is my own house."

The son sighed then and after a time he answered,

"You are rich and you may do as you like." And he sighed again and he said, "Well, I suppose one is not always enough for any man and there comes a day——"

He broke off, but there was in his look the tinge of a man who envies another man against his will, and Wang Lung looked and laughed in himself, for well he knew his eldest son's lusty nature and that not forever would the proper town wife he had hold the leash and some day the man would come forth again.

Then the eldest son said no more but he went his way as a man does who has had a new thought put into his head. And Wang sat and smoked his pipe and he was proud of himself that when he was an old man he had done what he wished.

But it was night before the youngest son came in and he

came alone also. Now Wang Lung sat in his middle room on the court and the red candles were lit on the table and he sat there smoking, and Pear Blossom sat silently on the other side of the table from him, and her hands were folded and quiet in her lap. Sometimes she looked at Wang Lung, fully and without coquetry as a child does, and he watched her and was proud of what he had done.

Then suddenly there was his youngest son standing before him, sprung out of the darkness of the court, and no one had seen him enter. But he stood there in some strange crouching way, and without taking thought of it, Wang Lung was reminded in a flash of memory of a panther he had once seen the men of the village bring in from the hills where they had caught it, and the beast was tied but he crouched for a spring, and his eyes gleamed, and the lad's eyes gleamed and he fixed them upon his father's face. And those brows of his that were too heavy and too black for his youth, he gathered fierce and black above his eyes. Thus he stood and at last he said in a low and surcharged voice,

"Now I will go for a soldier—I will go for a soldier——"

But he did not look at the girl, only at his father, and Wang Lung, who had not been afraid at all of his eldest son and his second son, was suddenly afraid of this one, whom he had scarcely considered from his birth up.

And Wang Lung stammered and muttered, and would have spoken, but when he took his pipe from his mouth, no sound came, and he stared at his son. And his son repeated again and again,

"Now I will go—now I will go——"

Suddenly he turned and looked at the girl once, and she looked back at him, shrinking, and she took her two hands and put them over her face so that she could not see him. Then the young man tore his eyes from her and he went in a leap from the room and Wang Lung looked out into the square of the darkness of the door, open into the black summer night, and he was gone and there was silence everywhere.

At last he turned to the girl and he said humbly and gently and with a great sadness and all his pride gone.

"I am too old for you, my heart, and well I know it. I am an old, old man."

But the girl dropped her hands from her face and she cried more passionately than he had ever heard her cry,

"Young men are so cruel—I like old men best!"

When the morning came of the next day Wang Lung's youngest son was gone and where he was gone no one knew.

34

THEN AS AUTUMN flares with the false heat of summer before it dies into the winter, so with the quick love Wang Lung had for Pear Blossom. The brief heat of it passed and passion died out of him; he was fond of her, but passionless.

With the passing of the flame out of him he was suddenly cold with an age and he was an old man. Nevertheless, he was fond of her, and it was a comfort to him that she was in his court and she served him faithfully and with a patience beyond her years, and he was always kind to her with a perfect kindness, and more and more his love for her was the love of father for daughter.

And for his sake she was even kind to his poor fool and this was comfort to him, so that one day he told her what had long been in his mind. Now Wang Lung had thought many times of what would come to his poor fool when he was dead and there was not another one except himself who cared whether she lived or starved, and so he had bought a little bundle of white poisonous stuff at the medicine shop, and he had said to himself that he would give it to his fool to eat when he saw his own death was near. But still he dreaded this more than the hour of his own death, and it was a comfort to him now when he saw Pear Blossom was faithful.

So he called her to him one day and he said,

"There is none other but you to whom I can leave this poor fool of mine when I am gone, and she will live on and on after me, seeing that her mind has no troubles of its own, and she has nothing to kill her and no trouble to worry her. And well I know that no one will trouble when I am gone to feed her or to bring her out of the rain and the cold of winter or to set her in the summer sun, and she will be sent out to wander on the street, perhaps—this poor thing who has had care all her life from her mother and from me. Now here is a gate of safety for her in this packet, and when I die, after I am dead, you are to mix it in her rice and let her eat it, that she may follow me where I am. And so shall I be at ease."

But Pear Blossom shrank from the thing he held in his hand and she said in her soft way,

"I can scarcely kill an insect and how could I take this life? No, my lord, but I will take this poor fool for mine because you have been kind to me—kinder than any in all my life, and the only kind one."

And Wang Lung could have wept for what she said because not one had ever requited him like this, and his heart clung to her and he said,

"Nevertheless, take it, my child, for there is none I trust as I do you, but even you must die one day—although I cannot say the words—and after you there is none—no, not one—and well I know my sons' wives are too busy with their children and their quarrels and my sons are men and cannot think of such things."

So when she saw his meaning, Pear Blossom took the packet from him and said no more and Wang Lung trusted her and was comforted for the fate of his poor fool.

Then Wang Lung withdrew more and more into his age and he lived much alone except for these two in his courts, his poor fool and Pear Blossom. Sometimes he roused himself a little and he looked at Pear Blossom and he was troubled and said,

"It is too quiet a life for you, my child."

But she always answered gently and in great gratitude,

"It is quiet and safe."

And sometimes he said again,

"I am too old for you, and my fires are ashes."

But she always answered with a great thankfulness,

"You are kind to me and more I do not desire of any man."

Once when she said this Wang Lung was curious and he asked her,

"What was it in your tender years that made you thus fearful of men?"

And looking at her for answer he saw a great terror in her eyes and she covered them with her hands and she whispered,

"Every man I hate except you—I have hated every man, even

my father who sold me. I have heard only evil of them and I hate them all."

And he said wondering,

"Now I should have said you had lived quietly and easily in my courts."

"I am filled with loathing," she said, looking away, "I am filled with loathing and I hate them all. I hate all young men."

And she would say nothing more, and he mused on it, and he did not know whether Lotus had filled her with tales of her life and had threatened her, or whether Cuckoo had frightened her with lewdness, or whether something had befallen her secretly that she would not tell him, or what it was.

But he sighed and gave over his questions, because above everything now he would have peace, and he wished only to sit in his court near these two.

So Wang Lung sat, and so his age came on him day by day and year by year, and he slept fitfully in the sun as his father had done, and he said to himself that his life was done and he was satisfied with it.

Sometimes, but seldom, he went into the other courts and sometimes, but more seldom, he saw Lotus, and she never mentioned the maid he had taken, but she greeted him well enough and she was old too and satisfied with the food and the wine she loved and with the silver she had for the asking. She and Cuckoo sat together now after these many years as friends and no longer as mistress and servant, and they talked of this and that, and most of all the old days with men and they whispered together of things they would not speak aloud, and they ate and drank and slept, and woke to gossip again before eating and drinking.

And when Wang Lung went, and it was very seldom, into his sons' courts, they treated him courteously and they ran to get tea for him and he asked to see the last child and he asked many times, for he forgot easily,

"How many grandchildren have I now?"

And one answered him readily,

"Eleven sons and eight daughters have your sons together."

And he, chuckling and laughing, said back,

"Add two each year, and I know the number, is it so?"

Then he would sit a little while and look at the children gathering around him to stare. His grandsons were tall lads

255

now, and he looked at them, peering at them to see what they were, and he muttered to himself,

"Now that one has the look of his great-grandfather and there is a small merchant Liu, and here is myself when young."

And he asked them,

"Do you go to school?"

"Yes, grandfather," they answered in a scattered chorus, and he said again,

"Do you study the Four Books?"

Then they laughed with clear young scorn at a man so old as this and they said,

"No, grandfather, and no one studies the Four Books since the Revolution."

And he answered, musing,

"Ah, I have heard of a Revolution, but I have been too busy in my life to attend to it. There was always the land."

But the lads snickered at this, and at last Wang Lung rose, feeling himself after all but a guest in his sons' courts.

Then after a time he went no more to see his sons, but sometimes he would ask Cuckoo,

"And are my two daughters-in-law at peace after all these years?"

And Cuckoo spat upon the ground and she said,

"Those? They are at peace like two cats eyeing each other. But the eldest son wearies of his wife's complaints of this and that—too proper a woman for a man, she is, and always talking of what they did in the house of her father, and she wearies a man. There is talk of his taking another. He goes often to the tea shops."

"Ah?" said Wang Lung.

But when he would have thought of it his interest in the matter waned and before he knew it he was thinking of his tea and that the young spring wind smote cold upon his shoulders.

And another time he said to Cuckoo,

"Does any ever hear from that youngest son of mine where he is gone this long time?"

And Cuckoo answered, for there was nothing she did not know in these courts,

"Well, and he does not write a letter, but now and then one comes from the south and it is said he is a military official and great enough in a thing they call a Revolution there, but what it is I do not know—perhaps some sort of business."

And again Wang Lung said, "Ah?"

And he would have thought of it, but the evening was falling and his bones ached in the air left raw and chill when the sun withdrew. For his mind now went where it would and he could not hold it long to any one thing. And the needs of his old body for food and for hot tea were more keen than for anything. But at night when he was cold, Pear Blossom lay warm and young against him and he was comforted in his age with her warmth in his bed.

Thus spring wore on again and again and vaguely and more vaguely as these years passed he felt it coming. But still one thing remained to him and it was his love for his land. He had gone away from it and he had set up his house in a town and he was rich. But his roots were in his land and although he forgot it for many months together, when spring came each year he must go out on to the land; and now although he could no longer hold a plow or do anything but see another drive the plow through the earth, still he must needs go and he went. Sometimes he took a servant and his bed and he slept again in the old earthen house and in the old bed where he had begotten children and where O-lan had died. When he woke in the dawn he went out and with his trembling hands he reached and plucked a bit of budding willow and a spray of peach bloom and held them all day in his hand.

Thus he wandered one day in a late spring, near summer, and he went over his fields a little way and he came to the enclosed place upon a low hill where he had buried his dead. He stood trembling on his staff and he looked at the graves and he remembered them every one. They were more clear to him now than the sons who lived in his own house, more clear to him than anyone except his poor fool and except Pear Blossom. And his mind went back many years and he saw it all clearly, even his little second daughter of whom he had heard nothing for longer than he could remember, and he saw her a pretty maid as she had been in his house, her lips as thin and red as a shred of silk—and she was to him like these who lay here in the land. Then he mused and he thought suddenly,

"Well, and I shall be the next."

Then he went into the enclosure and he looked carefully and he saw the place where he would lie below his father and his uncle and above Ching and not far from O-lan. And he stared at the bit of earth where he was to lie and he saw himself in it and back in his own land forever. And he muttered,

"I must see to the coffin."

This thought he held fast and painfully in his mind and he went back to the town and he sent for his eldest son, and he said,

"There is something I have to say."

"Then say on," answered the son, "I am here."

But when Wang Lung would have said he suddenly could not remember what it was, and the tears stood in his eyes because he had held the matter so painfully in his mind and now it had slipped wilfully away from him. So he called Pear Blossom and he said to her,

"Child, what was it I wanted to say?"

And Pear Blossom answered gently,

"Where were you this day?"

"I was upon the land," Wang Lung replied, waiting, his eyes fixed on her face.

And she asked gently again,

"On what piece of land?"

Then suddenly the thing flew into his mind again and he cried, laughing out of his wet eyes,

"Well, and I do remember. My son, I have chosen my place in the earth, and it is below my father and his brother and above your mother and next to Ching, and I would see my coffin before I die."

Then Wang Lung's eldest son cried out dutifully and properly,

"Do not say that word, my father, but I will do as you say."

Then his son bought a carved coffin hewn from a great log of fragrant wood which is used to bury the dead in and for nothing else because that wood is as lasting as iron, and more lasting than human bones, and Wang Lung was comforted.

And he had the coffin brought into his room and he looked at it every day.

Then all of a sudden he thought of something and he said,

"Well, and I would have it moved out to the earthen house and there I will live out my few days and there I will die."

And when they saw how he had set his heart they did what he wished and he went back to the house on his land, he and Pear Blossom and the fool, and what servants they needed; and Wang Lung took up his abode again on his land, and he left the house in the town to the family he had founded.

Spring passed and summer passed into harvest and in the hot

autumn sun before winter comes Wang Lung sat where his father had sat against the wall. And he thought no more about anything now except his food and his drink and his land. But of his land he thought no more what harvest it would bring or what seed would be planted or of anything except of the land itself, and he stooped sometimes and gathered some of the earth up in his hand and he sat thus and held it in his hand, and it seemed full of life between his fingers. And he was content, holding it thus, and he thought of it fitfully and of his good coffin that was there; and the kind earth waited without haste until he came to it.

His sons were proper enough to him and they came to him every day or at most once in two days, and they sent him delicate food fit for his age, but he liked best to have one stir up meal in hot water and sup it as his father had done.

Sometimes he complained a little of his sons if they came not every day and he said to Pear Blossom, who was always near him,

"Well, and what are they so busy about?"

But if Pear Blossom said, "They are in the prime of life and now they have many affairs. Your eldest son has been made an officer in the town among the rich men, and he has a new wife, and your second son is setting up a great grain market for himself," Wang Lung listened to her, but he could not comprehend all this and he forgot it as soon as he looked out over his land.

But one day he saw clearly for a little while. It was a day on which his two sons had come and after they had greeted him courteously they went out and they walked about the house on to the land. Now Wang Lung followed them silently, and they stood, and he came up to them slowly, and they did not hear the sound of his footsteps nor the sound of his staff on the soft earth, and Wang Lung heard his second son say in his mincing voice,

"This field we will sell and this one, and we will divide the money between us evenly. Your share I will borrow at good interest, for now with the railroad straight through I can ship rice to the sea and I . . ."

But the old man heard only these words, "sell the land," and he cried out and he could not keep his voice from breaking and trembling with his anger,

"Now, evil, idle sons—sell the land! He choked and would have fallen, and they caught him and held him up, and he began to weep.

Then they soothed him and they said, soothing him,

"No—no—we will never sell the land——"

"It is the end of a family—when they begin to sell the land," he said brokenly. "Out of the land we came and into it we must go—and if you will hold your land you can live—no one can rob you of land——"

And the old man let his scanty tears dry upon his cheeks and they made salty stains there. And he stooped and took up a handful of the soil and he held it and he muttered,

"If you sell the land, it is the end."

And his two sons held him, one on either side, each holding his arm, and he held tight in his hand the warm loose earth. And they soothed him and they said over and over, the elder son and the second son,

"Rest assured, our father, rest assured. The land is not to be sold."

But over the old man's head they looked at each other and smiled.

About the Author

PEARL S. BUCK devoted her life to the creation of better understanding between the peoples of Asia and the West. She was born in Hillsboro, West Virginia on June 26, 1892, but spent her childhood in China, where her parents were Presbyterian missionaries. Living in the historic city of Chianking, she learned Chinese before English. When she was fifteen she went to boarding school in Shanghai, her first formal schooling before she returned to America to enter Randolph-Macon College. After graduation in 1914, she married John Lossing Buck, a teacher of agriculture, and went to live in a town in North China. Here she lived for five years, gathering the memories that became the basis of *The Good Earth*.

The publication of her first article in the *Atlantic*, in 1923, confirmed a childhood interest in writing and led ultimately to her first novel, *East Wind, West Wind*. Less than a year later, the appearance of *The Good Earth* established her reputation. The novel was an extraordinary best seller and was awarded the Pulitzer Prize, translated into more than thirty languages, and made into a play and a motion picture. After that she wrote over eighty books, including such famous novels as *A House Divided, Dragon Seed, Pavilion of Women*, and *The Time is Noon*.

In addition to the Pulitzer Prize, Mrs. Buck was awarded the Nobel Prize for Literature in 1938, the Brotherhood Award of the National Conference of Christians and Jews, the Wesley Award for Distinguished Service to Humanity and more than a dozen honorary degrees from American colleges and universities. She died in Danby, Vermont on March 6, 1973.

Bestselling

Classics

Here's a selection of the finest in literature from Pocket Books.

_____	48941 ALICE IN WONDERLAND AND OTHER FAVORITES Lewis Carroll	$1.95
_____	42636 ANNE FRANK: DIARY OF A YOUNG GIRL	$2.50
_____	82561 BASIC KAFKA	$3.95
_____	49101 CANDIDE & ZADIG Voltaire	$2.25
_____	49126 DAVID COPPERFIELD Charles Dickens	$2.75
_____	43342 THE GOOD EARTH Pearl S. Buck	$2.75
_____	48955 IVANHOE Sir Walter Scott	$2.95
_____	43132 LEGEND OF SLEEPY HOLLOW Washington Irving	$2.50
_____	49108 MADAME BOVARY Gustave Flaubert	$1.95
_____	42243 LOST HORIZON James Hilton	$2.95